THE FALL O

D0779036

"I'm in awe of this book. Ella Patel is a fantastic, flawed, sympathetic protagonist who pops off the page from the moment you meet her and leads you on a breathtaking adventure that is at once poignant and wondrous."

Ken Liu, Hugo, Nebula, and World Fantasy winning author of The Grace of Kings

"Tipping his hat to both science fiction novels and comic books, Chu delivers a narrative that is at times pulse-pounding, laugh-out-loud funny and thoughtful. Part James Bond, part Superman, part *Orphanage*. There's something here for everyone."

Myke Cole, author of The Armored Saint *and* Shadow Ops

"*The Rise of Io* is great ride, and I desperately want a Quasing. The idea of a cosmic cheering section in my own head sounds delightful. Not to mention my Quasing would make me totally boss. Another hit by Wesley Chu."

Melinda Snodgrass, author of the Edge series

"Years after a killer debut, Wesley Chu keeps leveling up. Storytelling that seems so effortless you never see the punches coming."

Peter V Brett, bestselling author of the Demon Cycle series

"*The Rise of Io* is the perfect SF adventure! A scrappy young heroine, a highlight this terrifi ries. Fans of Pierce E e new SF underdog

Christoph r of

Snowbli

PALM BEACH COUNTY
LIBRARY SYSTEM
3650 Summit Boulevard
West Palm Beach, FL 33406-4198

"The India slums after the Alien Wars might seem like a hell of a place to kick off a series, but Chu's explosive storytelling and firecracker new hero make opening *The Rise of Io* feel like tumbling into an action movie. I'd follow Ella Patel – or Chu – anywhere."

Melissa Olson, author of the Boundary Magic series

"Damn, this is a great book. Wesley Chu may have created his best character yet with Ella – a scrappy, savvy street urchin, who he tosses into a world of hidden aliens, political maneuvering, and possible treachery. *The Rise of Io* is a fun, fast, beautifully written book that grabbed me on page one and didn't let me go."

Peter Clines, author of The Fold *and the Ex-Heroes series*

"Wesley Chu keeps getting better and better. Ella Patel is engaging and exciting, and her story grabs you by the front of your shirt and drags you along for one heck of a ride."

Diana Rowland, author of the White Trash Zombie series

"Ella Patel of Crate Town is my favorite kind of hero, a young person struggling to survive on a diet of tough living and petty crime who gets swept up in world-spanning intrigue and danger. Wesley Chu's funny, confident writing never sacrifices good science fiction world-building for the sake of action. While the bullets fly and knife blades flash, Chu also gives us body-jumping aliens and poignant characterizations. *The Rise of Io* is a fast and furious ride piloted by an author rising to the top of his field."

Greg Van Eekhout, author of California Bones

"Ella is a strong protagonist, scrappy and determined. You're going to love her!"

Laura Lam, author of False Hearts

"It's like *Men in Black* and *Blade Runner* had a baby, and it took over the world."

Dan Wells, bestelling author of the Partials novels and I Am Not a Serial Killer

"Wesley Chu gets better and better with every book. Action-packed and full of surprises, *The Rise of Io* is his best work yet."

Richard Kadrey, author of the Sandman Slim series

"With rich world-building, twisty politics and plot, plus some kick-ass leading ladies, *The Rise of Io* had everything I look for in sci-fi, and more. I loved this book!"

Susan Dennard, bestselling author of Truthwitch

"A fun, rollicking adventure, with a unique and charming heroine. *The Rise of Io* gives us a fresh look at the world of Campbell Award Winner Wes Chu's witty, action-packed, globe-trotting Tao series."

Ramez Naam, author of Nexus *and the Philip K Dick Award-winning* Apex

"An absolute blast of a book! With fresh characters, incredible world building, and buckets of humor, *The Rise of Io* is everything you want in a sci-fi novel."

Suzanne Young, New York Times bestselling author of the Program series

"Wesley Chu is my hero... he has to be the coolest science fiction writer in the world."

Lavie Tidhar, World Fantasy Award winning author of Osama *and* The Bookman Histories

ALSO BY WESLEY CHU

The Lives of Tao
The Deaths of Tao
The Rebirths of Tao
The Days of Tao (novella)

The Rise of Io

Time Salvager
Time Siege

WESLEY CHU

The Fall of Io

ANGRY ROBOT
An imprint of Watkins Media Ltd

20 Fletcher Gate,
Nottingham,
NG1 2FZ
UK

angryrobotbooks.com
twitter.com/angryrobotbooks
To catch a thief

An Angry Robot paperback original 2019

Copyright © Wesley Chu 2019

Cover by Ignacio Lazcano
Set in Meridien by Argh! Nottingham

Distributed in the United States by Penguin Random House, Inc.,
New York.

All rights reserved. Wesley Chu asserts the moral right to be identified as the author of this work. A catalogue record for this book is available from the British Library.

This novel is entirely a work of fiction. Names, characters, places, and incidents are the products of the author's imagination or are used fictitiously. Any resemblance to actual events, locales, organizations or persons, living or dead, is entirely coincidental.

Sales of this book without a front cover may be unauthorized. If this book is coverless, it may have been reported to the publisher as "unsold and destroyed" and neither the author nor the publisher may have received payment for it.

Angry Robot and the Angry Robot icon are registered trademarks of Watkins Media Ltd.

ISBN 978 0 85766 787 8
Ebook ISBN 978 0 85766 788 5

Printed in the United States of America

9 8 7 6 5 4 3 2 1

To Mom and Dad

CHAPTER ONE
Retirement

The first day of your career is often the hardest. The last, the most difficult. The worst, however, is the week after retirement when you have nothing to do and realize that the world has moved on without you.

BAJI, PROPHUS KEEPER, EIGHT DAYS AFTER HER RETIREMENT

The announcement for the emergency all-hands meeting came right as Josie Perkins sat down to eat her crème brûlée without the burnt caramelized sugar on top, which honestly made it just a rather mediocre custard. Gourmet was not an accusation anyone had ever leveled at the kitchen here at the Prophus Academy in Sydney. The nearest dessert shop, however, was a good hour's drive away, so this place was it. Beggars, choosers, and all that. Josie stuck a spoonful in her mouth and scowled at the blinking notification on her phone. Nothing in the world was important enough to skip dessert, but here it was.

Josie hated emergency meetings; no good news ever came from someone telling you to drop whatever you were doing to listen to them talk. Her first emergency meeting had been when she was six years old. Her parents had brought her and Parker to the dining room and told them that dad was moving to Perth while mum was staying in Sydney. Both had decided that they couldn't stand the other, and that Josie and Parker weren't good enough reasons to try to make things work. Her life had been pretty much a mess ever since.

Since then, every emergency meeting had steered her life in a worse and worse direction. Josie had been ordered to an all-hands emergency meeting when the Alien World War broke out. She had been called into another when Parker's spy plane went down behind enemy lines in Thailand, and he was presumed captured or dead. Josie found out a year later that he had been tortured and killed at the hands of Thanadabouth, a Genjix Laotian general wanted for war crimes.

She was summoned for an emergency meeting to cancel her operation the night before she was to lead an attack on Thanadabouth's stronghold. The war had ended one day too early. Australia, along with every other country involved in this global disaster, signed the armistice. All the humans were sick of fighting. The only ones who wanted to keep killing each other were the Prophus and Genjix. Everyone else just called it a draw, packed up their toys, and went home. Josie was informed that General Thanadabouth, vacationing less than two klicks away in his summer villa, had immunity and was now completely off-limits. She had to be physically restrained and dragged out of that meeting.

Josie quit the Australian Defense Force the next day and joined the Prophus. One dead Laotian general and nearly a decade later, Josie had pulled herself away from the front lines of this now not-really-shadow war between the two alien factions, and was Head of Security at the Prophus Academy in Sydney. It was a cushy job, perfect for someone on the tail-end of a distinguished military career, and a relatively safe way to head off into the sunset.

The pace at the Academy was often molasses. She admittedly missed the action and chafed at being put on the shelf, but overall Josie had had more than her share of violence and war, and was content riding the last few days of her service educating fresh eager recruits and busting delinquent ones.

To this day, however, her nerves tingled every time some asshole called an emergency meeting. She was tempted to duck out and take a nap. Pretend she missed the call entirely. Still, all-hands was all-hands, and she was never one to shirk duty. This time, it was from the high-and-mighty Keeper herself. Maybe it was good news for once. Maybe they were handing out bonuses and paid holidays.

Fat bloody chance.

Josie jammed the rest of the limp custard into her mouth and watched the steady flow of instructors, administrators and security personnel stream into the faculty lounge. She greeted everyone and made room at her table. Niko and Frieda, her two sergeants, sat down either side of her. They were joined a few moments later by Lauren, the Academy's commandant, Genny the explosive weapons instructor, Ahman the military history professor and a few other faculty members. Makita Takeshi, the new Asian Relations instructor who had only arrived last week, walked into the lounge and stared at the remaining seat at the round table before retreating to the far corner.

Josie snorted. Asshole. Makita was awfully unfriendly for a communications expert. He had transferred in from the San Francisco Academy to take over Instructor Ying's job, but if anything, Makita looked older than the person he replaced.

"Do you know what this is all about, Colonel?" asked Niko, peering at the blank three-dimensional screen floating at the front of the room.

Josie shrugged. "Who knows? Maybe we've unconditionally surrendered. Whatever it is, it's probably not good."

Niko ran his fingers through his thinning hair. "Damn, surrendering? I just renewed the lease on my condo."

The room was abuzz as everyone floated their own theories.

Half the room thought layoffs were coming, while the other half was pretty sure the war was back on. A few of the more panicked ones were positive Australia had just declared for Genjix, which meant every single person in the room was one step away from becoming a prisoner of war. Several bets were made. Alien World War II had ten-to-one odds.

Josie really didn't care. She was weeks from retirement and walking away from all this. Even if an all-out war broke out tonight, she'd be fishing off the coast of Rottnest Island by the end of the month. Eventually, the lights dimmed and everyone settled into an anxious anticipation.

Jill Tesser Tan, the Keeper and current leader of the Prophus, appeared three-dimensionally in the air at the front of the lounge. Josie was pleasantly surprised. She could tell right away it was good news. She had spent the last years of the war working intelligence and had developed a keen eye for a person's physical cues. She could predict almost exactly what someone was going to say simply by seeing how they stood, what they were doing with their hands, and how their eyes moved. The Keeper did not have the posture of someone who was about to send them all to war. She was relaxed, smiling, jovial almost, as if a great weight had been lifted off her shoulders.

"Oh my lord," murmured Josie. "I think she's out."

"No way," said Frieda. "The Prophus is like a gang. No one gets out alive."

The Keeper began to speak. "Thank you everyone for attending on such short notice. Working and fighting alongside you has been the greatest honor of my life." She hesitated, shook her head, and crumpled the paper in her hand. She tossed it aside. "This speech sucks. I had to scribble it down on the way from my office."

A chorus of chuckles filled the faculty lounge.

"I consider you all family, so I'm not going to beat around

the bush." A smirk grew on Jill's face. "I am officially stepping down as Keeper, effective immediately. Twenty-some odd years ago, the original Keeper asked me to take over the reins of the Prophus on an interim basis while her new host was literally learning how to ride a bike. Well, now Angie has grown to become a fine young woman and has proven herself a capable leader in her own right. The Prophus are in good hands for many years to come. As for me..." She grinned openly. "I have a ranch up in Oregon that needs attending. You are all invited to stop by once you retire, but not a day before."

More laughter followed. A loud screech from the back of the lounge cut through the air, interrupting the Keeper's speech. All eyes turned to the rear of the room where Makita had stood up abruptly, his eyes shining with fury. He slammed a fist on the table and kicked his toppled chair, sending it crashing into the corner. He cursed in an odd accent and stormed out of the room.

"What got into Instructor Makita?" frowned Lauren, the commandant.

Frieda craned her head back. "That new guy is sort of a grump."

"He must really dislike the new Keeper," said Niko.

"Wouldn't you if you were some seventy year-old guy reporting to a twenty-something who was just elevated by alien nepotism," chuckled Frieda. "I know I would be."

"Is he really that old?" asked Niko.

Frieda shrugged. "He looks pretty worn down."

Josie's gaze lingered at the doorway. She had sniffed something dishonest about Makita the moment they met. For one thing, for someone hailing from the Japanese Defense Force, his Japanese was laughable. For a supposed career soldier, he was terribly unfamiliar with military protocol. For a war vet, he was very close-lipped about his service.

Most importantly, his demeanor and comfort in front of the classroom was raw and unrefined considering his 'twenty years of teaching experience'.

When she looked into him, she found irregularities. Most might have passed other eyes but not someone like her. Josie dug a little deeper to corroborate her suspicions and concluded that his entire personnel file was so doctored it was insulting. But Makita had been assigned to the Academy from Prophus Command. The commandant couldn't question or refuse his posting. He had to be some general's grandfather or something.

Josie turned her attention back to the screen as Jill introduced Angie and passed the mantle of leadership. She wrinkled her brow. Good God, that girl was young. Josie reminded herself that this "girl" had an eternally wise alien inside her, one with a million years of experience and knowledge. Not just any Quasing, but one of the original leaders of those aliens here on Earth. That practically made Angie Cleopatra, Genghis Khan, Caesar, Howard Florey, Napoleon and Kylie Minogue all wrapped up into one.

Josie herself had been close to earning a Quasing several times throughout her career, having made the shortlist as a prospective host when the opportunity arose. She never made it to the next step though, and one day woke up realizing it just wasn't meant to be. It didn't bother her too much, not any longer. She had accomplished what she had set out to do, defended the things that needed defending and killed the people who needed killing. Most of all, she knew she was fighting for all the right reasons. That was what mattered.

Frieda leaned forward, her eyes wide as she rested her head on her elbow. "The new Keeper is pretty good-looking."

"Totally," agreed Niko. "Not quite Genjix Adonis cute, but she's got spunk."

Josie rolled her eyes. "Why do you always compete for the

same women?"

Frieda chuckled. "You mean Niko always helps me find dates."

The man shrugged. "I can't help it. I am attracted to women who end up going for Frieda. She's literally the world's worst wingman."

Frieda jabbed him playfully with a finger. "Or perhaps you're the best."

Josie raised her mug to her lips to hide her smirk. "I'm sure the new Keeper is out of both your leagues."

Mai, one of the older instructors, stood up on the other side of the room and raised his mug. "To Jill Tesser Tan, and to the new Keeper."

Most followed suit and raised their glasses. Jill was a beloved leader and the only one most in this room had ever known. The next few years were going to be very interesting. But that bumpy ride was for someone else to worry about. Josie had not seen eye-to-eye with Jill on many of her policies, especially during the war…

Josie's wrist communicator began to blink yellow. She hovered a finger over it. "Perkins."

"Sorry to bother you, Colonel. This is Simmons over at Ops. The network just flagged. Someone's probing us."

"Is it a student?"

The Academy required their students to become proficient at various computer systems before graduating to agent. Security hacking was one of the more difficult classes at the Academy. They actually encouraged students to try to break into the system, offering automatic passing grades to anyone who could successfully hack in and change their grades.

The challenge meant the Academy had some of the best network security on the planet despite its low-level status. In fact, no student had ever successfully penetrated the system, but it wasn't for want of trying.

"I'm not sure, but it looks external," said Simmons. "They're not using the usual backdoor sniff and key log attempts. I think they're trying to drill into the virtual socket."

"I'll be right there." Josie stood up. The room was still animated. She made eye contact with Frieda and Niko, and tapped the communicator on her wrist. Both nodded.

"Is anything the matter?" asked Lauren.

"I'm sure it's nothing, Commandant. Please enjoy the festivities." Josie excused herself and took her time weaving through the crowded room. She said several long goodbyes to a few of the instructors she mingled with only during holiday parties, grabbed a croissant and coffee from the counter, and strolled out of the faculty lounge. She headed to the stairwell at the far end of the building, leisurely taking the stairs down to the basement, passing through a security checkpoint, and proceeding down a narrow hallway, past the Academy's lone server room to the Operations Command Center deep underground.

Ops was a wide, shallow windowless room with a reinforced blast door. There were two rows of stadium-style workspaces arrayed in front of a long wall of outdated monitors on the opposite side. The Academy had served as an army depot in its previous life during the war, but that was a long time ago. Its clearance meant now it was a glorified training room.

Josie took a chair at the top of the room and nodded at the four people seated at their stations. It had been over a year since an incident required her presence here. The only one she recognized was Simmons, the engineer on duty. The others were likely students or staff taking their turns training to run operations.

"Report."

"Someone managed to tunnel through the firewall," said Simmons. "Sophisticated enough that I don't think it's one of our students. However, they're not covering their tracks well either."

"Any chance they'll break in?"

"It's too soon to tell." Simmons shook his head. "Wait, whoever it is just tried to hack the surveillance system on the outer perimeter."

A moment later, the main electrical grid went down. The room dimmed briefly as the backup generators kicked in. The network began to flicker. The main alert console started lighting up like Australia Day. Josie stared as a fresh batch of alerts came alive. "Any chance one of our students is a genius?"

"Not bloody likely, ma'am."

Chatter from the night watch began to filter through the comm. Searchlights down. Reports of suspicious activity. Gunfire. Suspected or confirmed. The locations were garbled. Coming from everywhere.

Josie stood up and barked orders in rapid succession. "Inform the commandant of our status. Call up security teams. Lock down campus and enact the curfew. Reinforce the perimeter. Send all civilian personnel to the bunkers."

"Yes ma'am."

A map of the Academy grounds appeared in front of her. A couple dozen blue dots formed a rough circle around the center of the campus. Small numbers appeared next to each dot, corresponding with a column of faces on another screen off to the side. The circles began to grow as the bulk of her security teams expanded to sweep the campus. Gradually, the blue dots drifted to the edge until they formed a scattered perimeter around the entire campus, anticipating an attack.

A voice blared over the speaker. "This is Niko. I'm getting a frequency signature on the south end, a hundred meters from the edge."

"I'm getting something too on the east end," added Frieda. "Also hitting several signatures."

Jimmin, on the north side, confirmed the same thing.

"Colonel," said Frieda. "We're detecting – and then – not sure how–"

More static interrupted the comm. Josie stared at the chaos that was erupting all over the grounds. The lights flickered before shutting off. Emergency floodlights kicked on a second later. "What's going on, Simmons?"

"The comm is on the fritz," he replied. "We just lost main power. Backup generators have kicked in."

"We're experiencing a technical malfunction," she said to her security teams. "If we lose contact, hold the lines. We have students' lives to safeguard."

A series of broken confirmations fought against the static coming through the speakers.

"We're deaf here," snapped Josie. "Get that fixed."

She drummed her fingers on the chair. Something didn't feel right. An imminent attack would find little resistance. Her security forces numbered less than forty, and most were on the tail-end of their careers. Why would anyone even want to attack the Academy? It held little strategic value. There was no stockpile or armory of significance, nor a blacksite or a surveillance center. There wasn't even a Prophus safehouse on site, and its only server room was classified non-sensitive, the lowest level of clearance.

"Cut the main line to the Prophus data network and sever the gateway to the outside," she said abruptly. During the war, the Genjix had enjoyed huge initial success infiltrating and poisoning the Prophus network whenever they took over a facility. Safeguards had since been implemented, but Josie preferred to err on the side of extra caution.

Simmons stopped typing and looked back her way. "Are you sure, Colonel? It'll take at least two days to bring that back up."

She nodded. "Do it."

"I'll need your access." He held out his tablet.

"Colonel Josalin Cecelia Perkins." She touched the tablet, punched in her thirteen-digit access code, and waited as the tablet measured her biometrics, scanning her eyes and recording her fingerprints.

Simmons typed several more commands before hitting the last button with a solid whack. He let loose a long breath and stood up. "It's done, Colonel. The main line is severed and will require a manual fiber hookup to reestablish uplink to the Prophus network."

"Ma'am," said the operator next to Simmons. "Waterhen just radioed in asking about the hard connection break. They're asking for a status."

"Tell them it's just a precaution," said Josie. "We'll send a full report once–"

A hollow clicking sound pinged through the room. Simmons froze, face full of surprise as he stared down at the red stain blossoming on his chest. He looked up at the man standing at the other end of the room holding a pistol, and then collapsed to the floor.

He moved smooth and quickly like a snake. He jammed the silenced pistol into the shoulder of the woman sitting next to him and pulled the trigger twice. He finished the remaining operations controller, who barely had time to look away from their screen. Once all three were down, the assassin focused his attention on Josie.

It had been many years since Josie had been in a live combat situation, but instincts never die. She wasn't armed, and she was locked in this room behind a reinforced steel door. That left her only one choice. She leapt out of the chair and attacked.

Unfortunately, while her instincts and decision-making were still as sharp and decisive as ever, her body was far less so. The first punch she threw in years could have been timed on a stopwatch. Her follow-up wasn't much better. The assassin dodged both blows with nary a shift of his head. He caught her third punch with his palm, and then cranked her arm behind her back.

Pain shot up Josie's shoulders, and she saw the near wall flying toward her face. Josie managed to turn as her head smashed into it, momentarily causing the room to blacken and her knees to go limp. A hand grabbed a fistful of hair on the back of her head. She spun, throwing an elbow out, and was pleasantly surprised when it connected with his face. Unfortunately, she was only rewarded with a muffled grunt as he pressed his elbow forward, pinning his forearm against her exposed neck. The pistol appeared and ground into her temple.

The killing shot never came. The man spoke. "I need your access to the server room." He spoke strangely perfect American English with a flat delivery that often came from news anchors.

"Go to hell," she spat. "Just kill me now."

The man grabbed her by the neck again and swiveled her over to the operative slumped over the console, whimpering and shaking. "She still breathes, as does that one, although not for long. Cooperate and all three of you may live. No one has to die tonight. We both know there is nothing in your server room worth dying over."

Josie was about to tell him to go to hell again when she stopped. He was right. There was data in the Prophus network absolutely worth taking a bullet for, some even worth every life on this base. That was a call she knew she had no trouble making. However, this wasn't one of them. The main line to the Prophus network was severed. The server room held only information relevant to the school's operation: student profiles, curriculum, health records. Some of it confidential, but barely classified.

It made sense. He was exploiting their protocol. This whole thing was a setup, a carefully orchestrated ruse, and she had fallen for it. Josie closed her eyes; she hated getting played. She was tempted to refuse him just to deny him this victory, but she had more than her ego to consider.

"How do I know you'll let us live once you have what you want?"

He pulled out several plastic ties. "You don't, but I will kill one of you on the spot if you refuse."

If there were any chance to save her people, she had to try. She swallowed her defiance and nodded. "Let's go."

The man released her and backed up, the muzzle never drifting far. He took the plastic ties and trussed up the three still breathing. Once they were secured, he waved the gun at the door. "Lead the way."

Josie kept her hands up as she unlocked the reinforced door and stepped out. She had half-hoped to encounter some of her security out here, since the armory and server room were both in the restricted area. If they weren't already deployed to the perimeter.

Damn. The Genjix had really played them like a fiddle. What could he possibly be after? She led him next door to the entrance to the server room and was about to begin punching in her access when the cold muzzle pressed against the back of her skull. "Don't even think about putting in a distress code. I memorized your finger strokes."

"Damn you're good," she muttered.

Josie completed implementing her biometrics and the door swung open. The assassin nudged her inside, closing it behind her. He pushed Josie against the corner as he hardwired himself into the nearest console. The seconds ticked away. Josie couldn't quite make out what was on the screen, but it seemed the Genjix got what he wanted. After he finished stealing the data, he disconnected from the system and spoke softly into his comm, no doubt already working on his extraction.

He turned to her and raised his pistol. "Thank you for your assistance, Colonel."

Josie was expecting a messy death now that he was done with her. There was no point leaving any loose ends, and she *was* a colonel. It would be almost insulting if he didn't kill her. Josie was fine with this. She had saved three people's lives in exchange for her own. It was a good trade. She squeezed her eyes shut and thought about Parker, her folks, and that dream vacation to the Maldives she never got to take.

A muzzle flash erupted in the darkness, followed closely by the deafening clash of a gun discharge in a tight space. The Genjix operative whirled and somehow dodged a gunshot as a bullet punched into the wall behind where he had been standing moments earlier. Two more shots: one just missed when he dropped to a knee and the other he miraculously blocked with his gun.

The ricochet from the bullet twisted the pistol from his hand. The Genjix reached down to pick it up. Josie leaped forward and kicked the gun, skidding it across the floor. She followed up with another to his face. The assassin trapped her leg in his arm and kicked her feet out from under her. The newcomer fired again, but the Genjix took cover behind a server shelf.

"Crap, it's a freaking pretty boy," a voice cursed. A figure stepped out from around the corner with a pistol in hand.

Josie's mouth fell open. "Makita? What–"

A shadow leapt out from Makita's blind side. To Josie's astonishment, the Japanese man sidestepped the lunge and countered the punch with a surprisingly fluid block. His foot shot out and tripped the Genjix, knocking him momentarily off balance. Then, Makita raised his pistol and fired at point-blank range. Somehow he missed again. At this point, Josie wasn't sure if the Genjix operative was superb or Makita badly needed glasses.

The assassin executed a spectacular looping spin-kick that connected with Makita's face, throwing him all the way across the room. The old man bounced off the wall and slumped to the floor. Somehow he remained conscious. He'd even held onto his gun and fired two more shots, missing both times but nearly hitting Josie.

The Genjix disappeared again behind the server racks.

Grunting, Makita grabbed a shelf for support and wall-walked to his feet. He tried to spit, then decided instead to pull his dentures – cracked – out of his mouth. He swept his gun across the room, and waved for Josie to approach. Once she got close, he pulled her behind him and they made their way toward the door.

"We need to get out of here. We can't fight this guy. Best we can do is lock his ass inside," he muttered under his breath. "When we get out, run for help. I'll hold the door."

Makita pawed for the handle.

No sooner had the door opened a sliver than the Genjix appeared, streaking toward them. This time, Makita was ready for him. Two more pulls of the trigger. Two more misses.

"You are an awful shot," remarked Josie.

"Not helpful," he snapped, his arms jerking left and right.

By the grace of God and probably blind luck, Makita's next shot finally hit the Genjix, striking him in the bicep. At such close range, Josie expected any man to crumple, but he kept coming. His body jerked from the impact, but he barely slowed as he covered the distance between them in two steps. A kick to Makita's mid-section sent him flying out of the server room.

Josie cracked the assassin once in the ribs with an uppercut and then tried to smother and drag him down. The Genjix shucked her off as if she were nothing and then slammed her to the floor. The breath escaped her body.

He towered over her, his fist drawn back, ready for the killing blow. For the third time in ten minutes, she thought she was going to die, but Parker must have been looking down on her. The Genjix looked away distracted, and then took off. Makita tried to grab his legs, but was rewarded with a kick to the head that knocked him back down. The hallway was soon silent save for Makita's groans and Josie's faint gasps as she tried to catch her breath. A few seconds later, the Japanese instructor got to his feet and offered a hand.

"Are you all right?" he asked gruffly.

She nodded. "I haven't had this much fun in years. You?"

He helped her to her feet. "Cracked my dentures, maybe a rib too, but I've had worse. Any time you fight an Adonis vessel and live to tell about it is a good day."

Josie looked in the direction the Genjix had fled. "So that's what he was. I have never seen one up close."

"We're lucky to be alive."

She frowned and studied Makita's bloody face. "What happened to your accent?"

CHAPTER TWO
Break In

So you wish to learn about Ella Patel. Why is this relevant? Her past is inconsequential to her circumstance. It will not change your perception of her, nor will it affect her actions moving forward. But since my opinions on the matter are not relevant either, I will comply.

I have searched her mind and experienced her earliest tangible memories.

Let us start at the beginning.

When Ella was young, she used to love metal briefcases. That was before she was inhabited by a Quasing alien named Io, before she became hunted by the Genjix, and before the two of them were forced to flee Ella's home in the Crate Town slum of Surat, India. A lifetime had passed since she innocently believed that shiny metallic briefcases carried a life of comfort, riches and beautiful hunky men. She was now more seasoned, wiser and hardened, practical. Any lingering fondness for those bulky, unwieldy containers with their sharp corners was long gone. It had been a long two years.

These days, she loved vaults: big, shiny walk-in bank vaults with cool locks and cylinders and large circular knobby protruding metal bolty thingies.

It is called a hand wheel.

Vaults with lots and lots of storage. Vaults holding cash and gems and other things that people valued enough to hide behind thick metal doors. Valuables to fence on the black market.

It just happened to be Ella's lucky day. She was standing in front of one such vault this very moment.

The large metal circular door, complete with cylinders and dials and that hand wheel thingy, looked out of place in the gray damp stone. It came alive as she punched in the emergency code and gave the hand wheel a turn, its metal heartbeat speeding up with the spin of the dial. It finally came to a stop with a loud hollow thunk that reverberated through the underground sewer tunnels. The vault door swung inward with a loud creak, revealing a dingy room that faded into darkness.

Ella's flashlight crawled into the pitch black interior, but couldn't pierce a sea of disturbed dust particles. She looked down; a thick even layer of dust caked the floor.

The last recorded use was three months ago when the facility was restocked. It appears it has not been occupied since.

"Perfect."

Somewhere in the void, a ventilation system hummed to life. Rows of ugly fluorescent ceiling lights kicked on one by one, illuminating a long room that stretched far to the right. A gust of rot and stale air blew past. Someone must have left food out the last time they were here. Ella wrinkled her nose. Cleaning up after yourself was a lost art these days. She took two steps inside.

Left upper corner.

Ella spied the security camera nestled near the ceiling. She bit down on her lip and drew her pistol.

Like we practiced. Steady breath. Soft pull.

She stared down the sight and softly squeezed the trigger,

once, twice. Dust kicked up from the cement wall next to the camera as it continued to pan toward her position.

Relax your shoulders. Stop tilting your head. Remember, center line.

"Why don't you center *your* line," she growled.

Ella exhaled forcefully, loosened her shoulders and readjusted her aim. Her mind drifted to the many times that Nabin had patiently trained with her. His body wrapped around hers as he guided her arms. His soft voice preaching relaxation as his southern drawl paced her breathing.

She was even more off on the third attempt. A guttural cry crawled up her throat. Ella twisted her body and sent a throwing knife streaking from her thigh to her hand to the air in one fluid motion. The blade point punched through the center of the camera lens, killing the feed.

I do not know how it is possible you can make that throw with a knife but cannot hit the same target with a gun.

"That's because guns suck."

Guns do not suck. You are just an awful shot.

Ella twirled the pistol and tried to holster it fancy, like in those American cowboy movies. It slipped straight off her finger and nearly crushed her toes. Luckily there were no witnesses. She put a finger to her ear. "I'm in. How do things look outside?"

"The alley is clear, Ella," grumbled a high-pitched voice. "In fact, no one's even walked past the entrance in over an hour."

"What was that, Pek?"

"Sorry, I mean Big Bosu."

"The crew's ready, Bosu," piped up Hinata.

Sweep the room first.

"Give me a second." Ella did a quick pass of the main room, disabling a camera in the opposite corner and another pointing at a samurai sword mounted on a wall. She poked her head into the kitchen at the far end, the dining and living quarters in the center of the open area, and the three side rooms stacked with bunk-beds.

The interior was surprisingly nicely furnished for a lair hidden in an old sewer tunnel far beneath Tokyo. Ella sort of wished she could just move in and take over the place. Sure, walking through sewer tunnels was pretty disgusting, but it wasn't worse than the garbage-strewn streets in Crate Town, and she wouldn't have to pay rent.

This particular lair was carved out of a long-forgotten storage facility now only accessible through a maze beneath the city's railway network. It was well-hidden and nearly impossible to navigate unless someone knew exactly which paths to go down, which turns to make, and what conce niche to examine.

After both she and Io were sure they had swept the room clear of surveillance devices, Ella gave the signal. "Pay attention, Burglar Alarms, I want us in and out. We should be eating noodle soup in thirty minutes."

A chorus of "OK, Big Bosu" echoed in her ear.

A few seconds later, Ella's handpicked outfit of highly skilled and hardened operatives spilled into the lair. She had christened them the Burglar Alarms. She used to run a one-person operation in Crate Town, but now Ella had far greater ambitions. She wanted to build and expand a fully-fledged criminal empire. That meant she needed help.

Stop calling it a criminal empire.

The Burglar Alarms would have been called a street rat gang in Crate Town. The outfit was a crew of six, counting Ella. They were around her age, give or take a few years, and though they were of different ethnicities and from different places, there was one thing that tied them all together: they were dirt-poor.

More than that, though, they were young people struggling to find their place in the world after the adults had wrecked it with a massive war. All of them had broken families and no more than one parent, save for Hinata – but that didn't count, because his father was in prison. The rest of them had lost at least one mother or father during the war. Lee had lost both and been raised by a great-aunt.

Ella liked to think she was elevating others out of their hopeless situations, bringing them up alongside her. Not that she was running a charity. Each of the Burglar Alarms was quick-thinking, street-smart, ambitious and hardworking. The best people she could find on the streets. Most importantly, they were loyal to Ella, and they were going to help her get rich.

How loyal could they be? You only met them five months ago.

"As long as they get paid, they'll be loyal."

That much was true whether she was in Crate Town or Tokyo or on the Moon.

"Can I come too, Ella?" pleaded Pek. "I mean, Big Bosu? I'm so bored."

OK, maybe they weren't *all* the best and brightest. More like the leftover kids she had managed to convince to give her a shot. In any case, she was going to make the Burglar Alarms the envy of all the streets.

"Stay with the truck, Pek," she ordered the newest and youngest member.

Pek whined. "I always stay behind. I think I should get to–"

"That's the problem. You think too much," said Ella. "Now shut up, unless you see something suspicious."

Go easy on the boy. He is fourteen.

"I ran my own criminal empire by the time I was fourteen."

Is that what you call your racket back in Crate Town? Pek has been sitting in that truck staring at the alley entrance the entire evening. When we first met, you could not stay still for more than an hour.

Ella grunted. "I still can't."

She moved briskly across the facility and began to direct

her troops like a general on the battlefield. "Lee, to the supply closet. Kaoru, find the armory. Daiki, medicine closet, get only the scarce stuff. Hinata, dig up anything else that's useful."

"What do you consider useful?"

"I don't know. Stuff that looks like it'll sell. Nothing stupid." She clapped her hands several times. "Hurry up. Military and medical first, then survival, and Ganesh help me if I catch one of you stealing DVDs again."

"What about electronics?" asked Hinata.

Ella shook her head. "Nothing stupid, I said. We're not here to decorate your apartment. Nothing bolted down."

The oldest and largest of the Burglar Alarms, with spiky hair and a broad frame, pointed with a heavily tattooed arm at one of the large screens mounted to the wall above his head. "That one's mine."

"Nothing. Bolted. Down." Ella stood near the center of the room and oversaw the score as each Burglar went about their assignments. Lee climbed a ladder and disappeared into a crawl space. Kaoru began to run her fingers along the walls, searching for hidden latches. Hinata started pilfering a metal workbench stacked with assorted tools and gadgets.

Ella scanned the premises. "Where did Daiki go?"

Kaoru frowned. "He's supposed to be checking the closet on the opposite wall."

Ella saw a yellow light shining from the kitchen. Scowling, she went to investigate, and caught the boy hunched over an opened refrigerator.

The very best people, hm?

She crossed her arms, leaned against the door frame and cleared her throat. "Find anything in the fridge worth selling?"

Daiki gave a start and turned toward her, his mouth messy with a dark brown substance. "I was just checking what's here."

"Really?"

He had the decency to look abashed, and hung his head. "I'm about to fall over," the smallish boy protested, his mouth already half-stuffed with food. "Okaa-san had to work double shifts all week. I've eaten nothing but ramen packs for two days straight."

"You should learn how to cook." Ella stopped herself. Not knowing how to cook wasn't why the boy was eating only instant noodles. "Make it quick. We're not here to stuff our faces."

"Hey, why does he get to eat?" Lee yelled from the other room. "I want..."

"Back to work," roared Ella. "Unless you're about to pass out from hunger, you can wait until the job is done."

"Bosu," called Kaoru. "I found the guns."

Ella let Daiki stuff a few more bites in his face before hauling him by the sleeve to where Kaoru had uncovered a hidden room behind the false wall with the samurai sword. The secret door creaked open. Kaoru stared inside, her eyes widening. Lee, who was passing by with a bundle of thermal blankets in his arms, stopped and whistled. "That's a lot of killing."

Ella broke into a grin. Shelves and drawers lined the walls inside what appeared to be a fully stocked mini armory. Atop each shelf were rows upon rows of guns. Guns of all shapes and sizes. Big ones, long ones, funny-looking ones, even a tiny cute one in the corner.

That one is not even a gun.

"Does it shoot things?"

Yes, crossbow bolts. They are like arrows.

Daiki rushed inside and came back out hefting a large cylinder on his shoulder. "Look at this funny fat thing."

"Put that back," snapped Ella. "No one is going to buy a bazooka."

Technically that is a surface-to-air missile launcher.

"It looks expensive," said Daiki, defensively.

"It's junk if no one buys it."

"There's a lot more stuff here than we figured, Bosu," said Kaoru. "Should we clear it out?"

Take a little bit of everything so as to not arouse suspicion. Remember what I told you. Make it a garden. Harvest it little by little. Take no more than a fifth. The best victims do not realize they are victims.

Ella did some quick math in her head. She really hated leaving anything behind at all, but they had already agreed the best way to handle this facility was to bleed this place slowly instead of cleaning it out. That way they could come back in a few months. Still, assault rifles fetched a lucrative price on the black market in a country where guns were illegal.

Leave the medicine.

"What? You're crazy. Medicine always sells."

Not in a country with universal healthcare. There is no market for medicine if everyone here gets it free. The inventory is just going to sit on the shelves.

Io's words almost swayed her. Almost. Medicine back in Crate Town was always in high demand and awfully expensive. Ella had a hard time believing something so valuable in her old home could be worthless somewhere else, especially since the one time Io gave her horrible advice during a heist involving stolen tetanus and hepatitis doses from a bunch of gangsters. Besides, guns, ammunition and armor were heavy. Medicine was small and light, and would probably fetch the most money by weight. The Burglar Alarms weren't exactly the burliest group.

Ella decided to trust her gut. She pointed at the medicine cabinet. "Clean out the medicine. Go equal parts on the guns and military hardware. Spread out your pickings though and don't get too greedy."

You are making a mistake.

"I'm a businesswoman. I'll find a way to unload it. You'll see."

In a short amount of time, her crew had efficiently worked through the facility, skimming just enough from the supplies to accumulate a decent haul. Ella took a quick inventory: nine cartons of medical supplies, four crates of guns, six cases of ammunition, five boxes of clothing and survival equipment, and an assortment of high-end surveillance instruments, including two Penetra scanners. This was more than enough to keep them afloat for the next few months. Best of all, they could come back in three months.

Better make that eight months to be safe.

"That's forever from now. Let's compromise on six."

That is not how it works, Ella. Remember what we talked about.

Ella gave the room one last scan. Satisfied, she slapped the nearest crate. "Load the goods onto the truck. We still clear outside, Pek?"

"Yes, Bosu," came the sullen reply. "Did I hear that right? Is there food down there? I'm hungry too."

"You'll get noodles soon enough." Ella did one last pass of the area, grabbing a few random knickknacks. She watched as the Burglar Alarms left the facility single file, two to a crate as they made their way above ground. She took up the rear hefting a duffel bag. "Remember, right, another right, then a left to the truck," she called, her voice bouncing through the tunnels. "I want to be out of here in fifteen. I'm getting hungry."

Fifteen minutes may have been ambitious. That or the Burglar Alarms had tried to steal a bit more than they could handle. Transporting the heavy crates down three hundred meters of sewer tunnels, then up a rusty ladder through a manhole, and then onto a truck, and repeat, took far longer than she originally anticipated. Their getaway vehicle was a rickety flatbed truck with a worn canopy full of holes parked next to the sewer manhole. There were actually several entrances closer to the surface, but this one was near the back of an alley and offered better privacy.

They finally finished forty minutes later. Hinata and Lee were struggling to push the last crate onto the truck bed when Kaoru tapped Ella on the shoulder and pointed at the alley entrance. Someone was coming. Ella furiously motioned to Hinata to drag the crate under the truck and for everyone to hide. The two boys followed orders and scampered underneath the truck. The rest ducked inside the bed while Ella pulled the canvas flap down.

She crouched and slowly drew a knife in each hand, the blades hissing free. Kaoru, next to her, pulled out a rubber mallet, while Pek behind her nearly dropped a broomstick. Ella signaled for him to just stay still. The Burglar Alarms was not an outfit built for fights, but it didn't mean they weren't ready to mix it up if necessary.

A gun would be more suitable in this situation. In just about every situation.

"I don't want to push my luck tonight."

Point taken. One day, you will bring knives to a gun fight. Then the last thing you will hear before you die is me telling you I told you so.

"At least I'll be rid of you then."

The footsteps grew louder and were soon joined by chaotic voices. A man and woman were exchanging sharp words. Several silhouettes sped past the canvas and then the outside quieted. Someone moaned. Another argument erupted. The woman began barking orders in a stern voice. Ella couldn't quite make out what language they were speaking.

It is English.

"It doesn't sound like English."

That is because your English is awful. In your defense, they are speaking with a heavy Icelandic accent.

Kaoru, who was peeking through a slit between the canvas, whispered, "They stopped right behind the truck."

Ella tensed and adjusted the grip of her knife. Her heart

hammered in her chest. If these strangers laid even a hand on the truck or poked their heads through the tail cover, they were going to get a knife right in the face.

"I think one of them is hurt," whispered Kaoru. Seconds passed. Finally, she signaled that they were in the clear. "They're gone. They went down through the manhole."

Ella flipped the tail cover up and stuck her head out. "Everyone here?"

Hinata and Lee's heads poked out from under the truck. Lee made a face. "We parked over a puddle."

She turned to Kaoru. "How many were there?"

"Two, three, or four."

"Which is it?" she snapped. "There's a pretty big difference between two and four."

"I couldn't get a good look," said Kaoru. "They were in a hurry and carrying something heavy."

They are without a doubt heading down to the lair. We should leave as soon as possible.

Ella couldn't agree more. "It doesn't matter anyway," she said. "We're done here. Load up the last crate. We'll drop it off at the World-Famous and get some noodles."

Kaoru looked around. "Where's Daiki?"

The rest of the Burglar Alarms exchanged looks.

"I thought he was with you," said Hinata.

Lee shook his head. "He was still down in the room when I left with the last crate."

"Does he have a comm?"

Kaoru shook her head. "We only had three so you, Hinata and Pek got them."

Ella checked the front of the truck. The stout, bald teen with the bottomless stomach was nowhere in sight. She cursed.

He must still be down there. Leave him.

Ella was awfully tempted to do just that. It would serve him right. The boy had the attention span of a koi. Maybe he would learn to listen. Problem was, if he got caught, there probably wouldn't be a next time for him. Ella had also met Daiki's mother just last week. The old woman had fed the crew cake, told them how happy she was Daiki had friends.

She clenched her fists. "Keep the engine running. I'll be right back."

Lee frowned. "You're going after him alone?"

Ella ignored him and climbed back down the manhole. She landed in ankle-deep water and carefully crept down the curved tunnel toward the lair. It didn't take her long to catch up to the strangers who had so rudely interrupted her heist. She slowed and waited until they were just about to turn the second corner. These strangers were making a lot of noise as they splashed through the sewers.

She kept to a safe distance, hugging the wall and using the running water to mask her footsteps. There were three of them. The woman was in the lead while the two men were encumbered carrying a heavy load. She hoped they would get lost down here so she could cut ahead of them and find Daiki, but they knew exactly where they were going and headed straight to the lair. They stopped at the entrance.

"Something is wrong," said the woman. She pushed the vault door, watching as it lazily swung open. She drew a gun. The others began to put down their load.

"No," the woman shook her head. "It's filthy out here. Put Asha down just inside and sweep the room."

The group disappeared into the facility. Ella held her breath, waiting to hear the immediate outcry. When none came, she crept closer to the facility and peered inside. There was a woman lying just inside the door. Her clothing was wet, and a moan escaped her lips as she writhed in pain. The remaining three were spread out inside, weapons drawn as they swept the room.

"You two finish sweeping," the woman in charge yelled.

"Asha's bleeding through the dressing and losing too much blood. Look for an abdominal tourniquet." There were more sounds of doors slamming open, drawers opening, and cabinets banging. The leader woman cursed. "It's gone. There's nothing here."

"What do you mean, nothing?" yelled one of the men.

"I mean, I'm staring at the medical cabinet and it's completely bare."

Ella bit her lip. "Damn."

I told you to leave something. What did I say?

"How was I supposed to know someone was going to come here bleeding like a stuck pig?"

That is the whole purpose of these facilities.

A moment later, the high-pitched squeal that Ella was expecting carried across the room. One of the men appeared out of the kitchen, yanking a sniveling Daiki by the collar, a pistol to his head.

"Who is that?" asked the woman.

"A thief," the man said. "I caught him stuffing his face with chocolate cake."

"How can he eat that stuff?" the other man said. "That dehydrated crap taste like rubber."

"You, boy," the woman demanded, speaking in Japanese. "Where are our supplies?"

The man cuffed Daiki and knocked him to the ground. "Talk, boy. Where is all of the stuff that belongs here?"

Daiki began to blubber.

You need to leave. Now.

"They're going to kill him."

It is too late. You will only get caught if you intervene.

Ella almost obeyed Io. She took two steps backward and was nearly out the door when she hesitated. As much as she knew leaving the boy was the right thing to do, she just couldn't. Instead, she pulled out a knife and dropped to a crouch. She moved up to the injured woman and pressed a blade to her throat.

"Let him go," she yelled.

Every set of eyes turned toward her, as did three sets of guns.

Now you have done it.

Ella did her best to look mean. "Let him go or your friend gets it."

"Let her go," yelled the woman.

"I said it first," yelled Ella back.

None of them moved a muscle. In fact, they looked like they were taking aim. Ella flattened as close to the body as possible. The woman's breathing was shallow and her face pale. Ella hoped she didn't die on her before they were done with the standoff. The injured woman was her only leverage. "We just want to leave. Let him go and no one gets hurt."

For a moment, it appeared as if these people were going to call her bluff. Then the woman exchanged looks with the others and lowered her gun. The two men followed suit. Daiki picked himself off the ground and sprinted to Ella.

"Thank–" he said.

"Shut up and get to the truck," she snapped.

Once Daiki was safely out of sight, Ella slowly released her hold on the woman and retreated out of the vault entrance. She ran at full speed through the sewer tunnels and then back up the ladder and out the manhole. The truck was waiting for her. Daiki was already inside. Kaoru and Lee were waving for Ella to climb on. No sooner had they grabbed her arms and her feet left the ground than it began to roll away. The adrenaline drained from Ella's body, and she slumped over.

Good job. I still would have left him, but you did well.

"Shut up, Alien." She paused. "And thanks."

Ella leaned against one of the medical cartons and stared at the red cross painted on the side. She closed her eyes. "Crap."

No, Ella. It is too risky.

She should. She couldn't.

"Stop the truck," she ordered.

"What?" said Hinata.

"Stop it. Now."

The truck screeched to a stop just before it left the alley. Ella grabbed one of the medical cartons and lugged the damn thing back down the sewers and backtracked to the safe house. The people inside had closed it this time, but the code remained the same. The vault door swung open and Ella wobbled in carrying the heavy carton.

The group had moved their injured friend to the kitchen table and were huddled around the body. Ella dumped the contents of the emergency field kit onto the floor. The three people looked at her, alarmed. One of them pulled a gun, and then slowly lowered it when he saw what she had brought.

"Here," said Ella.

The woman saw the medical supplies and then rushed to pick up what she needed.

Ella turned to leave.

"Wait, stop," said the woman. "Who are you? Why are you helping us?"

Ella ignored her. "I'm nobody, and none of your business, Prophus." As she closed the door behind her, she yelled out, "And change the locks on your front door."

CHAPTER THREE
Makita

Ella Patel is the daughter of Anu and Ada Patel. The Prophus have scrubbed her official identifications and records, but there was not much that was useful anyway except for her extensive arrest record. Her parents were in the military and fought on the side of the Prophus during the Alien World War when it enveloped the entire globe.

Her mother was a major in the Republic of Singapore Air Force. Died during the Genjix Third Wave blitzkrieg. Her father was a havildar with the Indian Army. Declared MIA after the fall of Gujarat.

Both are presumed deceased. Ella became an orphan at ten years old. Their deaths have made her naturally biased against the Genjix, although her trust of the Prophus is nearly as tenuous.

The man known as Makita leaned against the wall and felt the dull ache all through his body. He hunched over to rest on his knees, and took a couple long breaths. In, out, in, out. Pain, pain, sharp pain, oh-that-last-one-really-hurt pain. After a few more labored breaths, he stood up and threw his head back, letting the air rush into his body. The ache in his chest softened.

Makita closed his eyes. He was angry. There were several people he could blame: the Genjix – the pretty boy Genjix assassin – the Prophus, Jill Tesser Tan, his own rotten luck, or that little missing punk. Take your pick. Just about everyone he could point at for putting him in this situation.

Most of all though, Makita blamed terrible television programming. Bad programming, boredom and those damn weeds in his garden that just wouldn't die. He had never been a patient man. People were supposed to become wiser and more patient as they aged. Makita found the exact opposite to be true. Maybe it was because he had used up all his patience over the course of his long life, or maybe it was because he knew his days were running low. Regardless, he could no longer tolerate wasting time.

Like he was right now. Standing here outside the office waiting to be disciplined. Fortunately, the wait was not too long.

The door opened, and the commandant of the Academy poked her head out. "Thank you for your patience, Instructor Makita. Please come in."

He gave the commandant a curt nod and followed her inside, but not before noticing security guards appearing at both ends of the hallway. There were no such things as coincidences.

"I'm glad to see you up and about," said Lauren, walking around to the other side of her desk. "The medics reported you took quite a beating."

"I am as good as can be expected," he replied gruffly. "Thank you very–"

"You can quit the fake Japanese accent," a gravelly and now-familiar voice chirped from somewhere behind him.

His hesitation was brief. The woman never liked him. Not since he first stepped foot on campus. He didn't much care for her either. Makita figured he could play this one of three ways. One, try to maintain his cover by feigning ignorance. Two, accuse her of lying or mishearing him. Three, quit this stupid charade.

Or four, head back home to his boring life watching bad television. Especially in light of recent developments.

Four almost won out. Almost. Makita decided against any of the above. Josie had an exemplary record. Trying to throw her under the bus wouldn't work. Lauren wasn't a slouch either. She was much more likely to believe her head of security than a visiting instructor who had been on campus all of one week. Besides, he had never been that good of a liar. Option four wasn't a possibility anyway, unless he was willing to fight his way off Academy grounds. In the end, he decided to try to keep both his identity and enlist their aid. It was time to pull the get-out-of-jail-free card.

"Pull up my personnel file," he said finally in his normal voice. "You'll find an encrypted hidden attachment under the miscellaneous notes. Open it with base binary code: one, one, zero, zero, one, zero, one, one, zero, zero, zero, one."

"I knew you were a fraud," heckled Josie, chuckling. "Smelled it a kilometer away. What kind of remedial language for dummies did you use to learn Japanese? I mean–"

Lauren's face went deathly white, and then the commandant flicked her hand and sent the hovering display over to the colonel. The snark died and was replaced by a period of extended silence interrupted by an occasional uncomfortable cough.

Makita tried to bury his smugness and keep his gaze locked on the commandant, but his smirk won out. He couldn't stop himself from turning to preen once at Josie. Twice actually. He berated himself for not keeping his cool. It had been a while, and he was out of practice. He was never that great at keeping it in anyhow.

The commandant's response was exactly as he expected.

"What can we do to help support your mission?"

"Thank you for your cooperation," he replied. "The first thing I require is my anonymity. It's imperative I maintain my cover. Next I need to know what the Genjix–"

An orange flew past Makita's head. Josie's response, on the other hand, was not what he expected. "This is crap. Who are you and what are you doing here?"

Makita turned to her. "Were you not listening? I just said my identity needs–"

"I heard you, and I don't believe you for a flaming second." Josie hopped to her feet. "First of all, I'm a twenty-year operative with the highest clearance. Any official operation would go through me. Second of all, I'm the one on the ground. You don't operate under my nose without my say-so."

"Yeah but…" sputtered Makita holding up the commandant's tablet. "I have a missive from the Keeper…"

Josie knocked it out of his hands. "That's what I think about your stupid directive. If you were sent here, that means you must have known something was coming. Keeping me in the dark was a security risk. If I had known of a possible attack, I could have been prepared. We lost ten good people last night, including those in the ops room."

"Lana didn't make it?" asked Makita quietly.

Josie shook her head. "Lost too much blood by the time the medics got to her."

"I'm sorry to hear that. We couldn't risk it."

"Who is we, and what is this all about? If you don't come clean, I'm going to arrest you and ship you back to Prophus Command in a straitjacket."

Makita didn't blame her for being furious. He would be too, in her position. His need for secrecy had a cost, and left the Academy unprepared for an attack, but it couldn't be helped. If the Genjix had caught wind of his activities at all, he might as well have just sent them a telegram letting them know where to look.

Part of being undercover meant the operative had to know who to trust and when to divulge his mission. He decided to trust Josie. Makita looked up and waggled his finger in a circle. "Can we get a cone of silence up?"

Lauren looked at Josie, who nodded. The commandant reached under her desk. A moment later, a low-pitched resonance filled the room. The three waited as the noise grew gradually higher and quieter until it was no longer audible to the human ear. Satisfied, Makita sat down opposite of Lauren. He pointed at the empty chair. Josie chose to remain standing.

Makita shrugged and made himself comfortable. "Eight weeks ago, a location contract was put out on the black market for the whereabouts of one of our hosts. There's usually a dozen such long-standing contracts, so it's not a big deal. However, this one was for three million US dollars."

Lauren's eyes widened. "Just for a location?"

"Somebody really wants to find them," said Josie.

"In any case, Command decided to do nothing," continued Makita. "The whole thing felt like a fishing expedition. The host was a new one in training, well-hidden and part of the Host Protection Program. Command surmised that any activity – relocation, movement or a protection detail – would simply draw attention."

"Why couldn't they do it quietly?" asked Lauren.

"Because our network security sucks," he said. "Infiltration tech has far outpaced defensive firewall measures, so our data is always potentially vulnerable. That's why protocols are in place to cut main lines at the slightest intrusion. Speaking of a sieve..." Makita stood up abruptly and headed for the door. He swung it open and caught the guard standing outside by surprise. "Hello." He reached for the man's holster.

The man caught Makita's wrist way before his fingers got

close to the sidearm. "What do you think you're doing?"

"Let him go," said Josie.

"I really have lost a step." Makita rubbed his bruised wrist when the man complied. He turned to Josie and threw a thumb at the guard. "Can you send your man away?"

"I've seen you in action, fake instructor," she replied. "Niko stays."

Makita shrugged. "You're just creating more paperwork for everyone. You might as well come on in then, Niko."

He closed the door behind Niko and returned to his chair. "Where was I?"

"You were explaining about the host with the location contract, but you haven't explained what you're doing here," said Lauren.

Josie glared at him with narrowed eyes. "You're not supposed to be here. At least not officially. You're off-book, aren't you?"

Makita pointed at Josie and grinned. "Nothing gets past our head of security here. Someone close to the Keeper has a special interest in this host and was concerned enough about the giant price tag to ask the Keeper for a favor. Since we can't use an active agent, especially one who may leave a paper trail, she dipped into the retired pool and asked me to babysit."

"So how goes it?" asked Josie.

"How goes what?"

"The babysitting."

Makita hesitated. "I ran into a snag. I was unable to pull the host's identity from the HPP's database without making it an official request and raising a bunch of flags, so I thought I'd do it the old-fashioned way. I snuck a Penetra scanner onto campus."

Lauren's eyes narrowed. "Those are strictly forbidden on campus for the hosts' safety. If the enemy discovers the identity of new hosts who are not ready to defend themselves, then their Quasing's lives could be at stake. It also negatively impacts a student's training if their peers know they are a host."

"I'm aware of that," said Makita dryly. "But I had no other choice. The only information I have on the host is a name. Once I realized the name was washed, all I could do was to scan for them."

"And?" asked Josie.

Makita shook his head. "I couldn't locate them. I blanketed the entire campus over the past week and couldn't find any host who fit their description."

"It's a pretty large campus, and we have thousands of students," said Lauren.

"It isn't that big," he replied.

Josie frowned. "As head of security, I know the identity of all our host students. I accounted for all four last night after the attack. "

"Actually," said Makita slowly. "There are six."

"What?"

"Six," he repeated. "There are different levels of confidentiality in HPP. Four are in the regular program. Two are special need-to-know cases. One is the second son of the Bhutan royal family, and the other is the one I'm supposed to be looking out for."

Josie threw her hands up. "All that snow in Greenland has frozen their brains. Fine, there's six hosts. Which one are you looking for?"

Lauren pulled up an image of the Bhutan royal family on her comm. Her eyes widened. She pointed at one of the boys. "That's Ugyen, one of our third-years. I should have guessed. That boy is literally the perfect young man." She scanned the royal family's profile. "His real name is Dorji. That suits him."

"My only option," continued Makita, "is to match the host's encrypted serial identifiers to the master historical call list.

Which I believe is what the Genjix were after last night."

"I can pull it up." Lauren tapped a few buttons on her tablet and handed it to Makita, who began to match the numbers.

"So who is this host?" asked Niko

"My money is on that Ling boy," said Josie. "He's always a little too smart and polished for a student."

"Mine is on Ruskov," said Lauren. "That boy has impeccable manners."

"Ruskov has two left feet," chuckled Josie. "Maybe it's Kim."

The three nodded in consensus. All eyes turned to Makita.

"You're all wrong," said Makita as his program began to filter out the candidates. "First of all, it's not a boy. Second of all, she's..." His face noticeably drooped "...aww man."

"What is it?" asked Lauren. "Is there a problem with our mystery host?"

"You can say that." Makita slid the tablet across the table toward the commandant. "This explains why I can't find her. You expelled her six months ago."

CHAPTER FOUR
Home

India, one of the major battlegrounds, was devastated during the war. Ella, along with millions of other refugees, was abandoned and forgotten by the rest of the world. She found her way to a slum known as Crate Town, where she eked out a meager living, begging and stealing on the streets.

Ella was eventually taken in by the owner of a laundry and bath house named Wiry Madras. The woman was strict and used Ella as a slave, forcing her to work long hours cleaning, folding and carrying water. Wiry Madras, however, also kept Ella safe from the dangers of the streets and allowed the girl to grow and mature. It was a difficult and formative period of her life, and the reason that to this day Ella chafes at authority.

Ella melted into her seat as she rode the Tozai Line toward the east end of Tokyo. The night had lasted much longer than she had anticipated. The truck had gone straight from the Prophus safe house to the bar they used as a storage facility. It took almost as long to unload the goods as it did to load in the first place.

By the time they had finished, Lee had to take the truck back to work. Kaoru was late for the night shift at the lab at the university. Daiki and Pek had to hurry home to get some sleep before school. Ella sent Hinata to speak with a few parties who could be interested in the guns, leaving her to do all the organizing by herself. It was closer to sunup by the time she finished moving the goods from the loading area into the store room. She had considered just sleeping on the crates like a dragon on her pot of gold, but she wanted a soft bed. That, and she smelled like she had been wading through sewage the entire night.

Ella was so exhausted, she almost passed out on the way to the station. Io had to help keep her upright as she staggered into the train car to find a seat. She definitely would have missed her stop if Io hadn't woken her. She left the Nishi Kasai Station and weaved through the lightly trafficked street, which was not uncommon at this time.

Home was a tiny worn-out low-rise in the Nishi Kasai district, affectionately named Little India. She hadn't intentionally sought out her people in this sprawling city of thirty-four million when she first decided to settle in Tokyo; they just had especially cheap rent. The entire neighborhood was shut down for the night with the exception of a few twenty-four-hour convenience stores and breakfast shops.

Devanagari letters scrolled down the signage, and the smell of curry and marigolds and sandalwood drifted into her nostrils. An elderly couple passed by on their morning walk speaking Hindi. The familiar foods, sounds, and words were tremendously comforting in this alien world. No pun intended.

Pun totally taken.

Ella sighed. Homesick didn't even begin to describe how she felt. She could never go back to India. It was now thoroughly Genjix-controlled. Crate Town no longer even existed. Shortly after she had fled, the regional government bulldozed and flattened the slum, and evicted all of its residents. It was now just one massive Genjix base.

Ella bit her lower lip. She wondered what had happened to all the people she had grown up around: Wiry Madras, Manish, Melonhead, Congee, Mogg, even the Fabs family, who had tried to sell her out. They were probably scattered all over the place like dandelion seeds in the wind. Crate Town was gone and would likely never rise again.

"Not like that's a bad thing," she grumbled. "Crate Town was a dump."

But it was her dump, her home. She missed it. Badly. And Japanese food sucked and was weird. Who eats raw fish?

Sushi is popular all over the world.

"Barf."

As always when her thoughts wandered back to Crate Town, which was almost every day as she made the six-block walk from the train station to her apartment, Ella ended up thinking about her outfit's namesake, the mutt who used to live outside her old container home. The moment that mangy dog entered her consciousness, she would work herself up into tears and rage. Her eyes watered, and her hands balled into fists as she stomped all the way home. She had technically avenged her dog's death, but her revenge felt incomplete.

Because revenge is hollow. Nothing good comes from it.

"I should have been the one to kill him."

It would feel just as hollow regardless.

Ella finally reached her building, a raw concrete structure with flaking paint. Iron bars covered every window in the front, and only half the ceiling lights were working. The streets were immaculately clean, but that was common across much of Tokyo. She dragged her tired body through the wrought-iron gates and up the stairs. Stale dampness filled her nostrils. Water dripped from the ceiling, and a blinking fluorescent light flickered around every corner. A baby cried somewhere above her. Someone was shouting something incoherently on the third floor. A television was blaring from the side.

As she walked down the hallway to her fifth floor unit, a door to her left creaked open. One of her elderly neighbors, Luna or Roona or something like that, poked her head out and eyed Ella suspiciously, as if she were a thief trying to break into her home, never mind that the two of them had crossed paths dozens of times since she moved in. At Luna-Roona's feet was her yappy jerk Pomeranian, appropriately named Yappy. The little fuzzy ball of asshole had a bark that could shatter eardrums.

Ella hurried past. She could feel the old woman's accusatory gaze follow her until she reached her apartment door. She had tried to be friendly when she first moved in, and was rewarded by Yappy drawing blood from her ankle and Luna-Roona somehow blaming her for the bite. Ella had stopped trying to be friendly to her neighbor when Luna-Roona accused her of being a prostitute.

Her apartment was a small dilapidated room facing the back alley. There was barely enough space for a bed and a cooking range on one side of the unit and a toilet on the other. Her only window opened to a rusty fire escape that obstructed almost all of her view. She didn't mind it that much, since the view was the building on the other side of the alley, and it was just as ugly as hers. Living directly across from her was a weird mustached man who would stare out of his window for hours on end. Ella was at first disturbed by his continued presence, but eventually came to the conclusion that he was probably mostly harmless.

She locked all four locks on the door and pushed her dresser in front of it. It was partially for added security – mostly out of habit – but also because her place was so small the dresser blocked her toilet and refrigerator.

She unstrapped the harness that sheathed the half-dozen knives looped around her body, ankles and thighs, and then gently hung it on the stand next to her bed. Her big dagger stayed strapped to her lower back; that one stayed on her person except for when she bathed. She tore off her sweat-soaked sewer-drenched shirt and pants and tossed them haphazardly into a corner bin. Ella sniffed her shoulders; speaking of bathing, she badly needed a shower.

First, she needed to decompress. Ella opened the fridge and took out a blue can of barely-chilled beer. She had taken a liking to it from her unfortunate stint at the Academy. This particular brand of beer was rather difficult to find. Supposedly the name of the beer was Australian for beer, although she had always thought the word "beer" was already the Australian word for beer. The English language was inexact and confusing.

She climbed out of the window onto the fire escape and tucked herself into the corner where the staircase met the wall. Ella cracked open the can and took a long swig. She wiped her mouth with her sleeve and stared up at the hazy sky. She used to climb onto her roof back in Crate Town and star-watch for hours. That felt like a million years ago. So much had changed, yet everything still felt the same.

"Worse actually," she grumbled, taking another sip.

I think you are looking back at your time in Crate Town with rose-colored glasses.

Ella didn't bother answering the alien in her head. Her old home may have been a dangerous slum, but it was home. It felt like home. And in Crate Town, she was someone, the Black Cat, the Samrãjñī.

You realize you were the only one who called yourself the Samrãjñī.

"At least they knew who I was." Here in the endless expanse of the largest city in the world, Ella was just another small-time nobody packed like a rat once again living hand-to-mouth.

At least Tokyo, compared to Crate Town, was relatively safe. That didn't mean there weren't plenty of bad guys here. One neighbor found her alone out here the first week she moved in and got a little too close. She kissed his shoulder with the tip of her blade and sent him crawling away less one pint of blood. They had an arrangement now; he paid her a hundred yen every time they ran into each other. It was unfortunate for him they were next-door neighbors.

She was nearly finished with the second beer when the window three units down opened. Her hand instinctively drifted toward the dagger at her lower back. An old woman stuck her head out, eyed Ella, and then hung some shirts on the railing. Strangely, that comforted Ella. Hanging clothes was a time-honored tradition in every impoverished place, no matter where in the world.

"It seems my lot in life is to never escape these places," she grumbled, hefting a third beer, debating whether she should crack it open. That was probably a bad idea. She was already getting tipsy, being a tiny person who still wore kids' clothes.

You had a chance when you went to the Academy.

She closed her eyes. "But I screwed it up."

Ella had tried; she really did. She just wasn't cut out to be a Prophus agent, no matter how much she and everyone around her tried to make it work. Even with Io in her head helping her, or perhaps in spite of Io, it just wasn't a good fit.

You might have a problem with authority, but that is not the real reason you got expelled from the Academy. There are those thirty citations you manage to rack up in a span of eighteen months.

"Their stupid rules are stupid."

That one time you brought a knife to a hand-to-hand sparring match.

"Perkins had it out for me. She put me up against Shepherd, and he outweighed me by ten stone!"

And then there was that black market and gambling ring you ran in the dorm rooms.

Ella shrugged. "OK, that probably wasn't my best idea, but I was broke and bored. We weren't allowed to have jobs and everyone else got their money from home. What did you expect me to do?"

Not embezzle from the Prophus.

"And now look at what we're doing."

Io laughed, which to be honest was awfully unsettling. Quasing laughter sounded like tussling dogs. It was strangely infectious though. Perhaps it was because Io's creepy laugh was echoing in her head, or perhaps they were finally starting to get along.

Their initial meeting had been tumultuous, to say the least. A fervently stubborn Ella and a demanding asshole Quasing. What could go wrong?

Hey!

They had eventually come to an understanding, which led to a reluctant partnership forged by their survival being tied to each other, first in Crate Town and then during Ella's colossal failure at the Academy. The two had almost formed a friendship, or at the very least a stable working relationship.

Whatever. Classrooms and studying and rigid schedules weren't for her. Not to mention the dozens of rules they had tried to make her follow. The streets were more her natural habitat. Ella preferred it, honestly. She swung her legs back through the window and into her musty, stale room. She shut it behind her, locked it, and threw the curtains closed, enveloping her apartment in darkness.

Ella climbed over the small table next to the window and rolled onto her bed. Yawning, she positioned her body so her back was against the wall and, as part of her nightly ritual, touched the dagger still strapped to its holster against her lower back, just in case. Comforted, she closed her eyes and allowed herself to fall asleep.

• • •

Io waited until Ella's breathing fell into a steady cadence before sitting her body up. She wasn't very good at controlling hosts, and the girl was an annoyingly light sleeper. Io moved over to the table and painstakingly pushed the clutter aside. Teaching the girl to put things away was an ongoing struggle that would probably take the rest of one of their lives.

Once she was satisfied with the work space, Io pulled a laptop out from a cardboard box tucked under Ella's bed. She booted it up and tapped into the Prophus network with her previous host, Emily Curran's, account. The Prophus administrators must have forgotten to close it after her status moved from missing to KIA, so now Io was using it as a back door.

She was hesitant at first, thinking the omission intentional. However, after a year of intermittently logging in and finding the account truly dormant, her confidence in being able to leverage this oversight as a back door grew. As long as she was careful with Emily's account and did not initiate changes that raised flags, Io should be able to continue working the Prophus network to her and Ella's advantage.

That was how the Burglar Alarms had been able to break into the Prophus safe house tonight, and how Ella had been able to skim from them ever since she was expelled from the Academy. She had been miserable there, and her tenure cut short prematurely at eighteen months. Io had thought Ella was actually making solid progress and was on her way to becoming a competent agent, but her old habits and ways eventually crept back in, and she fell apart.

The girl was a caged bird, chafing at the curfews and rules, struggling to get caught up with the other students, many of whom were military recruits from all over the world. All while trying to learn to write and speak English. It wasn't for her lack of trying. She just never had a chance. Throw in a bad breakup, and the whole experiment was a disaster.

Just like Io had planned.

Not that Io had necessarily wanted the girl to fail. Ella's failure was Io's as well. They shared a body after all, and there were many skills that the girl needed to learn if they were to survive. Io wanted Ella to have the abilities of a Prophus agent without necessarily having to wear the yoke of being a Prophus.

The Quasing had known her days with the Prophus were numbered from the moment Tao had laid out his threat to Io's life if anything ever happened to the girl. One could argue that Tao was simply ensuring Ella's safety, but there was a greater implication to Tao's words. It told Io that she was expendable. The Prophus may keep her around now, but for how long? If her life was contingent upon that of a short-lived human, Io did not believe she had any value to the Prophus whatsoever.

So while she did her best to help Ella grow, assisting her with language, technical and combat skills, Io did little to help Ella adapt to the Prophus organization, which honestly was more alien to the girl than having an actual alien inhabit her body. When the situation came to a head and Ella was faced with expulsion from the academy, and by association the entire Prophus organization, Io embraced it.

Now, the two were on their own, no longer beholden to either the Prophus or the Genjix. They were free to carve their own paths forward, and accountable to no one. That is, as long as they could stay hidden. That was where Io's work came in.

For the next hour, Io scoured the Prophus intelligence network. Things had been quiet on this front between the two factions for the better part of a year. The Genjix had been busy consolidating their hold on India. The Prophus had mostly abandoned the entire Asian continent and had moved to defending the countries around Australia. Japan was technically neutral territory, but it trod a delicate line to keep its neutrality due to its close proximity to China, which was the center of Genjix power.

As of this very moment, a little more than a hundred Prophus teams were operating in all of Southeast Asia on some three dozen assignments, with three specifically located in Japan. One was a large team managing an extensive surveillance network embedded into the nation's fishing industry. Another was supporting the actual fishing industry, in which the Prophus silently held a large financial stake. Io pulled up the summary on the third team. They were working in a Hokkaido Wolf refuge.

There was strangely no information on the team that had crashed that safe house earlier tonight. If Io had the aptitude to make Ella's face frown, she would have. If she hadn't needed to stay under the Prophus network's radar, she could have submitted a query to Command to glean more information, but that would be a dead giveaway. This team wasn't supposed to be here. Something must have happened. She made a mental note to have Ella stay low for a few days until things blew over.

Io switched over to the channels on Genjix activities and flags. There were few alerts out of the ordinary, other than the occasional security chatter picked up by surveillance. Wait, Io had spoken too soon. The safe house that the Burglar Alarms had raided tonight had just been flagged as compromised. She read the report the team just sent.

"Really, a gang of thugs?" muttered Io. "That is giving the Burglar Alarms far too much credit."

The report contained a pretty accurate description of Ella, but the odds of anyone matching that to her were slim. More importantly, Command would probably shut down the safe house now. Io had hoped it was a location they could farm for months, but Ella exposing herself to the agents had put an end to that opportunity.

Other than that, the region – this city specifically – was relatively quiet. That was what was most important. Io's primary focus these days was to just stay out of everyone's way. She no longer wished to be the pawn of either faction. If she and Ella could live out the girl's remaining days in obscurity and stay out of history, Io would consider this a life well-lived.

The screen flickered and dimmed. Io checked the battery level. The laptop was about to shut down. She must have forgotten to charge it last night. Io reached for the power cord and fumbled trying to plug it into the tiny grooves. It was like trying to do brain surgery in mittens. It reminded Io of her brief frustrating stint inhabiting arctic seals.

It took seven tries before Io managed to fit the three prongs into the tiny holes, but then she accidentally elbowed the screen, knocking the laptop off the table. Fortunately, it was a military-grade machine and could easily withstand the impact if it hit the floor. Unfortunately, it did not hit the floor but rather Ella's foot. Io cursed as she lost her balance. She bounced off the table, then off the bed cornerpost, and ended up sprawled onto the floor. Io felt herself lose control as the girl roused.

Ella opened her eyes and frowned when she discovered that she was wedged between two pieces of furniture. She sucked in her breath and scrunched her face together. "Ow. Why am I sleeping on the floor? Why do I hurt all over?"

I had a little mishap. Go back to bed.

Ella groaned and pulled herself to her feet, making another round of hissing sounds when she put weight on the bruised foot the laptop had smashed. "What did you do to me, Alien?"

Sorry about that.

Ella looked down at the laptop flipped open on the floor. She picked it up and pieced the events together. "Anything on the radar?"

A small blip, nothing that should not pass. Lay low for a few days. Make sure nothing comes out of the night's events. The Prophus have no reason to think it was you, but you did us no favors by showing your face and opening your mouth. I will need to dig further. Go back to bed.

"I'm not sorry. I had to do it."

We can agree to disagree, but you are wrong. Daiki was likely in little danger. The Prophus agents would not have harmed the boy, and the odds of them handing him over to the police was nil.

Ella stretched her arms in the air and turned toward the small mirror hanging crooked on the wall. Her fingers instinctively brushed aside a loose strand of hair. The hair on the top of her head had grown down just past her shoulders, but it was still too short for the style she was aiming for. She had fawned over it when she found this particular hairstyle in a fashion magazine. Her sides were shaved with horizontal lines that wrapped around her head. That did not turn out as well as she had hoped. That was the last time she listened to Daiki's fashion advice.

"How much longer do you need to use my body?"

An hour, maybe more. Now that the safe house is compromised, we need to locate another Prophus mark. Can you do me a favor and plug the laptop in?

Ella did that and then climbed over the bed frame like a cat and burrowed herself into the sheets, pulling her knees to her body until she was curled into a ball. "Don't forget to wake me up tomorrow. I have a meeting with those Kuhn guys."

I never forget. I am millions of years old and have more knowledge and experience than all the humans in this city put together, but sure, I can be your alarm clock.

"Yeah, yeah. Just don't make me late." She yawned and closed her eyes. A few minutes drifted by. Ella opened her eyes again. "Io?"

What is it now?

"I can't sleep."

I do not care. I have work to do.

"Tell me an alien story."

No.

CHAPTER FIVE
The Hard Peace

Ella not only survived Crate Town, she thrived. She left the safety of Wiry Madras's nest at thirteen and set off on her own. For the next few years, she worked the streets, establishing relationships with the locals, running cons and brokering contraband transactions.

She became known as the Black Cat and developed a reputation as a savvy operator, someone worth knowing in the streets of Crate Town. She managed to save up enough to purchase her own container home by the time she was fifteen. By nineteen, she had graduated to large-scale cons.

That was when we met.

A shadow loomed over Alexandra Mengsk, blocking out her sun. Shura the Scalpel, or just Shura to the people she wasn't trying to kill, pried one eye open, then the other. The silhouette of a dark, bald, stocky man in black military armor towered over her. An assault rifle was slung behind his back and a gas mask hung around his neck.

"Adonis," he bowed stiffly. For some strange reason, he was looking off to the side. "The black market dealer has arrived at the hotel."

"Did they bring the merchandise?"

"It appears so, but it is not verified. Three rectangular crates with dimensions consistent with our intel." He continued to avert his eyes.

"What are you doing, Kloos?" she asked.

Mayur Kloos was her second in command. The two had met during the construction of the India Bio Comm Array two years ago when she was consolidating her hold over India. He had fought alongside her ever since, earning himself a position as general of all of her forces in India. While he had ridden her coattails to increase his standing within the Genjix, it was Shura who benefited most from the relationship. Kloos was a cunning tactician, an independent thinker and most importantly a fiercely loyal commander. It would only be a matter of time before she lost him to his own command.

Or a Holy One with sufficient standing.

That was true. Several Quasing had already inquired about his availability to become their next vessel. Shura had so far managed to rebuff their overtures, but likely not for much longer. That was the unfortunate cost of competent underlings. The only way she could retain Kloos's services after he was raised to a vessel was if the Holy One was willing to report to her. Unfortunately, Shura's Holy One, Tabs, did not play well with most of her kind.

"You are unclothed." Kloos continued to stare past the balcony and held out her translucent shift.

Shura rolled her eyes and sat up from the lounge chair. "Kloos, you've saved my life countless times. You've held my intestines in your hands. I think we're well past modesty. Look at me when you address me. That's an order."

"Yes, Adonis." He moved his eyes to lock on hers. He was technically following her order.

Shura grabbed the shift and wrapped it around her shoulders. She glanced at the two balconies to her left that would be her stepping-stones. The deal was running late, which was fine with her. It gave her more time to work on her tan. "How is he handling the delay?"

"Badly. We don't even need surveillance. His yelling is audible through the walls. We were worried he might back out when the dealer was fifteen minutes late."

Shura smirked. "He probably wouldn't have stayed if he weren't desperate for this to go through."

Rurik Melnichenko was Shura's chief rival for a seat on the Genjix Council. He had an obsession with punctuality and what he considered his "valuable time," one of the many failings she had taken advantage of on numerous occasions. The Russian oligarch was from a very old and influential family, and controlled a large and powerful swath of Russia within the Genjix sphere of influence. Shura, on the other hand, controlled only the war-ravaged resource-deprived India territory. There should not have even been a contest between them, but due to her competence and his lack of it, the battle for the lone open seat on the Genjix Council was tightly contested.

For the past two years, the two had struggled for control of the global Bio Comm Array initiative, one of the most important projects on the Genjix docket. What she had lacked in resources she had more than made up for in small victory after small victory, slowly whittling away the oligarch's once-vast advantages. Now the two of them stood at nearly equal standing. It was only a matter of time before she marginalized his diminishing power, seized control of the global array and took her rightful place on the Council.

Shura raised her glass of Côte de Beaune to her lips and leaned against the railing overlooking the metropolis's vast sprawl. Hong Kong was an interesting city. Her gaze followed the constant hive of activity flowing through the streets like blood coursing through veins, the curved buildings that could be mistaken for gargantuan organs, and the many bridges that linked them together. The city was a living, breathing being, not unlike how she envisioned the Holy Ones' home world looked.

She could just make out the ocean at the tip of the horizon. The last time she had been here, Shura's division of Genjix soldiers had evacuated the coast just three hours before a Prophus orbital barrage had leveled the southern half of the city. After humanity had lost its appetite for war, the Genjix and Prophus had once again moved their conflict into the shadows.

The Genjix had not only rebuilt the broken parts of Hong Kong, but done so in the image of their home world Quasar. The scars of the Alien World War were now healed with fresh new skyscrapers towering out of the ruins of the devastated island.

For Shura, it was a symbol of what the world was and what it would be once the Genjix fulfilled this planet's destiny. The northern part of the metropolis, untouched by the war and molded by human hands, was an unsightly cluster of rectangular structures randomly shooting up into the sky like broken jagged teeth. Each building was its own noisy entity begging for attention. There was little symmetry, beauty or flow to those districts, and movement through them was inefficient and messy.

The southern half of the city, the region remade in the image of the Holy Ones, appeared organic, alive. Buildings rose gracefully into the sky, fitting together like tall blades of grass on the plains, forming giant flowing waves like the currents of the Eternal Sea. Bridges spider-webbed hundreds of meters in the air while tunnels underground integrated everything like a giant ant farm. It was a beautiful and awe-inspiring display of divine technology and vision, an island in perfect harmony, a glimpse of the true potential that the Genjix could bring to this world. Before that paradise could manifest, however, the rest of this old world had to be burned away.

Kloos studied the screen wrapped around his forearm. "The dealer has reached the corner unit. They've temporarily moved out of camera range."

"Are the rods with him?"

"Near the side wall. Three of Rurik's operatives are verifying. He is currently threatening to gut the man for being late for their appointment."

Shura smirked. "That will go over well with their negotiations. Are my cadres in place?"

"Second team is waiting in the room opposite Rurik's. The rest are here awaiting your orders."

Shura looked inside and saw half a dozen operatives in full combat gear standing at the ready. "How many are inside that penthouse?"

"The dealer brought four. Rurik has twenty."

"Twenty bodyguards? In the heart of Genjix territory?" That man always did love bodyguards. Shura couldn't risk smuggling this many operatives into the hotel without raising suspicions, but she was confident the element of surprise would even the odds.

Shura measured the air between the balconies and the sixty-story drop below. She drained the last of her wine and let the glass fall. "Very well. Let's begin."

The shift fell off her shoulders. An updraft caught it, and it fluttered away, dancing into the clear, blue sky. Kloos held up her one-piece armored suit. Shura slipped it on and pressed a small button at the base of her neck. The suit energized and shaped itself to her body. She refused the rifle Kloos offered, opting instead for her two modified handguns and a baton. The fighting, if it was to come to that, would be close-range.

After she was ready, Shura stepped onto the side railing. The rooms closer to the corner unit had unfortunately already been booked, and she didn't want to raise any suspicion by leveraging her standing. Traversing the balconies of a skyscraper was not her preferred method of insertion, but it wasn't the worst either. The two meters between the balconies was an easy jump, but the sixty stories down made things interesting. Especially on the second and third jumps.

Withdrawing her hand from the side of the building, she leaped. Her lead foot touched the railing on the other side, and then she gracefully stepped down to solid floor. She landed softly, one hand palming the floor, the other near her waist.

Two witnesses to your left.

She looked inside the room and saw a surprised young couple, eyes wide, staring back at her. The man was wearing his bathrobe and the woman held several shopping bags in her hands. In the near corner was a pile of gifts. They must have just gotten married at the hotel. How nice. The shopping bags fell from the woman's hands, and she opened her mouth to cry out.

Shura blurred into action. As one reached for her handgun, the other pulled back the balcony door. She squeezed the trigger twice, carefully placing her shots. The silenced gun puffed twice: one military-engineered electrically charged chloroform pellet striking the woman in the leg, flipping her forward onto her face; the other to the man's chest, knocking him back onto the bed. Shura reached for the chloroform wraps in her pocket and raced inside. The pellets themselves should get the job done within seconds, but she had to be extra careful neither honeymooner made any noise.

By the time Kloos and the rest of her cadre had extended a bridge and crossed over, both were unconscious and trussed. They would wake with harsh headaches and nasty lacerations from the non-lethal pellets, but they would have her mercy to thank.

"You're too slow," she quipped, heading back out to the balcony.

"You're too quick," he retorted. "You should let us do the heavy lifting."

Shura shrugged and placed another foot on the railing, ready to make the next jump. "Try to keep up this time."

Watch the wind!

That was a surprisingly harsh warning from Tabs, who in all their years together was consistently even-keeled. Unfortunately, the warning came too late. A strong gust crashed into Shura just as her foot left the railing, pushing her into the building. Her shoulders skimmed the wall and the friction soaked up much of her forward momentum, landing just short.

The toes on her lead foot caught the railing, but in this situation that didn't count for much. Small errors a kilometer above ground made for grave mistakes. For a split second, she was falling through the gap between the balconies with nothing but an unceremonious and rather humiliating death waiting for her, one unbefitting a vessel of her standing. She just managed to snake a hand onto the railing to dangle precariously.

Steady your breath. Use the wall to walk back up.

Years of training and combat in life-and-death situations took over. Shura steadied her nerves, glanced once to the side and then swung her legs over, pushing off as soon as they touched the surface. Her other hand got a hold of the top of the railing and, with a quick graceful swing, she pulled herself over the side and fell to her knees in a not-so-graceful landing.

She took a deep breath. Panic was nothing more than a human response to stress, but just because she had learned to control and harness it did not mean she was impervious to its effects.

When Shura was done collecting herself, she looked up to see a wide-eyed little girl holding a ragdoll just on the other side of the door. Kloos landed behind her a second later. He noticed the girl and pulled out a chloroform wrap. Shura put a hand on his arm and shook her head. She moved a finger to her lips with her other hand and winked, giving the girl a knowing smile. The little girl wrapped her arms around her doll tightly, nodded, and then wandered away from the window.

Shura rose to her feet and smacked him on the shoulder. "You can't drug little girls!"

"Apologies, Adonis." He did not sound apologetic at all. "The mission comes first."

The rest of her cadre soon followed, crowding in a crouch on the balcony. Shura peered over the top and waited as the lone guard patrolling the corner balcony came into view. Fortunately, his attention was focused more on what was outside the building than to the side of it.

"Is the second team ready?" whispered Shura.

Kloos tapped the comm on his wrist and nodded. "Sixty seconds lead time. On your mark."

Shura studied the lone guard's movement as he meandered toward her. Her fingers drummed her thigh as anticipation surged through her body. Elder Mother at the Hatchery would be disappointed with her careless lack of body control, but Shura lived for this thrill.

She waited until the patrolling guard turned away, and then put one foot on the railing and leaped, clearing the gap in one quick motion before she was on top of him. A downward kick to the back of his knee dropped him to the ground. She put an arm around his neck and pulled him away from the glass doors while at the same time pushing a chloroform wrap over his mouth. The larger man fought back violently, twisting and throwing his elbow. Shura bent his neck at an awkward angle, cutting off his breathing, and held on tightly as his protests weakened. Once he went limp, she dropped him onto the floor and waved for the rest of her team to follow.

Shura glanced through the window at her perspective audience. "Start the timer. Two minutes." She took out her compact and checked herself in the mirror.

Kloos frowned. "Is this an appropriate time, Adonis?"

"I haven't seen my dear brother in over a year," she remarked with an impish grin. "He needs to know how effortless it is to crush him."

You are toying with your opponent again. It will be the death of you.

"It's the small joys that make this dark world tolerable."

Shura saw a cluster of shadows on the left side of the room, and one near the glass door. She calmed her breathing and then opened the sliding door, strolling into the corner penthouse as if she didn't have a care in the world. She made it half a step before the nearest bodyguard gave a start and reached for his weapon. One of Rurik's captains recognized her immediately and barked a warning to her associate, saving him from making a very foolish and fatal decision.

Shura stared the man down. "You should heed Nilaksh's advice. She's looking out for you."

Nilaksh actually gave her a slight bow for the recognition. Being acknowledged by an Adonis vessel by name, even if it was someone considered a rival, improved her standing. Shura took note of the unknown bodyguard's physical description and filed it to her memory, or rather Tabs did. Shura had a detailed dossier on every member of Rurik's inner circle, from his allies, closest advisers and bodyguards to the landscapers at his Summer Palace in Saint Petersburg. It was this level of thoroughness that had allowed her to play chess to Rurik's hopscotch.

The rest of the room, caught off-guard by her sudden appearance, swarmed with activity. Three to her right drew their weapons. Two moved between her and Rurik. Four backed away. One guard to her far left was trying to creep up on her from behind. The rest were just confused.

Shura held her ground, staring each of them down like only an Adonis could. Even if they did not know who she was, they must know what she was, and that made her invulnerable.

Tread carefully. You are severely bending the rules of the Hard Peace. The rules must be observed.

"Bend, not break," she murmured under her breath. She flashed Rurik a smug smile. "I'm sorry, was I interrupting something? Brother, it has been too long. You look like you have seen better days."

Indeed, Rurik looked tired. He had aged visibly over the past two years. His left arm was wrapped in a large cast that climbed all the way up to his shoulder, and he moved stiffly. What had he been up to lately?

Stop antagonizing him before he decides to risk shooting you. Countdown at ninety seconds.

Rurik, who was sitting opposite the arms dealer, rose to his feet. Shura noted the slight grimace as he stood. "You have some nerve, Shura. How dare you show your face here."

"What is the meaning of this, Mr Melnichenko?" Shah, the arms dealer said. "Is this bitch with you?"

Shura filed the man's words away. She would have to pay him back during negotiations.

"She's an uninvited guest," spat Rurik.

"As long as I'm a guest, one way or another," said Shura cheerfully. "Excuse me, Shah. I believe you were discussing trading my dear brother Rurik several cases of catalyst reaction rods that you acquired from the IXTF. I have interest in those as well. Would you be open to multiple bidders?"

Shah was taken aback, and then took on a sly look. "I think we can come to an arrangement."

"Absolutely not!" Rurik rounded on the arms dealer, going so far as to reach for his gun. Everyone else in the room drew their weapons and pointed them at each other. All except for

Shura, who stood near the center, reveling in the chaos she was sowing.

Countdown thirty seconds.

"What's the matter, Rurik?" she purred. "Afraid of a little competition?"

"I should just shoot you right now and deal with the consequences," he snarled, swinging his gun back her way.

The bodyguard who had drawn on her – Shura believed his name was Halston, something like that – reached for his weapon again. This time, Shura was not so kind. Her arm shot out and trapped his hand to his body. Her other hand speared him once in the soft flesh of his throat and then she slammed his head into the wall.

"You should have listened to Nilaksh," she growled.

Nilaksh got between her and the rest of Rurik's men. "Put your guns down. The Hard Peace forbids this violence. Put your damn guns away, you fools."

Her response was a tad too emphatic. Shura brushed her hair out of her face, stood up and then crossed her arms. "Now Shah, where were we? What is Rurik offering you?"

Rurik stabbed a finger in the air at her. "I won't allow it. The Hard Peace may spare you from injury, but it has limits. Take the Adonis to the next room. If she resists, knock her unconscious."

Five of Rurik's bodyguards holstered their weapons and closed in on her. She noted that Nilaksh wasn't one of them. Shura should consider recruiting the woman to her side after this mission.

None of them individually were a match for her, but five skilled Genjix operatives in an enclosed space was too much for any Adonis vessel to handle. Shura sidestepped the first bodyguard who tried to tackle her. She sliced him with an elbow across his temple. Another came from the side, grabbing her arm. He was rewarded with a punch to the mid-section, crumpling his body to the ground.

More hands pawed at her. They eventually smothered and managed to subdue her. Shura glanced around the room. Everyone was distracted, staring at her tussle as she got dragged down to the floor. Exactly as planned.

"Time, Tabs?"

Five seconds… now.

The front door exploded inward, and her second team poured in. Kloos and the first team simultaneously burst through the windows. Rurik's guards, who were completely focused on her, were caught by surprise. Shah, eyes wide as saucers, stood frozen in the center of the chaos.

"Stop," screamed Rurik, throwing his arms out. "Put your weapons down. No one is shooting anyone. You know the consequences. The price of violating the Hard Peace is death." He turned to Shura, his face painted with fury. "You may have us surrounded, but I still have the numbers. We can't shoot each other, but I'll win in a melee."

"That's true," conceded Shura. "It's a good thing we're not fighting the Thirty Years War."

Shura's cadres opened fire, catching Rurik and his bodyguards in the middle, making short work of them with a hail of electrically charged chloroform pellets. Within seconds, all of Rurik's people were in different states of unconsciousness on the floor or slumped over couches and tables. Rurik, splayed on the sofa, groaned as his hand crawled to the parts of his chest where he was struck. The man, in his arrogance, had decided to forgo armor and could now be overdosing from a half-dozen tranquilizers.

Shura waved at the haze of smoke drifting in the air as she stepped over bodies and overturned chairs. Shah's ashen face followed her path as she came to a stop across from him. She pushed Rurik's limp body off the couch to make room, and then sat down gracefully, crossing her legs. She motioned for the arms dealer to join her.

Shah hesitated, then slowly lowered himself to her level. A smile broke on Shura's face as she studied him: early sixties, ex-Revolutionary Guard, muscular with a slight paunch, but surprisingly soft hands. A few seconds ticked by. Slowly, Shah began to match her smile with one of his own. Shura's arm flashed, slapping him hard across the face and knocking him to the floor.

"That was for calling me a bitch." The smile was still plastered on her face. She gestured for him to sit back on the sofa. "Now, let's start over."

CHAPTER SIX
Laying Low

When I met Ella Patel, I was residing inside a Prophus agent named Emily Curran. I was contacted by the Genjix operative Surrett Kapoor and had come to Crate Town to learn about the Bio Comm Array, which, if true, was the most important initiative the Quasing could have ever attempted on this planet. As you are no doubt aware, nothing went as planned. Emily was ambushed by a Genjix kill squad. Neither she nor anyone in the squad survived the fight. My options were Emily's cowardly auxiliary or Ella, who at the time had robbed a group of Pakistani gangsters and was hiding in a nearby trash heap.

Ella tried to follow Io's orders and lie low in her tiny studio. She tried to convince herself she was taking a staycation; a much-deserved respite after a job well done. Having woken up and finally showered around late morning, she was even able to find something to eat in her fridge and spent the afternoon watching bootleg Korean soap operas. She managed to maintain her positive outlook throughout the day, in no small part because she slept through most of it. Eventually, she had to call this what it actually was: lock down. This was prison. Io was punishing Ella for disobeying her.

That is absolutely untrue. You can actually leave if you want. I just would not recommend it until you know it is safe.

Ella paced, which was really nothing more than walking in a very small circle. She bounced a ball off the wall and stared out the window as the rain plinked the dirty glass. This voluntary incarceration would be a lot more bearable if she could sit outside and have a beer. Of all the awful times for bad weather.

You could spend this time being productive, like working on your English. Or better yet cleaning your room.

Io had been working diligently with Ella on her English and Mandarin ever since they met. It was still a work in progress.

Finally she couldn't stand it any longer. She rolled out of bed and snatched her knife harness from its hook, grabbing a wad of cash and sheathing three knives. She adjusted the strap holding her large dagger, and then took a black garbage bag sitting in the corner of her apartment.

This is it? This is as long as you can lay low? It is not even dinner yet. You cannot even last a day.

"You're the one always telling me not to keep score."

That is not… never mind. Can you at least agree to stay in Little India?

"Fine, whatever."

You know I can read your thoughts.

"I mean I'll try."

Still lying.

"It's close enough." Ella barged out of her apartment, whisking by Luna-Roona's place before the old meanie could open the door, and sped down the stairs two at a time. She sent texts to her outfit for an update and then hurried to her favorite noodle shop a block out of the Nishi Kasai district. It was technically not in Little India, but like she and Io had agreed, why keep score? Besides, it was only a little bit outside. That didn't really count, right?

I will remind you of this next time Asao shortchanges you.

She grunted. "Not if he's a fan of his blood staying in his body."

Ella arrived at the aptly-named Go-To Udon and took her usual seat in the corner booth. The proprietor Kite gave her a familiar wave, and a piping hot bowl of soup arrived as if by magic a few minutes later. Ella thanked him in her heavily-accented Japanese and handed him a garbage bag filled with slightly-dated textbooks from the neighborhood juku.

Kite's daughter Yuki was studying to get into university, but their family could not afford to enroll her into the local cram school. It didn't take too much digging around for Ella to discover that the chain-smoking owner of the juku enjoyed a special brand of Caribbean cigarettes that were heavily tariffed and difficult to obtain.

One more inquiry to a contact at the docks, and everyone was happy. The juku owner got discounted cigarettes. Ella made a small profit and got some old books thrown in for free. Yuki got the books she needed for her studies. And as an added bonus, Kite gave her free udon whenever she came in.

It was a lot of legwork for free noodles, and Ella made sure not to abuse his generosity. She had made a friend though, and friendship was infectious. She was starting all over again in a new city with new people. If she ever hoped to achieve the same success she had had in Crate Town, she had to build relationships and become a known person. Kite had already referred a few of his customers to her. A woman was looking for a cheap source of quality knock-off designer purses, a university student was looking for some Star Wars Lego set, and an old lady badly wanted opium. Ella wisely left that last request alone. The drug trade was its own brand of extra nasty.

Let us not get carried away with your degree of success in Crate Town.

"Says the alien with the worst track record in history. Or is that the universe?"

The two continued to jab at each other, mostly good-naturedly. They were finally comfortable enough to give each other grief and not take offense. At least not too much. There were a handful of times, especially during Ella's stint at the Academy, when they had pushed each other over the edge. It had given Ella a bad reputation among the students. It had made her appear moody and volatile. None of them ever suspected that it was because she was a host. It was considered inappropriate, even forbidden, to discuss who may be a host. Everyone gossiped though; it was the most talked-about thing at the Academy after one-night stands.

It honestly also wasn't hard to guess who were the likely hosts. They were usually the stand-out students, the brightest, the most polished, and the best trained in just about everything. No one, in the eighteen months that Ella had attended the Academy, had ever accused her of being a host.

You are just very good at hiding my abilities.

"You are just very good at not having any."

That set off another round of insults over wagashis and boba tea. Kite stopped by her table to offer her some fruit sandos as well, which was super nice of him. He was still very appreciative of all the textbooks and knew how to show it. The deal with the school was paying dividends even after all these weeks. Kite had also become used to the verbal outbursts that happened when she was having an especially animated discussion with Io.

After about an hour of ribbing, Ella's phone began to play an 8-bit anime theme song. She stared at the screen: Yakuza Reject. She picked up the phone. "What's up Hinata?"

"Hey Big Bosu, I have buyers lined up. The Bakkas are interested in the guns."

Of course those Neanderthal clowns would be.

The country had seen a resurgence of these bosozoku gangs after the Alien World War, and the Akai Bakus were one of the larger gangs that loosely reported to the local yakuza running the Kabukicho District. Most called them the Bakkas, but never within earshot of the Akai Bakus.

Ella scrunched her face. She preferred to sell weapons to someone else, anyone else, just about everyone else. The Bakkas weren't the most stable bunch. She almost told him no. Almost. But Ella was a businesswoman, and their money was as good as any. She shrugged. "Make it happen. Cash deal. No questions. We get free and clear from the Yakuza for the transaction and immunity with the Bakkas for any trouble."

"They want to make the deal today. Right now."

So much for the day off. Ella rapped the table as she decided what to do.

You do not have to sell to the first interested buyer. The Bakkas are not trustworthy. The guns will sell themselves to many parties.

Ella hated sitting on merchandise, especially weapons. Gun running was serious business and, like drugs, a trade she didn't particularly enjoy partaking in. If any word leaked about that stash, someone would likely try to rob them this very night. She also didn't trust Io's business sense. "Set it for in an hour," she said to Hinata. "Meet at the World-Famous."

"You got it, Bosu."

You still have not forgiven me for that briefcase deal back in Crate Town, have you?

"And I never will."

Ella checked the time. It was a long train ride. She should have said two hours. She got up to leave and looked down at the tasty-looking fruit sandos. It would be criminal to waste good snacks. She stuffed two in her mouth and waved goodbye to Kite as she hurried out of the restaurant to sell illegal guns to a bunch of psychotic bikers.

CHAPTER SEVEN
The Search

I knew Emily's auxiliary would abort the mission and flee India once he became a host. I could not allow that to happen, so I took the risk and chose Ella. It was my intention to connect with the Genjix in order to defect. However, I had to walk a fine line with Ella, because she blamed the death of her parents on the Genjix.

I began training the girl, building our relationship and biding my time to make a move. Things progressed well at first. She was initially easy to manipulate, but the situation became more complicated with the arrival of the Prophus Adonis vessel, Cameron Tan.

The customs agent studied the photo, eyed Makita's worn and misshapen bald head, and then stared back at the passport. His face scrunched. "Purpose of your visit?"

Makita put his arms around Josie's waist. Her entire body tightened. "Been promising the missus a vacation for years. Just trying to keep my word. You know how it is–" Josie elbowed him in the ribs. He winced and coughed.

The agent ran them through a Penetra scan, and then returned their passports. "Heed the restricted zones. Always carry your passports with you. Obey all Genjix officials. You can identify them by their yellow lapels. You will be arrested if you are found after curfew. Welcome to Singapore. Enjoy your stay."

"In that order of importance, obviously," grumbled Makita, as he linked elbows with Josie and led her away from the checkpoint.

She whispered out of the corner of her mouth. "Are you having a stroke?"

"No, why? This is my Australian accent. I'm staying in character."

She scowled. "Well, cut it out. You sound like a drunk cowboy who forgot his lines in a low-budget American western."

"Isn't that what Australians sound like?"

She elbowed him again. His already-broken ribs were getting more tender, not less. Makita and Josie hailed a taxi to the Geylang district. They settled back into their seats as the car sped down the East Coast Park toward Downtown Core. Bright, flashing neon signs and flurries of videos and sounds assaulted their senses. Makita turned away from the window. It had been years since he had last done any fieldwork. On the one hand, this was the most thrills he had had in over a decade. On the other, he forgot how overrated excitement was.

He pointed out the Penetra scanners placed at major intersections, and the various blue-uniformed local police and yellow-lapelled stateless officers who held jurisdiction over every Genjix-controlled country. Makita noticed Josie holding her breath as they drove down the coastline. Her eyes looked far away. "When was the last time you were here?"

"The first time we retreated off the continent." She pointed at the harbor. "I was on one of the last ships that pulled away right there after the beachhead in the fourth wave. That was a disaster."

Makita shook his head. "The early years of the war were especially bad, and full of stupid."

"That's the nice way of putting it." Josie turned away from the window as they passed by another checkpoint, their third in fifteen minutes. "So, if you're retired, how did they rope you back into active duty?"

Makita chuckled. "When the Keeper asks you for a favor, it's hard to say no. Besides, retirement sucks. There's only so many flowers a guy can plant and so many walks the dog can take before you get the itch to do something stupid just so you feel like you're still alive. Like getting back into the field."

"No one to keep you company?"

"Not every couple gets to retire at the same time. Wife still has a career to wrap up, and the kid's long flown the coop, blazing his own trail." Makita swallowed his bitterness. "Most of my friends are dead, and all my old hobbies hurt my back. So when the Keeper said jump, I thought, what the hell, why not?"

"And here you are behind enemy lines looking for a runaway host who doesn't want to be found. All because of boredom."

"More or less," he grinned. "I just thought I was going to teach a bunch of dumb kids for a few months. You know, get a free vacation out of it. Visit the Outback and see what's left of the Great Barrier Reef. This trip here is a bit more than I expected. Not gonna lie, I'm having more fun than I've had in years."

"You're a fool."

"You've just never been retired. You'll understand once you get put out to pasture. If we survive this mission."

The taxi deposited them on a narrow street filled with skinny four-story buildings sandwiched together like books on a shelf. Makita and Josie kept their faces down and wore their duffels over their backs like tourists. They turned onto an even narrower street and navigated more crowded alleys and slender walkways between sagging stone structures. They had just crossed one of the major streets when something caught Makita's eye. He stopped and squinted.

"What is it?" asked Josie.

"Are you hungry?"

She looked as if she were about to snap at him for sleeping on the job, paused, and gave it a second thought. "I could eat."

"My kind of partner," grinned Makita. "I need to keep my blood sugar up. I get pretty hangry." He led her to a small porridge shop off the main street called Miss Congee-neality. They sat in the far corner adjacent to the kitchen so they had a clear view of the front entrance and the hallway to the back. They settled in and placed their orders.

"You said there's a lead to the host in Singapore," asked Josie. "We're here. How do we find her?"

"First stop is to hit up our contact at the safe house."

Josie's eyebrows rose. "In a Genjix city on the main continent?"

"In every city, *especially* on the main continent."

"I've heard so many things about Prophus safe houses. I've never had the opportunity to actually see one."

He rolled his eyes. "Prepare to be disappointed. They're all dumps. Definitely not the Four Seasons. In fact, I don't think I've ever been to a safe house that wasn't in the sewers or some crappy re-purposed warehouse."

"It really can't be worse than..." Josie stiffened and clammed up when a yellow uniform wandered into the restaurant. Her reaction was so abrupt, it attracted the Genjix officer's attention. The young woman threw them a curious glance, and then decided that lunch was more important.

Makita reached out and gently laid a hand over hers, giving it a gentle squeeze. "Relax," he mouthed silently. They kept their eyes locked on each other.

The young woman ordered carry-out and chatted familiarly with the owner. She waved at a few more patrons who walked in and then lounged at a table on the opposite side of the restaurant while she waited.

"Have you ever worked clandestine operations?" asked Makita after the coast was clear.

Josie shook her head.

"There's nothing to it. Relax and follow my lead," he assured her. "It's all just acting. Pretend you're in a play."

"I was once in a play in secondary school. I didn't have a speaking part." She sneaked a glance at the youthful uniformed woman staring at the menu on the wall. "That young thing is an actual Genjix operative?"

He nodded. "In a way, yes. Stateless officer likely recruited from the local office, probably from the youth core. Not the hardcore serial-killing assholes we know and love."

"She looks barely grown. It's shocking how normalized things have become. I still remember being utterly shocked when the news broke that aliens live among us. Now people seem to readily accept the aliens as overlords. I don't understand how they ignore that the Genjix's end goal is to destroy and remake the world."

"It's not so black-and-white," said Makita. "Most folks just want to go about their lives. As long as they provide stability and jobs and technology, people are all right with the consequences of some distant future. Humanity can be very shortsighted."

"Take the penny now. Pay the pound later."

The waitress delivered their drinks and porridge. Josie had hot tea while Makita had black tapioca boba tea with the giant straw. These were joined a few minutes later by two large bowls of steamy, gooey congee.

Makita waggled his jaw from side to side, checking if his cracked dentures were going to hold, and then dug in. He slurped noisily for several seconds, then eyed Josie curiously. "If this sort of work isn't your thing, why did you decide to come with me? You could have sent one of your officers."

Josie burned her tongue spooning the hot porridge into her mouth. "You're an over-the-hill retired agent going into enemy territory on what I consider a suicide mission. I'm not letting you go by yourself, but I'm also not about to order a direct report to go on some off-book job. We are a school. Most of my guys are just cruising until retirement."

"Aren't you a couple months from retirement yourself? In fact, you were eligible for full benefits two years ago. What are you still doing out here? You've done your time."

"A few weeks actually." Josie stared as she stirred her congee. "Guess I'm afraid of what you're going through. Parents and brother long gone. No other relatives. I just have an empty house in Perth waiting for me. All my friends are in the service. The Prophus and that Academy are all I have left." She sipped her tea and smacked her lips. "Besides, one last hurrah sounds like fun."

Makita held out his cup of boba tea. "Then you're a fool too."

Josie chuckled. "To the foolish couple." They touched glasses.

After their meal, they set off on foot again, navigating the maze-like alleys. Dusk was setting, and what little daylight was left in the slits between the buildings was barely reaching ground level. They passed several more blue-uniformed and one more yellow-lapelled officer.

"There's police all over," muttered Josie. She checked her comm. "This entire city is blanketed by scanners. I don't see how any host can move through here without getting caught."

"She's not," said Makita, beckoning her to follow.

"Then what are we doing here?"

"Following a lead."

They followed the map on their comms until they reached a large and busy commercial plaza nestled between several skyscrapers. Makita stopped and stared. "These coordinates must be wrong. According to the GPS, this building in front of us is the safe house rendezvous point."

"Why do you think it's wrong?"

Makita pointed at a large sign off to the side. "Because this is literally the Four Seasons Hotel."

Josie looked up at the glass-paned, gold-and-silver building that curved taller than the eye could follow. She double-checked his numbers and codes, and then scanned their surroundings. "This looks right."

An astonished grin slowly grew on Makita's face. "Finally, a decent place. I was expecting some wooden shack behind a dumpster or a hole in the back of a laundromat or an underwater cave underneath the fishing dock. Could you imagine if we can get room service?" He was positively giddy.

They entered the massive lobby of the richly adorned hotel. A towering piece of gleaming metal and stone resembling a staircase climbing into the clouds was on display to their left. The art piece formed a babbling waterfall that cascaded into a pond on the ground level. Then, through some optical illusion, the water continued to stream down another set of staircases beneath the water's surface.

"Fancy," said Josie, leaning forward and looking into the depths.

"You should see some of the stuff they have in Hong Kong," said Makita. "They might be world-destroying assholes, but the Genjix love their art."

"You've been to the heart of the Genjix Empire?"

He walked away from the elaborate display. "The entire city looks like it's from another planet."

They first stopped in the front lobby, and then at the concierge, and then down to the lower levels where the maintenance and support staff worked. Two bribes and one comedy sketch of them playing lost tourists later, Makita and Josie finally made it to a small laundromat reserved for employee uniforms in the far corner of the second basement.

Makita walked up to a tiny gray-haired woman. "Are you Madam Lucy Ong?"

The old woman crossed her arms, saying nothing. She looked as if she were etched from marble.

Makita coughed and bowed. "A man who falls off a cliff…" He waited for a response. Nothing happened. A few uncomfortable seconds passed. Makita tried again, this time with looping hand gestures. "A man falls off the cliff…"

Still nothing.

"Uh did I do it wrong?" He muttered. "Was it dives or fall? A woman? That's what I get for not writing it down. Stupid rules."

Josie palmed her face and pushed him aside. "A man who jumps off a cliff…"

"…Jumps to conclusion," finished Madam Lucy Ong. She beckoned for them to follow. The three proceeded through the room filled with thousands upon thousands of uniforms and past an unobtrusive door in the back that led to a dusty unfinished cement staircase. At the bottom was a rusty metal door that opened into an underground walkway.

Any hope that Makita had harbored regarding staying at a five-star safe house evaporated as they walked through the long, drab tunnel under a seemingly endless row of harsh fluorescent lights, a chorus of water drops joining the echo of their footsteps.

He sighed. "We are definitely not at the Four Seasons any longer."

Josie looked around. "It's not so bad. During the war, we were often lucky if we slept with a roof over our heads."

"That's a pretty low bar. During the war, we were just lucky a day passed when no one got gassed."

They continued for several more minutes. By his calculations, they must have traveled a good kilometer underground, which meant this walkway had likely taken them several city blocks out of Downtown Core. Along the way, he noticed several metal supports rigged to collapse. This must have been one of the forgotten tunnels used during the war, when the city was a heavily contested hot zone.

"What are we doing here?" asked Josie. "The last known whereabouts of Victoria Khan was Manila. At least that was the one-way ticket that we purchased for her at her request. You've seen how tight security is. There's no way any host can avoid detection in this city."

"Manila is a neutral city and a major hub for illegal smuggling throughout the entire South China Sea," replied Makita. "She likely went there to find a way to smuggle herself home. If that's the case, she'll be near-impossible to track."

"So I ask again: what are we doing here?"

They reached a set of damp stone stairs and went up one level through a rickety wooden door, appearing in a small restaurant kitchen filled with line cooks and dishwashers. None paid them any heed as Madam Ong circled around the back to a rickety stairwell.

After climbing what seemed like six or seven stories, they reached a door at the top. Makita had lost count. He was slightly embarrassed to see that he was the only one among them breathing a little heavily.

He knocked on the door and turned to Josie. "I don't know where she is, but I know someone who should."

The door creaked open a sliver and a squat, dark-skinned man poked his head out, the barrel of a pistol floating just below his chin. He saw Madam Ong and the gun disappeared immediately. His gaze drifted to Josie and then to Makita.

His eyes widened. "What are–"

Makita stuck his hand out. "Agent Nabin Bhattarai, I'm special operative Makita Takeshi, under special instruction from the Keeper. This is my associate, Colonel Josie Perkins. You're Ella Patel's boyfriend, right? We'd like to have a word with you."

CHAPTER EIGHT
World-Famous

Cameron Tan and my former host, Emily Curran, were old friends. He had disobeyed orders and came to India to investigate her death. With his help and guidance, Ella and the Prophus began investigating the Genjix presence in Crate Town. They managed to uncover the plans for the Bio Comm Array facility under construction.

The rest of the events that unfolded are well-documented. In the end, the Genjix Adonis vessel Shura gained control of India. Ella Patel fled the country with Cameron. Crate Town was eventually demolished to pave the way for the Bio Comm Array facility.

Ella struggled with balancing the eight bottles of beer on a serving tray as she carefully tight-roped across the bar to the corner booth. Eight may have been a little ambitious, but Tsuki, the regular waitress, had carried far more than eight at any one time using only one hand. Ella was a trained secret agent. Well, sort of trained. Regardless, waiting tables should be a piece of pie.

Cake.

"What?"

Now that she had been kicked out of the Academy, Io was

using cooking and lifestyle blogs to teach Ella English. The results had been mixed.

The American saying is "piece of cake," and just because you can throw a knife does not mean you can wait tables.

"Isn't a pie and cake the same thing?"

Ella carefully placed the tray on the table and distributed the beers to the same number of men clustered in the booth. She caught eyes with Hinata as he laughed and negotiated with the Akai Baku leader seated across from him. He looked completely relaxed and at ease among the seven murderous gangsters, but she knew his tells: that fake overly wide grin, the exaggerations and overacting, that super-annoying laugh as he tried to act cool, and his intensely wide-eyed enraptured stare when any of the gangsters spoke.

Ella listened, understanding maybe a third of the Japanese. Io filled in the rest. One thing that was perfectly clear, however, was the numbers.

Two crates of American-made military assault rifles, four cases of ammunition, and six sets of body armor. All for a million yen and change, no protection levies for the bar for the next two months, and the Burglar Alarms would stay in the clear with the Akai Bakus if any problems arose. The Kabukicho District was their turf, so a lot of the underworld activities had to run through them.

Close the deal.

"You sure?"

Why do you always ask me if I am sure?

"Because you're always wrong."

Look at the one on the far end. He is about to jump out of his seat.

Ella did. Io was right, this one time. The Bakkas weren't the savviest bunch, often restless and easy to rile. If they got rowdy, things would get unpleasant for everyone else. She caught Hinata's eye and tapped her middle finger and thumb together twice. The terms were good enough. Wrap it up.

He finger-tapped back and continued drinking with the Bakkas. Ella grimaced; she was footing the bill for all of those drinks. Eventually, Hinata and the Bakkas got around to making their final toast to seal the deal. Ella turned away and signaled to Kaoru and Lee waiting in the back room to start moving the goods from the storage room to the loading area.

Ella put the tray down and kept her hands near her knives as the payment was made. She stayed tense and alert until the merchandise was loaded onto the Bakkas' bikes, and they rumbled loudly down the alley. She was half-expecting a rival gang to jump them before they made it out to the streets. Military guns attracted that sort of attention in Tokyo.

Once they were out of sight, Ella allowed the tension out of her shoulders. She pumped her little fists and high-fived the Burglar Alarms. "Are you guys staying?" she asked.

Hinata shook his head. "Talking to the Bakkas was stressful. I need to go home and stare at a wall for a few hours."

Kaoru and Lee exchanged looks, and then excused themselves. Ella let a small grin grow on her face. The two were trying to keep it a secret, but it was getting harder to hide every day. She wondered if she could get a matchmaking fee for putting them together. She sent everyone home and stayed back to take inventory on the still-unsold goods.

Well done. That should keep us afloat for a while. We almost have enough to get our own place. We should go aground for a few weeks at least and make sure there is no chatter from the Prophus. There is bound to be blowback from your little heroics.

Ella doubted it. What were the Prophus going to do? Try to find her in the largest city in the world? Please. She allowed herself to breathe as she turned back to the bar, staying in character as she wiped the counter with a rag.

Asao Sato, the owner of the World-Famous Bar & Udon came up to her from behind the bar. "Are the Bakkas gone? Is the deal complete, Beektoria?"

Ella grimaced. For the life of her, she didn't know why she had chosen that stupid name. She hated it. Hated everything about it. It sounded ugly. It had too many syllables. Worse of all, like Asao, she couldn't even pronounce it half the time. It unfortunately was the first thing that popped into her head when the stupid Prophus signed her up for the Host Protection Program and asked what alias she wanted to go by. She had blanked and the only thing she could think of was that stupid song from the silly British girl band that was playing in her head at the time.

I told you not to be hasty. Take your time and think it over.

"I know. I panicked, and now I'm stuck with it forever."

"Yeah, we got a fat million yen for the stash," she said aloud.

"You said you'd clear one and a half."

"Don't be a greedy asshole, Asao. That's still five hundred thousand more than you were going to get. I also got you out of protection money for two months."

A gravelly grunt erupted from deep within the ex-bosozoku bar owner. Asao cut an imposing figure, but Ella knew better than to judge him by his bulk and his tattoos. Asao was a fraud, a big fluffy coward who nearly soiled himself the first time she pulled a knife on him. She had later learned that although he looked the part of a bosozoku gang enforcer, he had actually only been their accountant and had wanted to fit in.

Ella was also surprised to learn he had two Masters degrees, one in Waka and one in the Muromachi Dynasty, which made him far more educated than she would ever be. Even criminal enterprises needed good bookkeeping and poetry, she guessed.

The two had worked out a pretty unreasonable business arrangement. Asao allowed her to use the back of his bar as storage and for the Burglar Alarms' home base of operations. In return he got half of all business done on his premises. It wasn't a remotely fair deal by a long shot but when she first arrived in Tokyo six months ago, nearly homeless, penniless and very much not Japanese, Ella had been shunned by practically every other disreputable business. It was this arrangement with Asao and a couple free nights sleeping in the storage room that had kept her safely off the streets. It also gave her the base she needed to start her own crew.

"Good job. If you're done, quit taking up space and get on out of here," said Asao. "Unless you want to keep working. I'm a server short."

Ella thought about her busy schedule that night, and then slung the rag over her shoulder. She checked the chalkboard with the specials, which was really the week's leftovers: tempura udon. She slapped a smile on her face and got to work.

On top of being allowed to run her deals through his bar, Asao allowed her to network and scope out new jobs. The World-Famous was where she had met and recruited Hinata, her first Burglar, and also where she found leads for clients to buy her ill-gotten goods.

Unfortunately, the bar wasn't big, and Asao didn't allow loitering, so either she had to be buying drinks the entire time or working. Ella chose to work, mainly because she couldn't hold much liquor. Working also allowed her to keep her ear to the ground on new leads and contacts. She didn't have a network like she did back in Crate Town – that took years to build – so this was the next best thing.

For the next two hours, Ella hung around, lazily cleaning up the place and half-heartedly serving drinks, mostly to a few regulars and folks stopping by after work. Business was fairly light, but slowly improved as the night progressed. Asao occasionally threw her scowls from behind the bar, but only because she kept raiding the salty finger foods he laid out for the customers.

During her shift, she learned that the Akai Bakus had been losing ground in their turf war with their neighbors to the north, and that the local yakuza, who supported both groups, had decided to sit this one out to see who came out on top. That was probably why the Bakkas needed more guns and armor. One of the factories making counterfeit tablets had a surplus they were looking to unload. Ella wondered if she could use her newfound money to buy the lot and then sell that to the night markets. Or better yet, if she got ahold of some of her old contacts from Crate Town…

Do not even think about it. We are not going to risk that level of exposure simply to make a little side money on cheap knockoffs. To your right, the two women sitting by themselves are talking about needing to find a fence for gear and recruiting a getaway driver for a museum robbery. Perhaps they could use some surveillance equipment.

The two women sitting at the table were at the far end of the bar. Too far for Ella to make out what they were saying, but a Quasing could leverage a host's senses better than they could themselves. Ella continued pretending to wipe a table with a rag as she craned her head to the side.

How very subtle.

The two women looked as if they were up to no good. Their body language made clear that they preferred to be left alone. That didn't stop a few idiots from trying though. Each was sharply rebuked.

Perhaps it was time for a woman's touch.

Ella grabbed a serving tray and was about to scoot over closer to make a casual introduction when a commotion caught her attention. It was the unruly group of six who had come in an hour earlier: four weirdly dressed men in their early twenties and two girls who looked a little younger, probably in their late teens.

One of the girls had refused her drink and tried to stand. The boy sitting next to her had grabbed her arm and tried to pour the shot into her mouth. When she shied away, the drink spilled all over the table. He yanked her back into the chair and began to yell.

Ella, no. Remember what we agreed about. Keep quiet. Do not stick your neck out.

Ella bit her lower lip. Her fury burned like the sun, but the damn alien was right. Mind her own business. Remember what was at stake. Look out for number one. Not doing that was what had gotten her this stupid alien in the first place. She forced herself to look away and focus on the two art thieves in the corner. She almost succeeded. Almost. Then the punk went ahead and smacked the girl. A loud sharp slap.

Ella, no, no, do not–

"Shut it, Alien." She stomped over to the table.

The boy had let go of the girl and had a bottle of beer raised to his lips. He saw her approach and pointed at the mess of alcohol pooled on the table dripping off the side. "Just in time. Clean this up, and get us another round."

Ella gave him a cold glare and then looked at the girl. "Are you all right, sweet potato?" That wasn't actually what she was trying to say but her broken Japanese needed a lot of work and sometimes Io was a little late with the translations and pronunciations.

"This is none of your business, gaijin," the boy spat.

If he makes a move, it will be with his left hand. His right is holding a drink.

Ella leaned in and offered her hand to the girl. "Why don't you go home? Come on. I'll walk you out. The rest of you scram."

"Who the hell do you think you are? Do you know who I am?" The foolish boy grabbed at Ella's arm. Almost before his fingers clamped around her wrist, she twisted out of his grasp with a sharp tug. At the same time, her other hand, the one holding the serving tray, swung out and smashed his face with the flat side. The boy's head snapped back, and a spray of blood splattered down his shirt.

To your near right. Just above your head.

One of his friends had stood up and was reaching into his jacket. Her long dagger appeared in her hand almost like magic, and she pressed it to the center of his chest.

A little higher.

Ella adjusted her arm until the blade pressed against the guy's neck. That was one good thing about having an annoying alien in her head; it often made her look like a total badass, at least more so than she was normally. She buried the smirk growing on her face; that would have ruined the effect.

Please. Get over yourself.

The rest of the table froze, except for the boy with the bloody nose. He moaned, swaying left and right as he cupped his face.

The entire time Ella never took her eyes off the girl. "As I was saying, get–"

"–another round of drinks." Asao looped a beefy tattooed arm around her neck and dragged her backward so sharply she nearly lost her balance, and in the process almost accidentally slit that guy's throat.

Ella's gut instinct was to stomp on Asao's toes and then jam the pointy end of her dagger into his forearm. Then she remembered that Asshole was her business partner and gutting him would likely end that arrangement. She still needed the bar until she got her own operation up and running.

Ella, enough!

Ella saw the crimson handprint on the girl's cheek and tears rolling down her face, and agreed with her alien. She relented, allowing Asao to manhandle her back behind the bar. When he finally let go, she spun on him and jabbed him in the chest with a finger. "Don't touch me like that again."

"I will if you go on beating up my customers," he replied

just as hotly. He seemed strangely unnerved. "Do you know who you were messing with?"

"Some jerk face beating up his girlfriend. Who cares?"

Asao looked over her shoulder and turned sheet white. The group had gotten up and appeared to be leaving. "Please sit, sit," he waved furiously. "Let me get you a bottle of sake. On the house."

The group passed them as they headed toward the exit. The girl who got slapped was helping her jerk boyfriend. The boy looked unsteady on his feet as he leaned against her for support. His nose was definitely broken, and was fountaining blood. He looked like a butcher after a hard day's work. The other boys in the group shot her murderous looks as they passed.

"I hope he bleeds to death," Ella shouted.

You should be quiet... Asao is overreacting to this situation. Something is wrong.

Asao kept staring at the exit long after the group was gone. He shook his head, muttered furiously under his breath, and then whirled on her. "You idiot! What have you done?"

"What do you mean?" said Ella defiantly. Her fingers itched for her blade. "That punk was beating up that girl. What did you expect me to do?"

"I expect you to shut up and not cause trouble," growled Asao.

What part of keeping a low profile do you not understand?

The bartender and the alien were both laying it on her pretty thick, and Ella had just about had enough. "You two are a bunch of idiot cowards," she screamed. "And both of you stop telling me to shut up."

"You two?" frowned Asao. "What are you talking about?"

"I mean you," she replied lamely.

Keep your head on straight. You are going to blow our cover.

"Shut it, Alien!"

Asao pointed toward the doorway. "Do you know what you've done? You just smashed the face of the local yakuza boss's son."

"Huh?" The full gravity of her actions dawned on her. "Oh? Oh! I see. Now you tell me. I wouldn't have done that if I had known he was someone important."

That was a lie. She totally would have.

Yes you would. We may need to find a new partner.

Asao buried his head in his hands. "It may not be that bad. I'll make some calls. The boy may not wish to bear the shame of being beaten by a serving girl. He may be too embarrassed to report this to his elders. As for you, go home and do not show your face until I clean this mess up. You've caused enough problems for one day."

Ella, scowling, was about to shoot off another volley of retorts, and then thought better of it. She took off her apron and spiked it on the ground. She turned to leave and then stopped. "Uh, can I stay for dinner at least?"

"Go!"

CHAPTER NINE
Directive

Ella and I were given several choices to relocate. Prophus Command wanted to bring Ella to a safe haven, either their headquarters in Greenland or another Prophus-heavy country like Canada or South Africa. Ella did not want to travel to the opposite ends of the world. In truth, she did not even want to leave India.

I also did not relish living under the overbearing hand of the Prophus. Much to my dismay, Cameron had taken the girl under his wing, and stymied my influence over her. Tao, Cameron's Quasing, was already suspicious of my intentions.

The compromise for our new home was Australia, close enough to India but far enough away from the Prophus's central strongholds.

Shura strolled past the long line of passengers at Hong Kong International waiting to board the commercial liner to Sochi. The Black Sea beaches were breathtaking this time of year, and she was looking forward to working on her slalom. She had half-serious aspirations of making the national team. It was a bit outlandish, but making the Olympics had always been a childhood dream.

In any case, she wasn't young any more and had too many

responsibilities pulling her in too many directions. Her duties governing India, hunting the Prophus and trying to crush her rivals for the last Genjix council seat left little time for a hobby. Still, it was a nice goal to work toward, especially when she needed to take a break from waging her multiple battles.

Sochi was technically under Rurik's sphere of influence. However, because of the Hard Peace, Shura could now walk freely in her rivals' territory without fear of violence. Until its implementation, she would have had to worry about her safety if she were discovered. It had gotten so bad over the past few years in the battle for standing among the vessels, that for many, their fellow Genjix were almost as dangerous as the Prophus.

Conflict breeds innovation.

After Weston was elevated to Zoras's vessel, he had instituted the Hard Peace. The Hard Peace reminded them that the true enemy was the Prophus and the humans, and that the contest for standing among the vessels was meant to hone their abilities, to keep them sharp and innovative. It could go on, but only to the degree before true violence, whatever that meant.

Different vessels interpreted "true violence" differently. Shura tended to push the boundary as far as possible. She personally thought Zoras was being hypocritical, seeing as how he had climbed to the top of the Genjix hierarchy by essentially waging a civil war. Shura had technically been forbidden from even stepping foot on Russian soil until just two years ago because her family had backed the wrong side when Zoras's previous Adonis vessel, Enzo, bested Councilman Vinnick for control of the Genjix.

Do not be sacrilegious.

"My sincerest apologies, Tabs."

You are not being sincere.

She sighed. There was no hiding from her Holy One, but that had been the case since she was a little girl. Tabs knew Shura better than she knew herself, which was often frustrating. However, Shura liked to think she knew Tabs almost as well, including how her Holy One did not put much stock into ceremony, so she was oftentimes just as sacrilegious as Shura. Gods were not infallible.

You are being sacrilegious again.

"Must be my poor upbringing."

Shura entered the first class cabin. The large commercial liner was just beginning to load its passengers. She smiled and waited patiently in the row as a little girl ran down the aisle. She helped an elderly couple store their carry-on, and then, once the aisle cleared, continued past the cabin and proceeded upstairs to a private lounge reserved for Genjix operatives.

She was fortunate the plane was delayed, since she had run late wrapping up her business in Hong Kong. Ordering another plane to take her to Sochi would have delayed her at minimum another hour, and she had a vacation schedule to keep. The plane could have been ordered grounded, but the process was frowned upon and considered an abuse of power by their allied governments, not that the Genjix cared.

Shura held a high enough standing to maintain a private plane, but she preferred piggybacking on commercial liners for one very simple reason: the Prophus did not shoot down civilian planes. This year alone, their enemy had located and shot down three Genjix planes carrying high-ranking Adonis vessels, and currently there was very little defense against such an attack.

The technology for low-orbital surveillance and warfare had improved by leaps and bounds, and there was a burgeoning war in the exosphere. It would only be a matter of a few years before they took their conflict into space. The Chinese government was already in the late stages of designing a permanent moon base to house another Bio Comm Array that would free them of atmospheric interference.

Shura felt it the moment she entered the darkened quarters reserved for her. It was a sixth sense, an awareness of a presence. One behind her and the other off to the side. Her instinct was to change levels, drop to a knee and become a difficult target. Her pistol was at the small of her back, and she had a blade cached in her sleeve. A glimmer of metal reflected the light outside.

Behind you and to your left.

This could be an ambush, in which case she was likely dead. However, the odds of this being a Prophus attack were low, if non-existent. Any enemy assassin who managed to sneak in here deserved the chance to try to kill her. Hong Kong was the heart of Genjix power. If an Adonis vessel wasn't safe here, she wasn't safe anywhere. That could only mean one thing.

Humming, she closed the door behind her and reached for the light. Then, as calmly as if she were taking a stroll along the beach, she turned and smiled at the three intruders in the room. Only the one lounging on a sofa in the far corner required her acknowledgment.

"High Father Weston."

The leader of the Genjix tilted his head and eyed her with a steely gaze. He brought a cup of tea to his lips and sipped. There was no steam; he had been here a while. Weston placed the cup on the console table with a loud clink. He leaned back in his chair looking relaxed but alert, like a snake ready to strike. "I'm very cross with you, Shura."

Shura didn't blink. Elder Mother would have been proud.

"Give me a situation breakdown, Tabs."

The two men at your flank are Hamil and Stephenson, both elite bodyguards. Both are wearing body armor underneath their suits, and Stephenson has a blade tucked near his ribs. Hamil's finger is on his trigger. You have little chance of defeating both together. Weston is at least as skilled as you, and definitely stronger, so you have no chance if this conversation results in conflict. My recommendation is to accept your fate if Weston orders your death, so just kill yourself gracefully. I prefer Hamil as my next vessel, so try not to kill him.

"Thanks. I'll try to keep that in mind."

"Your words distress me, High Father," she replied aloud. "How have I displeased you?"

Can you sound any less sincere?

"Of course I can, Tabs."

A small chuckle escaped Weston's lips. He knew the game as well as anyone. She correctly assessed that he appreciated her skirting protocol so brazenly. "Rurik informed me of what happened at the hotel. You broke the Hard Peace."

Shura considered her next words very carefully, making sure to run them by Tabs before voicing them. "I assure you I have done no such thing."

"You ambushed his meeting with the Iranian dealer, shot his guards, and then hijacked his transaction." Weston appeared amused. "Did I miss anything?"

Shura delicately dabbed a finger in the air. "Actually, High Father, I took special precautions to avoid lethal violence. The only injuries were to the guards who attacked me, so if anything I have a stronger case to argue that Rurik's people were the ones who broke the Hard Peace. I could make an issue of it, but I'm not a snitch who feels the need to whine to you every time he is unable to manage his own affairs. It is hardly becoming for an Adonis vessel vying for a seat on the Council."

Shura took her time crossing the room to the chair opposite Weston. She paused for dramatic effect. "My bargain with Shah was not made under duress and, if I may add, is on far better terms for the Genjix than what Rurik had arranged."

"Hardly no violence, however," murmured Weston.

"I said no lethal violence," she responded softly.

"You may not have technically broken the Hard Peace as written," he said, "but you certainly bent the rules quite badly.

You are too clever for your own good, daughter. You violated the spirit of the order. Your actions for personal gain have been a detriment to the Genjix. It also sets a poor precedent for other vessels contending for standing. After the internal strife that the Council has endured the past few years, we need stability. Conflict breeds innovation, but uncontrolled conflict is a waste of our resources."

When exactly did your Holy One decide that? she thought. She wisely kept that to herself.

Wise indeed.

Shura had a glib retort on the tip of her tongue, but she held back. What was the point? Why bother defending her position when they both knew he was right? Weston was as intelligent and cunning as any vessel, one of the top students at the Hatchery. That was why he had been chosen to be Enzo's heir, to be Zoras's vessel.

The leader of the Genjix wasn't here for her to plead her case. He was her judge and executioner. This conversation was a formality. Her fate had likely been sealed before she even walked into the room. The only thing left to do then was to go on the offensive. Either defend her aggressive tactics or show that she was too valuable to the Genjix to be put to death. That, or she could try to kill all three in the room.

She leaned forward and poured herself a cup of tea. "When one's enemy holds three times one's territory and wealth, and five times one's forces, one has to think outside the box. Because of the Hard Peace, Rurik has enjoyed every tactical advantage in our conflict. But then, you want him to win, don't you, High Father?"

"And yet you still stand." Weston spoke without emotion, but it was a great compliment.

His respect is irrelevant. He fears you.

Shura knew where she personally stood with Weston, and where Rurik stood. She and Weston had a relationship spanning back to their days at the Hatchery, though he was a few years her junior. Still, personal affection and childhood relationships only went so far when it came to the Genjix hierarchy. She knew he thought little of Rurik, but the Russian's family had its own advantages, while Shura's name bought nothing.

Weston stood up and moved out of her peripheral vision. She forced herself to keep looking forward. His hand squeezed her shoulder as he leaned in close. "You're talented and dangerous, and far too ambitious."

Stay in control. His gesture is relaxed.

Shura felt her hand drift closer to one of her knives. That movement was not lost on Weston's guards. She reversed course and, instead, put her hand over his. She lightly caressed and stroked the back of his arm. It was comforting and sensual, and brought back memories to them both.

"Overwhelming odds nurture strength," she replied. Another of Elder Mother's sayings.

The two had history, physically as well as mentally. Sex was just another tool at the Hatchery. The children often experimented with each other, sometimes using it for pleasure, other times learning how to wield it as a weapon.

"I should make an example of you," said Weston, his lips lingering close to her ear. The tips of his fingers brushed her cheek as he pulled away. Shura continued looking forward, but she tracked his voice in the room. "However, that would not serve the Holy Ones." He returned to her line of sight and sat back on the sofa. "Tell me, Shura. Are you up-to-date on the current progress of the Bio Comm Array project?"

The politically expedient answer would be some degree of affirmation. It was one of the Genjix's most important projects. Unfortunately, she had a full plate and Tabs was not fond of reading dry status reports when Shura was asleep either.

"Not a clue," she admitted. "The outcome of the project

is your responsibility. I am tasked with making sure that the facility wants for nothing, and that nothing interrupts its operation." She paused. "Which is why I did what I had to do to obtain those catalyst reaction rods. My facility has need of those."

"As do all the Bio Comm facilities," replied Weston. "But in commandeering and hoarding a source of catalyst reaction rods for one facility, you have deprived Rurik's three arrays of the necessary materials to maintain operations. You have forced them offline."

"Do you believe the Holy Ones would like for me to take over responsibility for those arrays as well?" Shura said that with a completely straight face.

A tight smile broke the plane of Weston's mouth. "Perhaps you should. Rurik has already been informed that the arrays being offline are unacceptable. However, that is not why I am here today."

"How may I serve the Holy Ones?" said Shura automatically, bowing her head.

"The Bio Comm Array initiative has succeeded far better than the Holy Ones could have possibly hoped. We are already entering the next phase of the project. We now require the talents of a Receiver," explained Weston. "Unfortunately, there are no Genjix alive who possess that ability."

"And the Prophus?"

"We are uncertain," he said. "As far as we are aware, there is only one Quasing alive on record who has this ability, who was a Receiver, but no one knows where she is, and it appears you are to blame."

"I have no idea what you're talking about, High Father."

Weston approached Shura and looked down at her. "A Holy One named Io. She was the Prophus double agent who tried to defect to the Genjix two years ago, the one you let slip from your grasp."

It took a moment for those words to sink in and for Tabs to get her caught up to speed. Shura stiffened and her face turned ashen. The room felt warm, but Shura was not going to break her composure in front of him. She sank into the chair, relaxed. "I see."

Weston leaned forward. "I had already assigned Rurik to locate the girl, since India was originally under his domain, and it was his people who were handling the defector. I want you to join the hunt."

"Why both of us?"

"Because you two have been headaches for me, albeit for different reasons. Also for redundancy. One of you had better get the job done, or I'll send you both to the Eternal Sea."

Shura stood up and bowed. "I won't let you down." She really meant it this time. Weston stood and walked toward the door. The two guards took to his flank. "High Father Weston, wait," she called out as Weston was about to leave the room. She pursed her lips. "Are you expecting Rurik and me to work together?"

Weston chuckled. "Of course not. I want this mission to succeed."

"What happens if we cross paths?"

"To the victor the spoils. And in this matter, the gloves are off. I am exempting you both from the Hard Peace until someone recovers the Receiver. Your conflict with Rurik has gone far past amusing and is beginning to hamper Genjix goals. It will end once and for all." Weston gave her a small nod. "I hope it's you, Shura, for personal reasons, but also not you, because I know what you are capable of. In either case, I will have peace between your territories one way or another. Good hunting, daughter."

A few moments later, after Weston had deplaned, the commercial liner was finally allowed to take off. Shura's gaze stayed on the open doorway. Fifteen minutes after the plane was in the air, the captain came on the loudspeaker. He apologized for the inconvenience but informed them that the plane would be forced to divert to India due to an electrical malfunction of the aircraft's disposal system.

CHAPTER TEN
Exes

With Cameron's support and sponsorship, Ella enrolled at the Prophus Academy in Sydney to train as an agent. The girl's status as a host was kept secret from the Academy's administrators.

The Academy has a strict policy about not disclosing who hosts are. Penetra scanners are not allowed on campus. Many new hosts train at these academies and their safety is a top priority since new hosts are at their most vulnerable and often hunted by the opposing faction. It is also to aid their training. The instructors want to insure that the host students do not receive any special consideration or privilege.

To Makita's disappointment, Nabin and Ella had broken up over half a year ago, shortly after she was expelled from the Prophus Academy. He wondered if her getting expelled precipitated the separation. The two hadn't been in touch. Even worse, it wasn't an amicable sort of breakup.

"Does that mean you'll dish on your ex?" he asked.

To Makita's even greater disappointment, Nabin was a stand-up guy. He maintained an intense loyalty to Ella and refused to volunteer any information regarding her whereabouts. It was not up to him to reveal where she was living, he declared.

She was no longer with the Prophus, and therefore out of their jurisdiction. It was up to her if she wanted to keep in touch.

In fact, Nabin knew for a fact Ella did not want to be found. She was done with the Prophus. No matter how much Makita relayed the urgency of his mission or emphasized how much danger the girl could be in, Nabin held his ground.

At least for the first day.

Makita would have gone as far as to physically threaten Nabin if he thought it would do any good. It wouldn't. Maybe thirty years ago. Still, Makita would have loved to try to box his ears, old age be damned.

Nabin was one of the Prophus's elite agents. He had turned down several promotions and a dozen offers to become a host over the years. The main reason, he had said, was that being a host severely hampered his ability to operate in Genjix territory, and he wanted to stay on the front line. He was also intensely loyal to Cameron Tan, his commander, who was considered the only Prophus Adonis vessel.

Makita was persistent, and he could be very persuasive in an annoying fly sort of way. He and Josie had spent a good portion of the day trying to cajole and shame Nabin to no avail, and then the rest of the afternoon threatening him. The only reason Makita finally gave up was because he needed a nap.

He had forgotten how exhausting running missions and staying on the move could be. He had sat behind a desk for the better part of the last decade, and while he kept himself in relatively good shape, the years of wear and tear were catching up with him. Plus, there was no fighting it: getting old just plain sucked.

By the time he woke up, it was bedtime. Makita yawned and cracked his sore neck. Sore neck, sore feet, sore back. He stared at the angled off-white ceiling with dark blotches where the roof had leaked and the paint had peeled. It took him a second to remember where he was. Sleeping on a couch. Somewhere in Singapore. Really far away from home in Oregon.

For a second, he cursed his idiocy for taking this job. He should be home chopping wood or fishing on the lake or watching a crappy game show on the television. Never mind that he detested all of the above. Makita considered staying in bed and power sleeping his way through to morning, but then another annoyance of old age forced him to reconsider. Sighing, he sat up and looked for the bathroom.

"It was supposed to be a cushy babysitting job. Go sightseeing in Australia. Swim the Great Barrier Reef. Smoke weed with the Bushmen," he growled, rolling off the sofa and walking across the room. Getting to his feet took far more effort than it should have. It was like a walk down memory lane of every injury and broken bone his body had ever suffered. Dull aches, popping joints, and just that general feeling that things weren't working the way they were supposed to. It was a not-so-gentle reminder that this body had trod through many miles, and that his remaining time was dwindling.

On the way, he noticed that Nabin's door was ajar, and the bed was empty and pristinely made. A bed with perfectly folded sheets was always a sure tell of a military career, which Nabin absolutely had. Unfortunately, all three bedrooms were already spoken for. Nabin's team of five had been squatting here for the past five months, two to a room, running a long-term recon mission. Not one of them considered offering the two old farts a bed. Makita looked over at Josie splayed out on the sofa at the other end of the living room, a leg and arm spilling over the side. Well, maybe just one old fart.

The safe house actually was nicer than usual. It was still not the Four Seasons, but it was a pretty solid rooftop unit in a mid-rise apartment building nestled in an upscale residential neighborhood in Singapore. It consisted of one generous open common space with a cathedral ceiling, three bedrooms flanking one side and a kitchen area against the opposite wall. The armory was cleverly hidden under the main floorboards, and all the other secret-agent tools were hidden in an attic space in the far back. Makita would have killed to have these digs back during his bachelor days.

After he emptied his tank, he wandered through the safe house looking for signs of life and something to drink, not necessarily in that order. Other than Josie passed out in the living room, no one was home. He wandered into the kitchen.

After a glass of water, he noticed a tall metal flask sitting on the counter. Curious, he popped off the top and sniffed. Makita perked up. He glanced around the kitchen like a first-time shoplifter. He had quit drinking a few years back, partially for his health, partially on his wife's insistence, but mainly because most of the people he enjoyed sharing a drink with were gone.

Being on a mission felt like the proper time for an exception. He took another deep sniff and let the burn climb up his nostrils. It was very good scotch. Whistling and feeling like he just found the perfect parking space, Makita pocketed the flask and strolled outside and up the stairs to the roof to look for someone to share the drink with.

He found Nabin and one of his agents in the far corner, poring over a map in front of a pair of tripods supporting high-powered binoculars aimed at the Singapore Strait about a klick to the west. The agent noticed him approach, tapped Nabin on the shoulder, and offered a little deeper of a bow than necessary. "Beautiful night for sightseeing, sir. Can we assist you with something?"

Makita smiled, but inside he grimaced. He was trying to sneak up on them. He must be losing his touch. "I'd like a few minutes of Nabin's time if he's available."

"Can it wait until morning?" asked Nabin. "We've just received the latest crack from our code breakers. We have a pretty limited window to verify the data before the algorithm resets the encryption."

Makita inhaled the cool night air deeply. "Would you mind if I join you? We can talk along the way."

Nabin hesitated. He pointed toward the port. "Uh, with all due respect, sir. I'm taking the most direct route. It's not an easy one. Are you... are you sure you're up for it?"

"I'll be fine." That was an automatic and emotional response, given without much thought. Makita looked toward the port, which was mostly just blurry lights after a hundred or so meters, and realized that Nabin literally meant moving across the rooftops, scaling walls and jumping over alleys.

"What's wrong with street level?" he asked.

"Too many checkpoints and patrols. The rooftops are pretty much a clear shot."

Last chance to back out. "I can handle it," replied Makita gruffly. Stupid pride.

"Suit yourself," shrugged Nabin. He handed the binoculars to the other agent. "Bea, keep an eye on it and let me know if any activity pops. We'll be back soon."

"Sure thing, Nabin." Bea saluted Makita.

"Don't do that." Makita took a few minutes to stretch. He had a feeling this wasn't going to end well. He signaled to Nabin when he was ready and followed the Nepalese's lead, hurdling over the side of the building and dropping down to the adjacent roof a few meters below.

The first landing rattled his bones, causing him to pitch forward and roll out on the gravel top. Every pebble stabbed into his back. He swallowed the groan climbing up his throat.

Nabin was there to help pull him to his feet. "Are you doing OK, sir?"

"I'm OK, and stop calling me sir. All this formality drives me nuts."

"My apologies, Makita."

That was one thing he really appreciated about Nabin. The guy was a consummate professional even when they were alone. He never took shortcuts or deviated from his script. Although in this era of constant surveillance, could anyone really be sure they had complete privacy any more?

They began to jog side by side, dropping another level to the next building before climbing a wall to the one after that. Next they hopped down to a fire escape and took it all the way up to the next building's roof.

Makita did his best to keep up. "How goes the assignment?"

"I've been staring at ships all day for the past five months. What do you think?" grunted Nabin as he bounded up the ten flights of stairs. The man wasn't even breathing heavily, which was more than Makita could say.

Stupid pride.

"Who did you piss off to get this gig? I thought Cameron's crew was untouchable. Why did you break with him?"

Nabin made a face as if he smelled something foul. "I didn't. He got tired of everyone on his team turning down promotions and hosts, so he threatened to apply for a transfer to guard the Svalbard Global Seed Vault unless we started taking them seriously."

Makita chuckled. "Don't mess with an Adonis, regardless which side they're on."

"Besides, he was the one who asked me to take this job," said Nabin. "Singapore is the Genjix's main sea transportation hub. All the collection points for the Bio Comm Arrays pass through that port. All the shipments are coded. My team has been grabbing snapshots of the manifests, tracking their destinations with a dozen other teams in the area, and trying to crack the codes. We're close. Once we do that, the encryptions will practically draw a map of every array in the entire world."

Makita signaled for a quick break when they got to the top of the fire escape. A lengthy silence passed as he labored to catch his breath. Nabin leaned against a chimney, looking perfectly relaxed as he waited patiently, which annoyed Makita even more. He wouldn't mind resting for another ten minutes, but motioned for them to start moving again. Thankfully, Nabin slowed and walked the length of the next building.

"Is that really what you wanted to talk to me about?" asked Nabin.

"It's about Ella Patel. I need you to reconsider your position. We need to get in touch with her."

"I can't do that."

"You know I could just give you a direct order, right?"

"You could," admitted Nabin, "but I don't think you will. From what I've heard, I don't think that's your style." He paused. "Didn't you say not six hours ago that you were retired and this whole mission is off-book?"

"Well, young man," huffed the old man, puffing his chest out. "I still have the authority, even if I've been put out to pasture."

"Technically you don't, so I'll probably just refuse."

"Off the record, what happened between you two?" asked Makita as they took a ladder down a few levels to a warehouse roof.

Nabin reached the bottom first and waited for him to catch up. "After she joined the Academy, we got together. We became serious enough I considered leaving the team to be closer to her." His voice trailed off.

They walked around two long rows of skylights and then jumped down onto a sky bridge crossing a main street. Staying low, they quickly moved to the other side. They paused in the shadow of the building until the traffic below died. Then

Nabin gave him a boost up to the next roof, and followed right behind.

"Relationships and service are tough things to juggle, especially if you serve the aliens," continued Makita. "My wife and I fought for years over the Prophus. I thought fighting the Genjix took priority over my family, that I was saving the world for them. It took her leaving me to realize that she was right. What is the point of fighting for your future if you destroy it? So why didn't you make the move?"

Nabin spread his arms. "And miss out on all this fun? Squatting here for the past five months has been so fulfilling. It had nothing to do with duty, if that's what you're thinking, and everything to do with Ella. She's... wilful. How's that saying go? You can take a girl out of the slum, but you can't take the slum out of the girl. She had a tough time adapting."

"Understandable," said Makita. "I was pretty lost before I joined the Prophus."

Nabin chuckled. "Oh, that's the problem. Ella's not lost at all. That girl knows exactly who she is, where's she's from, and what she's all about. Did you know she ran a gambling ring in the dorms? A cards table, game betting, dice, the whole deal." He leaned in and whispered as if he thought someone could overhear. "Pretty sure the dice were weighted."

Makita was impressed. "Entrepreneurship. Organizational skills. Clandestine operations. Business acumen. I'd think all of that would be a plus."

"Maybe in the old days," grinned Nabin. "Not sure if you've noticed, but the Prophus have gone a little corporate lately. I'm surprised the commandant didn't kick her out as soon as she got caught. I think the Academy gave her a pass because Cameron vouched for her. But then she injured a few students with her knives. Snuck them into a sparring session. She's pretty good with those."

"Real-life combat experience is always a plus." That sounded less convincing.

Nabin shook his head. "The final straw was when they caught her pilfering Academy supplies, electronics and weapons, and selling them on the black market."

"Holy crap!"

"She had an entire operation set up and just–" Nabin sliced his hand horizontally across the air "–was skimming off the top. Did it for an entire year. I mean, who does that?"

"You're kidding. That's colossally stupid," mused Makita. "That's ballsy as hell, but stupid."

"That was the last straw. They kicked her out then. I begged her not to do stuff like that. Offered to send her money, but that only pissed her off." Nabin sighed and made a face. "Ella Patel is beholden to no one, was what she said... screamed. She knocked the money out of my hands. Anyway, after she got expelled, we broke up. I'm a Prophus agent. I can't have a loose cannon risking my people's lives."

"Understandable." Makita stopped and stared at the space between this warehouse and the next building. The alley wasn't wide, and his younger self may have given this hurdle a shot, but not at this age. Now this gap might as well have been the Grand Canyon.

"Um, I'm not jumping that!" he exclaimed.

Nabin was already a step ahead of him. He went off to the side and returned dragging a metal ladder, which he extended over the gap. He pressed down on the ladder to check its stability and then climbed on. "If it makes you feel better, I can't make this jump either." He pointed down. "Short legs."

They climbed across the alley, threading down a series of shorter buildings until they reached the outer fenced perimeter of the port. They took position behind a billboard overlooking the streets. Nabin pulled out his monocular and began to scan the grounds.

Makita squinted at the main dock area on the other side of the fence. "This is a civilian dock?"

Nabin nodded. "There's a standing contingent of Genjix security onsite but most of the guards are just rent-a-cops."

"Why don't the Genjix transport their classified and sensitive cargo through military channels directly to naval bases?"

"Same reason why so many high-ranking officials on both sides fly commercial. Our satellite detection systems have gotten too sophisticated while stealth technologies have fallen behind. The enemy learned early on that it was more effective and far safer to mask their cargo through commercial shipping lanes than to use military transports. We kept finding their ships and blowing them out of the water. Now they just hide it with all the civilian transports. We have a lot harder time finding their needles in haystacks that way."

"Doesn't this make infiltrating the docks much easier?" asked Makita.

"Once we finally locate it, maybe," answered Nabin. "The hard part is wading through the mountain of crap. Took us almost a year to find this particular shipping node."

Makita looked over at the Nepalese and decided to give his pitch another go. This time with numbers to back him up. "Listen, I appreciate your loyalty to Ella. I know you care about her, and you think you're respecting her wishes, but her life is in danger. The Genjix are after her in a big way. They want her badly enough to put a very large location contract on her head."

"How big?"

"Three million US."

Nabin whistled. "Wow! At that price, she might just turn herself in."

"The Genjix are expending a tremendous amount of resources attacking the Prophus network and searching for her whereabouts. We need to get to her before they do."

"Damn it, we have a problem," said Nabin. He checked the time. "Someone is in the port master's office. We're going to lose the window."

"Can we wait him out?"

"The Genjix are careful with their paper. The encryption rolls in thirty minutes."

"Then take out whoever is in the office."

Nabin shook his head. "Can't. This is a white-glove operation. The moment the Genjix discover any foul play, they wipe everything and start over. We'll lose months of intel and probably the shipping node as well."

"What if we lure him out? Create a distraction."

Nabin frowned. "Throwing a rock at a window only works in video games."

Makita pointed at his own bulbous head. "I'm a little bigger than a rock."

"If they catch you, they'll hand you straight over to the Genjix. That is a poor trade, sir."

"Not if they just think I'm some drunk who wandered onto the docks."

"Through a barbed-wire fence, a guard house, and dozens of surveillance cameras?"

"I'll make it convincing." Makita grinned and fished out the flask. He unscrewed the top and took a long swig, feeling its raw goodness burn as it washed down his throat. Then, sacrilegiously, he doused himself with the peat-smoked drink.

Nabin just stared. "Wait... I was saving that. That's a twenty-four year Ardbeg!"

"Sorry." Makita actually did feel bad, albeit for a different reason entirely. By the time the flask was empty, he smelled like a boozy campfire. He ruffled what little hair he had left on his head for effect, and then pulled out a knife and cut a few slits into his shirt. Once he was done, Makita held his arms out. "What do you think? Do I look like I sleep on the streets and just finished a bender?"

"I don't know about this." Nabin furrowed his brow. "This is a terrible idea. If you get captured by the Genjix, the Keeper will kill me and court-martial my corpse."

"Don't worry, son, I have this handled. If I get captured, you can tell Command it was my idea and that you tried to stop me. They'll understand." Makita grabbed the nearest drainpipe, and began to shimmy down. He had made it halfway to street level when the world began to sway. His sensitive bowels were letting him know how unhappy they were. It had been so long since he last had alcohol, he was practically nine years old trying it for the first time again. Well, it made the act more convincing at least.

He crept to the gate and waited for an opportunity. There was only a lone guard managing the entrance as he watched television inside a small booth with windows on only two sides. Curved spikes were laid out in a row across the road, and the top of the fence was lined with barbed wire.

It took only a few minutes for a truck to pull up. Makita barely had to slouch as he strolled along the opposite side of the vehicle and then slipped in from the side. Whoever had designed the security for the front gate needed a new line of work. Within moments, he was lurking in the shadows of the large warehouses and making his way to the port master's office.

Makita found the perfect location for his distraction just outside the second-floor window. He bided his time inside a backhoe's loader bucket until he saw Nabin's silhouette creep up to the base of the exterior metal stairs leading up to the port master's office. Makita patted the ground and rubbed some dirt on his face, and then staggered out directly under one of the bright floodlights. He began singing too. Unfortunately, the only songs in Japanese he knew were theme songs to old anime.

It wasn't long before he got into character. Makita weaved left and right, bumping and bouncing off cargo containers, slapping the sides of machinery and humming loudly off-key. An old friend of his would have accused him of overacting – which was likely true – but that didn't make a lick of difference when you're trying to act drunk. He pretended to finish chugging the flask, and then he baseball-threw it as hard as he could at one of the containers, making it ring like a giant gong. Then he remembered that Nabin probably wanted to keep the flask, so he went to retrieve it.

He picked up a handful of rocks and began to pelt a dump truck as big as a house. Most of his throws sailed wide, bouncing off the sides of containers and warehouses, which was just as good.

Within seconds, he had caught the attention of two dockworkers. Within minutes, a small crowd had gathered. The silhouettes in the office hadn't budged. Makita turned up the decibels and began to yell, half in Japanese and broken English, and the other half in badly slurred made-up phrases.

Finally, after he had run out of things to say, two men exited the port master's office to investigate the commotion and the growing crowd surrounding him. One looked white-collar and the other looked military. Hopefully, those two were it and Nabin was clear to do whatever he needed. Makita kept his cool as the group closed in on him.

"What is going on here?" the man with the tie demanded.

"Old drunk ghost here," laughed one of the workers. "Moi and I have a bet to see if he pisses himself or passes out."

"What if he does both?" laughed another.

Out of the corner of his eye, Makita noticed a shadow move up the stairs to the second floor office. He began to drift in the opposite direction, pulling the dockworkers' attention with him. It didn't occur to him until he had a good look at the growing mob that he may have been too effective in attracting their attention. A dozen burly men now surrounded him. Escaping his little ruse may be a problem.

He had no choice; he was pot committed, as they say. Makita continued to stumble away, yelling incoherently and throwing clumsy swings at anyone who came too close. One dockworker managed to grab his arm. Makita moved with the fluid motion from thousands of hours of practice. He felt for the gap in between the thumb and the rest of the fingers and gave a hard yank, freeing himself. Then he stepped in and shouldered the man, sending him tumbling off his feet.

The rowdy group howled and whooped as their friend fell on his ass into a puddle of mud. The young man jumped to his feet and charged again. Makita remembered to act unsteady as the man tried to shove him. He shifted just slightly, causing the dockworker to push air. A little nudge to his back sent the man diving face first into the ground. Now he was caked with mud on both sides, much to the enjoyment of the audience. The young man growled as he picked himself up a third time and charged, his fists swinging. One almost connected, but Makita shifted his weight just in time, tripping the man back once more.

By now, the laughter had run dry and was replaced by suspicious stares and mutters. Once or twice may have been luck. Three was a pattern. Things were about to turn ugly. To make matters worse, the one in the military uniform just happened to be a Genjix stateless official.

Makita swayed and spun in a circle, hoping to catch a glimpse of Nabin. Failing that, he backed up until he bumped up against the hard ridged metal wall of a shipping container. He turned quickly to the side and banged his head into another shipping container. He had somehow effectively cornered himself.

"Great," he muttered.

Makita considered his dwindling options. Each was worse

than the previous. When he was younger, he maybe could have fought his way out. There was no chance now. The Genjix official pushed his way to the front of the crowd and looked as if he were going to order his arrest.

He closed his eyes. There was only one thing he could do that could remotely get him out of this situation. He turned to the young man that had picked himself up for the fourth time and threw a wide, lazy, looping swing.

Makita was ready for a punch in the gut. Ready for a follow-up to the jaw. It didn't hurt too badly. The secret of taking a punch was knowing it was coming and having your body prepared to receive the pain. It also helped tremendously that the guy whaling away at him couldn't throw a proper punch to save his life. Unfortunately, what the young man lacked in technique he more than made up for in enthusiasm. That, and a couple of his buddies joined in on the fun.

The beating was mercifully brief. It probably wasn't that enjoyable beating up a geriatric, and Makita did an excellent job of selling it, although it didn't require that much acting. By the time they were finished he was black and purple all over, and bleeding from half a dozen minor cuts. His plan worked. The dockworkers got bored quickly; some even took pity on him. Most importantly, the Genjix lost interest and wandered away.

The dockworkers tossed Makita into an ankle-deep pond just outside the front gates. It was actually more of a sewage ditch filled with refuse. The freezing water bit into his skin. It smelled worse than the Chicago River on a hot summer day, but Makita opted to lie in the pool for a little longer. It was less painful than moving.

A while later, Nabin's head appeared. "Holy hell, are you all right, sir?" The robust agent scrambled down the ditch and picked him up. "I knew I should have recorded you saying this was your idea. You better not be dead, you stupid old bastard."

"I'm alive," he coughed, his chest clenching as he breathed.

"Thank goodness, sir. I was very concerned for your wellbeing."

"You sounded like it."

Nabin sat him down in the alley across the street and looked him over. "Nothing appears broken. Your cuts are superficial."

Makita waved Nabin off. "I'll survive the night. Did you get what you were looking for?"

The agent nodded. "We got all the intel we needed. Thank you. I couldn't have done it without your assistance."

"See, I told you I had this handled." Makita grunted as Nabin pulled him to his feet and helped him walk. They retreated to cover.

"I was thinking about what you said," said Nabin, leading him down the alley away from the street. "I'll make you a deal. I'll tell you where Ella is under one condition."

"Which is?"

"I come with you. I should be the one who makes contact with her. The team can survive without me for a few days."

"Sounds fine by me," shrugged Makita. "How do you know where she is?"

"Cameron and I set up a backdoor to keep tabs on her." He paused. "And she, um, also sent me a birthday card."

Makita looked around the dead end. "What are we doing here? Call a cab or something to take us to the safe house. I need a hot bath then I'm going to bed."

Nabin pointed up at the fire escape that zig-zagged up the side of the warehouse wall. "Actually, sir, we have to go back the way we came. The checkpoints, remember?"

Makita hung his head. Every ache was reminding him of its existence, as were the new aches he knew he was about to get. He let loose a long sigh. "Of course it's always the hard way."

CHAPTER ELEVEN
The Hustle

In Ella Patel's case, they took her protection a step further. Because of Tao's suspicions and the events that had transpired in India, Ella was enrolled into the Host Protection Program. This program is usually reserved for royalty, celebrities, the wealthy and high-value Quasing. Ella was considered the latter due to possible Genjix interest in her. All information and images relating to her identity were scrubbed. Ella Patel was simply erased out of existence. From that moment on, she became Victoria Khan.

One of the first lessons drilled into students at the Prophus Academy was that mistakes happen. Everyone made them, and every agent had to learn how to deal with the consequences and fallout.

Could they correct the mistake?

Could they learn from it?

Lastly, could they quickly forget it?

That last bit was especially interesting and relevant for Ella. She hadn't understood it at first, but Io explained that forgetting the mistake wasn't so much forgetting that it happened, but not letting that mistake weigh too heavily on the agent moving forward. It was called "having a short memory," said Io.

That was one lesson Ella took to heart. She was very good at having a short memory. Too good, in fact. She became so adept at forgetting her mistakes that she often outright forgot that the event ever happened, lesson and all be damned.

She managed to stay away from the World-Famous for two whole days, and then she completely forgot about the episode with the yakuza boy, and then it was business as usual. Ella was soon back to masquerading as a waitress and working hard with the Burglar Alarms to unload the rest of their loot. Asao had given her a stern talking to, threatening to kick the Burglar Alarms out of the World-Famous if another incident occurred. Ella didn't take his bluff seriously and also promptly forgot his warning the moment the conversation ended. At the end of the day she wasn't really there to wait tables anyway, and he was far too greedy to make good on his threats.

Kaoru was the one who had lined up a sale today. She was a first-year student at Keio University, the only Burglar in higher education. She ran with the crew to pay for tuition. Kaoru had been working as a hostess at a kyabakura when they met. The two had hit it off right away. Ella had noticed how sharp the girl was when it came to noticing details and remembering names, and how deft she was navigating an ocean of slimy men.

When one particular patron got a little too handsy with Kaoru, Ella had gotten handsy with her knives. The two had become friends ever since. Eventually, she recruited Kaoru to help her build a criminal empire.

I really wish you would stop saying that.

"What's wrong with building a criminal empire?"

Because one, criminals do not refer to themselves as criminals, and two, you are not building a criminal empire. And while we are at it, I think it is very counterproductive to name your little group of thieves Burglars. It is honestly downright stupid.

"Burglar Alarms," growled Ella stubbornly.

Yes, I know they are named after your dog, but it is a silly risk to take and hits way too close to home. It is akin to a group of hired assassins calling themselves the Murderers.

Kaoru had just finished leading a group of her classmates to inspect the goods, and was bringing them back to the front of the bar to begin negotiations. The engineering club, or whatever they were, thought it would be fun to take apart military-grade electronics. It sounded like an awful waste of good gear, but as long as their money was good, what did Ella care?

Ella, serving plate in hand, guided them to the booth where the Burglar Alarms usually conducted their business. She returned a moment later, distributing each of the clean-shaved boys a mug of cold Suntory malt. She could tell the four were nervous, probably not used to patronizing run-down establishments of ill-repute. Ella gave Kaoru a knowing look before busying herself nearby.

Asao was giving her the evil eye as Ella, whistling, pretended to wipe the counter. She returned the glare. "What, Asshole?"

He turned away and began stacking glasses. The pouty man was obviously very bad at having a short memory. He was still peeved at Ella for her stunt the other day, but obviously not enough to prevent her from conducting Burglar Alarms business. He liked his take of the sales too much.

Asao is making way too much profit for simply offering us storage space. We need to set up our own shop soon.

Ella completely agreed.

Asao eyed Kaoru and the university students huddled in the corner, and his curiosity and greed finally got the best of him. He grunted at Ella. "What's the deal today? How much are those geeks paying?"

She shrugged, picking nuts out of a bowl and tossing them into her mouth. About half of them made it in. "Not sure yet.

Those geeks seem to want to take apart one of everything, so this might take all morning."

Ella apparently was very bad at estimating the amount of time things took to happen. All morning became long into the afternoon. It appeared these university kids were tougher negotiators than gangsters, clawing for every yen on every item. Twice, Kaoru threw up her hands in frustration and left the booth.

She stomped over to the bar next to Ella, her face scrunched in a scowl. Ella popped two bottles of Ramune and offered one to her. "What's the latest?"

Kaoru threw her drink back as if she were doing a shot. "I'm so angry. I can't believe I dated that jerk."

"Which one?"

"Ikko, on the right."

Remember your lessons. Being tactful is a skill. This is one of those times.

Ella squinted. "He's not *that* ugly."

Ella.

"What did I say wrong?"

Kaoru finished her drink, walked over to the recycling receptacle, and gently placed the bottle inside. She returned to Ella. "They want a return policy."

Ella spewed her Ramune all over the floor. "What? Are they nuts?"

"The engineering club wants a guarantee that everything works."

She clenched her hands into fists. "I'll show them guarantee…"

Ella, remember Asao's warning.

A memory of her smacking the girlfriend-beater flashed into her head. She stopped after three steps and stomped back to Kaoru. "They get twenty-four hours to return an item, but we charge a twenty percent restocking fee. And nothing if they've already tried to take it apart, got it?"

"Yes Bosu."

Kaoru marched back to the negotiating table. Ella chewed her lips and continued pretending to polish the bar counter, wiping so hard with the rag that it looked as if she was trying to drill a hole.

Calm down.

"Those kids are pissing me off. I worked hard to steal that stuff."

You need to not take everything so personally. Remember, it is just business.

Io was right. One of the few times Ella grudgingly admitted it. She ran through a few of her knife-throwing exercises, taking deep breaths to drain away her irritation. It took a little while to calm down, but after a frustrating morning where it seemed everyone was out to piss her off, she needed to clear her headspace.

Later that afternoon, Lee walked into the bar. He was the only American in the crew, Hawaiian or something, and the only one with a steady job, something to do with processing tofu. Hinata had brought him on board. Lee was quiet and laid back. That's what Ella liked best about him. He didn't argue with her like all the other Burglar Alarms. Most importantly, he seemed like a genuinely good guy. To be honest, Ella at first wasn't sure why he wanted to run with the Burglar Alarms. It wasn't until she saw him with Kaoru that everything made sense.

"Any of those boys giving her problems?" he asked as he took a seat at the bar.

"None she can't handle, and none I can't if she couldn't," she replied. "Any leads for the rest of the stuff?"

"I hit up all our local contacts, talked with a bunch of people and organizations." He spoke with a drawl that made every word twice as long as it needed to be. For some reason, it was very soothing. Lee was the only one Ella let get away with not calling her boss. He had a good head on his shoulders, so she never felt the need to exert her authority over him. Lee hesitated before speaking again. "Listen, Ella... I think you should just give away all the medical supplies."

The boiling blood rushed back into Ella's head. It really *was* one of those days. She took back all the nice things she said about him and thinking that he had a good head on his shoulders. "I'm going to kill–"

He held up his hands. "Hear me out. I went everywhere: hospitals, pharmacies, clinics, underground clinics, even the Shinto Church. Nobody wants to buy the stuff."

I will not say anything.

"You better not, Alien."

"All that stuff we got," continued Lee, pointing at the back room, "is for stuff like bullet wounds and cuts and injuries from someone trying to kill you. There's no crime in Tokyo. The only people who even have guns is us, and we're the ones selling them. Even if someone does accidentally cut himself gutting fish or something, there's literally a clinic on every other block." He pointed in both directions. "Ōkubo Hospital is two blocks away. And if that's too far, I can go to Kashi's on the corner. And everything is free."

Ella slapped her cheek with both hands. "I have nine cartons of this junk. What are we going to do with it?"

I told you so.

"You said you wouldn't say anything."

I cannot help it.

More angry words leaped to Ella's lips, but died before they left her mouth. Io did warn her. She didn't listen, and as much as she wanted to blame someone else – anyone else really – this one was on her. Something about admitting fault raised her spirits somewhat. She sighed. "Who do you want to give these goodies to? Can we get anything in return?"

Lee ticked one finger. "I recommend we give half of the goods to Dr Shinpei."

"The creepy yakuza doctor?"

"He'll have a use for it. He will also owe us a favor."

Ella nodded. "Sounds like a fair trade. What about the other half?"

"To the Shinto free clinic in Taitō."

"What's our angle with them?"

He shrugged. "Nothing. They're just nice people who take care of the old and the poor."

Ella swallowed her gag reflex. All of her hard work for nothing. Well, not for nothing. It was for a good cause, which was just about as useful to her as nothing. It still stung. If she had just skipped the nine cartons they could have taken more guns, or even that bazooka thing Daiki wanted to swipe.

Surface-to-air missile launcher.

"I'm not talking to you right now."

"Fine, I guess," she said aloud, crossing her arms. "But they have to come pick it up. I'm not lugging that stuff all the way across town through traffic."

"Fine," shrugged Lee good-naturedly. "I can do it myself. I'll pull up my truck in the rear and load them up. I'll be back in a few hours."

Lee disappeared into the back room. Ella's scowl deepened. Something was off. She felt a nauseous sensation in the pit of her stomach. Shouldn't she feel better after doing a good deed? She watched through the doorway as Lee struggled with the topmost carton.

Ugh. Guilt. What an awful emotion.

"Fine," she yelled after him. "I'll help you bring those stupid things over. Not like I have anything better to do."

My little Ella may finally be growing up.

"Shut it, Alien."

Ella checked on Kaoru before leaving. The girl's excessive

eye-rolling said all that needed to be said. They were still negotiating on only the eleventh of nineteen items the engineering club was interested in. Ella gave Kaoru a sympathetic pat on the shoulder before heading to the back room to help Lee load the truck.

An hour later, Ella and Lee were in bumper-to-bumper traffic to the Shinto clinic. The drive to the impoverished Sanya neighborhood in the Taitō District on the eastern end of Tokyo was typical of rush hour, slow and uneventful. Ella stewed for most of the trip, replaying all the bad decisions she had made on the job that led her to this very moment. Daiki almost got caught. She almost killed a dying woman. She could have taken more weapons to sell for money. Instead she took these stupid cartons.

Do not forget you stupidly exposed yourself.

By the time they got to the clinic, her mood, if possible, had worsened. She met the Shinto nuns with a hard grimace even as Lee embraced a few of them. Ella hated to admit it but as she and Lee unloaded the crates and saw the appreciative look in those nice old ladies' faces, she found herself feeling better.

The nuns doted on him – he obviously was a familiar face there – and treated Ella with a motherly care that she hadn't felt in a long time. In a way, the clinic reminded her of her early days when Wiry Madras helped get her off the streets. Being here made her homesick. The little black ball of fury in her gut began to dissipate. The nuns even fed her hot soup. By the time they were finished with their business, Ella wished they could have stayed a little longer. She promised the nuns she would come back.

Ella left the clinic feeling like she had done some good. Not quite as good as if she were able to sell the stuff, but she definitely got something warm and fuzzy out of it. Even if she couldn't spend it.

Unfortunately, their next stop was the oily and very creepy

Dr Shinpei, the chop shop patch-up doctor in the Roppongi District, and all the warm fuzzy feelings dried up like a wilted flower in a drought. Not only did he totally ignore her and insist on talking only to Lee – that sexist ass – he made sure to pointedly inform them that he owed them nothing. The jerk even gave them a hard time for accepting the supplies, as if he were doing them a favor instead of the other way around.

Technically he is.

"You are supposed to be on my side."

Do you want me to always agree with you?

It sounded like a trick question. Ella went for the honest answer. "Yes."

If I did, we both would likely be dead by now.

She barked a sarcastic laugh.

Lee, who was driving the truck next to her in the front seat, gave her a puzzled look. "Something funny?"

"No," she replied lamely. "Just an inside joke."

Lee didn't press. He was decent like that. He had offered to drop her off at her apartment after Dr Shinpei's. "You talk to yourself a lot. Sometimes Kaoru and I can't decide if you're a little crazy or if you have one of those Quasing alien things in your head."

The grin on Ella's face froze. So much for being a good undercover agent. She couldn't even hide being a host from a bunch of teenagers. What else does Lee know? Should she own up?

What? No. Are you insane? Laugh! Ridicule that idea right now!

Fortunately, they were saved by a phone call. Ella checked the phone: Nice Hair. She answered. "Hey Kaoru."

"They're here."

The girl was panicked and speaking so fast Ella's modest Japanese failed her. Io filled in the rest but it still took some translating. "Slow down. What's here?"

"There's a bunch of gangsters at the bar. They're yelling for you."

"Hah. It's a good thing I'm not there then," said Ella.

That was not the response I was expecting, but I approve. You are finally learning.

Kaoru's voice raised an octave. "They're trashing the bar. One of them hit Asao."

"Is he hurt?"

"No, it was more like a slap."

That didn't sound so bad. At least not bad enough to get involved. "They'll get bored. Just get him to a safe place. Tell him we'll help clean up afterward."

I see I am finally rubbing off on you.

"They're going to steal the rest of our stuff!"

I still think it is not worth–

Ella's hand involuntarily shot out and grabbed a fistful of Lee's sleeve. "Turn around. Get us back to the World-Famous. Step on it!"

CHAPTER TWELVE
The Search

Ella Patel's time at the Prophus Academy started out well enough. She was assigned to the first-year class and seemed to blend in. Ella was shy and reserved at first, and her English was poor. The Academy was a far cry from life in Crate Town. Her new life was practically an alien world. Because of that, she managed to stay on her best behavior and out of trouble for the first few weeks.

That civility did not last for long, however.

"I'm sorry, Shura, but I cannot help you. Your position is delicate, and I have my own standing to consider."

Shura glared at the floating three-dimensional projection of Anton Yoong, who was locked in a tight struggle with two other Adonis vessels for control of South Korea. "I'm not asking for you to take sides, brother. I'm just asking for access to your intelligence."

Anton gave her a meaningful look. "Doing so is taking sides, and I frankly do not wish to incur Rurik Melnichenko's wrath."

"We have a long history together."

"One that I cherish," he replied. "My answer is still no."

"How many times have I saved your life?"

"And I yours, or do you not remember Budapest?" replied Anton coolly. "Do not try to dredge up our past. It is long buried. What can you do for me now?"

"I would consider this a personal favor," said Shura. "One that you will find useful to call in in the future."

"You may control a larger territory," conceded Anton, "but it is a tired one, and you are going head-to-head with one of the strongest. Regardless of your many recent successes, the betting odds are that you will eventually make a misstep or that Rurik will wear you down. Russia also wields considerable influence in South Korea. I risk everything for that favor. I wish you luck, sister, but I will not go against my own interest."

Shura ended the communication and stared out the window overlooking the Yamuna River. It had been the same with every call. She had contacted dozens of Adonis vessels from all over the world, many with whom she had shared a long history, and had come up empty-handed.

You are at a disadvantage. Rurik has been searching for the girl for several months now, and likely has a formidable head start. The Russian spy network is arguably one of the best in the world, second to the Chinese and possibly the Americans.

"I have been at a disadvantage my entire life, Tabs. What makes this time different?"

Since her meeting with Weston, she had attacked her search for the Receiver with fevered vigor. This was the opportunity she was waiting for, and she intended to seize it. If she succeeded in capturing the Receiver, she could finally reclaim her birthright and restore her family's shame. More importantly, she would finally achieve her place on the Genjix Council.

It is different because this will be the last time, one way or another.

That was likely true. Weston's intentions were clear. The High Father wanted peace in his regions, and the only way there would ever be any between her and Rurik would be if the other was no longer there to fight. To the victors the spoils. To the loser, a forced transfer of their Holy One, of which there was only one way to carry that out.

He also still has vastly more wealth and resources.

"That has been true for two years since I tore India from his grasp, and I have still beaten him at every turn."

This mission is not the same. Intelligence gathering wages a different sort of war. You cannot build or purchase a spy network on the fly. It has to be carefully grown and nurtured.

Shura didn't realize exactly how different this world was until she began her search. She soon discovered that she was far out of her element. The Genjix spy network was incredibly complicated and insular. Information was power, and the vessels who controlled these information-gathering apparatuses guarded their territories zealously. Strong relationships were key in the spy world, and Shura had made little effort to establish them in her short stint on the world stage. There may have been an opportunity to reach an agreement if Tabs had a close relationship with another vessel's Holy One, but she did not play well with others.

The only other way to obtain access to these foreign spy networks was to purchase it, either through funds, resources or favors, all of which Shura possessed in limited supply. This, too, quickly became a moot point. When she contacted several vessels to inquire about buying access, she was informed that the Russians had already paid them handsomely specifically to deny her use of their intelligence.

Rurik had thoroughly choked off every spy agency available to her, therefore killing any chance she had of locating the Receiver. Shura hated to admit it, but she was impressed. The Russian had moved quickly the moment he learned she was joining the hunt and had effectively neutralized her before she even began. Russia's spy network had its hands in everything.

They were tightly connected in one way or another to every major government in the world. And with that integration came influence.

The odds were so stacked against her that at first Shura thought that Weston was actively working against her, possibly tipping Rurik off or even actively ordering the other vessels to not deal with her. She eventually came to the conclusion that the odds of Weston working against her were low. It just wasn't his style. If he had wanted her to fail, he would have just ordered her death. No, the Holy Ones were testing her mettle. Conflict bred innovation.

I did tell you to expend some budget on diplomacy the past two years.

"With what budget? I had more pressing issues to deal with at the time."

In many ways, she realized how much she had underestimated her rival. She may have beaten and outmaneuvered him in areas of operation and direct conflict, but he had expended his time and formidable resources cultivating allies and growing his financial empire, which he was now wielding freely against her. In focusing on winning every small battle, Shura may have lost the war.

By the end of the first week, she had gone from calling Adonis vessel-led countries to those who administered smaller territories, and even some non-Adonis vessels. She had come up empty in every case, and now was at a dead end.

The next call Shura made, the tenth of the day and the hundredth in a week, was to Abbi, a competent spymaster who managed a rapidly growing spy network in the Philippines. While Abbi was only a raised vessel, someone who had earned her Holy One in the field rather than being blessed through the Hatchery, she was a respected operative who had cultivated an extensive network throughout much of the South China Sea, and was making an outside claim for control of all the surrounding islands. That was unheard-of for someone of her relatively modest standing.

Shura knew ten seconds into the communication that the call would likely end in failure.

"Rurik told me you would call," said Abbi.

She kept her tone neutral. "Whatever he has offered you, I'm sure we can come to an understanding."

"Rurik has paid me quite handsomely to tell you no."

"How much?"

A number flashed across Shura's desk. Expensive, but not inordinately so, at least not considering the reach of Abbi's network. "I can match that," she said finally.

Abbi stared at Shura for several moments. She finally spoke, "I don't think you understand. I don't care if you can."

"He is weak, Abbi, vulnerable. You know I am not."

"That is why I support him," said Abbi. "Here's the difference between you two. Rurik is mindful that his power, the control he has over his territories, is built upon sand. This game he plays is easy to exploit, influence, control even. That was how you were able to carve India away from him. He was too busy minding other matters and dropped the ball."

"Your point?" said Shura, coolly.

"You, however, Shura, used to be one of us, regardless of the fact you are Hatchery-raised. You were of lower standing and assumed your lofty perch. Your foundation is a rock, self-made. There is much to admire." Abbi leaned back in her chair. "I do you this one favor, that is all you will pay. You do not need me. You never did, even when I offered my support in the past. That is your strength and your vulnerability. You are an island." She pointed to the side. "Rurik controls a vast kingdom he can barely hold together with tape, glue, and a pile of money ready for siphoning. I do what he asks, he pays me in perpetuity." She smiled. "Instability breeds opportunity."

Shura leaned forward. "Rurik can't pay if he's dead."

"Then I better make sure he wins."

You walked into that.

This was pointless. "In this case Abbi, I won't be wasting any of your time." She reached for the button to end their communication.

"I want you to know one thing, Shura," said Abbi quickly. "You think you're better than me."

"I *am* better than you," she replied. Raised vessels often did not know their place, thinking they were equals to Adonis vessels.

If you are trying to win her over, this may not be the best way to go about it.

"Rurik thinks he is your better as well. What is your point?" said Shura.

"That's the problem," the raised vessel replied. "You have a reputation of only improving the standing of those who directly serve you. You also have one of stepping on your rivals. You have never tolerated competition. Rurik, on the other hand, has a reputation of raising the standing of those who deal with him, even if it is unintended."

"Then serve me," said Shura.

"You know I won't do that," said Abbi. "However, ally with me. I may not be an Adonis vessel, but raise my standing as your equal. My network is extensive. If what you are seeking is in this part of the world, there is a good chance my people have picked it up. Support my claim for all the islands in the South China Sea, and perhaps we can both accomplish what we seek."

Absolutely not. How dare she make such a demand? It is outrageous and extremely dangerous. Another Adonis would demand her life for such a bold request.

Shura hesitated. The Philippines were a major transportation hub. There was a good chance the Receiver had passed through Abbi's region. The last known information on the Receiver was that she had fled southeast, likely settling in Prophus-friendly Australia.

It does not matter. Even considering it will disrupt the Genjix hierarchy and turn every Adonis vessel against you. It is not worth the risk.

Shura was raised in the Hatchery, and admittedly carried some of the prejudices that came with a blessed upbringing, but she was not as strident and arrogant as most Adonis vessels. Still, Tabs was correct in that supporting Abbi in her stake for the South China Sea Islands would cause an uproar, and likely make Shura many enemies. The number of Adonis vessels had only grown since the creation of the Hatcheries, with more seeking to lay their claims and raise their standing every day. The number of territories for them to claim, however, had stayed roughly the same or even dwindled as stronger Adonis vessels consolidated their gains. It would be outrageous and outright dangerous to give this position to a raised vessel over an Adonis.

"Good luck in your claim." Shura closed the connection and turned away. She buried her face in her hands and rubbed her temples. Now she knew what it felt like to be a failed politician cold-calling for contributions. "I don't think I've had this many people turn me down in my lifetime, let alone in a single day."

She was back where she had started, while Rurik was no doubt focusing all of his energies on locating the Receiver. It was a nearly insurmountable lead. She looked to the side and stared at the map of the world hanging on her wall. She had run out of options within the Genjix network. That left her with only one other choice.

Shura reached across her desk to open the channel. Her fingers hovered for several moments. She closed her eyes. A feeling of deja vu swept over her, and all she could think about was the dreaded weight of making this unwanted phone call.

Shura's first assignment after she was blessed with a Holy One was to command a reconnaissance company within the 45th Spetsnaz, a brigade that operated exclusively in Western Europe during the Alien World War. Technically, she commanded the captain who commanded the company, but that really was just a technicality. Genjix operatives – Adonis vessels especially – normally functioned outside the normal chains of command.

The position was considered low for someone from the Hatchery. Most of her Hatchery siblings who were activated during the Alien World War operated at the brigade level and commanded generals. This was because her parents had lost the Genjix Council power struggle a generation earlier.

Even though the position was beneath her, Shura took her first command seriously and personally made every death notification for each of her fallen soldiers. Tabs thought it ridiculous that she spent several hours every day notifying the family of her fallen when there was the captain and his lieutenants to perform this tedious, and what Tabs considered meaningless, task. Shura, however, refused to hand that duty off. It was one of the few times she directly disobeyed her Holy One.

Her diligence paid off in the long run as the casualties mounted. Even though it took many hours of her weeks to speak individually with the family members of the fallen soldiers, it fomented a fanaticism among her soldiers that no other Genjix operative enjoyed. Throughout the war, her company earned a ferocious reputation. She became known as Shura the Scalpel, and the division earned the moniker The Scalpel's Cuts.

Shura had to finally quit personally making death notifications when she was given command of an entire division. By then, late in the war when casualties on both sides were astronomical, death notification had become a full-time job, and she was far too preoccupied trying not to lose the war to handle it any longer.

The memory of making the notifications flooded back to Shura. She pulled her hand away and stood abruptly. She walked to the other end of her office, opened the liquor cabinet and pulled out a decanter with a dark amber liquid. She gave herself a generous pour in a crystal glass and threw it back, feeling the whisky burn her throat and the warmth spread through her body. She considered drinking another, or better yet just bringing the entire decanter back to the desk.

You will need your wits about you.

Shura returned to her desk and banged on the button firmly. A few moments later, an image appeared of a lounging Rurik Melnichenko, dripping wet and shirtless with a towel looped around his waist. Shura really wished she had had that second drink.

He does have a face that begs to be tortured.

"Hello, brother," she said, with just a hint of deference. As much as she hated it, it was necessary.

He scowled. "What do you want, Shura?"

She mentally added one more grievance to his docket. Rurik had never accepted her as his equal, especially after she stole India from him, and made a point to show his contempt publicly and loudly at every opportunity. One day, she was going to collect on this very large and still-growing debt.

Stick to the task at hand. He affects you the same way. The two of you are simply playing the game differently.

Shura stuck to her mocking formality. "As you are no doubt aware, dear brother, High Father Weston has tasked us with locating the Receiver, no doubt putting us in competition with each other. I'm sure you're aware that locating the Receiver is probably the most important thing either of us will do in our lifetime in service to the Holy Ones. I propose we set aside our differences and work together on this important matter. What do you say, a truce?"

He broke into a nasty smirk. "I see you've tried to access our spy network. Failing that, you now come crawling to me, begging on your hands and knees."

Shura locked her smile on her face. "I'm just looking out for the greater good. Regardless of our personal relationship, we are both still Genjix and serve the Holy Ones faithfully."

"You are bold, sister." He shook his head. "What makes you think I need you at all?"

Shura had an ace up her sleeve. "As you are well aware, I have recently come into a surplus of catalyst reaction rods. An embarrassment of riches. I hear that you recently had to close down several of your Bio Comm Array facilities for lack of these rods. I am prepared to offer from my existing supply in exchange for cooperation in finding the Receiver."

Rurik's face contorted in shock. His mouth fell open and stayed that way for a good while. For so long, in fact, that Shura had thought for a second that their connection had frozen, or better yet he was suffering an aneurysm. Finally, he laughed, a high trilling whine that grated on her ear.

Perhaps you read his reaction wrong.

Shura feigned innocent puzzlement. "Care to share the humor, brother?"

It took him several moments to settle down, though by the end his mirth came out a bit forced. Their acting coach back at the Hatchery would have rolled her eyes at that performance. He shook his head. "Trying to barter the very rods that you stole from me. I have to admit, Shura, you always had the biggest pair in the Hatchery."

"Think of it as my atonement for our misunderstanding the other week," she said mildly.

Rurik disappeared off-screen and returned a few seconds later with a drink in his hand. He took a long, slurpy sip and shook his head. "This is what's going to happen. I'm going to tell you to go to hell, and then I'm going to enjoy watching you flail blindly looking for the Receiver. After I hand-deliver her to the High Father, I'm going to watch you die, Shura. I will even beg to strangle you myself."

Shura forced a smile onto her face. "Is that how you think it's going to play out, brother?"

"I do. That is, of course, unless you cede India to me, renounce your standing as an Adonis vessel, and serve under my leadership. I could use an able commander in my Siberian holdings."

Shura's calmness broke, just for a flash. "Then may the best Adonis vessel triumph. Remember, we are exempt from the Hard Peace. You will be wise to not cross my path."

"That's fine," he replied. "You won't be anywhere close to mine when I find the Receiver. I will get to her first. I will be the one who presents her to the High Father. Remember my offer, Shura. It's your only hope of surviving this."

Rurik's projection faded, leaving her alone in the room. She was in grave danger; she knew it. This was also the most uneasy Shura had ever felt Tabs. Not when she was the little girl Alex escaping through the United States wilderness. Not when she was convinced to murder her father. Not during the global war that nearly broke the world. Tabs truly thought Shura was going to die. Even though most Holy Ones cared little about their vessels – just specks in their long existence – she knew Tabs cared about her. Strangely, Shura stayed calm, in control.

Your only option is to assassinate him. Make sure his Holy One has someone to transition to. Take your chances with Weston. Perhaps his fondness for you and your general competence will earn you some leniency.

Shura drummed her fingers on her desk and stared out the window again at the harbor in the distance and the ships passing down the river. She could continue to try to access a spy network, perhaps even the Chinese government's, but she knew Rurik would likely have those avenues covered. He was a very thorough man. She was loath to show weakness and beg Weston for a favor. No, he wouldn't give it. Not when he had already walked her down this path.

Perhaps we should consider Rurik's offer. You fell once and fought your way back. You can do it again.

Shura turned her attention to the map on the wall, looking for a way to unravel this conundrum. The drumming of her fingers increased in tempo until finally she was rapping her fist on the table. Then it stopped. The solution was clear. The drumming still echoed in her ears. Sometimes, the only way to solve an impossible problem was to do the outrageous.

Shura tapped on the comm and opened a new channel. A moment later, Abbi appeared on the screen.

"Yes, Adonis?"

"I've reconsidered my position."

CHAPTER THIRTEEN
Consequences

The first sign of problems at the Prophus Training Academy was on Ella's first day. She was placed in shared housing with a young woman named Amy Ng, whose parents were career Prophus operatives. Ella had not shared a space for many years, and did not take well to it.

Ella immediately took a dislike to the bubbly teenager from Yorkshire. She kept her feelings under wraps, and, because she was on her best behavior, managed to bear it for all of two weeks. Her restraint surprised me.

One day, Amy brought her boyfriend to their room and asked Ella to sleep outside. She finally snapped and threatened to stab them both. She would have made good on her threat if I had not stopped her. Needless to say, the roommates' relationship went downhill from there.

Ella and Lee reached the main street leading into the Kabukicho District. Rush hour had mercifully ended so the time it took to drive there wasn't too bad. The night life in Tokyo was just coming alive. The rest of the outfit was waiting in the shadow of an awning at the busy intersection. Ella jumped out of the truck and met up with her grim-faced crew. Lee came bounding from the other side a moment later, a traditional bo staff slung over his shoulder. Hinata, bouncing a lead pipe in his hand, waved them over. Kaoru had her rubber mallet, and behind her stood Daiki with his… Ella squinted. "Is that a tennis racket?"

"Racquetball." He looked crestfallen. "My brother has baseball practice."

"I should send you home."

He stammered. "What for?"

"For bringing a stupid weapon." She took a quick head count. "Where's Pek?"

Remember his test?

"Right. Good day to ask for time off, I guess."

Pek had a history exam today. Ella had promised his big brother that, no matter what, the crew's work would not interfere with their grades. She really should stop meeting everyone's family. It was affecting her business. Then again, she would rather Pek not be involved in something like this anyway.

"How many?" she asked.

"Five," said Hinata. "Pretty even."

Not even close to even with this sad bunch. I told you to recruit that big Mung boy. You need the muscle.

"We're not supposed to ever have to fight."

And now look at where you are.

"Where's Asao?" she said aloud.

"He's hiding in the shaved ice cafe across the street," said Kaoru.

"Coward," muttered Ella. "Where are the yakuza?"

"In the back loading up our goods," said Kaoru. "They found our stuff while ransacking the bar. They took a break to fetch a van."

"What's the plan?" asked Daiki.

I do not recommend a frontal confrontation. The gangsters are all likely older, stronger, more experienced.

Ella reviewed her scrawny, undersized team. Io wasn't wrong when she said that they were not built for a fight. She wasn't confident that the Burglar Alarms could even put up much of one. Definitely not against the yakuza. Perhaps not even against the junior team stealing their stuff.

When Ella put this team together five months ago, she wanted to avoid confrontations and violence. She went through great pains avoiding danger, scoping jobs where no one would get hurt. It had limited their options but also kept the outfit out of harm's way. She had aborted entire week-long jobs at the slightest hint of something going wrong. Her outfit had complained about her cautiousness, but after Crate Town, she knew better.

This time was different. This time they had no choice. Confrontation was not only at their base of operations, it was stealing their stuff.

You can cut your losses and just abandon the goods and this base of operations. Start all over. The goods are not valuable enough to risk everything. If you insist on fighting, this should be our strategy. We have the element of surprise. They will be clustered in the back room and guarding the alley. Use the clutter in the bar to our advantage.

For a split second, Ella entertained giving up all their loot and abandoning the World-Famous. Her face blackened, and then the split second ended. She began to rack her brain trying to come up with a plan where no one got hurt. There really wasn't one. A fight was inevitable. Unless…

Ella grabbed Hinata by the sleeve and pointed at the entrance to the alley. "I want all of you to stick together. That's the only way in and out. Stay near the entrance. Get their attention and distract them. Don't fight though. If they come at you, run away. I'm going to go around the bar and hit them from behind and try to take down one or two of them to even up the odds."

What? This plan makes no sense.

"If I get caught sneaking up on them, just get out of here."

Daiki ticked off his fingers. "But we have the same number of people."

Hinata frowned. "You're going to go in alone? That's the dumbest–"

Ella took off before the rest of her crew could protest further. She weaved through the busy crowds, packed with curious tourists and the sordid locals who frequented the Kabukicho District at this late hour. If anything, the constant assault of glittering lights and cacophony was the perfect cover, far more effective than darkness and silence.

You will get yourself killed if you do this alone. The odds are already bad with all of the Burglar Alarms helping. This is suicide.

"I don't want the others to get hurt."

This is what they signed up for. This is part of being a crew. It is not too late to just walk away from this.

Io was right. Going as a team heavy and hard was the right way to fight these thugs. However, she balked at sending the Burglar Alarms into danger. In the past, it had never bothered her when people she worked with got hurt, maimed, or arrested while on a score. Everyone knew and accepted the risks. It was part of the job. These kids, though, might have said they accepted the risk, but she didn't think they truly understood it.

Back in Crate Town, danger was part of survival, part of everyday living on the street. Life was cheap. After a person accepted that truth, they could overcome their fear of dying. Only then could they be free to take the risks they needed to survive. Ella had learned her lesson early. There was barely a week that she didn't hear about someone getting robbed and stabbed and left to die in a ditch, or someone starving to death or dying from getting rust in their blood. It was just the way things were. Everyone knew and accepted the stakes.

With these kids though, it felt different. Sure, poverty

and the desire for something better brought them together. Kaoru was at university; she had things to look forward to after this. Daiki lived at home with his mother who would be devastated if something happened to him. Hinata's girlfriend was pregnant and he was just hoping to give her a better life. Lee, well, she had no idea why he was here, save that his day job making tofu apparently didn't pay that well. Probably because of Kaoru. All of them had something more to live for. They all still feared death. For some reason unbeknown to her, their innocence and inability to accept dying made the danger weigh much heavier on her conscience.

Ella turned down the side street where the World-Famous was located. It was only slightly less crowded on this narrow one-way path. She unlatched all her knife holsters as she neared the entrance. A small clutter of overturned tables and chairs littered the ground. The floor just inside was wet and covered with glass shards and broken pieces of wood. One of the signs had been pulled off the wall.

"What a mess. Do you think Asao is going to make me pay for the repairs?"

At the very least. We will regardless probably need to find a new base of operations after this. He probably will not want to continue our relationship.

"In that case I'm not going to pay him a stinking yen."

That is fair.

Most of the passersby barely gave her a second glance. One look at her and at the wreckage in the bar told them that there was nothing but trouble brewing in the World-Famous, and these days the locals knew better than to pry. Japan, while sympathetic to the Prophus-aligned forces, had declared itself neutral during the Alien World War, which probably saved it from destruction, considering its proximity to the Genjix home sphere of influence. That did not exempt them from violence, however, as an entire proxy war was waged over control of this important geographical area. A French family walked by and stared at her curiously. Ella waved for them to hurry on. The last thing she needed was dumb tourists giving her away and ruining the only advantage she had.

Ella tugged at the long dagger strapped to the small of her back with her right hand. It was her last remaining blade from the set her old teacher Manish – "Iss Jiva ko Mukti Prapt ho," she whispered automatically – had given her when she began training with knives. The others she had slowly lost over time, which she guessed made sense since she threw them at people. This one, though, she was going to take to her grave.

Ella drew one of her longer throwing knives with her left hand, just small enough and weighted correctly to throw, but long enough to use in melee if necessary. She wielded the blades in both hands with equal skill, courtesy of her extensive training at the Academy.

The large wall-to-ceiling shelf on the side of the bar had toppled over, forming an overhang as it leaned against the now-shattered mirror on the opposite wall. Ella sneaked inside and stayed close to the left wall, using the bar counter as cover. She glanced over at the chalkboard out of habit: Zaru Udon. Ella shuddered; cold udon was gross.

The constant sounds from the street faded with each step, and were replaced by the chatter and barking of young asshole men. Their laughter grated on Ella's nerves as she crept closer.

She ducked under the hatch of the bar counter. Broken bottles and glass crunched under her feet. Half of the cabinet doors hung open, and all of the contents inside had been swept out, littering her path. A small river of liquor flowed down one side and emptied into the drain.

Ella, turn back. There are too many yakuza. You are not skilled enough to handle five armed men, no matter how bad they are. Please. I do not relish inhabiting another young, immature thug as my next host.

"You better start helping me then."

She was a few paces away from the entrance to the back room when someone strolled out to the front. Ella froze and did her best to blend into the cabinetry. She wasn't in position yet, and would have little room to maneuver if she was caught out in the open in the narrow space between the bar and the cabinet.

Her arms were crossed in front of her chest, the right hand gripping the longer dagger in a defensive posture while the left with the throwing knife was drawn back and ready to loose. If this sucker so much turned in her direction, he was going to get a knife to the face.

Fortunately – for him that is – he walked straight past her, his head thrown back as he chugged a bottle of beer, which he probably hadn't paid for. He finished and tossed it at the wall, shattering it into a shower of shards. Laughing, he grabbed a few more bottles and turned to head back into the other room.

Ella almost escaped detection. Instructor Niko, who taught concealed movement and tracking at the Academy, would have been proud. Or at the very least given her a passing grade. Unfortunately, *almost* avoiding detection didn't amount to much in this line of work. The man retraced his steps and was about to disappear from view when he looked her way. Their eyes met. He hesitated, just briefly.

That slight pause was the only window she needed. The throwing knife sprung out of her hand like a bullet, with Ella following close behind. The blade sunk into his forearm when he threw up his guard. Ella's second attack came a split second later. He barely had time to make a pained cry before her now-free left hand batted his arms aside, so she could slam the butt of her dagger into his temple in one fluid motion.

The yakuza's eyes rolled up, and his legs went limp. Ella plowed into his body, and her momentum carried them both clear of the doorway. They crashed to the ground in a pile. The good news was the man's soft midsection broke Ella's fall and saved her from cracking her head on the cement floor. The bad was that her midsection landed right on his bent knee. She was gasping like a fish as the wind whooshed out of her. Soft squeaks escaped her lips as she rolled off the man and onto her back, momentarily stunned.

Get up! Stop knocking yourself out.

"What's that noise?" a voice called from the back. "Ikuo, you there?"

"Fool probably passed out," another one said. "He holds his liquor worse than my kid sister."

Stop messing around. Now, Ella!

"I'm not messing…" She exhaled labored breaths between clenched teeth.

Ella pawed the floor for her dagger and grimaced as she rolled to her stomach. She took a few deep breaths and then got her knees under her. First she checked the man named Ikuo. He had an ugly red mark on the side of his face. He was a boy really, since shaving looked wasted on him. Chances were they were probably the same age. Ella wasn't sure if it was the strike to the temple or hitting his head on the floor that knocked him out, not that it mattered. He would wake with a beautiful welt and an ugly headache tomorrow.

Ella crept to the side of the doorway and peered in. The remaining four men were loading the Burglar Alarms' goods onto a van in the alley. Several of the crates were cracked open, and their contents scattered all over the floor. One of the yakuza had opened a case of assault rifles, and was examining one by holding it up in the air and staring into the muzzle.

"I think these are real," he was saying. "Why does a fat bartender have heavy-duty guns lying about?"

"He doesn't look like an arms dealer," he continued. He and a shirtless tattooed gangster were loading a crate into the van. She only recognized him by the large bandage on his nose, and his voice was very nasally. "I hope we didn't just wreck a family establishment."

That caused a level of consternation among his friends who began to yell at him all at once.

"You didn't check with your father first, Masato?"

"I'm not losing a finger over your stupidity," another added.

"I don't need my father's permission," the one named Masato retorted. "I speak *for* him."

The one who spoke first turned toward the doorway, "What happened to Ikuo?"

Ella pulled back and gripped the dagger close to her chest. The sound of footsteps grew louder.

He is two heads taller, skinny, and will have a much longer reach. Holding a machete in his left hand. Wearing sandals.

Ella processed this information. She reversed her grip on her dagger and lowered to a crouch, and then waited, watching the floor intently. A light shadow, barely perceptible unless someone was looking for it, told her when he reached the other side of the doorway. The tip of the machete poked into sight first.

"Ikuo, fool, where are you?" the man called out.

Ella's left hand shot out and grabbed his machete wrist, then she slammed her right hand downward. The blade pierced Tall & Skinny in the meat of his dorsal, right between his index and middle toe, hard enough for the tip of her dagger to go clean through the flesh and rubber and clip the ground beneath his foot. She pulled the blade up violently, sending up a spray of blood. That was what dummies deserved for wearing sandals.

Ella pulled his wrist with her left hand, sending Tall & Skinny tumbling forward. She charged into the room, screaming in a high-pitched roar as loud as her tiny body could muster. Her war cry did not quite elicit the response she had hoped. The three remaining yakuza just stared at her curiously, looking puzzled as she barreled toward them.

Though Ella had hated most of her time at the Academy, there had been one subject where she had prospered, and that was the deadly art of knife fighting. While she had initially trained under Manish in Crate Town, she had vastly improved her Escrima craft while studying at the Academy under some of the best instructors in the world. Cameron Tan had seen to that. Now, she considered herself pretty good, even an expert.

This is not the time for a big head.

"That's her! That's the one who broke my nose," yelled Broken Nose, the girlfriend-beater.

"That little thing is the reason you needed to bring four of us?" laughed Shirtless.

Wrong End of Rifle joined the derision, which only infuriated Ella. Growling, she jumped on him like a feral beast, the black blades of her weapon serving as her teeth. The laughter died in Wrong End's throat, and he stumbled backward as her opening thrust nearly disemboweled him. He swung the barrel of the assault rifle like a club and tried to take her head off, but Ella was ready for it. She shot low, cutting him once in the shin right below the knee, and then once more as she whirled, striking him a second time in the bicep. Wrong End howled, dropping the rifle as his leg gave way.

Broken Nose charged her next, swinging nothing but his fists. Foolish. Ella blocked his looping punch with her dagger, cutting his wrist in the process. When he yelped and flinched back, she followed up with a throwing knife that grazed his neck. The injury wasn't serious, but painful, sending him spinning to the floor.

To your left!

An image projected into her head of the tattooed gangster sneaking up just off to her side. He swung a metal rod toward her head. Trusting Io, Ella twisted blindly, narrowly dodging the swing as the rod bounced off the wall.

Now it was her turn. She was going to show Shirtless how a pro fought. Ella feinted left and then attacked: a jab to the wrist, a horizontal slice at his chest, a downward stab to his thigh, and then she tried to dance out of the way. To her surprise, she hit nothing but air on all her attempts, and then when she tried to escape to safety, Shirtless countered and immediately closed the gap. Metal clanged on metal as they exchanged blows.

For everything Ella tried, Shirtless had a counter. He was stronger and had a longer reach, and to her dismay, he was quicker as well. He grinned as he flared his weapon, taunting her. "You're not too terrible, girl," he barked as she, getting anxious, lunged for his chest. "But still not that good. Let me give you a free lesson."

Stay calm. You are panicking.

"What do I do? Io, tell me!"

He deflected her blade and veered it to the side, and then in one smooth circular motion, swung the pipe straight at her face. She reeled from a bone-numbing blow to the jaw, then a boot to the chest sent her flying until she bounced off a stack of beer crates. Ella's head hit the ground hard and everything blanked momentarily.

Shake it off. Hurry. He is coming in from your right.

"So you're the runt who messed up the boss's kid," he laughed. Shirtless was enjoying himself. He knelt down in front of her and poked her shoulder with the end of his rod. "You're going to have to pay for that. It'll cost you a nose, at the very least. There's also the matter of some very interesting stuff here in the back. I bet you know where it came from."

Ella exploded with a last desperate swipe, but her blade clanged against his rod. He knocked the dagger out of her hand and sent it skidding across the floor. He grabbed her wrist and swung her onto her back, and then pressed a foot down on the base of her neck.

Shirtless looked to the side. "Rest of you fools still alive? If I have to move the remaining crates by myself, I'm keeping all of the points."

"I'm bleeding all over," cried Broken Nose, clamoring to his feet. "Is it bad?"

Shirtless squinted. "I've gotten worse cuts shaving. Now–"

A tennis racket – no, a racquetball racket – came flashing out of the corner of her eye. Shirtless turned toward it just in time for the head of the racket to smack him in the face. He reeled backward, and then Lee was there, sweeping the yakuza gangster off his feet with his bo staff.

Kaoru rushed across the room with a surprisingly low-pitched snarl, not unlike an Amazon. She smacked Broken Nose once on the chest with her rubber mallet, and then followed up with another to the side of his knee. He crumpled to the floor screaming. Maybe Ella should call him Broken Leg from now on.

Wrong End of Rifle, limping badly, attacked Kaoru from behind with the butt end of the rifle. Hinata was there, however, still bouncing the lead pipe in his hand. The two men roared and feinted for several seconds, with neither daring to make the first move. It ended when Daiki got behind Wrong End of Rifle and smacked him hard on the side of the head with his racket.

He turned to Ella, grinning. "You owe me an apology. I got two with this thing."

"Is that the last of them?" said Hinata, coming over and helping Ella to her feet.

Daiki looked at the bodies on the floor. "Did you really take on three of them by yourself, Ella?"

The conclusion of the fight entailed the Burglar Alarms running off the junior yakuza squad, who honestly had their fill of fighting. The Burglar Alarms were happy to accommodate and get them out of the World-Famous as soon as possible. In fact, Hinata and Lee had to help Wrong End of Rifle to his feet and carry him to his van. Shirtless actually had the nerve to ask Kaoru if she wanted to have drinks later.

When the last of them was gone and the van had driven off, Lee turned on her, shaking his finger. "Don't do that again, or we're going to kick you off the crew."

"You can't do that. It's *my* crew," she replied indignantly.

"Not if you make another dumb decision like that, Bosu," said Daiki. The other Burglar Alarms, flanking him, bobbed their heads vigorously.

They are right. There was a better way to handle the situation. You almost got killed. More importantly, you would have left me with no desirable options for hosts.

Ella scowled, and then finally relented. When everyone was against her, even her stupid alien, she was probably in the wrong. "Fine, whatever. Daiki, fetch Asao and tell him it's safe to come back. We got rid of his rats. We have a lot of cleaning up to do."

Kaoru frowned and scanned the room. "Where's all our stuff?"

In their eagerness to get rid of those yakuza, Ella had totally forgot about the goods. She looked at the corner where the meager remains of their loot sat. The few containers still there were overturned and split open, their contents scattered on the floor. "Those yakuza were loading them into the…" She pointed at the empty space behind the opened garage door where the van was parked moments earlier. "Oh no."

CHAPTER FOURTEEN
Investigation

By the end of the third month, Ella had become an outcast. Many of the students at the Academy were from affluent backgrounds or were children of existing Prophus operatives. It is my suspicion that Amy Ng did not have any intention of following in her parents' footsteps, and was only enrolled here for the free education. Others had military backgrounds and were looking to join the organization. Ella had none of those advantages.

It did not help matters that she was looked down upon, considered inferior by the rest of her privileged classmates, someone unworthy of attending the Academy. No one was aware that she was a host, technically the highest rank among the Prophus. This only made her more defensive.

Makita stared as the vault door came to life: clicking, rumbling and hissing and doing whatever vault doors did when they opened. He kicked his feet as the ankle-deep water lapped up against its metal frame, and wondered if vault doors were rustproof. This particular door looked brand new. Was it in the metal or some sort of special chemical treatment? Whatever it was, he'd like to apply it to that bothersome samurai sword he had mounted in his study.

The stupid thing was a spoil of war, taken from a fallen asshole Genjix leader, an Adonis vessel, after a particularly long and difficult battle where Makita had broken both of his arms and lost several of his friends. Not knowing what to do with it – samurai swords really weren't his thing – he had kept it as a souvenir.

Because that was what old warriors did once they retired, right? They mounted trophies from their past on their walls to remember the glory and to commemorate their achievements. They showed off these mementos to visitors and grandkids, and regaled them with harrowing tales of their victories. But with those visitors – not having grandkids was a very sore sticking point for Makita and his wife – came fingerprints and accidental swings that sliced open his favorite reading chair and sent his next-door neighbor to the hospital for stitches.

And when those old warriors were alone in their studies with nothing but themselves, the sword and their memories to haunt them, they stared at it to reminisce about who they once were, and how they were once mighty and strong and full of purpose. Most of all, with reminiscing came the memories of friends who had fallen over the decades, some to that very sword.

Makita should just throw the damn thing away. He had gotten pretty tired of wiping and oiling the thing every few months. He considered letting it rust and wither, but something in him balked at the idea. Destroying historical relics felt like bad karma. Maybe he'd pass it along to his son one day. Who was he kidding? Nobody in his family wanted that cursed thing. He should just donate it to the Smithsonian, or sell it to a pawn shop. Whatever was closest.

A hand touched his shoulder lightly. "Are you all right there, old man?" said Josie. "You sort of spaced out for a second."

Makita snapped back to the present just in time to see the vault door finish its intended course. He pointed. "This is a really good vault door. I wonder who makes it." He took several steps into the safe house and spread his arms. "Now this is what a safe house should look like. A big storage room somewhere in the dank sewers designed by an architect who specializes in the aesthetics of prisons. Not that penthouse suite we were in yesterday."

Nabin trailed in after Josie. "Yeah, what a dump."

Josie harrumphed. "You two obviously have never lived in a military school dorm. This place is like the Taj Mahal."

Three figures, two men and a woman, one at each corner, emerged armed with assault rifles and what looked like a sniper rifle in the far corner, effectively catching them in a crossfire. "Hands where we can see you. Identify yourselves."

Makita remained un-fazed. He casually turned to Nabin. "Do you mind? I haven't bothered with any of the recent field passphrases."

"Not at all." Nabin kept his hands raised and walked forward a few steps. He looked at the woman in the far corner, and spoke in a loud voice. "I love you."

"I know," she replied.

"Wait, what?" sputtered Makita. "What the hell was that? That's the passphrase? When I was in the field, I had to memorize stupid philosopher quotes."

Nabin grinned. "You must be still using the old books. We've been slowly phasing the stuff out over the past few years. No one has time for that any more, sir."

The woman lowered her rifle and threw her cloak back, revealing a sharp pale face and a crop of short platinum hair. She motioned to the others to follow suit. The two groups met in the center of the room. The woman offered her hand. "Agent Hekla Einarsson, operating out of Osaka." She pointed to the other two. "The ugly shaggy one is Tarfur Hilmarsson and the even uglier shaggier one with the glowing smile is Pedro Rafaeli. Asha Okande is in the back room recuperating from a bullet to the gut."

"Colonel Josie Perkins, Chief at the Academy in Sydney." She pointed behind her. "That's Agent Nabin Bhattarai, out of Singapore, and Makita Takeshi, out of an old folks' home."

Makita let that slide. Barely.

"Well-met," said Hekla, shaking each hand. "Apologies for the theatrics, but this safe house isn't as secure as it probably should be. We had a run-in with some local thieves."

"We saw your report on the break-in," said Makita. "It's why we're here."

After the pleasantries were concluded, everyone did their best to settle in. This particular safe house only housed four comfortably and the other team had already lived here for over a week, so that left the three of them to scrap for one sofa.

Nabin was obviously sleeping on the floor. Josie didn't put up a fight either. She gave Makita one look and carried her sack to the space next to the younger man. To be honest, Makita was a little offended. Sure, he held rank and was the oldest, and of course his aching back was desperate for a cushion, but they should have at least let him put up a fight to save face.

"Excuse me, sir." Tarfur saluted and shot Makita a wide smile. Hekla was right. There was something unusually bright and shiny about his teeth. "That's an awfully lumpy couch. Would you like my bed? I can bunk out no problem."

Makita's pride almost prevented him from saying yes again.

"If you need your own room," added Hekla. "I can take the double with Pedro. He snores like an earthquake. Our team is used to it, but he's going to keep you up all night."

Makita didn't bother to hide the enthusiasm on his face. He somehow went from sleeping on the floor to his own room without saying a word. He felt like one of those people who parked in handicapped spots just because they could. "Being old does have its perks," he hummed cheerfully as he picked up his duffel. Lo and behold, Tarfur was there to pick it up and help him carry it in.

Later that evening the two groups gathered to debrief on the situation in the city. They sat around the kitchen table and passed around a couple bottles of cheap sake Tarfur had scavenged from the supply closet. Hekla and her team were planning on staying here for another week or two while their teammate recovered, but otherwise had no objectives in Tokyo.

"You said this place was robbed," said Makita. "And this happened while you were here?"

"We had just arrived at the safe house. Asha was minutes from bleeding out," said Hekla. "The vault door was ajar, so the three of us swept the room. We were shocked to find the medical cabinet wiped bare. The girl got the jump on us and held a knife to Asha. All she wanted was for us to let her friend go." She frowned. "After they got away, she returned with a first-aid kit."

Josie raised an eyebrow. "She came back?"

"Held a knife. Robbed the place. Heart of gold. Sounds like Ella all right," said Nabin.

"Do you know what she took?" asked Makita.

Hekla handed him a report. "We took inventory on what was missing and passed the information to Command along with a request to reset the safe house's security systems. We're cut off from the main network until then. The stuff they took looked pretty random, nothing specific."

Makita read it over and whistled. He handed the tablet to Nabin, whose face went a little ashen. The Nepalese slid the list to Josie, who simply shook her head. "Oh my. Last time I caught her selling contraband, it was Taiwanese whisky and forged weekend passes. She's playing in the big leagues now. Assault rifles can't be common in Japan. They should be easy to track, no?"

"This isn't the army, Colonel," said Nabin, shaking his head. "Covert ops does not keep identifiers on anything we use. That would make us pretty lousy secret agents."

Josie shrugged. "Then track weapons that don't have any tags then. How many American-made military-grade assault rifles without identifiers can there be? One of these suckers has to show up in the hands of law enforcement eventually."

Makita tsked. "Japan is neutral territory. We can make official requests through the government, but that will leave a paper trail the size of the Taiwan Strait. The Genjix will for sure pick that up. We might as well just advertise we believe Io is hiding out here."

Hekla was conversing quietly with Pedro and Tarfur at the other end of the table. They appeared to reach a consensus. She leaned forward. "We have discreet contacts in Tokyo law enforcement. We can make some inquiries and offer support if your team needs."

"That would be appreciated," said Nabin. "It's a needle in a haystack in Tokyo, but it's all we've got. She likely chose to settle in the largest city in the world so no one can find her."

"Are you guys in any position to assist?" said Makita gruffly. "What about your current mission?"

Hekla shrugged. "Our mission is red-lined and we're currently benched. Once we exposed ourselves, we became in danger of blowing everything up and exposing our larger mission goals. Especially with Asha out. She was our sneak. Tarfur and Pedro can't walk across a room barefoot without attracting the attention of everyone within a klick. The best thing we can do is lay low until things cool down. Then we'll reassess our situation and determine if we can continue."

Her team was operating out of Tokyo tracking Genjix shipments in the Sea of Japan, a counterpart to what Nabin's team was doing in Singapore. Their mission was to track and record the rotation encryptions from Genjix shipments passing through Tokyo Harbor and send the intel back to the Prophus codebreakers.

"What happened?" asked Nabin.

"We were discovered," she explained. "We came across an unusual shipment heading toward North Korea, and decided to get a closer look."

"It was an oil tanker with a veritable army guarding it," said Tarfur.

"At first we thought it was a biological weapon of some sort," continued Hekla. "Then, upon closer inspection, we discovered that it was filled to capacity with manufactured ProGenesis."

Makita's eyes widened. "You confirmed it? An entire oil tanker?"

All three nodded.

"What's ProGenesis?" asked Josie. "Some sort of biological weapon?"

"The opposite actually," explained Makita. "ProGenesis was invented by the Genjix a few decades back to emulate the Quasing home world's atmosphere. It looks like translucent ketchup, and has the same texture as well."

"That doesn't sound so bad," she said.

"It allows them to survive in it without a host, and more importantly lets them reproduce."

She blanched. "I take it back. That sounds horrible."

"Actually," explained Makita. "You were right the first time. When the Genjix first developed the ProGenesis liquid, they had planned to breed billions of Quasing in order to inhabit and overwhelm all living creatures on the planet. The plan backfired when they discovered that the newborn Quasing, without the osmosis of the shared experience and knowledge from their Eternal Sea, were barely sentient. It would require thousands of years to develop to the same level of consciousness as the Quasing who had crash-landed on this planet millions of years ago. They abandoned those plans shortly after."

"We haven't seen this much ProGenesis in quite a while," frowned Nabin. "What is it for?"

Hekla shrugged. "The disturbing thing, however, was that the vats weren't empty. They were filled with life."

"They're breeding again?" Makita leaned back and furrowed his brow. "They're growing something?"

"That's what we were searching for when we were discovered," continued Tarfur. "Asha took a bullet for our efforts. We fled Osaka with the Genjix hot on our trail. We finally lost them in Tokyo and made it here."

"Barely," grumbled Pedro. "Asha lost a pint of blood on the way over."

"Well, if you're willing to help, we'll take all that we can get," said Makita. "Do we have any other angles we can hit?"

"The yakuza, maybe?" said Tarfur.

Makita shook his head. "That'll be like pulling teeth. The Genjix will likely have a stronger bond with the yakuza than the Prophus will. What about the Japanese Defense Force?"

Josie smirked. "Aren't you the one with contacts there, considering you spent your entire career serving in the JDF?"

"Stop throwing my fake personnel file in my face."

Nabin was still scanning the report. "It says here that the vault door was functioning normally and that there were no signs of break-in. She must have used the backdoor we had set up to track her to obtain access to our safe house network."

"It seems everyone with a Wi-Fi connection can hack us these days," grunted Makita. "I swear, the security for most governments and corporations are sieves. The entire world needs a systems overhaul."

Josie reached for the sake and poured a glass. "Well, here's to new friends and bad networks."

The group toasted. They spent the rest of the night swapping stories and sharing news, which was a tradition among agents passing by in the night. Being a secret agent was lonely work. It was good for morale when two teams discussed their experiences. It reminded people that they weren't fighting the war alone, even though it felt that way. It often just degenerated into a grousing session to let out steam.

Josie talked about the reconstruction of Australia after the war, how many of the mines throughout the northern and western coast that formed the blockade were still in place, and that the government was seriously considering following in the footsteps of Japan and Switzerland in regard to this conflict.

"Those fools in Canberra," spat Josie. "Acting like scared babies, as if we had lost the war."

"I honestly can't blame them," said Makita.

"How can you say that?" she fumed.

"Just because the war ended in a stalemate doesn't mean there weren't winners and losers. The war had clear winners. Japan won by not being involved. Australia lost badly by taking the side of the Prophus. Now the neck of the entire country is under the Genjix's boot. Self-preservation is a powerful tool, even against the right thing." Makita picked up a freeze-dried ration bar and bit into it. "Hmm, pizza-flavored. I actually really miss these things. Look, I'm happy they fought for us. I totally understand if they don't the next time around."

"You really think there is going to be a next time, Mr Takeshi," said Pedro. "Wasn't the last time enough?"

"Well, until the aliens find a new common enemy, they'll keep fighting. And if you remember, before they were fighting each other, they were fighting us."

The atmosphere grew somber. A global stalemate with no end in sight, with the only resolution being another war, was rather disquieting news.

"What do you guys think about the Keeper retiring?" asked Josie, obviously trying to change the topic.

The conversation bubbled back up as everyone offered their personal analysis and predictions about the years ahead. Was Jill Tesser Tan pushed out? What was going to happen with the Prophus moving forward? Were they going to finally move Command out of Greenland?

Makita was the only one who didn't join the conversation. He became very interested in his pizza-flavored ration bar. Eventually, he tuned out and his mind wandered to a dark place, as it often did when left to its own devices.

Had he made a huge mistake in accepting this mission? Was he going to die romping around Asia looking for this girl? That would be the worst. In his surprisingly long life, Makita had been with the Prophus for longer than he had been without. He was honestly pretty shocked he had made it to pasture. It would be a fantastic and terrible irony if he died while on a mission after he had officially retired.

Makita felt a tinge of homesickness, which was strange, because his career as a Prophus operative kept him away from his home for longer than he had ever spent in his official residence. He still missed the swing; he should have rocked in it more. He missed the morning fog that drifted down from the mountains and curled around the trees in the forest like ghostly tentacles. He missed the dirt between his fingers when he gardened... what was he talking about? He hated gardening.

That really wasn't the point. None of it was. Being homesick was just a representation of the real worry running through his mind. Was he ever going to see his wife and kid again, or had Makita, like many of his long-dead friends, taken on one mission too many? What if...

He came to attention. A new concern hit him. Was he getting paid for this? He should be; he was so bored at home and eager to do something other than sit on his couch that he had just said yes. At least some sort of hazard pay. His thoughts continued to wander. Since this was an off-book mission, could he even call for an extraction?

Makita had had enough. He needed to go for a walk, clear his head. He stood up abruptly. The conversation around him died immediately.

"Is there a problem, sir?" asked Nabin.

"I just need some fresh air," he replied. "Is there by chance another way up to the surface that doesn't involve ankle-deep sewage?"

Everyone shook their head.

Makita sighed. "Of course."

He turned to leave. Just as he was opening the vault door, Nabin came running up to him with the tablet in his hand. "Sir. I have an idea. I think I may have another way to find Ella. Instead of looking for her in a city of millions, what if she came to us?"

"Why would she do that?" asked Makita.

"Remember how I said Cameron and I made a back door to keep tabs on her?"

"What about it?"

Nabin grinned. "Have you ever heard of a honey pot?"

CHAPTER FIFTEEN
Square One

Ella had come from a vastly different world from most of the other students. To make matters worse, the Host Protection Program meant she would never be able to speak freely of her past. This isolated her even more from her peers.

In hindsight, Cameron Tan made a mistake. He should have constructed her background in such a way that the Academy would have been more supportive of her situation. Instead, neither the Academy nor Ella were prepared for each other.

As expected, Asao threw a complete fit when he saw the state of the World-Famous Bar & Udon. He staggered through the wreckage of his establishment in a daze, soft moans escaping his lips every few steps as he fondled this broken frame, touched that shattered mirror, or stared at the cracked bottles slowly bleeding liquor.

Ella tried to look on the bright side. "We'll help clean it up. You'll be back up and running in no time."

"Clean. It. Up?" Asao's grief turned into rage, which he channeled at the Burglar Alarms, Ella specifically. He shook his fist in her face, spittle shooting from his lips as they curled into a misshapen snarl. "This is all your fault, Beektoria! You punks have ruined me. You'll pay for this!"

Ella instinctively reached for her dagger, but then she gave Asao the benefit of the doubt. He really wasn't threatening her, because that would be foolish.

Be patient with the itchy finger. Just in case, he has a bad leg and cannot turn quickly. Take out his other leg and he will become a beached whale.

"He better get his hand out of my face before he becomes a beached whale missing a flipper."

"Why are you mad at us?" she protested. "We're the ones who chased off those yakuza gangsters while you were eating a snow cone." Ella tried to sound more conciliatory. "Look, you're upset. I get it. We can work this out."

He pointed toward the street. "Get out. Get out. You and your stupid kids. I never want to see any of you here again."

Ella considered arguing, and then shrugged. "Fine. We'll just get the rest of our loot and leave. Have fun cleaning up yourself."

"No," he raged. "Whatever is left stays. Hand over whatever money you've made so far. That pays for repairs." She didn't realize he was being literal.

"What?" Ella's voice went up several octaves. Her dagger slid halfway out of its sheath. "Over your dead body."

Fortunately, the other Burglar Alarms were there to separate them. There were more shouts and threats. Words like "police" and "idiotic foreigner" and "lousy udon" were hurled back and forth. In the end, it didn't matter. Asao wanted them out, so they were out.

The two sat opposite each other at the only table still upright and haggled. How were they going to divvy up the business the Burglar Alarms had done so far? Ella was willing to pay him what he was owed and not a yen more. Asao wanted all of it to pay for his repairs.

What about the remaining goods, and all those promises she had extracted for the bar? She was the one who had arranged for the World-Famous to stay out of the Bakka's crosshairs. She was the one who had found a steady supply of American bourbon embezzled by the dockworkers, and she was the one who had found the super-cheap Indian handyman who Asao used daily. Ella felt she should be compensated for all of that. Asao couldn't care less.

"I'm serious," he yelled. "If you don't give me my share, pay for the damages, and then get out, I will call the police. That's my final offer – it's more than fair, considering how much business I've lost."

"How about I stab you in the gullet and dump your body into the Arakawa River, Asshole?" Ella's eyes shot lasers at the bar owner. The fact that he wanted her share and to kick her out too was downright greedy. It felt very much like a bad divorce.

I would not know. I have never been married.

"How is that possible? You have been around for billions of years, and none of your hosts have ever gotten married? That does not bode well for me."

Emily's parents were together for decades but were too busy working for the Prophus to bother. The life of a host is difficult, not usually conducive to marriage.

"That or you just pick a lot of unlikable hosts."

That appears to be true.

It took Ella a second to realize she had just owned herself, which she got over quickly. She never wanted to get married anyway. The only guy she had ever really liked wanted to change everything about her the second they got serious. 'Stop breaking rules, Ella.' 'Don't commit any more crimes, Ella.' 'Stabbing someone with a dinner fork is not a good way to resolve arguments, Ella.' She crossed her arms and slouched in her chair, her glare at Asao intensifying even though her anger was now actually aimed at someone else.

It became a battle of attrition and a very long night. At dawn, they were still sitting there arguing out of sheer stubbornness.

It wasn't until Io did the math and explained to her that the difference the two of them were quibbling over was the price of a nice dinner, that Ella finally relented.

By breakfast, the Burglar Alarms were out of the World-Famous Bar & Udon. Ella's mind was numb as she glanced back one last time. Asao, standing in the doorway with his fists on his hips, kept his glare on her all the way until she turned off the block.

What would they do next? Where would she go? Most of the money the Burglar Alarms earned over the past few months had been wiped out. She barely had enough to pay the team, let alone cover her rent and food. They were also homeless now. There was no way the Burglar Alarms could operate without a base. They needed a place to meet, negotiate their business and store their loot. Her tiny apartment couldn't even fit everyone, let alone store any goods.

You are working yourself up. Worry about it tomorrow. Go home and get some sleep for now.

"But Io. It took us months–"

Go home. Sleep.

"Fine."

That was probably the best advice Io had ever given her. Ella was so tired, she barely made it to the train station. She dragged her feet into the first train car heading home and plopped down in a corner seat, falling into a deep slumber by the time it began to rumble down the tracks.

Io didn't bother waking Ella when the train pulled into Nishi Kasai Station. When it came to a complete stop and the doors hissed open, she decided to do the girl a favor and let her get some much-needed sleep. She had been running pretty hard lately. Io took control of the body and walked her out of the station. It was a bold move for her, who usually could barely walk a host upright for more than a few steps before falling over. Most of her experiences in mammals prior to humans were of the aquatic variety.

The short trip to Ella's building felt like a marathon, and the walk up the five flights of stairs to her apartment climbing a mountain. By the time Io finally walked through the door, she was exhausted and vowed never to do the girl a favor again. She was tempted to park the girl in bed and just let her sleep for the next Earth day cycle. However, that would mean Ella would wake up the next morning refreshed and probably with nothing to do. Without direction, she would mope, then get bored and get into trouble. The girl needed goals.

Io grudgingly moved her to the table and pulled out the laptop. She began combing the latest Prophus reports in the region, looking for something, anything, that could earn them a little breathing room. They needed to land a quick job, preferably an easy score, and lucrative enough to make it worth their while. It also had to be a job that did not require the use of a storage room. Most importantly, it had to be close by. Io wasn't confident she could find something like this, especially on short notice.

Easy, fast, and good. Just two of the three would do.

To Io's surprise, a very promising opportunity presented itself in just a few minutes of searching. Io looked the report over and double-checked the corroborating data. She ran an online background check and then mapped out the location. Everything matched up.

"This girl is lucky to have me," smirked the Quasing. At least she tried to smirk. The symmetry necessary for a proper human smile was difficult to pull off. The best Io could manage was make Ella's face contort with a lopsided upward curve of the lips, as if she were suffering a stroke.

She gave up after a few attempts. There were more important things to worry about than stupid smiling. It was time to plan their next move.

CHAPTER SIXTEEN
The Law

For the first year, Ella tried to play by the rules. She attended classes and studied hard. It was a difficult and frustrating time. She had to learn and train while simultaneously studying English.

She chafed at the limitations imposed on her, but tried her best to stay within their bounds. She was someone who had grown up in the streets, unused to the rules of a structured life. She often complained that living at the Academy was worse than being one of Wiry Madras's girls.

In the end, no matter how hard she tried, the experiment was doomed to fail. The real Ella Patel could only be locked up for so long.

The announcement that Shura was backing Abbi in the raised vessel's claim for control of the South China Sea Islands came in the morning. This partnership, as Abbi insisted it be framed, whipped up a storm. Many among the Adonis vessels considered it no less than a full betrayal of their status as the gods' chosen. Shura spent the rest of the day inundated with calls from dozens of outraged Adonises, each begging or threatening her to reconsider her position.

Rurik was already leveraging this news to his advantage,

rallying the bulk of his kin to him, further isolating her from the rest of the Genjix. Even her Hatchery siblings, those she had grown up and struggled side by side with, had publicly denounced her.

Before the creation of the Genjix Hatcheries, the eugenics programs that bred and trained the Adonis vessels, all vessels were raised from ordinary humans. Now, Adonis vessels were the preferred method of transition for all Holy Ones. The success of this program had created a caste system among the vessels, the Adonises and the Raised. In a time when dozens of young and newly blessed Adonis vessels were clamoring for opportunities to serve the Holy Ones and lead, her support for a lowly raised vessel was bound to earn her many enemies.

As if these unproven Adonises consider themselves a whole other species.

Shura didn't necessarily disagree with her Hatchery brothers and sisters. "Are we not the next evolutionary step?"

You are still human. As you were raised to be an Adonis vessel, you can also fall from grace.

Fortunately, Shura had insisted on a condition to her agreement with Abbi. Their partnership would only go public if the spymaster actually found actionable information leading to the location of the Receiver. The spymaster quickly proved as good as her reputation.

Shura had an advantage over Rurik: she knew what the Receiver's vessel looked like. As they said, a picture was worth a thousand words, especially in the spy business. Shura was able to provide Abbi with a detailed and accurate description, which was fed into her networks.

Within a matter of days they got a hit with facial recognition, flagging a certain Victoria Khan matching the description of the Receiver's vessel traveling from Sydney to Ninoy Aquino, and then to Tokyo. From there, security cameras placed at the train stations were able to confirm the girl traveling throughout the city as recently as a few weeks ago.

Shura was able to further corroborate the information when they intercepted a Prophus report citing a robbery at one of their safe houses beneath the city. One of the culprits was a short, scrawny girl of mixed Indian descent.

Abbi had passed the information to her contacts within the Tokyo Metropolitan Police and was able to arrange a secret meeting for Shura with the police superintendent-general. Getting the local law enforcement on her side was a big boon in finding the girl.

The die was cast.

Shura was in the air within the hour. She arrived at Narita Airport in the dead of night, again by commercial liner and shrouded in secrecy. She brought only Kloos and four trusted bodyguards. Any more, and she risked alerting Rurik, which was likely inevitable no matter how hard she tried to mask her movements. His network was far too extensive for someone of her standing to escape notice.

If she wasn't detected at the major transportation hubs, she was bound to have been sighted by one of the many security cameras or facial recognition scanners, or even by a checkpoint officer on alert. For all she knew, Rurik could be having her tailed constantly. Still, time was critical, and every advantage counted.

Shura changed cars twice before departing the airport in an unmarked sedan. She headed immediately toward the Keishichō, the police headquarters of the Kasumigaseki district. There was no time to waste, and no such thing as business hours when dealing with the Genjix.

She changed cars once more and entered the underground parking garage in a utility van. Shura and her people emerged in the darkened garage and proceeded through a maintenance elevator. They exited on the sixth floor into the main hallway where they were greeted by an honor guard of twelve police officers in full uniform.

"So much for a secret meeting under cover of darkness," she muttered.

A proper sign of respect for someone of your standing. I am sure it is not often the police superintendent-general receives a visit from a high-ranking Genjix vessel.

"Nice of them to scrounge up so many bodies in the middle of the night."

The officers saluted sharply. Shura did her best to mask her irritation and walked past them in a manner expected of someone in her position. She was greeted by two more officers, women this time, also dressed in uniform. Shura noted, approvingly, that both women carried batons at their hips. They saluted and then gestured for her to follow, flanking her. The two rows of officers fell in behind them down a long brick corridor with large glass displays on one side with the uniforms of the Meiji Restoration and vending machines on the other.

The entourage continued up a set of stairs, through traditional wooden double doors, and right into an open central area filled with desks partitioned by glass walls. They passed several rows of low benches and lounge tables, two rows of waist-high bookshelves dividing the open area in half, and then entered a meeting room with all glass walls.

Five more officers stood at attention on the other side of a long table as Shura and her people walked into the aquarium. The fourteen officers who had accompanied them spaced themselves along the walls with their backs to the glass. They saluted together. It was all quite dramatic.

"A nice touch," murmured Shura.

The man standing in the center of the group inside the aquarium took charge. He was older, and obviously more seasoned than the fresh-faced officers. If nothing else, the extra shiny badges on his chest gave him away. Shura always thought such ribbons silly. All it did was give her a clearer target of who to assassinate.

While the military in the governments under their control did employ such rankings, the Genjix did not. Their ranks simply had a natural way of falling into place. It was said one could always decipher an individual's standing by was to simply seeing how they carried themselves. Shura didn't have to know the identifications on his uniform ribbons to know that this was not the superintendent-general.

"What is the meaning of this?" she exclaimed loudly.

The officer bowed. "I am Captain Kitaro Miko. Superintendent-General Hitashi sends his regards and apologizes for not greeting you in person. He has served for many years and is of limited health."

That is a plausible response.

Shura reluctantly agreed. "Send him my regards."

Kitaro waited until she sat down before joining her. "To what do we owe this honor, Adonis vessel?"

"I seek a fugitive residing in your city," she said. "Expat, likely hiding under several aliases. The Genjix require your force's cooperation."

"Has this individual committed a crime?" asked Kitaro.

"Irrelevant." Shura adjusted her tone. Unlike most Adonis vessels, she understood the power of not-being-an-asshole. "It is an internal matter. You would have my deep appreciation for your aid and discretion."

Kitaro pondered her words, and then nodded. "Very well. Please pass along all relevant information regarding your quarry. Do you have a photograph or description of this individual?"

"I do," she replied.

"That would be most useful. If you transfer that data to me, I can have it processed quickly."

That was easy.

"Indeed. Too easy perhaps."

Shura tapped the screen on her forearm and was about to cast the data file to Kitaro.

Hold. Something is amiss. Look to your sides.

Shura pretended to be busy on her comm and then casually glanced to her left and then her right. An image flashed in Shura's head: a female officer walked to the double door that they entered from, closed and locked it. Another quick flash: outside the aquarium, the hands one of the officers standing watch were shaking. He rubbed his fingers together, his palms sweating. One more flash: one of the officers mouthed silently to the man next to him. The words formed on his lips: get ready.

The final flash: it was a small gesture, barely perceptible, but Tabs missed nothing. Another officer moved his hand and loosened the straps of the baton holster around his waist. He gripped the handle as if preparing to swing. Shura could only come up with one reason. A gun was too lethal, a taser too limited.

They mean to take you alive.

For the police to attack a Genjix official, even during an unofficial visit, especially one with her standing, was no less than an act of war. Even Shura's most hated rivals would see it as a personal affront to their religion and their gods. The Genjix countries would likely have the island blockaded within a week.

That is, unless a higher power was providing cover. Shura should be as safe here as if she were soaking in her own tub at home. Though in all seriousness, she had survived assassination attempts in the tub before. That could only mean one thing. This was sanctioned. Only one person in the entire world would have the knowledge, wealth, and desire to arrange this trap.

Kitaro looked up expectantly from his tablet. "Is there a

problem, Adonis? I am still waiting for the image. We can proceed immediately."

Shura stared the officer down. She was still puzzled. If this was a trap, and the police were about to arrest them, then why the charade? Why not simply arrest them at the airport or the parking garage? Why lead them up here with this elaborate ruse?

Of course...

"Rurik needs an image of the Receiver," she remarked matter-of-factly. "He ordered you to get it before you captured me. How much did it cost him? I hope it was a princely sum, and I hope he paid in advance."

Kitaro was not a great actor. "I do not know what you speak of–"

Shura scrambled onto the table and kicked a heel out, shattering his orbital bone. He flew backward out of his seat and into the glass wall with a heavy crack. Shura's momentum carried her off the table. She landed on one knee and shot her hands outward, grabbing ahold of the two officers who were sitting adjacent to Kitaro. She torqued her body, pulling both men out of their chairs.

Try to avoid killing any of the police if possible.

Two successive strikes ended both their nights. The officer to her right barely had time to stand before Kloos was on top of him, his hammed fist coming down across the man's temple. The remaining officer to her left suffered a similar fate when Vitali, one of her bodyguards, picked up a chair and bludgeoned him with it.

"That is probably too much of an ask in this situation." She slammed the head of another police officer into the glass wall.

The rest of the officers outside charged into the room, only to be met by Shura's entourage. Several pulled out their batons and banged on the glass, causing the interior to vibrate like a roof under a hail storm. There were too many bodies to fight and not enough space to take them all down efficiently. There was only one way out of this room.

Shura had a fix for that. She grabbed two metal beads the size of her thumb hidden in her belt, and lobbed them at opposite walls. The beads exploded upon impact, cracking the glass as well as filling the room with a red, swirling smoke. A second later, the glass walls on each end shattered, and the choking smoke rolled out into the open area.

Shura's bodyguards spread out and attacked the remaining officers, like this had been their plan; as if this had been *their* ambush all along. Most bodyguards' jobs were to be meat shields for the ones they protected. Shura's people did not have to protect her; they were there to fight alongside her and to cover her flank against overwhelming odds.

Watch your breath count.

Several officers quickly fell into a coughing fit. Shura held a long breath in her lungs and slowly let it seep out through lightly clenched teeth. Genjix soldiers were trained to fight in this haze, offering them a significant advantage in close combat. She knocked the officers over easily as she mowed through their ranks.

One officer was stepping over the shattered wall when Shura barreled into him. The two fell, and she rolled to her feet. Shura immediately found herself surrounded. She ducked a swing to the head and sidestepped another to her body. She caught the wrist of a third attack – thrown lazily – and snatched the baton from the fool's hand then, changing levels, dropped near the floor and upended two of her attackers with blows to the achilles. The third came swinging from up top. Shura parried the blow, slipped in, and slammed her elbow into his face.

A female officer approached Shura head on, not bothering to sneak up. She brandished two batons, which she banged together in a challenge. Shura offered her a brief nod as she wielded her own baton. She liked this woman's moxy. The officer came at her with a coordinated flurry meant to overwhelm Shura's defenses. Hard metal clanged against metal. The woman was good, much more skilled than the boys Shura had just taken out. It almost strained her reflexes to block the strikes. Even then, two got through, one hitting her square on the shoulder and the other glancing off her chin. In another situation, Shura might have tried to recruit this woman. Instead, she waited for a slight opening and charged, jabbing a knee into the woman's gut, doubling her over. Shura finished her off with a baton blow to the jaw. She glanced down at the badge pinned on the woman's chest: Amaya 3144. Shura might decide to offer her a job yet.

Behind you to the left. Going low.

The warning came too late. A coward attacked Shura from out of the corner of her eye. The most damaging strikes are the ones you never see coming. Almost anyone else would have buckled under that blow. The last-second warning gave Shura just enough time to prepare for it. She moved her weight off one leg just as the baton crushed the back of that knee. The resulting impact swung her leg outward, dampening the damage. Shura allowed the blow to swing her around as she brought the baton whistling down on her assailant's head.

The officer, barely into his twenties by the looks of him, only had time to utter a strangled cry before he crumpled to the ground. When Shura put her weight back on her foot, it nearly gave. Grimacing, she raised the baton again to finish him off.

Shura. Remember what he is.

The baton came to a stop inches from cracking his skull. Nothing sets off a government like the killing of their law enforcement. She glanced up. The entire area was strewn with broken glass and bodies. Groans and pained cries filled the air. She took quick inventory: only four of her people were standing.

"Where's Vitali?" she asked.

Roxani, another of her bodyguards, walked over to the unmoving body of her fallen man. She looked up and shook her head.

"Burn his body," ordered Shura. "What about theirs? Casualty report?"

"All mine live, at least for now," said Kloos. The rest of her people offered similar assessments.

"Good enough. Let's go."

Shura looked at the locked door from which they had come. There was a good chance there was an army of Tokyo police officers waiting for her on the other side, and likely more below. Perhaps there was another way. She went over to the floor-to-ceiling window on the near side of the building and peered over the edge. Her memory of the facility's map told her this was the southwest end, which meant they should be just above the sky bridge connecting to the adjacent building. Sure enough. It was a bit of a drop, but nothing her people couldn't handle.

Shura reached into her belt and pulled out another bead. One explosion and several jumps later, the small group had managed to escape the building even as dozens of police cars swarmed around it. They watched as the night was lit up with red and blue lights.

"What happened, Adonis?" asked Kloos.

"It appears Rurik got to the police before we did," she replied.

"Do you think Abbi betrayed us?" she thought to Tabs.

Unlikely. Her success now hinges upon yours. A double-cross would reflect poorly upon her.

"Your orders?" asked Roxani.

Shura loosed a sigh. "It is only a small setback. We know

the Receiver is here in the city. We can clean this up in the morning. We'll just have to find the girl another way. There are other government resources we can contact for assistance. I have a meeting with the Minister of Defense and the Head of the Public Security Service tomorrow. For now, off to the Ritz. I could use a bath."

By morning, the small setback had grown significantly larger.

The news reported the incident at the Tokyo Metropolitan Police Headquarters as a bombing, a terrorist attack by a Russian separatist group. The city was now on high alert. The Japanese government had officially declared her a terrorist, and Shura was now a wanted fugitive with her photo plastered on every screen. They even gave her a catchy nickname: the Blonde Bombshell Bomber.

To add grave insult to injury, the reward for information that led to her capture was pitifully small.

CHAPTER SEVENTEEN
Second Score

Some of the best professors in the world were at Ella's disposal. She studied everything from languages to hostage negotiations to quantum physics to network security. She also spent hundreds of hours learning a wide variety of physical skills, from hand-to-hand combat to reconnaissance to clandestine tactics.

Unfortunately, Ella could not grasp even the fundamentals of linguistics, history or political affairs, which are enormously important for field agents. She was not technically savvy, nor was she skilled in math, science or law. To make things worse, she got bored and frustrated easily. It was a miracle and testament to my own coaching and nurturing that she was able to pass any classes at all.

"Are you sure this is right?" Ella teetered on the tree branch she was perched on and carefully adjusted her balance. She stared at the grounds of the estate on the other side of a low traditional Japanese wall. "This looks like the wrong address."

I used to help navigate a living starship that traveled across half the galaxy. I can read maps very well, Ella.

"Well, it looks wrong. This place looks like a temple or something. Are you sure this is–"

Stop asking me that. I agree with your assessment that this is not the usual sort of mark we hit, but my answer is not going to change.

Ella gave the venue one last suspicious glance before scampering out of the tree. The other Burglar Alarms were waiting near its base, looking very uneasy as well. Rightly so. They were slightly out of place in Azabu, one of the most affluent neighborhoods in Tokyo.

"Well?" asked Kaoru.

"This is it," said Ella.

Daiki's eyes went as large as saucers. "And we're going to live here?"

"This is going to be the Burglar Alarms' new headquarters," she replied. "You're still going to be living with your mother."

Hinata tilted his head. "If it's as rich inside as it looks out here, we're going to be rich."

Daiki looked down both sides of the street. "This is a funny place for a secret hideout, no?"

"Maybe that's what makes it such a good secret place," said Lee. "No one will expect it." He appeared dubious, however.

"Well, we're not doing ourselves any favors by sticking around," said Ella briskly. "Pek, stand watch. The rest of us are going in."

"Aww, me again? Why can't someone else stand watch?"

"What?"

"I mean, why me again, Bosu? All I do is–"

"Because I said so." She turned to the others. "Just like last time. I'm going to go in and check it out. When I give the all-clear, you guys follow."

The outfit exchanged awkward and hesitant glances, and then all crossed their arms at the same time. Ella scowled. They had obviously choreographed that.

"Not a chance, Ella," said Lee. "This going in alone thing to keep us out of danger isn't going to work any more." The rest nodded in agreement. They didn't nod in unison, at least.

They are right. A good leader would actually send an expendable underling in first. Send in Pek. Let him spring the booby trap.

"Not a chance, Io."

For a moment, Ella considered calling the whole damn thing off. Then she remembered what happened at the World-Famous. It was time to learn to trust her Burglar Alarms. "I'll make you guys a deal," she offered. "It's easier for me to move without you oafs clomping after me. I'll keep my comm open at all times."

They eyed her with suspicion, and then retreated to discuss her proposal. Ella felt like she was losing control of the team. Somehow, the Burglar Alarms had evolved from her dictatorship to some stupid form of democracy. For some reason, Ella didn't seem to mind this new development as much as she pretended, which surprised her.

Are you actually learning to trust someone? Little Ella is finally growing–

"Shut it, Alien."

The rest of the Burglar Alarms appeared to have come to a consensus. They returned and crossed their arms again in unison like some stupid Korean dance video. "Here's the deal," said Lee. "You need to let us know everything is OK. If we don't hear from you every minute, we're coming in after you."

"Hmm, fine," growled Ella, her face scrunched up. That was all an act on her part just to save face. "At least stop clustering around the front door looking so obvious."

The Burglar Alarms scattered in the most conspicuous way possible, each wandering off on their own in a different direction. Fortunately, the well-to-do inhabitants of this neighborhood were either too polite or couldn't be bothered to notice. They really could have used that clandestine training from the Academy though.

The class you barely passed?

"Passing is passing. It's like grenades."

You had to cheat on the final. If I had not given you all the answers on the multiple choice, you would have missed most of them.

"I did not cheat! You're part of me, so using you is not cheating."

There was a lengthy pause. Finally, Io spoke. *You just said I am part of you. That may be the nicest thing you have ever said to me.*

"Stop rubbing it in," mumbled Ella. She focused her attention on the security keypad next to the red half-moon-shaped double doors. Then, for the first time, she noticed the small security camera blinking in the corner. She reached for a throwing knife. "I thought you said the security system was off."

This location is not live yet. The feed is self-contained on a twenty-four hour recording loop. Mostly just to scare off vandals and girl scouts.

"What's a girl scout?"

Never mind.

Just in case, Ella partially covered her face from the camera and punched in the code. She was half-expecting this not to work, and was pleasantly surprised when one of the red doors swung inward with a high-pitched creak. She poked her head inside. "It is really nice in here. How did you come by this place again?"

I told you. Command shut down the underground safe house after your little stunt, and are moving it here. This one will not go live until the security measures are installed, and Command cannot get to that for another four months. In the meanwhile, I see no reason why we cannot use it as your headquarters.

Ella closed the door behind her and crept inside. She took three steps onto the grounds and felt as if she were transported to some weird alien planet. The estate looked as if it had sprung from a dream or fairy tale, like time had forgotten it existed. It was a picturesque scene of a traditional Japanese house sitting next to a babbling brook just inside the walls. Beautiful cherry blossom trees lined the perimeter, and several large gnarled and twisting oaks dotted the rest of the landscape. It looked very out-of-place nestled here in the center of Tokyo. Ella half-expected a samurai to walk out of that hut.

Minka.

"What?"

Those houses are called minkas, *not huts.*

Ella ignored the architectural lesson as she crept across the grounds looking for signs of activity. The interior of the hut – *minka* – was darkened, and the only sounds she could hear were the gurgle of the brook and the chirping of the birds. She paused behind a boulder and waited. Minutes passed. Still nothing. Ella was about to move closer into the house but something held her back. Her gut was telling her something was off about this place. Truth was, everything felt off.

Her earpiece buzzed. "Hello Ella? You there?"

"What is it, Hinata? Everything clear outside?"

"Yes, Bosu. Just checking in to make sure you're alive."

"You're supposed to check in every minute," added Lee.

"Is it really nice in there?" asked Daiki.

Everyone began chattering at once, jumbling the comm channel. Now she remembered why she had preferred to keep the thing off. "I need you guys to be quiet," she hissed.

A chorus of "sorry, bosu" followed. Ella made her way toward the *minka,* moving from cover to cover. The peace and calm broke as the chatter slowly grew again. This time Hinata was poking fun at Lee and Kaoru for dating. Daiki and Pek piled on. At least they weren't focused on her this time.

Push it out of your mind.

Ella did her best to do just that. She reached the *minka* and slowly slid the amado open. It was dark inside, musty. She swept a flashlight across the room. Half of it was empty, and the other half was filled with boxes. Her light rested on a familiar long metal tube leaning in the corner. It was the bazooka, no, the surface-to-air missile launcher.

To the left are the same supply containers from the underground safe house. The report checks out.

Ella waited several beats, listening for scraping or breathing or any other signs of life. Failing to pick anything up, she finally crept inside. Her gut was still telling her something was off. It was right more often than not, but perhaps this was one of those times when she was just being too cautious.

She walked to the adjacent *shōji*, slid it open, and peered inside. More boxes. She went across to the other end of the room and slid that door open as well. Furniture from the safe house was crammed into the corner and stacked in a pile.

Ella continued to the room on the far end. She slid that *shōji* open. "Hey Burglar Alarms, I think we're cle–" Her voice trailed off as her body froze. Her eyes bulged, threatening to fall out of their sockets.

There, standing in the center of a barren room, was Nabin. "Hello, Ella. How are you?" He waved his familiar lackadaisical wave and spoke with his weird American southern drawl that sounded like each of his words was falling down a well.

Ella opened her mouth. No noise came out. She forgot how to breathe.

Get out of here. Go, go now!

A dozen intense and conflicting emotions slammed into her one after the other. Ella did the first thing her heart told her to do. She reached for a throwing knife.

No time for that. You can stick him another day.

Nabin's eyes widened. He threw up his hands. "Whoa, whoa, babe. I just want to talk."

"Don't 'babe' me, you self-righteous jerk," she hissed reflexively. "Especially after what you did."

Nabin gave a start. "Me? After what *I* did?"

Ella's hand tightened around the handle of her knife, and

she readied her throw. Truth was, seeing him made her heart flutter. Seeing him also made it ache. By Ganesh, she missed his ugly face and his stupid wide smile and the stupid way the ends of his stupid lips almost reached his stupid oversized ears.

For a moment, fond memories of the only man she ever loved flooded her thoughts. His visits were the only highlights Ella remembered during her tenure at the Academy. She had no family or friends, so all of her spare time and energy were reserved for him. Their brief but passionate relationship had burned hot and bright.

Damn it, Ella! Stop daydreaming. This is a trap!

Of course Io just had to be an asshole and ruin the moment by reminding her of all the bad times as well. A series of quick scenes slammed into her head one after another. She relived it all in rapid succession, as if someone was fast-forwarding a movie and stopped at all the worst parts. All those moments when he had brushed her off as a silly girl, saying she was being immature. She wasn't immature; he was being a stubborn know-it-all. The several times he wasn't present with her because he was too caught up thinking about duty. The dozens of instances when he ignored her when she needed him. The fights… those dozens of fights.

Whatever Io was doing worked. Everything replayed vividly in Ella's head as if she were right there experiencing them again for the very first time. By the time the scenes had finished running in her head, she was grinding her teeth as the now-familiar rage bubbled up to the surface from a place she had thought long-buried. She focused on Nabin, who was now standing before her.

"Ella, listen please, babe," he said, offering his hand. "I really need to talk to you. This is serious."

She completed the motion and the knife flew from her fingertips. Her heart really wasn't in the throw, so the knife flew lazily and sunk into the floor right between his legs. Ella pulled out her long dagger and took two steps forward.

No, no. Just leave. Get out before it is too late.

"Ella?" Lee's voice blasted in her ear. "What's going on? You're breathing awfully heavy. Who is that talking?"

"I thought the place was empty?" chirped Daiki.

The crew began to clamor in her ear again. It all just became background noise. Ella's attention was on Nabin. Finally, she found her voice. She couldn't quite process all her emotions. She was somehow enraged and ecstatic to see him all at the same time. "What do you want?" she hissed.

He wants to haul you back to the Prophus.

"The Genjix are after you. You need to come with me so we can protect you," he replied, taking a step toward her. Ella took a step back.

He probably has orders to take you in for raiding the safe house.

"We know it was you who robbed the safe house. If we could determine that, then so can they."

See! You need to flee now.

Ella wavered. Everybody was yelling at her. Io, the Burglar Alarms, even her conscience, and they were all telling her to do different things. She pushed all the voices out of her head and asked what was really on her mind. What really mattered to her. "Did you come looking for me because you love me?"

There was no hesitation. "Yes."

By the Eternal Sea, do not fall for that, Ella.

She took a step closer to Nabin. "Are you trying to get back together with me?"

Slight hesitation. "Maybe. I don't know." He paused. "I do miss you."

That was good enough. It wasn't exactly the answer she was looking for, but Nabin was stupidly truthful with her, which was often annoying. She sometimes – most of the time – preferred he tell her what she wanted to hear. She took another step forward. Sure, the two of them had technically broken up, but there was still something there. And he came looking for her. That had to mean something. Ella took a few more steps forward. She was almost at arm's length.

Ask him if he is under orders to find you. Ask him!

Io seemed on the verge of panic. That was a good question. It never occurred to her that he was here for any other reason than to see her because he loved and missed her, and was really, really sorry he broke up with her, and wanted to make up and be together.

Ask. Him.

"Oh fine, Io." She was absolutely convinced he came only for her, regardless of all that negativity Io was putting into her head. It took Ella a second to find her voice again. "Are you on the job?"

The hesitation was long this time. "Yeah, Ella. I am."

Her heart stopped. "You're not here for me?"

"I am. It's both. You're in danger. The Prophus need to take you to a safe place."

Remember what I told you about how they want to control and imprison you?

His words cut into her chest. She whispered. "Io was right."

"What? No. Don't listen to that asshole."

They had never gotten along. A few months ago, Ella would have agreed with Nabin. Now that she was on her own again, and Io was the only one in Ella's life who hadn't abandoned her – even if it weren't by choice – Nabin speaking badly of Io felt like a personal attack. Ella's rage ticked back to boiling.

She stomped up to him, shaking her fist. "Don't you dare talk about my Quasing that way. Only I can. What are you even doing here? You don't want to be with me any more, remember? Go do your stupid important Prophus thing."

I appreciate you coming to my defense, but I would much rather you just follow my instructions for once.

Nabin took a step backward, just staying out of her blade range. "Can we sit and talk? In private?"

"If you're on the job, then we have nothing to talk about." She bent down and picked up her knife. "I just wanted this back." She turned to leave.

Nabin's hand shot out and grabbed her wrist. "Ella, you have to hear me out. You're in danger. The Genjix are looking for you."

"You better watch what you're doing with your hand." Her voice quivered with rage.

Nabin hastily let go. "There's a price on your head."

"How large?" That was the first question that popped into her mind.

"Big enough that every bounty hunter, mercenary, and probably a few governments are looking for you."

"It seems I'm finally moving on up in life. No thanks to you."

More like I am. I wonder why.

"Why are they after me?" she asked.

"We're not sure," admitted Nabin. "It has something to do with the Bio Comm Array, but we haven't cracked it yet. In any case, you need to come with us. We need to protect you."

Her eyes narrowed. "Who is we? Did a whole bunch of you come to kidnap me?"

"No," he stammered. "Look, we're just trying to keep you safe."

"How would you do that?" she asked. "How would you go about protecting me?"

"We'll move you someplace where they can't reach you. We'll hide you to make sure they can never find you."

Ella's eyes narrowed. "Some place like Greenland? With guards watching over me all day?"

Nabin nodded. "Around the clock security for your protection."

Ella loved him, but he could be so dumb sometimes. "No thanks."

She sheathed the knife with a hard push into its sheath and stomped toward the exit. She was just about to leave the room when a figure appeared at the doorway, blocking her path. "Why don't you sit down and we can talk this through, maybe starting with exactly why the Genjix are looking for you."

"I told you I don't know," she spat. "Who the hell are you?"

"Maybe you should take a breath and think it over. Dig a little deeper."

"I don't need to–" Ella squinted at the wrinkling, old man. Where had she met this fossil before? "You look familiar. Have we met?"

"No," said the old man, rather defensively.

Ella furrowed her brows. "Yes we have."

He crossed his arms. "I don't know what you're talking about."

Oh no.

"Oh no what, Io?"

This is more serious than we thought. You may have to fight your way out of here.

"I'm not going to beat up this grandpa. My ancestors will never let me live that down."

That was when it hit her. Ella's eyes widened and her mouth dropped. "Hey, we *have* met! On the plane out of India! You're Cameron's old man! You're Roen Tan!"

CHAPTER EIGHTEEN
Watchers

Not only was Ella at a disadvantage with her studies due to her lack of education and poor grasp of English, she was also far behind most of her classmates when it came to the physical aspects of her training. The girl was also small of stature and strength. Her health was delicate from a lifetime of malnourishment. She lost every single sparring match when she played by the rules. She was also the worst shot with a gun I had ever seen.

Most of her peers had at minimum some level of military or combat training. Ella learned by surviving on the streets. That did not translate well into the classroom. Lacking the physical and intellectual tools, Ella's opportunities at the Academy were rapidly diminishing. That was not even considering the most important tool of all, which she of course lacked as well.

"What did she say?" said Josie through the earpiece. "Did she just say Roen Tan? Who is Roen... oh crap. *That* Roen? He's here? Where?"

Roen Tan, currently undercover as Makita Takeshi on an off-book mission (sanctioned by his wife, until recently the Keeper of the Prophus) to the opposite end of the world to find and protect Ella Patel, sighed. He had a pretty terrible track record when it came to maintaining his cover. This time was no exception. He closed the sliding door behind him. "I guess we can skip the introductions. Why don't we all have a seat? I'll grab some beers. We'll put our feet up and all have a nice chat."

Ella continued to stare at him. "You look awful. What happened?"

"It's called getting old and retiring. Something you'll have the pleasure of not having to deal with if you keep up the stupid stuff you've been pulling."

"What happened to all your hair?"

"It kept falling out, so I shaved it."

"You don't look very good bald. Your head is lumpy."

Roen pointed at a cluster of chairs. "Thanks for that. Why don't we sit down so you can tell me more about my ugly head."

Ella whirled on Nabin. "This is talking in private? You bring the Prophus boss?"

"I was never the boss," said Roen. "I'm also retired, so I'm not anything really."

"I'm retired too," she spat. "So I'm leaving. You two can have your stupid Prophus talk by yourselves."

For a moment, Roen considered letting her go. Nabin obviously couldn't even get the girl to have a conversation, let alone convince her to come with them. Roen had a feeling that if he did let her go, it could be the last time they ever saw her, and he couldn't let that happen. But what was he going to do? Kidnap her and smuggle her to Greenland? That was probably the right call, but Roen didn't sign up for this supposed vacation to kidnap little girls. Besides, he was pretty sure Jill wouldn't approve.

Damn Cameron and his "Dad, I can tell you're bored. Want to do me a favor? You'll get to go on vacation. To Australia!" And damn Jill and her "you should go. You need to get out of the house anyway. Every time I get on a video call with you, you look like a hobo who hasn't showered in weeks." His wife's assessment wasn't exactly inaccurate.

Roen continued to block the exit as Ella tried to push past him. "Ella, at least hear what we have to say. If you don't owe it to Nabin, you at least owe it to Cameron."

She scowled. Roen could tell Io was talking up a storm to her. The girl hadn't learned to mask her internal conversations. Still, she hadn't tried to flee or knife him yet. The Quasing must have convinced her to at least listen to what he had to say.

Ella shook her head. "No, I have nothing to say to any of you." When Roen didn't budge, she reached for her knife. "Don't tempt me, old man."

Roen rolled his eyes. "What are you going to do, draw your blade? Try to cut me? Sure." He crossed his arms to prove his point. He added, a little bitterly, "And I'm not that old."

Ella drew her blade. She tried to cut him.

The girl was fast, but years of experience and dumb luck had kept most of Roen's blood in his body. Also, her heart probably wasn't really into eviscerating him.

Roen backpedaled to avoid a slice to the gut. As soon as the blade cleared, he scooted back toward her and gave her a little hip check, bouncing her off balance. He grabbed her wrist and looped an arm around her neck, then spun her around into a rear naked neck choke. She yelped and squirmed, but Roen held on.

"Now," he continued. "The Prophus aren't in the business of kidnapping, so I'm going to let you go, but not before you hear what we have to say. Do we have a deal?"

"Sir," said Nabin, approaching. "I would move my arm if I were you. Ella has a habit of–"

Ella opened her chompers and tried to take a chunk out of his arm. Roen let out a sharp cry and loosened his grip. Another blade materialized in her hand – she had gotten quite good with them – and she slashed horizontally, narrowly missing his carotid artery. She wasn't messing around this time. That was a killing blow.

Roen caught her return swing and twisted the blade out of her hand. "Look, we can do this the easy way, or we can do this the fun way."

He was about to drag her down to the ground when something semi-hard struck him in the back of the head. Roen pitched and tumbled forward. It was not a graceful landing. He missed catching his fall and ended up face-planting on the bamboo floor. He found himself sprawled with his hands and legs spread out. He rolled onto his back to retaliate against his assailant and stopped. It was a kid, barely a teenager.

He stared at the weapon that struck him. "Did you just hit me with your tennis racket?"

"Racquetball," the kid snarled. He leveled the racket at Roen with conviction. "You leave Bosu alone."

The room became uncomfortably packed as several more kids filed in, all wielding assorted sports equipment.

"What the hell is this?" he sputtered. "Gym class?"

"Wait," yelled Ella. "Stop it, you guys!"

It was too late. Both sides appeared to have lost control of the situation. One kid, the smallest in the group, pulled out a butcher knife and charged Nabin. Nabin looked more bemused than threatened as he yanked the knife out of the boy's hand mid-swing and then flicked the kid across the side of the head with a finger as if he were testing a melon's ripeness.

Roen jumped back to his feet and stared down a young man charging at him with a lead pipe.

"Here, sir." Nabin tossed Roen the butcher knife.

"Thanks." Roen gently lobbed it at the onrushing teenager, sending it flying in a high graceful spinning arc. "Catch."

The young man's eyes widened at the throw. He stopped dead in his tracks and actually tried to catch it, juggling both the butcher knife and lead pipe. Roen was in his face a moment later. Distracted, he grabbed the guy's shirt, pulled him sideways, and then yanked hard in the other direction to send him flying off his feet.

The boy with the racket charged him. Roen waited until the last moment, then stepped to the side and stuck his foot out. The boy continued running right past him and went flying into the opposite wall.

Roen turned to Ella. "Are these jokers with you?"

He never got his answer as a heavy thud to the side of his head sent him crumpling to the ground. Fortunately, whatever hit him was soft, and whoever hit him didn't hit that hard. It was still hard enough to ring his head. Roen blinked away the ache and looked up to see a girl wielding what looked like a black rubber mallet. The girl grabbed Ella by the wrist and hauled her out of the room.

Ella yelled to her little friends, and the rest of the kids began scurrying out. Roen considered giving chase but thought better of it. There was no way he was going to beat a bunch of teenagers in a footrace. He rubbed the welt growing on the crown of his head. His lumpy head was about to get lumpier. A sigh escaped his body. Roen was getting his butt kicked a lot on this mission. In fact, he couldn't remember taking so many beatings since he first met Tao.

He clambered to his feet and was immediately shoved aside by that smallest kid, whom he had tripped a few seconds before. Roen teetered, lost his balance, and fell on his rump a second time. He shook his fist after them. "That was unnecessary, you damn kids! Yeah, you keep running. Get out of my…" Roen closed his eyes. He promised he would never say that phrase.

Nabin was at his side a moment later, offering his hand. He hauled Roen to his feet. "Should we go after them, sir?"

He considered their options and decided to test an idea. "I'm not above kidnapping."

Nabin gave him a look.

Roen sighed. "Fine. As long as she's not in danger, we can bide our time. She needs to want to come with us. I thought you said you could talk to her."

"I thought so too. I think Io got in the way. She has always hated my guts."

Roen put on his earpiece, which had slipped off during the melee. "Are you guys tracking the nerd herd?"

"Yes, sir," came the chorus of replies.

"Follow them."

"Which ones?" asked Hekla.

"All of them. Definitely Ella, and the rest if you can. Find out where they live, where they hang out, and where they eat their meals. If we couldn't catch them this time around, we'll nab them next time."

"Copy that."

"Hey, sir," said Pedro, his voice breaking. "Did you guys wreck the place?"

Nabin looked around. "No, your family's summer home is still standing."

Josie burst into the room a moment later. She stared Roen down and put her hands on her hips. "Makita," she scowled. "I need to talk to you."

That was not a request.

"Sure," he said. "What can I do for you Ms Perkins?"

"Why did that girl call you Roen Tan?"

He shrugged. "Probably because that's what she knew me by."

Josie's face darkened. "You're the Keeper's husband."

"For now," he quipped. "We'll see if that remains the case after she finds out what I've been up to."

"You're a high-profile figure. You're literally on every Genjix's kill-on-sight list."

"Flattery works every time." Roen offered her a slight bow.

"To be fair, that list is a little outdated. After I retired, they moved me to the kill-when-convenient list."

"And I let you go first to Singapore, a central Genjix territory, and now Tokyo. Do you know how careless and stupid this is?"

"I guess you're going to tell me."

"We're heading back to Australia right now."

"Yeah, I don't think so." Roen pulled out the note with the Keeper's authority. "Remember, I'm in charge–"

Josie stomped up to him, knocked the tablet out of his hand, and then socked him in the face. For the second time in so many weeks, Roen's dentures cracked.

CHAPTER NINETEEN
Narrow Escape

The most important tool Ella Patel lacked – something which was crucial for all agents – were soft skills: emotional intelligence. The girl just could not get along with anyone. Amy Ng may have been her first roommate, but Ella went through three more before the end of her first year.

She was naturally suspicious and did not make friends easily, which only made others suspicious of her. She always angled for an advantage, which, while common on the streets, burned bridges at the Academy. Everything was stacked against her. It became obvious early on that she was not cut out for such a profession. No one expected her to succeed.

The Burglar Alarms parted ways shortly after the incident at the Japanese estate. Everyone had standing instructions to go to ground and lay low for a few days whenever a job went bad. Ella usually would let them know when to meet up again. This time was a little different.

Get back home. Pack your things. With luck, we can be out of the city tonight.

For Ella, the whole world now felt like enemy territory. During the train ride home she kept replaying her encounter with Nabin over and over in her head. She had always imagined that the next time they met, if ever, she would be rich and hardly even remember who he was.

Nabin? Ella would tap her chin deep in thought. That name sounded familiar. Oh yes, that guy, Nobhead or Nab-idiot or something like that. He was some guy she dated back in her younger years when she hadn't known better. If she remembered correctly, he had told her that she would never amount to much. Ella would shrug and chuckle, and then sip her champagne as she lounged on the deck of her yacht while her really handsome and tall Australian boyfriend prepared lunch.

That was how Ella imagined it would be like the next time their paths crossed. Instead, when she actually did run into him, all she wanted to do was wrap her arms around his barrel-shaped body and bury her head in his furry bear chest and tell him how much she missed him. That, as much as she wanted to dredge up all the times he had infuriated her, all she could think about was all the many more times when he had made her happy. She recognized that all the flashes of bad memories were Io just being a jerk.

I was trying to keep you grounded.

"You were trying to keep me away from him."

Technically, both were true. Ella wasn't naive or blind enough not to see why. Although they had never spoken to each other directly, Io and Nabin held diverging views on life; their goals were direct opposites to each other. What they each wanted for Ella was very different.

Nabin was Ella's first and only love, and she never thought she could love someone so much. When they first started dating, he used to fly down to Sydney at least once a month, no matter where he was or what mission he was on at the time. He was always so patient and caring and thoughtful with her. Nabin, who sat and listened endlessly as she ranted about the Academy. Who once hid in her dorm room for three hours to surprise her. Who spent his entire R&R tutoring her during her finals the first year.

He cooked the best pancakes and always made a big production of serving her breakfast in bed. She would curl into a ball and nestle into the crook of his arm as he drank coffee and read intelligence reports. They would spend the mornings jogging and practicing knife work, the afternoons eating ice cream and frolicking in the ocean, and the evenings counting stars next to a bonfire. That was when times were good. Great, even. It was fresh love and bursting hearts, and she was sure they were going to be together forever.

Forever was unfortunately far shorter than she had anticipated. Like all relationships, the honeymoon period eventually ended. Reality began to creep into their perfect life. Nabin had to eventually rededicate his focus back to being a Prophus agent. Ella slowly became, well, Ella Patel again.

It started with small things: Nabin leaving the toilet seat up, oversleeping and being late for date night, forgetting her birthday, etc. To be fair, Ella had her bad moments as well, since it takes two to start a fight: Ella picking out and eating all the wontons from the soup they were sharing, leaving the dirty dishes piled up, rummaging through his things out of boredom.

She could still hear his annoyed, snippy comment. "It's not about the stupid wontons, babe. It's about being considerate!"

Over time, their quarrels grew more serious and volatile. She missed him terribly when he was away on missions and begged him to stay. He chastised her for cheating on her tests and for stealing Academy supplies. That last incident hit Ella particularly hard. Nabin had yelled at her about embezzling tablets from the Academy and selling them on the black market. He told her that being a con woman was wrong, and that she was ungrateful to the Prophus.

He never once bothered to consider that being the con

woman that he so disdained was the only way she had managed to survive Crate Town as a child, that scrounging and stealing was how she managed to stay afloat. That even though Ella was now living safely in an air-conditioned dorm, she was terrified that, just like everything else in her life, she could lose it all with a snap of a finger.

Which she did. Her nightmare came true.

Things came to a head when she was expelled. Nabin had taken a break from his mission to fly in specifically to see her. Ella had thought he was there to console her as she, weeping and beside herself, was ordered to pack her meager belongings and given a one-way ticket. Instead, he came and kicked her while she was down. He broke up with her. Ella could still hear his hurtful words.

"I can't be with you any longer," he had said. "You will never change. You will endanger everyone around you. I won't let you destroy everything I fight so hard for."

His last words lingered in her thoughts. Ella sat still in her seat as the train rumbled along, tears welling in her eyes as she relived those painful memories as if they were newly fresh and raw. The minutes passed. She looked out the window as the cityscape flew by. Brightly lit skyscrapers gave way to warehouses, and to residential buildings in turn. Slowly, the city coaxed her back to the present.

She was going to miss Tokyo.

Io was right about one thing though. Ella could not stay here any longer. Maybe she should move to another part of Japan, like Osaka or just a little further out to Nagasaki. Kyoto was beautiful. Perhaps she should just flee Japan entirely. She could head out to New Zealand or Argentina or America, and hole up in a place where no one would ever find her.

Ella jumped out of the train as soon as the doors opened and pushed her way through the light crowds toward home. If she hurried, she could pack and be out of the city in an hour. Maybe even out of the country. She was halfway to her apartment when she stopped.

What is it?

Ella glared at the quiet streets of Nishi Kasai, the place she had made her home over the past six months. "Why am I the one who has to leave? I was here first, and I actually *live* here. In this custody battle, Japan is mine. Nabin's the one who should go."

Being here first is not relevant. What is important is they have found you and may try to forcibly take you.

"Kidnap me? They wouldn't dare, would they?" Ella wasn't so sure. Nabin definitely wouldn't. She didn't know about Cameron's dad. "How did Roen Tan even find out I was here?"

The Prophus are after you. They must be tracking you somehow.

"You were right. I shouldn't have sent him that postcard." She made a sad face. "But it was his birthday."

We must have left them a trail to follow. We need to be more careful next time. Cut off ties to everyone in our past. The Prophus must want something from us. If you want them to leave you alone, we have to leave now.

Ella crossed her arms. She had worked hard to make a life for herself. She had friends, a job – sort of – and people who were counting on her. Nabin should be the one to leave. She should talk to him about their breakup arrangement, like custody during a divorce. Except in this case, her custody was Tokyo.

Ella, this is about more than your boyfriend. If the Prophus are after us, they will not quit.

"So what?" she snapped. "The Prophus are all over the world. If they are looking for me here, they are looking for me in Peru and Tanzania. I shouldn't have to scurry off and hide every time one of those stupid alien heads shows up on my lawn." She paused. "No offense."

I see your point. Maybe we should have listened to what they had to say.

Ella made a face and huffed. "Of course not. I want nothing to do with him. He said I was dragging him down."

All her emotions bubbled up again. Ella quickly buried them. Nabin was the only person in the world who could set her off like that. As much as she hated him, she knew deep down inside it was just a protective shell. That meant Io knew as well.

My advice, if you choose to accept it, is to stay away from him. The Prophus obviously want to bring me back into the fold. They want to involve me in their war, and we want nothing to do with that. We dictate our own future.

Ella worked herself up and shook her fist in the air. "You're right. We're our own boss. We call the shots."

We decide where to live and what jobs we work.

Ella nodded furiously as she stomped into her apartment. "I like this craphole. I think I'm going to stay here forever."

It probably is not a bad idea to update your go bag in case things go poorly.

Ella shrugged and fell into bed. "I don't think that's necessary."

Just in case.

"I'll take care of it some other time."

That is what you said last time.

"Well, next time."

Ella's adrenaline finally drained, and she found herself bone-weary. She yawned and curled herself into a ball, her back pressing to the wall. She reached behind her – yep, the dagger was there. "Can you check and make sure everything is all right?"

Sure, Ella.

In seconds, she was sound asleep.

Io sat Ella up a few minutes later. The girl was in a deep slumber. Io had been sorting through her emotions and knew they were in trouble. Ella was not physically tired. Stamina was one of her strengths. She was emotionally drained; seeing Nabin had sapped much of her energy.

Ella loved him. More than she realized. Io might not know humans well, but she could tell he loved her too. He held enormous sway over Ella. It had taken all of Io's subtle and not-so-subtle prodding to split them apart in the first place. She couldn't afford to go up against him again. Sooner or later, Ella was going to choose him over her.

Io knew that love was simply a series of chemical reactions in the brain; she had seen it firsthand in dozens if not hundreds of mammals. However, that didn't mean it made humans any less foolish for following these emotions. Most of the greatest senseless acts in history were done in the name of love.

Io knew better than to allow that to happen. While she had come to an understanding with Ella and actually considered the girl her partner, or at the very least her ally, Io was still looking out for Io. And if it was to her benefit to keep Ella and Nabin apart, then that was what she intended to do.

The question was, how far could she push the girl? If it were up to her, they would be on a flight out of Tokyo tonight, fleeing to a rural area with few humans and even less Quasing conflict. Io had never been truly comfortable staying in heavily-populated centers in neutral countries.

That was why all of their passports were from several third-world countries. Io had almost succeeded getting Ella to go to Tanzania the first time around, her preferred outcome. The girl just couldn't bear being so far away from people. The compromise had been Tokyo, a city so densely populated that it would be just as difficult to find someone there as in the middle of a rainforest. An urban jungle was the next best thing. At least that was what Io had reasoned. Apparently she had been wrong.

The question now was, how had Nabin located them? What else did he know? What was Roen Tan, a very important and influential human, doing with him? His presence obviously made it important Prophus business, especially if he was being supported by a full team of agents. The Prophus wanted something from them, but what? It had to be from Io; what could they possibly want with a street kid like Ella?

Io set herself to find out. She moved the girl over to the table and powered up the laptop. A few keystrokes and authentications later, she was back in the Prophus network. The first thing she did was tap into the missive about the safe house under construction. Everything looked by-the-book in the report. However, Ella did make a very good point; that was an awfully strange safe house, far too nice. Which meant it wasn't one. And that the whole thing was a setup.

Io began to cross-reference the background information on the estate where they had run into Roen Tan. The first unusual thing that popped up was the lack of relevant information regarding it being in such an affluent part of the city. That meant the Prophus had scrubbed it. That made sense, since the location was being re-purposed, but again, why was such a relatively extravagant and ostentatious location chosen in the first place to be a safe house?

It took several layers of sleuthing for Io to find out who owned the address. It wasn't the Prophus, but the Rafaeli, a wealthy Brazilian family that operated the revived Kolynos Oral Care Company, the largest toothpaste company in South America. The Kolynos also happened to be one of the large corporate backers for the Prophus.

It didn't take too much more digging for Io to discover a certain Agent Pedro Rafaeli, five years out of the Rio De Janeiro Academy. Report: Hekla Einarsson's field scout team. Specialty Operations: surveillance. Current location: classified. Recent reports: classified. This was strange. Emily Curran's status as an active host agent should have given Io full access to Pedro's personnel files.

None of the background information mattered. How had they tracked Ella to Tokyo? More importantly, how had they known Ella would try to raid that estate?

Io stopped typing. Of course. She slammed the laptop shut. Emily Curran's account being left open was not an oversight. Tao never did trust her after India. She really hated to prove that smug low-standing Quasing right.

Io looked at the go bag haphazardly tossed in the corner. She could be on a plane to Africa – anywhere on the continent – by the time Ella woke. Actually she doubted that. It had been hard enough maneuvering Ella's body from the train station home. Trying to move her body to Narita from here would likely get them both run over by a car.

No, there had to be another way.

Io began to formulate another plan.

CHAPTER TWENTY

The Other Law

Training at the Academy was not without its merits. There were areas in which Ella excelled. She was deadly with knives, possessing quick reflexes and having a natural talent for gauging range and reactions. She had training from Crate Town in Escrima, but she took these skills to new heights at the academy.

Ella also developed a sharp eye for detail and was quick on her feet. She was decisive and adaptable, and rarely cracked under pressure. She often thought outside the box and found unique solutions and effective angles to problems. In essence, she possessed the intangibles that were important in a good agent. She just did not possess any of the tangibles.

It took less than a day for every door in Tokyo to shut in Shura's face. Every government agency that Shura had ever engaged with canceled their scheduled meetings. All attempts through her Genjix and Indian government channels were met with silence or outright hostility. Shura was not only completely cut off from the Japanese government, but any attempt to establish new lines of communication were likely to get her arrested.

Rurik had laid a clever trap. If she had failed to escape it,

Kitaro would have delivered her. But since she had escaped, she was now wanted by every major agency in the country. He had outmaneuvered her. He may have even succeeded in trapping her in Japan. She had to hand it to her rival – he was thorough. Frankly, Shura was more impressed than angry. She didn't think Rurik had it in him. She appreciated cleverness, something he had failed to display again and again over the past few years.

Now that the government was closed off to her, Shura turned her focus to the other ruling structure of Japan. In every country, every province, every city, there were two rulers: the elected officials, and the crimelords. If Shura had any hopes of finding the girl – especially in a maze as dense and massive as Tokyo – she would need to enlist the yakuza.

The Genjix had historically not worked well with the criminal elements of human society. Too messy, too inefficient and too difficult to control. Those tended to be more a Prophus sort of relationship.

It took a few days for her to leverage Abbi's contacts to request meetings with all four of the major crime families in the country. Shura was beginning to understand and appreciate the power and advantages of a strong and resilient spy network.

She was disappointed but not surprised to learn that Rurik was also a step ahead of her here. The two largest yakuza families, the Yamaguchi-gumi and the Sumiyoshi-kai, flat out refused to meet with her. She was not given the opportunity to plead her case or outbid her opponent. They offered their apologies, and told her messenger that honor would not allow it. Chances were it was also because the Japanese crime families were notoriously conservative and careful, and a civil conflict between two powerful Genjix brought too much heat for them to bear. At least they were polite about it, which was more than she could say for the Japanese government.

The third family, the Inagawa-kai, had demanded an astounding sum just to arrange a sit-down, citing the risk of talking to a terrorist, as well as falling into the crosshairs of the police, the military and Rurik's faction. At first Shura was furious, but the more she considered their position, the less she could blame them. She was radioactive right now.

By evening, Shura and her remaining people had fled their swanky arrangements at the Ritz Carlton and had moved into a small pod hotel on the northern fringe of the city. Their temporary home was now three stacks of two pods each that served as their beds and living arrangements. The five of them shared a single bathroom and tiny kitchen. Their only pieces of furniture were a two-person sofa and a four-person dining table that only had two chairs.

It was a steep drop from what Shura had grown accustomed to, but she didn't mind. It was still a far cry better than many of the nights she had spent during the war. Currently, four of them were clustered around the table, watching a projection of the news off a tablet while Kloos hogged the bathroom. The man had been spending an inordinate amount of time in there lately. Apparently Japanese food did not agree with him.

The news was displaying a three-dimensional video of Shura, in a sheer shoulderless peach dress with a plunging neckline, holding a champagne flute limply in her hand. Shura couldn't be certain when that image was taken, but she guessed it was from a surveillance video taken during the Adonis vessel networking retreat at the Forbidden Palace four months ago. Rurik was playing dirty by using internal footage.

Shura ground her teeth. This was unacceptable. She had a mind to complain to Weston about it. Not only was Rurik aiding the enemy by releasing possibly sensitive information about a high-standing vessel, she would likely never be able to work undercover again, much to the detriment of the Holy Ones.

You have not gone undercover in two years. Besides, you have done far worse to Rurik than make him Internet-famous.

That was true. She had burnt down his yacht last year.

And stolen what amounted to nearly three hundred million euros worth of goods.

"And killed his uncle."

You also stole his uncle's dog.

"I did no such thing. I rescued the poor thing. Little fuzzy Vitali would have eaten the corpse and starved if I had not done so."

Renaming the dog after the uncle was in poor taste.

Shura shrugged. She continued staring at the surveillance video of her standing next to a champagne waterfall. She would engage with a small gathering of ambassadors before heading for the door. Shura remembered assassinating the North Korean Minister of Information shortly after leaving the room. Rurik at least had the decency to blot out all the other Adonis vessels. Only the projection of her was clear for the whole world to see.

She walked to the window and looked out onto the streets below. She would stick out like a sore thumb in the city. If her long blonde hair and sharp nose didn't give her away, her athletic build and deep eyes would. There were just too many ways to mark her in one of the most CCTV-ed cities in the world.

She twisted her neck around. "Haucer, Valié, I need supplies."

Her people were back within the hour. Shura got to work. The first thing she did was take a blade to most of her hair, leaving just enough for her to dye dark brown. She had considered going full bald – she had always wanted to – but that would attract unwanted attention as well.

Next, she took several types of makeup and made her face less like that of an Adonis vessel. Symmetry was the foundation of beauty, so she set out to disrupt the mirror halves of her face. With clever use of cosmetics and minimal prosthetics, she made one eye much larger, made her mouth appear to drop off on one end, and made her high cheekbones uneven. Lastly, she dirtied her complexion, making it angry and blotted, busy and attention-seeking to the point it pushed the prying eyes away.

She turned to the others. "What do you think?"

Kloos gave her one look and grunted. "You're still pretty good-looking, but at least you don't look quite like you any more."

"Good enough." Satisfied, she wiped the work clean and started over, meaning to practice until she was able to apply it within minutes.

There was a knock on the door.

Four sets of weapons were drawn. Shura put down her cosmetics reluctantly. "Someone answer it. If it were the police, they would have kicked the door down by now."

A few seconds later, Valié returned with a boy of about ten or eleven. The boy walked up to Shura and offered her a deep bow. "The honorable Aizukotetsu-kai agree to a meeting. Because of your delicate situation, they require the meeting to be at a time and place of their choosing."

A trap?

"It is likely. Nothing comes easy in Tokyo, it appears," she thought to Tabs. She held her sarcastic remark at the tip of her tongue when she spoke as she waited for the inevitable outrageous demands to meet. "What are the terms?"

"No other, Adonis. They only offer their word."

That was good enough for Shura. Leave it to the yakuza to have more honor than local law enforcement. Shura looked at the boy. "Tell your oyabun I look forward to meeting him."

The boy bowed. "You are to come with me now."

Shura exchanged glances with Kloos. "May we have an hour? Not all of our people are here."

That was a lie, but neither Shura nor Tabs knew much about this particular yakuza family.

The boy shook his head. "You must come now. Leave your weapons."

"What's the hurry?" asked Kloos.

"Oyabun says come now or come never," replied the boy.

That is clever. It puts us at a disadvantage, gives you no chance to prepare and puts them fully in control.

"Very well," said Shura finally. "Lead the way."

Are you sure about this? I do not like it.

"I do not either, Tabs, but we have few other options."

The boy was patient enough to at least let them get dressed. After that, he ordered them around as if he were a fledgling crime boss himself, marching them at a brisk pace into a waiting limousine. Shura and her people climbed inside an interior with fully tinted windows.

Haucer tapped a fist on the glass. "Bullet- and shatter-proof."

Roxani fiddled with the sunroof. It was bolted shut.

Kloos checked the window divider to the front seats. It was the same. He shrugged and sunk into the cushions. "It appears we've willingly crawled into a cell."

"A cell with champagne." Shura reached over and plucked a bottle from an ice bucket. She poured herself a drink and offered a glass to the others. If the yakuza were planning on double-crossing her, at the very least they were doing so with class.

The limousine began to move. The tint in the windows was so dark they couldn't even see the shadows outside in spite of the sunshine. All they could feel was the acceleration, deceleration and centrifugal force when the limousine made a turn.

Even traveling blind, it didn't take long for Shura to determine where they were heading. Tabs was able to match their movements to a map of Tokyo she had memorized. What they lacked in a tangible body, the Holy Ones more than made up for with an eidetic memory and breathtaking analytical abilities.

We are heading south toward downtown Tokyo. The business district, likely the Aizukotetsu-kai corporate headquarters.

While she was confident things wouldn't take a turn toward violence, Shura and her team prepared as if they were wading into another fight. The Aizukotetsu-kai was still a powerful organized crime family, and she had been completely wrong about the Tokyo police.

By the time the limousine had come to a complete stop, Shura and her people were ready for all contingencies. The first surprise came when the doors opened and sunlight bathed the dark limousine interior. They were greeted by two rows of yakuza forming a line to the door.

The yakuza bowed, knees bent and hands resting on their thighs. Shura noted the scabbards hanging off each yakuza's hip: ceremonial swords, which, while a nice touch, were a bit unusual. Yakuza were neither ninja nor samurai, and while they were steeped in tradition and ceremony, they were not nostalgic. In previous centuries, the yakuza had ditched their swords the moment guns made them obsolete, and had quickly transitioned to hand grenades – or pineapples, as they were called – the moment Japan outlawed guns.

They entered the office building and were promptly escorted up an escalator to an elevator. The Aizukotetsu-kai were the fourth-largest yakuza family in Japan, although they were more of a loose conglomeration of smaller gangs than their larger counterparts. Still, they followed a strict code of honor along with the other families, unlike the Tokyo police.

You do not intend to let that go, do you?

"Not until the day I die. God help them the day I take control of this country."

A woman with some degree of authority, in her mid-twenties by the look of her, greeted them at a section of the hallway that clearly delineated the public and private areas of the offices. She offered Shura a deep bow and held it for just a moment longer than necessary, then bade them to follow.

"Who is she, Tabs?"

According to our limited intelligence on the Aizukotetsu-kai, she is Bashira Nishiki, the granddaughter of the leader, heir to the crime family.

"So she is someone worth knowing?"

Possibly. The report also says that the oyabun is in poor health, and his granddaughter has only tenuous support among the other bosses in the family. The odds of her surviving the succession are low.

"Pity." Shura wanted more female leaders in the world, even in a crime family. Especially in a crime family, actually.

They were escorted through a modern and updated corporate space to the private offices of the Aizukotetsu-kai. Shura hid her amusement with how loudly, proudly, and publicly these offices were kept. Leave it to the Japanese for even their organized crime to hold office hours.

They passed several sections filled with state-of-the-art systems and monitors hanging from the ceilings displaying everything from up-to-the-minute information from the Nikkei indexes and commodity trades to the latest celebrity gossip and weather. All of this information was being absorbed and analyzed by a small army dressed like they worked at an investment bank. These were the modern yakuza.

Shura and her team were escorted through a set of double doors that transported them into the past. Gone were the technology and screens, the marble floors and luminescent white lights. The room they entered was candle-lit with shoji screens on all four sides and tatami mats on the floor. In the center was a low table with a set of steaming tea cups.

An older man, handsome, with a long face and short sheet-white hair, sat at the table. He looked exactly how one would expect a yakuza to look: tailored black suit and a pocked clean-shaven face. Tattoos fell out of his cuffs and crawled up his neck above his semi-unbuttoned collared shirt. His pinky finger was a stump.

"Wait outside," she said to her people.

Kloos nodded, and Shura closed the screen door behind her. She walked to the center of the room and bowed, keeping her eyes lowered until the man gestured for her to join him. Shura did as asked, making sure to apply just the right amount of deference. Her efforts were not lost on her host.

Shura picked up the pot. "May I?"

The old man appeared amused. "Please do."

She poured them both tea, displaying perfect training in the traditional tea ceremony. Tabs, who had spent several centuries in Japan during the Tokugawa Shogunate, was on hand to help.

He chuckled as he accepted her offering. "I see the Genjix prepare their diplomats well."

"I am not a diplomat," she replied. "I am a warrior."

"War is the last resort of diplomacy."

"Or the lack of it. In any case, I trust that will not be necessary today."

"Let us hope."

She raised her cup. "I am Shura Mengsk, Adonis vessel of the Genjix and ruler of the India territory."

"I am Tanaka Nishiki, leader of the Aizukotetsu-kai. You have made large problems since you arrived in Japan just a few days ago. If this is the way the Genjix operate, then I fear our business is already concluded. The yakuza cannot have this trouble."

"A series of unfortunate events," she replied. "I assure you, upheaval is not my intent. I wish to complete my business and be on my way."

"That is not what was broadcast on every television screen. Explain yourself."

Shura did, and in great detail. All of this Tanaka probably already knew. One did not rise to the top of a yakuza family by listening to one-sided truths. He was comparing her account to his own information, and probably testing her trustworthiness. The leader of this family was also putting her through the motions in order to glean more information about her. Was she hot-headed? Angry? Nervous? What were her verbal tics? Did she talk fast? Did her hands quiver?

In every case, Shura showed him exactly what he would want in an ally and partner. Someone calm, resolute, tested, practical. The only thing she gave away was that she would not be closed off. Closely guarded allies made for poor ones. By the time she had finished speaking, she knew she had him.

Tanaka pondered her words in silence for a good spell before speaking. "I understand your predicament. Now understand mine. You are one of the most wanted fugitives in all of Japan. Doing business with you carries a great deal of risk and could prove costly, so the price for the Aizukotetsu-kai's cooperation will be high.

"I have made inquiries, and my family may have what you seek. Your fellow Genjix made the same request. What he lacks in grace, he more than makes up for in wealth, which he assures me you cannot match. So what else can you offer the Aizukotetsu-kai?"

The man was prepared.

Shura considered his words, thinking about what Tanaka in his old age really wanted. She doubted someone in his position cared much for material things.Wealth and power were drivers for everyone, government and yakuza alike, but Tanaka did not reach this level by pursuing only wealth and power. His health looked questionable, but no more than many his age. He looked to be pushing seventy or eighty easily.

This yakuza family is the only one who has agreed to speak with you. Raise their standing.

Shura bowed. "First of all, I thank you for the great honor of sharing tea at your table. It is one that none of the other yakuza families have bestowed upon me."

"They are cautious," said Tanaka. "Rightly so. For the moment, you are, to put it delicately, an individual most would rather not be seen around. The yakuza of today prefer to move with more subtlety."

"For that," she continued, "I offer your family favored status on all shipping contracts from Indian ports."

Tanaka cracked a chuckle. "That is hardly a generous offer."

"You misunderstand, Oyabun. It is a gift, given freely regardless of the outcome of today's talks."

To Tanaka's credit, he didn't blink, although she could see the calculations behind his eyes. The old man held a good poker face. Finally, he spoke. "Your generosity is appreciated."

That *gift* was amortized to about a billion yen a year, at least according to Tabs's calculations.

"As for your assistance in finding this individual hiding in your city, you are correct. I cannot match Rurik's offer. I won't even try. However, once he pays you, your business with him will be concluded. The next time you cross paths with the Genjix, you will again be a stranger, possibly even an enemy. If you ally with me, then the Aizukotetsu-kai will have a friend for life."

"Friendship is a valuable currency," said Tanaka, "but one that cannot be spent."

"One day soon," said Shura, "the Genjix's influence will fall over Japan. It is inevitable. We understand that the yakuza have a place in this society, but the Holy Ones do not tolerate inefficiencies or disruptions. When that day comes, we will require all yakuza to fall in line."

"Yes," said Tanaka dryly. "We have closely observed what

has transpired with many of the Triads on the mainland."

"The Genjix require order. We need only one representative, one voice who will speak for all yakuza. Those who refuse will be cleansed." Shura paused. "When that voice is chosen, I would prefer to work with those I consider friends."

Tanaka frowned. "Do you have such authority?"

"I will if I find the individual I seek."

Tanaka stared at her for a long while. Finally, he picked up his tea cup. "The Aizukotetsu-kai are always ready to aid a friend."

CHAPTER TWENTY-ONE
Exit Strategy

Not all of Ella's education at the Academy went to waste. As difficult as it was for her to socialize and connect with her peers, she discovered the value of teamwork and operating within a group. She had for most of her life been a lone operator unbeholden or responsible to anyone else. That changed at the Academy. Squad-based work was an important aspect of Academy training. It was here that Ella began to reassess the benefits of running with a crew.

Not all of Ella's experience working with a team was positive. She was once assigned as a squad leader for a three-day exercise in the Outback. Her actions contributed to one of her squadmates getting badly injured. Ella blamed herself. The accident weighed heavily upon her and influenced many of her decisions from that point on.

Ella actually spent the next two days listening to Io and staying close to home. She needed to figure out how to get out of the city and where to go if things went further south, although she wasn't sure how that was possible short of her deadbeat father showing up at her door and asking to move in and borrow money. Her fingers itched for a knife every time his memory popped into her head.

Planning a graceful escape should have been the first thing she did when she arrived in Tokyo. Prepare for the worst. That was what Instructor Frieda, the woman at the Academy who taught mission survival, continually preached in class. Guess she had been right.

Ella should have treated this like a mission all along and prepared for all contingencies. Io had harped on about it constantly, but Ella just couldn't be bothered. It was too much hassle, too much busywork. She had more important things to do. She could take care of it some other time. She didn't realize how soon "some other time" would be.

I told you this a hundred times.

"Yeah, but you like to worry about silly things."

I am obviously right.

"Lunch happens once a day."

That does not even make sense. Besides, that is not even true. There have been many days when you were forced to skip lunch.

"Hush, Alien."

Ella did finally refresh her go bag. She cleared the space in the center of her room and pulled the bed away from the wall. She flattened her stomach, pried the vent free, and pulled out her emergency stash.

As much as she lamented her experience at the Prophus Academy, she had learned quite a bit in her time there. There was an entire class on surviving in enemy territory, and a large segment of their curriculum was dedicated to exit strategies and the art of the escape. Instructor Frieda had always told the class to update their bags once a month. Ella hadn't touched this thing since she had moved into this place.

She rummaged through the contents, pulling out the four passports stowed away. She picked the two for Victoria Khan and tossed them. She really should have found a good forger and updated everything as soon as she had settled, but she never thought she would have to leave so quickly.

The two remaining passports were for Canada or Italy. Both neutral countries, although Canada was a hotbed of Prophus activity. Ella put her passports aside and pulled out the stacks of currencies: euros and dollars, easily changeable. She did a little math in her head on living standards and how much the cash would stretch. It wouldn't go far.

She replenished the dried rations and water bottles, and made sure the clothes she had stashed still fit; they didn't. It appeared she had experienced a mini growth spurt in the past half-year.

After that, Ella spent several hours searching online for a new home. She looked at several major cities: Rio de Janeiro, London, Oslo and Paris. She had always wanted to see the City of Lights. She envisioned some magical city with pretty museums and cafes, full of art, culture and charming men who sat around those cafes all day being charming.

You will run into the exact same problem in those cities as you did in Tokyo. Perhaps it is time to consider less metropolitan locations.

Ella reluctantly agreed. She began going through places she had always wanted to vacation. Places with warm weather and parties on beaches and good-looking buff guys. She especially took a liking to Jamaica. Something about the culture and lifestyle in the brochures really spoke to her. She could already imagine herself lounging on a towel while the clear waters lapped the sand and crawled up her legs.

Again, you will run into the exact same problem. I do not think you understand how this works. A vacation destination filled with tourists constantly streaming through is just as bad as a large city. This is what I was thinking.

An image of a green valley punctuated by rocky crags with a backdrop of snowcapped mountains filled her head. A clear blue lake reflected the clouds rushing across the sky. It was awfully pretty, but also looked awfully boring and lonely.

But safe.

Ella sighed. "Fine. Where is this place?"

Argentina. You will love it. We can go someplace where you will not find another soul for a thousand kilometers.

The next day, Ella checked the exchange rates and looked up ticket prices to Buenos Aires. She didn't even have enough money to buy a ticket. She spent the rest of the afternoon searching for a cheaper route to Argentina. Flying to Chile and then going by bus could work. Perhaps even Columbia. There were really no good options. The fact was Ella just didn't have enough funds left over to escape Japan let alone start over in a new country.

She was just about to break for dinner at Go-To Udon when she received a phone call. A name flashed across the screen: *Fat Leech.* She picked up the phone. "What do you want, Asshole?"

"Beektoria, listen. I've been thinking it over. I was too harsh with you. The damage at the bar isn't too bad. Now that I've had time to cool off, maybe we can try to fix things."

She stared at the phone suspiciously. Even on their best days Asao wasn't this nice to her. "Why?"

Perhaps the money was too good.

"It wasn't that good, Io."

"I just realize that I overreacted in the moment," pleaded Asao. "You and your little friends did come to my bar's defense."

"We ended our arrangement. You threatened to call the police on me," she replied.

"I was angry and hasty," said Asao. "I am wrong. I am sorry. I want to make things right, like before our misunderstanding."

"You called me a worthless irritating hangnail that you were going to clip the next time our paths crossed."

"Don't hang up, please," said Asao. "OK, I admit. I also came across a job. One I think only your Burglar Alarms can pull off."

Ella didn't believe that for a second. "Only us? Stop lying, Asshole. What's the truth?"

"OK, OK," he replied hastily. "Uh, the job is a one-time gig on short notice, and there's no other crews available. You're the last one I can call. The score is just too good."

Greed got the better of her. She did need the money. "How good?"

"Millions of yen. Possibly tens of millions. We need to talk in person. It's safer."

Ella didn't trust Asao. He could be trying to pull a fast one on her. Still, tens of millions sounded nice, and it wasn't as if she had anything else going on. She needed the money badly. If the job was as good as he claimed, then it could get her to Argentina and set her up comfortably with a fresh start. Also, she could leave a good portion for the rest of the Burglar Alarms. Ever since she had decided to relocate, Ella had been feeling a little guilty about abandoning them; leaving them high and dry. At least she could get them one last score to help secure their future, kind of like severance.

Still, Ella was tempted to refuse Asao. They had left on awful terms. Both had said things that made it difficult to look the other in the eye.

Is this your ego or sensibility talking?

"Both," she admitted. "Maybe a little more ego. What do you think, Io?"

I do not like it, we do not seem to have a choice. The money he is offering is the difference between starting over in another country and getting captured by our enemies. Take the meeting, but be wary. Make sure it is in a public place. Asao has always been too greedy for his own good. What is the worst that could happen? If the job is bad or too dangerous, just walk away.

"What's the cut?" she asked Asao.

"Same as always."

"Twenty-five percent for you."

"What?" he sputtered. There was some mumbling and cursing away from the phone. "Fine," he answered finally.

He had capitulated awfully fast. Ella had been prepared to negotiate all the way up to forty percent. He must be desperate. "I'll stop by tonight. You serving dinner?"

"Great, Beektoria. I'll have fresh soups waiting for you!"

Free soup was the best soup, and she was starving. Ella hung up the phone and sent texts to the rest of the Burglar Alarms, asking them to meet her at the World-Famous. The way she figured, it should be up to all of them to decide if they wanted to do this last job together. They had earned that.

No they have not.

"Hush, Alien."

Ella strapped on her blades and hurried out of her apartment. She paused at the front door of the building and waited a few beats. She had been feeling a little tense every time she left her building the past few days. Io had said it was simply a hint of paranoia from the shock of running into Nabin. It was expected and actually healthy for Ella. Her alien was probably right, but she was having a difficult time shaking the unease crawling up and down her arm.

Just in case, when she thought the coast was clear, Ella hugged one side of the street, doing her best to stay hidden and inconspicuous. She thought she did a pretty good job moving from shadow to shadow, crossing the street behind a young family. She reached the train station feeling confident no one saw her.

The train car was crowded with tourists and partygoers heading downtown to start the weekend. Everyone was polite and the passengers orderly as she stepped through the sliding doors. She easily found a seat between a wrinkled grandma with a shopping cart and a kid with a tall mohawk. Both moved aside politely as she sat down.

Ella continued to shift restlessly as the train pulled out of the station. She couldn't shake off the feeling that she was being watched. She looked at the grandma. Could Nabin be following her? Maybe it was him hiding under a lot of makeup sitting right there. A thought occurred to Ella. She would be kind of glad if he was.

A scowl bubbled up on her face at this line of thinking.

I agree. Stop letting your emotions get the best of you.

The short trip from the stop to the World-Famous was a similar exercise. The crowds here were thicker, which made it easier for Ella to move undetected. She reached the World-Famous pretty sure that no one was the wiser. Old, mean Instructor Perkins – who incidentally had flunked Ella in the concealed movement class and forced her to retake it – would have been proud.

She saw Asao standing at the entrance to the World-Famous Bar & Udon, staring into the crowd, tapping his foot in that nervous way he did when business was slow. She waved. He noticed her and tensed. He waved for her to come inside, and then headed back into the bar.

"Does he think I'm going to stab him or something?"

You already tried to do that once. That does tend to leave an impression on someone.

Something gnawed at Ella. She passed by a fancy black car and peeked around to get a better angle to look inside. Nothing seemed out of the ordinary. It looked like a pretty slow night at the World-Famous. She was about to walk into the bar when she decided at the last second to do just one pass around. She crossed to the other side of the street and glanced inside. The bar was mostly empty save for several businessmen in suits at the counter and a few small groups sitting in the booths.

Asao was behind the bar talking to a few of the suits. He looked decidedly stiff. Their eyes met briefly, and then his face reddened and he nodded.

Ella scanned the sparse clusters of patrons and noticed Lee and Hinata's heads. Upon closer inspection, she noticed the rest of the Burglar Alarms were already there as well. A large hotpot was steaming in the center of the table. Asao was true to his word.

Ella began to cross the street to head into the bar. Just then, she noticed Kaoru sitting at the end of the booth. The girl's hands were resting in her lap in a submissive pose, and her head was lowered. She raised her head and looked straight at Ella. It was very slight, but Kaoru shook her head.

Ella stopped in her tracks. The bar was too quiet for the number of patrons in there. There was a weird tension in the room. The businessmen in suits didn't look like businessmen. She caught a glimpse of the ends of a green tattoo falling out of one of the sleeves. Then she noticed a young man trying to hide in the opposite corner. A white bandage was wrapped across his face.

"Oh no."

This is a trap. Get out of here.

She should run. She had no choice, but that meant leaving the rest of the Burglar Alarms to their fates. That never ended well. The yakuza wanted her, not them. If she ran, they would pay for her deeds. The old Crate Town Ella would have been gone in a heartbeat. It was the smart decision, one every lone survivor made every single time. Live to fight another day, or something like that.

Do not be foolish. You help no one if they catch you.

Io was probably right.

Ella retreated two steps, then stopped. She wasn't the old Crate Town Ella any more. That girl without attachments had grown attached to people, to causes. She had made friends, found a family. People who looked out and cared for her. People who had charged into a trap when she was in trouble. Regardless of it all, walking purposely into a trap was dumb beyond all means, and was probably the wrong thing to do. However, doing wrong and dumb things for the right reasons was more important.

"Hey Beektoria, are you coming in or not?"

It was Asao. She had been so lost in thought she hadn't noticed him approach. He tried to sound friendly and casual, but his shaking hands betrayed him. His eyes looked terrified, shifting constantly. They were yelling at her to run. This was her last chance to back out and escape.

Ella, do not go in. If there is ever a time to consider my wisdom, now is it.

"Yeah, for sure," said Ella. "What's for dinner?"

CHAPTER TWENTY-TWO
Survey

To almost universal shock, Ella passed her first year at the Academy. The administrators had considered washing her out of the program several times. No matter what, though, Ella Patel was a survivor, and she did whatever she had to do to see the next sunrise.

I did not think it possible. It meant I had to work harder.

Roen and Nabin lounged on the lawn chairs they had just purchased from the Seico Mart around the corner. Their legs were hanging over the balcony railings, a six-pack of Asahi Extra Dry was chilling in a bucket of ice on a small table between them, and both were holding cups of steaming instant noodles.

Now *this* was starting to feel like the work vacation he had imagined when he accepted Cameron's stupid gig.

He held up his cup of noodles. "What do you think?'

Nabin touched cups. "I can't believe something like this exists."

"I can't believe you've never tried instant noodles before," said Roen. "How is that even possible? What kind of hole have you been living in all your life?"

"One obviously derelict of joy and happiness."

Roen had been outraged when he sent Nabin to bring back dinner their first night in Tokyo, and the guy brought back American fried chicken. Upon closer interrogation, he was appalled to learn that Nabin, who was born and raised in the American South, was a steak, potatoes and American barbecue guy, and rarely explored outside those culinary lanes. The guy liked what he liked and went out of his way to stay in his comfort zone.

"How can you have operated in Asia for five years and only eaten American food?" Roen ranted.

Nabin had shrugged. "What can I say? Asians love fried chicken."

"You're going to die of heart disease by thirty," accused Roen.

Nabin shrugged. "I'm a Prophus agent running missions in Asia. Thirty's optimistic."

That much was true. Roen still felt that it was wrong that Nabin was operating in this region without at least trying some authentic Asian food, so he had been plying Nabin with every sort of Asian cuisine he could get his hands on. Most of the stuff Nabin couldn't stand; the guy had a gag reflex like an infant. He had a visceral reaction to sushi, literally threw up when he tried duck, and somehow even disliked congee. Who the hell hates congee? Roen had called him the worst Asian ever. The Nepalese did not disagree. Fortunately, Nabin did like beef noodle soup, or Roen might have had to kick him out of the Prophus.

Nabin squinted and sat up in the lawn chair. He looked through a pair of mounted binoculars standing between them. "Nope, not our girl." He sat back down and continued failing at using chopsticks as he slurped his cup of noodles.

Tarfur had followed Ella all the way back to her home the night after the incident at the Rafaeli family summer home. Afterward, the team had decided to move from the sewer safe house to the palatial estate. Pedro had protested profusely. The estate was his mother's favorite vacation home, and he hadn't asked for permission to use it. Roen had pulled rank, making up something something eminent domain something. He was loving living above ground, and the only way he would move back underground was if they were burying his decomposing body.

They also rented a tiny place in a mid-rise three blocks away from Ella's apartment, giving themselves a clear line of sight to her building off the main street in the Nishi Kasai district and the train station. The team was now running around-the-clock surveillance on Ella, tracking her every movement, which honestly was pretty disappointing.

They could have just nabbed her, but then what? They couldn't just roll her up in a carpet and toss her into a cargo hold. Besides, there would be big problems if they were caught. He had to admit, he was almost willing to suffer the consequences of kidnapping Ella, except it was illegal and risky and he would likely end up somewhere with a long prison sentence.

Japan was technically a neutral country, so they couldn't depend on the government for help. Even more so, the government probably wouldn't take too kindly to kidnapping. Roen was pretty sure the new Keeper would let him and his team rot in jail, if anything just to teach them a lesson. They needed to convince her to come willingly. Roen figured as long as the girl was in no danger, they had time to wait and see what she would do next.

Apparently, Ella's next move was to flee the country. They easily learned about her plans after tracking her to a couple local stores, a currency exchange, and several pawn shops that the girl was planning to flee to South America. The dead giveaway was when she bought a tourism guide from the local bookstore. Hekla was standing right next to her when she made the purchase. They hadn't pegged exactly which country – she appeared to be exploring several possibilities – but they were fairly confident she was preparing to make her move soon.

That suited Roen fine. Grabbing Ella right when she got off the plane in South America was much easier than trying to nab her here in Tokyo. He initially thought she was going to immediately flee, but for some reason she never pulled the trigger.

Roen was beginning to get impatient. He was eager to end this stupid little mission. He wanted to go home and be with his wife. Jill's retirement had changed everything. Since Jill accepted the job as Keeper, the two of them had spent more time apart than together. Both were married to their work with the Prophus, and true family time was just a few days a year when the world wasn't burning to the ground. It was amazing they had somehow raised as good a kid as Cameron with their crazy schedules, although it was likely more because of Tao – Cameron's Quasing – than anything else.

Jill was probably already back in their home in Oregon. They had the rest of their lives to make up for lost time. Roen could not wait to get started. If that meant he had to do a little kidnapping, would it really be the worst thing he had done for someone's own good?

Cooler heads prevailed, and Roen took kidnapping Ella off the table. He had agreed to let Nabin try it his way, for now, but he was keeping the rope short. For the past two days they had been watching Ella, waiting for her to either make a run for it or find the right opportunity to reestablish contact.

"How will you know when it's the right moment?" he complained for the tenth time.

"It's like porn. I'll know it when I see it," replied Nabin.

Roen grunted as he plucked two more beers out of the ice bucket, and tossed one to Nabin. He was making up for not having drunk a drop of alcohol for the past five years. Jill wouldn't have approved, but Jill wasn't around, was she? "Maybe once she gets over the shock of seeing you. Didn't you know she was going to freak out when she saw you?"

"I honestly didn't think she cared enough to freak out," said Nabin. "I'm a little touched, frankly." He sat up again and peered through the binoculars. "That's her. Did you get that, Josie? Black Cat has just left the nest."

"Damnit, every time I sit down for dinner," Josie's voice blasted into their earpieces. It was her turn to be on the ground level. "Give me a second." Sounds of disquieting slurping came across their comm.

"Where's Hekla's team?" asked Roen.

"She's at the police station talking to her contact. Tarfur had to take Asha to the hospital for a staph infection, and Pedro is getting yelled at by his mum." Nabin grinned. "Apparently his mother was not too pleased that he loaned out her favorite meditation home without permission and now they are threatening to cut him off."

"Poor Pedro and his first-world problems. Can you imagine being so rich that you have a bonus home just to meditate?" grunted Roen. He took the binoculars from Nabin. "Our girl is heading north to the train station. You following, Josie?"

"I have eyes on her," said the Australian. "Oh, oh my." It was followed by muffled chuckles.

"What is it?" asked Roen.

"Victoria is actually trying to utilize some of the concealed movement training I taught at the Academy. I thought she slept through most of my class. Bless her heart."

Roen followed Ella through the binoculars. "She's doing a pretty lousy job."

"I wish I could record this so I could flunk her all over again."

Roen and Nabin eventually lost visual contact with Ella

and relied on Josie to fill in the gaps. The colonel's running commentary of everything Ella was doing wrong all the way to the train station kept them pretty entertained. The girl moved predictably. She was splashing her guilt all over the place. She glared when she scanned the area. She walked in a rush.

"We just got on the train," said Josie. "Victoria is staring intently at the train announcements. She's going someplace downtown. I don't have a good angle."

Roen frowned. "How close are you?"

"We're in the same car on opposite ends. She's so oblivious."

Nabin cracked open another Asahi. "You would think Ella would notice a large Australian woman tailing her, especially considering Josie taught three of her classes."

"Or at the very least Io would pick all that up," muttered Roen.

The door opened behind them and Hekla walked out onto the balcony.

Nabin tossed her a beer. "Come join us."

She cracked it open and pulled up another lawn chair. The apartment didn't contain anything but the lawn chairs and an upside-down cardboard box they used as a table.

Hekla sat down next to Nabin. He offered her a cup of noodles, which she refused disdainfully. "We may have a problem. You heard about the terrorist attack at the police station that's all over the news? Turns out it was Genjix."

Nabin turned to her, two noodles hanging out of his mouth. "Why would they attack the local police? That's the opposite of how the Genjix operate."

"My source is trying to find that out as well," she replied. "He suspects a cover-up and possibly multiple Genjix factions involved."

Nabin looked worried. "Do you think the attack has anything to do with Ella?"

"I don't believe in coincidences," replied Roen.

"The girl got off at the Kabukicho stop," said Josie. There were sounds of shuffling and heavy breathing. "She's moving quickly. Having a hard time keeping up with her. That girl is quick."

"That's the red-light district," said Hekla.

Roen and Nabin pulled out a map.

Josie continued to update her status. "She stopped by a bar. The establishment is called World-Famous Bar & Udon. She's circling the entrance. I'm going to get a better view." More shuffling and microphone static. "Oh, oh."

"What's the problem?" asked Roen.

"We have a situation here. Yakuza by the looks of it. I think our girl's in trouble."

Roen dropped his half-empty beer bottle into the bucket and reached for his coat. He stood up and tried to remember where he had left his boots. By the time he found them, Nabin was already out the door.

CHAPTER TWENTY-THREE
Paying the Piper

Three factors contributed to Ella passing her first year at the Academy. The first was a trait she possessed in abundance that few of the other students could match. The girl had grit. She was, if anything, extraordinarily resilient. That grit had been forged by her difficult childhood, honed to razor sharpness by years of living on the streets in one of the largest slums in the world. Ella Patel had nothing in abundance if not grit and determination.

The second factor was Nabin.

A wave of dread coursed through Ella as she walked into the snake pit that was the World-Famous Bar & Udon. She glanced at the chalkboard out of habit; today's special was Kitsune Udon. Her favorite.

Io was barking rabidly in her ear, imploring her to change her mind and run.

It is not too late. They cannot catch you. You can still flee and start fresh in Argentina if you turn and leave right now!

Begging turned to derision.

Why are you so stupid? Go ahead and get your throat slit. I was tired of your puny body anyway.

As usual with Io, when that failed, it led back to begging.

Please, Ella. For once. Listen to me. I promise things will work out.

There wasn't time for Io to move back onto threats again.

"Too late for that, Alien. Stop yelling and help me figure out how to get the Burglar Alarms out of this mess."

Every single suit at the bar got up and converged on her. Within seconds, she was completely surrounded. Ella chewed on her lip to hide her nervousness. The men clustered around her looked nothing like the ones she had tussled with last week. She didn't realize how young and juvenile Broken Nose and his friends were until she compared them now with the real deal. These yakuza looked like something straight out of one of those crazy gangster movies: older, scarred, seasoned, downright mean.

They are also armed. Half with clubs. The other half have knives. A couple guns. I also count quite a few pineapples.

"The fruit?"

Grenades. The Japanese government has harsh gun laws. They unfortunately have very few on grenades.

"What? That makes no sense."

Ella involuntarily backed up as they crowded her. Two of the yakuza cut off her exit. Not like she was really trying to, but whatever escape Io was hoping for was now officially dashed. Those two shoved her deeper into the bar. Lee and Hinata made to move toward her, but they were quickly crowded out by more rough-looking tattooed men.

There are two behind you, two guarding the other Burglar Alarms, and six surrounding you. I also saw one of the yakuza head into the back room.

"That is a lot."

Yes. You should have listened. Again you did the exact opposite of what you were told. You deserve this.

"Shut it, Alien."

No you shut it. If you had just listened, just this one damn time, we would have been safe. You could have even saved your friends another time. Instead, you knowingly walk directly into the trap with no plan whatsoever. That is the height of stupidity.

"You're the one who told me to meet Asshole in the first place!"

And to walk away if the job was bad. What part of walking away do you not understand?

A figure at the bar who had had his back to her turned around. He had to be the boss. It was an older man, mostly bald with an uneven lumpy head and a horseshoe of white hair along the sides and back of his head. Intricate red tattoo flames crawled up his neck from beneath his shirt. He was wearing a pair of sunglasses that at first made Ella wonder if he was blind. Who wore their sunglasses at night? The man's eyebrows rose and he approached until he towered over her. He lowered his sunglasses and gave her a hard squint.

Ella squinted back, mainly as an act of defiance, but also so she wouldn't stare at the two missing fingers on his left hand.

The older, balding yakuza with the misshapen head and bad hair summoned Broken Nose with a finger. "Masato, is this the one?"

"Yes, Otousan. That's her," said Broken Nose, his head still bowed and his cheeks red. He at least had the decency to look ashamed.

"She's the one who broke your face?"

"Yes, Otousan."

"This is the runt you and your stupid friends couldn't handle on your own?"

"Yes, Otou..."

"Baka!" Lumpy Head slapped his son across the face, sending Broken Nose careening into a booth. For a second, Ella felt sorry for him. Then she remembered him doing the same to his girlfriend, and then she got angry at both of them. With a father like that, no wonder the kid turned out to be such a dirtbag.

Lumpy Head took off his glasses. He wiped them with a handkerchief and slipped them into his breast pocket. He pulled out a cigarette. One of his men lit it, and he took several short drags, his eyes never leaving Ella. "I brought twenty men to deal with one little girl? You don't seem so dangerous."

"Apparently neither is your son," she snapped back, almost reflexively.

Lumpy Head grinned, and then burst into a loud chuckle. His men around him followed suit. It was almost comically villainous for the room to erupt in laughter in such a way. It was also strangely contagious. They weren't laughing at her, but with her? She wasn't sure. In any case, Ella caught the bug and began to chuckle as well.

That was when Lumpy Head smacked her. His backhand swept from his far left and crossed the length of his body. Ella saw it coming a mile away. She could have dodged it. She was about to when Io barked in her head.

Do not move!

This time Ella obeyed her alien; she wasn't sure why. She assumed Io had a good reason to say that, so she stayed still. The back of Lumpy Head's beefy right hand – also missing a pinky finger – struck across her cheek. She felt her feet leave the ground, and then she crashed down hard on her side. The entire right side of her face felt afire. More laughter followed.

"What the hell, Io? Why did you tell me to stay still?"

You are in no position to do anything right now. You will only anger him if you duck his blow. I can also tell you were about to reach for your dagger. That is a death sentence.

Lumpy Head knelt down in front of her. The jerk could really use a breath mint. "I was enraged when I learned that someone had dared attack my son. An attack on him is an attack on all of the Yoshi yakuza. It is a shame that cannot be overlooked."

She sneaked a peek over at Broken Nose. To be fair, he

looked just as terrified and miserable.

"Now I see a runt has caused this shame," continued Lumpy Head. "My son's dishonor cuts far deeper than I imagined."

Ella was confused. "Wait, is that good or bad?"

Keep your mouth shut. Antagonizing him may not be the best solution. You are in enough trouble already.

That was the most obvious and least useful thing Io had said all day in a long list of obvious and un-useful things.

"You are a peculiar creature." Lumpy Head ignored her question. "The western half of Shinjuku district is my territory. Nothing happens here without my approval."

"But I got approval," muttered Ella under her breath, as if that would make any difference. The approval she got to fence goods probably came from a smaller local boss. Definitely not from someone at Lumpy Head's level.

"One of my vassals recently began running around with assault rifles," said Lumpy Head. "Better my people have the weapons than a rival. Still, the Akai Bakus are not the most reliable gang; I prefer those fools not be armed at all, so I questioned how they came across such lethal weaponry. Imagine my surprise when I learn that the same girl who beat up my son also supplied my men with military-grade weapons."

He is being rhetorical. Do not speak. Do not speak. Do not–

"What a strange coincidence," said Ella, exaggerating a shrug. She squeezed her eyes shut and waited for the next smack.

What did I tell you? Why do you never listen?

"I don't know what rhetorical means."

Then ask next time!

To her surprise, the blow never came.

Lumpy Head stood and turned his back to her. "Do you now see my dilemma?"

Ella shook her head. "I have no idea what you're talking about."

"Do I have you beaten for injuring my son, or do I hire you to supply my men with guns?"

Ella spoke slowly. "Both options don't sound that great. How about we just forget all of this and let my friends go?"

Lumpy Head suddenly turned to her rather dramatically. "And then there is one last thing. On top of beating up my son and selling some of my more unreliable men weapons, I receive an order from the head of my family about a certain short, dark-skinned girl, who–" he waggled a finger at her "–fits this description."

Oh no.

The yakuza boss ticked his fingers. "A dangerous girl who not only is unafraid to quarrel with yakuza, but also turns around and sells them weapons. Who is being sought by the head of the Aizukotetsu-kai, with quite a handsome sum on her head." He tsked. "You are an interesting girl. Especially once I discovered what makes you so very special."

He signaled to his men. Two picked her up by the arms while a third approached with a Penetra scanner in hand. The stupid thing began to scream beeps at her.

Ella's stomach sank. This was worse than her worst-case scenario. She was prepared to get beaten up for what she had done to Broken Nose, or have to pay restitution. She was even ready to accept a job from the yakuza. But what she hadn't considered at all was getting kidnapped and sold to one of the Quasing factions. If this was Nabin's doing, she was going to kill him.

Ella tried to make a break for it. It was far too late. A smack to the side of the face stunned her, and then a pair of big meaty hands lifted her off the ground. An arm wrapped around her neck like a vice, locking her head in place.

"Let me go," growled Ella, thrashing futilely. "At least let my friends go."

Lumpy Head looked over to his side and nodded. "We have

no more use for them. Consider their freedom payment for your cooperation."

I cannot believe you are going to sacrifice me for your stupid friends. The yakuza would have let them go anyway. All you had to do was disappear until this blew over.

"I can't risk that, Io."

Lumpy Head turned his back to her. "Take her to the warehouse and put her under guard. Make sure no harm comes to her until that Genjix woman arrives."

What Genjix woman?

Ella repeated Io's question.

Lumpy Head smirked. "You are apparently quite popular. Not only is there a price on your head, it appears the fortune of the Aizukotetsu-kai rests upon your capture. Take her away."

This is worse than I suspected.

Ella began to holler as six burly yakuza picked her up. They disarmed her by unstrapping her harness off her body and carried her to a waiting van. One opened the doors and the others tossed her inside. Ella landed roughly on her side and groaned. The five climbed in while the sixth closed the door.

There was a loud bang, and then the doors swung open violently. A pair of hands reached into the van and yanked one of the yakuza by the collar, sending him flying out into the alley. A large pale woman in a tracksuit jumped inside, her arms swinging. The van became a tornado of bodies and punches and screams. They dropped Ella to focus on the intruder.

Ella caught a glimpse of a familiar face and froze. "Instructor Perkins?"

The Australian was currently tangled up in a weird wrestling match with three of the yakuza in the small enclosure of the van. She yelled at Ella, "Stop standing there and get out of here, you bloody idiot!"

This time, Ella didn't hesitate.

She grabbed her knife harness that had been haphazardly tossed in the corner. She dove out of the van and took off, straight into the waiting embrace of someone who wrapped his arms around her waist and lifted her off the ground. Ella wiggled her arms free and slapped her hands on his ears. The man's knees buckled, and they both crashed to the hard cement. Ella rolled to her feet first and stomped on the man's face. She looked back at Perkins, who was still tussling with the three.

"Should I help her?"

Forget her. Just leave.

Another enemy appeared and charged. This time, Ella was ready. She drew one of her throwing knives from the harness and brandished it. Big scary yakuza thugs bleed just the same as their baby versions. The man saw that she was armed and pulled out his pistol.

"Your boss says you can't hurt me," she yelled.

The guy hesitated and momentarily lowered his weapon. Ella swung the harness at his head as a diversion and then attacked. A poke to his side made him drop his gun. A slash to the front of his knee sent him falling face first into the ground.

Time to go.

"Right."

Ella made it halfway down the alley when two more yakuza blocked her escape. She skidded and tried to run back. She had returned to the van when another suited tattooed asshole appeared. Ella juked left. The man mirrored to block her path. She pulled her dagger and aimed straight for his gut.

You are leaning too far forward.

The man stuck a leg out and tripped her, sending Ella flying head-first into the wall. She barely had time to throw her arms up to cushion the impact before she bounced off and fell to the ground. Groaning and groggy, she reached for her blade, but he kicked it away.

He pulled out a baton and was about to crack her skull when all of a sudden he flew out of view. There was Instructor Perkins again, breathing heavily and bleeding from the side of her head. The instructor scowled at Ella. "Seriously, what the bloody hell are you still doing here? I told you to run." She offered her hand.

Ella hesitated, but allowed Perkins to help her to her feet. When she tried to release her hand, Perkins held on tight.

"You stay with me," her former instructor growled.

"Let me go." Ella tried to pull away, but Perkins's vicelike grip held.

Ella threw a punch. That was a mistake. Instructor Perkins brushed it aside and pushed her hard into the wall. "I am not in the mood for one of your tantrums, Victoria," she spat. "You're staying right next to me until we get out of this mess."

Something hit Instructor Perkins from the back, staggering her. She let go of Ella as more yakuza poured out of the World-Famous. They were joined a second later by two men who rushed to Instructor Perkins's defense. The alleyway had turned into a full-on battlefield. Ella scrambled to her feet and looked at the alley entrance, where another melee had erupted.

"Who are all these people? Why is everyone fighting? Did a war just break out?"

Sort this out later. You need to not be here. It seems the Prophus and Genjix and yakuza are all after you. This city is too dangerous for you to stay even one more day. You need to be on a plane tonight.

That sounded like awfully good advice. Everyone was too busy fighting everyone else to notice her. Ella crawled under the van and moved to the opposite side. When the coast seemed clear, she scrambled to her feet and took off, running away from the fighting. She reached the end of the alley and glanced back one last time. Perkins was still there, alongside those two men. On the opposite end to the alley, more fighting had spilled into the street.

For a second, she thought she caught a glimpse of Nabin. Part of her wanted to stay and help him, but Io was right. It didn't matter. They were all after her. She had to get away from everything. Ella sprinted as hard as she could away from the World-Famous.

This time, she didn't look back.

CHAPTER TWENTY-FOUR
All Hell

Nabin Bhattarai was a Prophus agent on Cameron Tan's team. Ella had met him when the team conducted the Crate Town operation, and they had struck up a friendship that led to a romantic relationship.

Human relationships, of course, are difficult enough as it is without having to deal with distance and immaturity and the presence of an alien being. Times were turbulent, and the odds were stacked against them.

They were deeply in love, however, and they made it work. At least for a little while.

Roen punched a long-faced yakuza squarely in the jaw, and shook his hand. That nut was a tough one to crack. Roen must have punched him a dozen times before the guy dropped. Once, he could do it in one. Two, tops. Now... He stared at his throbbing hand. He may have broken it on the guy's face.

Roen looked around him for someone else to fight. Fortunately, he was fighting alongside Nabin and Hekla. In the time it had taken him to knock out this one gangster, the two had managed to take down five between them.

"Where's Ella?" shouted Nabin.

Roen pointed down the alley. "There's Josie."

The colonel was getting the worst of it against a lone assailant, he had size on her, not to mention there were already half a dozen bodies lying in the street. The colonel folded from a punch to the gut and fell to a knee. The yakuza, towering over her, drew a long knife.

Roen took off, sprinting as fast as his tired legs could take him. He knew right away he wasn't going to make it in time. It was in situations like this that he wished he had a gun, but the team had decided it was too risky to carry one on the streets of Tokyo. Not to mention poor Roen's eyes made any target over ten meters away and smaller than a hatchback a risky proposition.

Just as the yakuza was going to bring the point of the knife down to the back of her neck, Pedro appeared from behind the van on one side, Tarfur on the other. The two men, built like linebackers, rushed and smashed into him, sending him flying through the air. He was actually limp and unconscious before he even hit the ground. They helped Josie to her feet, then all three were immediately swarmed.

Roen tried to reach them, but he was attacked by another guy who looked young enough to be his grandson, if his damn son would ever get around to meeting a nice girl. Had he even finished puberty yet? He was tall and gangly, but he moved as if he had two left feet.

He made short work of the kid. Roen slid outside an amateurish punch and stuck out his hip to knock the boy off balance. Roen grabbed the poor sap's wrist, folded his elbow, and threw him onto his back. A stiff elbow to the temple finished him off.

He paused for a moment to admire his handiwork and perfect technique. "Whattaya know," he grinned. "I still got it."

He continued a couple steps toward Josie before encountering a mountain of muscle. The guy-who-still-got-it assessed this new beefy threat and wondered how much "got" he actually had left. A hip-check wasn't going to work on this big boy. He looked as if he stole everyone else's lunches. The yakuza no-joke pulled out a pair of nunchakus. Roen almost laughed in his face until the guy started whipping it around his body. Big Boy here may have watched too many Samurai Sunday flicks, but he knew how to use them.

"I will never live it down in the afterlife if I get sent to the Eternal Sea by a guy pretending to be Bruce Lee," he muttered, trying to measure his distance.

Big Boy was surprisingly fast. Roen felt the wind kiss his chin as the end of the nunchaku just missed breaking it. He barely dodged a vertical swing and gave the man a sharp punch to the liver that would have dropped most people. At least in his younger days it would have. Big Boy barely registered the blow as he swung the nunchaku outward. It clipped Roen on the elbow, making his entire arm go numb. He stumbled, and Roen's foe pressed his advantage. Roen fell onto his backside and crab-walked backward as Big Boy barreled toward him. He watched the man's churning feet and then snapped his foot out, nailing the yakuza in the balls. Roen was never one who worried about fighting dirty, especially as he got older.

Big Boy didn't take the groin shot well. He stumbled forward and collapsed onto Roen, completely pancaking him. Then he began to flail in pain. Roen was in very real danger of suffocating under the weight. He managed to grab a fistful of Big Boy's ear and pull. Big Boy shifted just enough for him to scramble out. Roen grabbed the discarded nunchaku and swung it down on Big Boy's head, ending his night.

All the yakuza were down in various states of consciousness. Tarfur was treating a pretty beat-up Josie, Pedro was checking the bodies to make sure they weren't getting back up, and Nabin was frantically searching the alleyway, presumably for Ella.

"Everyone alive?" he asked.

"More or less," said Hekla. "Colonel Perkins's ankle is swollen. You look pretty beat up." She held up a hand in front of his face and moved it left and right. "Can you follow my finger?"

He wouldn't be able to follow a finger that close on a clear-minded day, let alone after getting his head banged up. He tried his best anyway. He passed, barely. Hekla helped him up.

"Are the premises secure?" he asked. His answer came in the form of eight more yakuza flooding out of the bar. The two groups lined up and glared at each other. Weapons were pulled out. Aggressive eye-rolling feints of intimidation were displayed. It was like a low-budget racist version of *West Side Story*.

"Where's Ella?" growled Nabin.

"Where is the girl?" shouted the oldest and best-dressed, who Roen reckoned was their leader, at the same time.

Both sides looked confused, and then testosterone took over, and they began to inch closer to each other. Nabin, fists clenched and veins bulging out of his neck, snarled like an enraged badger about to tear through a hen house. Conflict appeared inevitable.

But for what, if neither had Ella?

"Whoa, whoa, stop," barked Roen, throwing his hands out and stepping in between the two groups. He pointed at Nabin who was by far the most aggressive right now. "Especially you, peacock. Put your feathers away."

"Why are you singling *me* out?" sputtered Nabin.

Roen turned to the one he presumed was the leader. "You don't have her?"

The bald yakuza looked taken aback and shook his head. "No, I thought she was with you."

"I thought we were rescuing her from you," answered Roen, looking at his people, and then back at the yakuza. They were outnumbered, but he was pretty sure the Prophus could take them. There was a brief, awkward silence. "Well, if neither of us have her, do we still have to fight?" he asked.

The yakuza pointed at the bodies on the ground. "You attacked my men."

"Fair enough but…" Roen held out a finger. "We don't actually know who attacked whom first. Since we're both after the girl and she's not here, let's just call it a draw and go our separate ways."

For a moment, Roen thought he had gotten through to them. One of the underlings whispered in the main guy's ear. He shrugged and nodded and seemed to be telling his men to stand down.

Roen grinned and turned to his people. "See, who says diplomacy is dead–"

One of the yakuza pulled out a pistol. Someone cried out a warning, and then a sharp pain punched him right above his heart. The Kevlar underneath his jacket dispersed most of the impact and probably saved his life, but it still hurt like hell.

Roen gritted his teeth as everything went black, the shock of pain threatening to shut down his brain. Patience, experience and will took over, pushing through the noise from his screaming nerves. He allowed himself two short beats to catch his breath, then he forced his creaky, achy body to move.

A younger Roen would have tried to get up and join the fight immediately, and would have likely fallen over or gotten shot again before he had gathered his wits. Older Roen rolled onto his side and tucked his knees under him, giving himself one more beat for the wave of dizziness to subside. When he was ready, he surveyed the battle that had unfolded after that sneak attack.

The yakuza were paying dearly for their actions as the Prophus agents ripped through their ranks. Tarfur had tackled the jerk who shot him and was slamming his head into the ground. Hekla had somehow found a broomstick and speared a chubby man with the dull end, which was actually quite an impressive feat. Nabin was going berserk and had barreled straight into the bulk of the yakuza and was making silly putty of everyone within arm's reach.

For the first time, Roen got a front row seat of Nabin in action; he moved a bit like Cameron, albeit a shadow of his son. Slightly slower, less powerful and not quite as fluid. Roen's chest puffed a little. That was expected, since Cameron had personally trained his elite team. And everyone knew who had trained Cameron. Actually, everyone assumed Tao had trained Cameron, but Roen knew better.

He was about to join the fray when firm hands held him down. Josie hovered over him, shaking her head. "Stay down, Makita... I mean, Roen." She almost spat the last word. She still had not totally gotten over who he actually was.

It wasn't long before the professionally trained soldiers sent the gangster rabble fleeing. Both Tarfur and Pedro had a yakuza in each hand, but Roen ordered them to let them go. What were they going to do with prisoners, lock them up in the bathroom?

"Are you injured, sir?" asked Hekla, once the last of the yakuza were gone. "There's a hospital four blocks away. We can–"

Roen waved her off and hid his grin. He tried to appear nonchalant. "I've gotten worse hoeing my garden."

That was a big fat lie, but he would be damned if he showed weakness or age in front of his subordinates. Besides, there was something weird about getting shot that made him feel alive. It had been almost ten years since it had last happened, and he sort of stupidly relished the pain. At the very least, he could brag about it to Jill when he got home. She was going to be so mad. He couldn't wait. If he ever got home that was.

Nabin was rummaging through the van and searching the ground, repeatedly calling Ella's name. There was a heartbreaking desperation to his voice. Hekla appeared a moment later with a scared group of young people. Roen instantly recognized the girl who had clubbed him a few days ago with the hammer. Then he also recognized the little one who had so rudely pushed him aside.

"What are you kids doing here?" he demanded.

"Where's Ella?" asked one of the young men.

"That's the question on everyone's mind," he replied. There was an awkward pause. "So, where is she?"

The group crossed their arms in unison, each staring back defiantly at him. They must have practiced that. In the distance, the sound of a screaming siren began to grow.

"We can't stay, sir," said Hekla. "Remember, neutral jurisdiction, gunshots reported. There's also the matter of a dozen yakuza bodies lying around, and I can't attest to whether they are all still breathing."

"We're about to get more company," said Tarfur, eyeing the red flashing lights at the end of the block.

Nabin, who was still searching for Ella, stomped toward the group. "If anything happens–"

Roen grabbed his arm and held him back. "Don't go off all half-cocked, peacock. These aren't the ones you should be focusing your rage on." He passed Nabin off to Josie, and then turned to the kids. They looked like cornered animals. Roen held his hands up as if surrendering. "You're all free to go. I assume you're Ella's friends. Look, we're on the same side. If you really want to help Ella, help us. There are some really bad people after her."

The kids began to retreat. One of them, an older boy – young man really – turned back and asked, "How do we find you?"

Roen grinned. At least one of them was considering it. "You can find us where we first met."

Then they were gone, scampering back into the bar and out of sight.

"Why did you let them go?" Nabin was still frantic. "They're our only lead to Ella."

"What do you want to do?" Roen shot back. "Haul them into a cell? Interrogate them? They're kids. They'll help us when they're ready." He paused. "Besides, we know where they all live."

"Guys," said Tarfur more urgently.

"Where to now, sir?" asked Hekla.

Roen stared at the flashing lights, then at the other end of the alley. "Ella's last known whereabouts."

"Where's that?"

"Home," he replied, "although I doubt she's stupid enough to go there."

CHAPTER TWENTY-FIVE
Escape From Tokyo

Nabin and Ella's relationship was equal parts bright burning love and hurricane destruction. After India, Nabin was taken off the front line. For a while, he was able to visit Ella often at the Academy.

Nabin helped her study for her tests. He trained her how to shoot. He did whatever was necessary to help her succeed. Most importantly, he had a calming influence on Ella, and was a steady familiar face in a new world where nothing was familiar.

Upon Io's forceful recommendation, Ella had run straight home. Literally ran, as in deciding not to take the train or bus or even hail a cab. She kept to the back streets. The main streets of Tokyo were speckled with cameras, and she couldn't be too careful. Not after what had happened. It seemed the whole world was after her. Her paranoia confirmed. She saw eyes staring at her from everywhere.

Ella took those back streets home as fast as her short legs could carry her, which meant it took over an hour. It was well into the evening by the time she reached the Nishi Kasai district. Her legs burned and her feet ached, but the adrenaline and fear had kept her running the entire time.

She turned onto her street only to find a police car parked at the end of the block. For once, she was happy for police presence. Cops usually set her senses tingling in all the wrong ways, but this time she was grateful for a little law and order close by. They would hopefully deter all the people coming after her.

Why couldn't everyone just leave her alone?

Ella bounded up the front stairwell two at a time, her footsteps clanging on the metal stairs. She only paused to catch her breath once she reached the fifth floor.

A door cracked open and Luna-Roona poked her head out. She scowled. "You're so loud you woke up Yappie." Yappie trotted into the hallway as if he owned the building and began to let Ella have it. The little dog tried to charge her but Luna-Roona scooped him up before he got very far.

"I'm..." began Ella, and then she stopped. No, she was not going to apologize to Luna- Roona for waking up her dumb asshole dog. She exhaled, kept her head up and face straight, and walked past Luna-Roona and Yappie as the old woman and her dog yapped away.

Ella didn't let herself relax until she was in her apartment and the door closed behind her. She poked her head out to the fire escape and checked for anything suspicious. Once she was sure everything was quiet, she reached under her bed and pulled out her go bag.

She couldn't delay any longer. It was time to leave Tokyo.

Ella only needed to add clothing, her laptop and other meager electronics, her weapons, her stash of valuables, and whatever cash she had left and then she was ready to leave. It wasn't much, but it would last her a few months, at least long enough for her to start over again.

By the time she was done, the bag was bulging and stood half her height. Ella slung it over her back and tightened the straps to her body. The weight almost tipped her onto her backside. She shifted it side to side and back and forth until it settled in a comfortable resting position on her back and hips. Ella pressed a button on her left shoulder and the bag slipped off in one smooth motion. Good.

She picked it back up by the straps and stared at its bulkiness. Her entire life was in this bag. She was leaving Tokyo with less than what she came with, and it made her feel as if she had failed. As much as Ella agreed with Io and tried her best to trust the Quasing, she hated the idea of leaving.

She had no choice, however. After what had happened today, she was ready to disappear from history. Argentina was not her favorite destination – not even in her top ten – but at the very least it was far away from everyone, and hopefully peaceful and safe.

I have been trying to find that for us for years. I am glad we are finally on the same page. Trust me, it is for the best.

Ella practiced reaching for her dagger and had a difficult time squeezing her hand between the bag and her back. Growling, she adjusted the holster so the handle stuck out a bit.

Once she was ready to go, Ella gave her home of the past half-year one last look. The place was a dump, but it was *her* dump. She moved the dresser away from the door one last time, and left her apartment for good.

Ella walked to the end of the hallway and proceeded down the front stairs. With luck, she would make it to Narita within the hour, and be up in the air by tonight. She had just reached the landing to the last flight of stairs leading down to the first floor when she noticed a group just outside the front exterior door clustered around the intercom. They were all foreigners and some of them were quite large and muscular, and looked like they meant business.

They do not belong in the building. Go through the alley.

Ella backed away and raced across the length of the second

floor toward the rear stairwell. She had just made it to the stairs when she heard a sharp crack.

Someone just broke the back door lock.

Ella panicked. She retreated up the stairs to her floor and sprinted down her hallway. She stood in the middle, unsure what to do.

Go down the fire escape from your apartment. Hurry.

Ella patted her pants. "I can't. I left the keys in the apartment. I didn't think I needed them."

Well that is just great!

She spun in a circle, frantic for some place to hide. She caught Luna-Roona peeking out from her doorway and bolted for her only chance. The old woman tried to slam the door and nearly succeeded in slicing off three of Ella's fingers. Ella bit her tongue and pushed her way inside.

"What are you doing? Get out of here!" yelled Luna-Roona. "Help, help, I'm being robbed." She began to beat Ella with her throw pillow. Yappy danced around her feet working himself into a tizzy with high-pitched ear-shattering barks. The tiny dog had an amazing set of pipes on him.

Ella ran to the window, hoping the stomping on the stairs would be enough to drown out the shouting and yelping. She yanked it up, and nothing happened. She tried again, the panic creeping up in her gut.

Take a deep breath. Try to break it. Take that sculpture…

Ella wasn't listening. She took a few steps back and made a run at the glass. She heard a crunch, but it wasn't the window. Both her shoulder where she hit the window and her hip where she hit the floor throbbed.

From the ground, she tried to plead with Luna-Roona to be quiet, but the old woman continued to hack away at her with the pillow. Getting to her feet, Ella tried intimidation. She muttered an apology to all three hundred and thirty million Hindu gods and pulled out her dagger, sticking it near the woman's face. She really hoped to not have to use it on the old woman, or worse, the dog.

Ella was planning on threatening Luna-Roona to get her to shut up, but the only words coming out of her lips were, "I'm very sorry about this, but be quiet or I'll–"

Her apologetic tone ruined the effect. If Luna-Roona was intimidated by the blade, she didn't show it. In fact she looked straight at the knife and beat Ella harder. "You disrespectful, horrible girl with your street walking and your drugs…" The old woman raised her voice even louder and smacked Ella with the pillow even harder.

Shut her up. By the blade if you have to.

Ella resisted stabbing an old lady, regardless of how mean she and her dog were. The barking and yelling continued. The stairs did not echo loud enough to block this out.

We are in trouble.

"How much trouble?"

We are screwed.

Ella looked for any place to hide. She tried the closet; it was overflowing with clothing and suitcases. She tried the cupboard; bags and bags of rice. She even tried the refrigerator. That was overflowing with kimchi and curry.

Just incapacitate her and the stupid dog, and then wait out whoever it is.

The thought of clubbing or choking out an old lady was even more discomforting. While Ella was distracted, Luna-Roona went for the door. Ella rushed toward her, but it was too late. The door opened.

Ella played the only card she had left; she begged. She sheathed her knife and dropped to her knees, her hands clutched close together. She mouthed silently. "Please."

The old lady was about to flee the room when she looked down and stopped. Their eyes locked. Ella mouthed her plea again. The hateful woman opened the door anyway and stuck her head out. Ella was resigned to her fate. She heard a woman's voice on the other side. Her name was mentioned.

If the old woman opens the door, get ready to bolt out and run straight for the staircase.

"Do you think I can make it?"

Not a chance. It is too late. I told you to knock the old lady out when you had the opportunity.

"Well that's really helpful."

To Ella's shock, Luna-Roona didn't give her away. She gave the woman on the other side some curt, insulting answers, and then slammed the door. She turned to Ella and pointed at the laundry hamper. "Hide, just in case."

Ella didn't hesitate. She slid her go bag under Luna-Roona's bed and jumped inside the hamper. A moment later, the mound of dirty clothing was tossed back on top of her. The smell of soiled undergarments and body odor and old people immediately clogged Ella's nostrils. As far as hiding places went, this wasn't too bad. It wasn't great by any stretch, but nothing compared to some of the garbage heaps she had had to use in Crate Town.

Ella focused on a bead of light shining through the wicker basket. When she was at the Academy, there was a class on torture. They had spent a whole week on controlled breathing. At the time, like most of the classes, she thought it was stupid. Everyone knew how to breathe, right? Now she appreciated the lesson. She forced her body to relax, sucking in air on a five-count through her nostrils and then letting it seep out quietly through clenched teeth.

One of Ella's hands found the other and squeezed in a futile effort to calm her shaking. She lost track of her breathing and made the mistake of holding her breath, which made everything even worse. Ella's entire body clenched. Her vision blurred and her lungs burned. She fought the urge to kick out and pop her head out of the hamper for air.

Focus on my voice. Close your eyes and push everything out. You are calm and peaceful in your safe place. There is–

"Shut the hell up, Alien! Saying that just makes me want to scratch your eyes out."

The door never opened again, but shouting erupted in the hallway. The walls shook. Screams – from both men and women – soon followed. The noise continued for a few minutes and then fell into a lull. A window shattered. More yells, this time a voice tinged with panic. Then silence. The quiet seemed to last forever, and felt nearly as nerve-wracking as the noise.

Finally the door opened and shut again. Luna-Roona spoke. "You can come out now."

Ella tipped over the hamper and fell out, gasping. She rolled over onto her back and stared at the water-stained ceiling, blinking away the spots in her eyes. Then she noticed that Luna-Roona had a skylight, and she was momentarily very jealous.

The old lady appeared a moment later with a butcher knife in hand. "Have you killed anyone, girl?"

Ella shook her head. She was pretty sure she hadn't, at least not in the past year or so.

The butcher knife disappeared. "That's good enough for me, otherwise I'd open the door right now and throw you to those wolves. That's a big racket for just one girl. What did you do?"

Ella shook her head. "Nothing. There's some bad people after me because of who I am."

That wasn't a total lie.

"And who might you be, Victoria? Princess of the Nile?"

The amusement in Luna-Roona's voice almost made Ella want to tell the truth. "Actually," she replied, "Egypt may have been a monarchy when you were young but–"

She can still throw you out.

That was true. Ella swallowed her retort and sat up. "Why did you help me?"

"I lost a son to gangsters," grunted Luna-Roona. Her voice fell. "It happened almost like this, except at the time they said they just wanted to ask him a few questions. Hasim said things were going to be fine. I didn't want any trouble, so I let him go with them. I never saw my boy again." She wiped her eyes. "Come girl, you're obviously going on a long journey. Do you want to take a couple gulab jamuns with you?"

Ella got to her feet and offered a very traditional Indian bow. "Thank you, Luna. That would be lovely."

Luna-Roona squinted. "What did you call me?"

"Er, Roona?"

"My name is Zoya. I lived next door to you for so long. You know my dog's name, but not mine? You know what? Forget the treats. Get out of my house."

Ella barely had time to grab her go bag. She found herself standing in the hallway, or what was left of it. There were holes in the drywall. Someone had broken a floorboard. The door to her apartment was hanging off its hinges.

"There goes my security deposit," she grumbled, sticking her head into her apartment. She gasped at the destruction inside. All of her furniture was broken and turned over. The window was shattered. Blood was everywhere. "What happened?"

Nothing good. I recommend we get as far away from here as possible. You should have left days ago.

Io was right. She should have run at the first signs of trouble. Her apartment was now a crime scene. Not only were the yakuza, Genjix and Prophus after her, the police would be as well. Ella fled. She bounded down the back stairwell and peeked out the door on the ground level. The alley was deserted. Whoever was here earlier appeared to have left.

Ella's confidence grew. She might actually get away from all these people looking for her. All she had to do now was get to the airport and she'd be free to start her new life, hopefully some place where no one would ever find her again.

A small part of her wished she could have said goodbye to the rest of the Burglar Alarms. She was going to miss them more than she cared to admit. They were a good group of people. Perhaps she could send them a postcard…

No, Ella. No, you will not. In fact, you can never contact them again. Promise me.

"Fine," she sighed. Io was right. That was probably what got Nabin on her trail to begin with. Damn that guy. Damn birthday cards.

Io had been violently against her dating Nabin back at the Academy, often citing how important it was for Ella not to have any baggage to tie her down. She hadn't quite understood at the time but she did now. She had lived alone most of her life. Only in the past few years had she tried another approach and joined a community. She moved to another country and joined the Prophus. She found someone to love and tried to belong to something larger than herself. When that didn't work out, she tried again here with a smaller group. It almost worked, but almost was never good enough. Now Ella realized. People weighed a person down and held them back. Friends and lovers were baggage. Io had been right all along. The best way to survive in the world was by yourself.

I am glad you finally see it this way.

Well, if she was going to start a new life again, she might as well start with a clean slate. This time, she wasn't going to make the same mistakes, and she was going to listen to Io's advice.

You do not know how much I appreciate that.

No sooner had Ella pushed the door open and taken a step outside something flew over her head and her vision darkened. Rough arms wrapped around her body from behind, and she felt the world turn sideways. She tried to scream and kick her legs, but more hands grabbed at her, preventing her from shaking loose. The world jumbled and rocked as she was carried toward the rumbling of a waiting vehicle.

Her captors grunted something she couldn't quite make out, and then Ella was flying. She landed hard a moment later on the ribbed metal bed in the back of a van, knocking the wind out of her. She rolled onto her back and tried to sit up, and then someone cuffed her on the side of the head and everything stopped.

CHAPTER TWENTY-SIX
Doing Things Correctly

Nabin was loving and patient, but at the same time unbending. This was Ella's first love, the first time she thought of someone before herself. It made her a better person, but also a more vulnerable one.

Couple that with the sometimes weeks they had to spend apart from each other, and their relationship was doomed to fail.

There were only two things in the world that absolutely infuriated Shura: cilantro and incompetence. Nothing set off her murderous streak like the taste of soap and the sight of ineptitude. Although she had never killed anyone over cilantro, she certainly had over incompetence. The sad display of the yakuza in action had made her want to commit mass murder.

Tanaka Nishiki, the leader of the Aizukotetsu-kai, had reported that one of his underbosses, Hito Kinata, had information regarding the whereabouts of Io's vessel. The man claimed that his son had personally interacted with the girl. Tanaka had assigned Hito and his gang to assist Shura in the capture. This had all made perfect sense until Shura saw Hito and his group of clowns in action. The number of fingers he was missing on his hand should have been enough of a sign to not hold any faith in that man whatsoever.

As much as Shura had wanted to run point herself, the yakuza had insisted that she stay out of sight. This district was a popular tourist area and Shura had the small problem of being wanted by the Japanese government on terrorism charges. Her picture was plastered all over the city, so keeping away from the action seemed like a prudent move. The local yakuza could talk down the police, but if they caught her at the scene of the crime, nothing would save anyone. Shura was relegated to watching the events unfold behind tinted windows in a black car down the street from the bar.

The trap had started out well enough. The bar owner apparently had some sort of relationship with the girl, and called her in for a meeting. A few of the girl's friends were added as bait. Everything was going according to plan until they dragged the girl to the van to spirit her away to the underboss's warehouse. That was when everything fell apart. Shura's view of the alleyway was partially obstructed, so she didn't get a clear view of what happened next. No sooner had they tossed Ella into the waiting vehicle, a tall Caucasian woman charged in. There was a brief scuffle, but it appeared that the woman single-handedly took down half a dozen yakuza. Then the woman's friends appeared and things got ugly.

It looked like all of the Village People descended upon the yakuza. A dark stout one took down two in that many seconds; an old man who looked like he belonged in a retirement home fought in a way that belied his age; two blond Vikings who looked like they had jumped straight out of history; and a light-skinned Hispanic fought as if he were dancing.

They are moving and fighting like a well-trained military unit, but they each fight very distinctly.

A quick image of a Viking man, the older woman, and the

Indian flashed in her head. *Those three fight in a military fighting system.* A flash of the Hispanic. *Combination judo and capoeira attacks.* Another flash of the old man. *I could be mistaken, but I believe that is tai chi.*

"Can't be another Genjix unit. Unless there was an Adonis involved, none would dare cross my operation, and none of them fight remotely well enough to pass for an Adonis." Shura added. "None of them are attractive enough either."

The yakuza were losing. Shura moved to open the door.

No. The brawl has already attracted a sizeable crowd. Your picture is on the screen just to your left.

Shura looked up at a not-very-flattering image of her scrolling across a ticker. That particular picture of her was taken right after she had crossed the finish line of the Altai Ultra Marathon in Sibera. She scowled; damn that Rurik. That was petty. He was going to pay dearly.

The fighting finally ended with a single gunshot. The gawkers panicked and dispersed immediately. The crowd stampeded in every direction. The driver must have thought along those lines as well, since he began to pull away.

Shura reached over to the front and put a hand on his shoulder. "Not yet."

"We cannot stay," he replied. "We cannot risk being discovered. The police–"

Two of her fingers pinched a nerve at the base of his neck. "Stay, or being discovered will be the last concern you ever have."

A few seconds later, the few remaining yakuza fled out of the alley. A guttural growl crawled up her throat. Good help was so difficult to bribe these days. Shura released her pinch and was about to tell the driver to go when she saw a group of young people run out of the alley and scatter. The bait. They had to be the girl's friends. She chose one of the smaller ones at random and pointed. "Follow that boy."

"But..."

The pinch returned, this time with an added twist that should have made the man feel like his neck was getting hacked off. The driver shrank into his chair with a pained hiss, and obliged.

Shura sat back in her seat and sucked in a long breath. It was just one of those irritating missions when nothing was going her way. First, she got framed as a terrorist, then she learned the people she was working with were completely incompetent, and now her driver wouldn't even drive where he was told.

The car pulled into a slow tail half a block behind the boy. Following him through pedestrian traffic was difficult, but the crowds thinned out the further they moved from the tourist areas.

He is heading to the train station. Cut him off at the next intersection or you will lose him.

Shura waited for a good moment to engage the boy, but realized that she wouldn't get an opportunity in this dense of an area. She instructed the driver to go around the corner and pull up next to him. The car turned just as the boy stepped into the street. Shura jumped out with a bright smile and her arms opened wide.

"Hachikō! I thought it was you. I miss you so!"

Really? That is the name you choose?

"He was a good dog."

Shura roughly embraced the confused boy, smothering his mouth before he could utter a cry. She wrapped her arms around him and pulled him in, burying his head in her chest. He tried to break and push her away, but she held him close, restricting his squirms.

"Come my dear, I'll give you a ride home," she said cheerfully, turning and throwing him into the car. She slid back inside and closed the door. Before he could yell for help, she had the claws of her finger pinching his larynx. "Do something to displease me and I'll rip your throat out."

Tears welled in the boy's eyes.

"Crying displeases me," she said.

He sniffed hard and held his breath, his shoulder-wracking sobs reduced to pitiful whimpers.

"Good," said Shura. "I'm going to ask some questions. You will answer truthfully and directly. Deviating from my questions displeases me. Do you understand?"

He nodded, and then recognition filled his eyes. He looked out the window past a giant screen with her face on it, and then stared back at her. "Aren't you the Blonde Bombshell Bomber?"

Shura kept her face passive, but her entire body clenched in irritation. "Asking questions displeases me."

"You're super pretty."

She let that one slide. "I have a few questions for you, boy. What's your name?"

"Why would someone as beautiful as you want to bomb the police station?"

"I didn't," she said. "I was framed. That was your free question. Where is your friend Ella Patel's home?"

"Was he like an ex-boyfriend? Why aren't you blonde any more?"

Shura slapped the boy. She grabbed and dug her thumb into the soft flesh of his collar at the base of his neck. "Tell me where the girl lives."

It was a trick she had learned during the war. Torture, at its foundation, was little more than catering to a human being's base instincts: embracing pleasure and avoiding pain. All an interrogator had to do was strip away the nuances, the distractions and other motivations, burn away all thoughts and emotions until all that was left was the pure truth. To do so was simple: associate the truth with pleasure. Everything else with pain.

With the practiced movements of a skilled interrogator, she extracted everything she needed to know in two minutes. She learned that Io's vessel Ella Patel lived in the Nishi Kasai district on the second left turn off the main street. Her building had a red awning. She also learned that Pek and Ella met when he had tried to pickpocket her, that she was allergic to mushrooms, always smelled like heavy incense, and that the crew had a running bet on whether she was crazy.

Furthermore, Pek volunteered that he and Ella were part of a crew of thieves called the Burglar Alarms and that they used to work out of the World-Famous Bar and Udon, but then Ella got into a fight with some gangsters, and then she got into a fight with the owner Asao, and then she got into a fight with her ex-boyfriend, and that there was a weird underground apartment with weird vault doors in the sewers between the night market and the docks. He continued to volunteer that he had joined the gang to help his mother pay the bills, but then he realized they were good people and he liked having friends.

Shura learned all of this in the span of ninety seconds. The last thirty she spent getting him to shut up. It was an impressive deluge of information.

When she was done with Pek, Shura pulled out his identification card and cellphone, and held it up. "I know everything about you. Displease me again and I'll do the same to your family, and then I'll slit their throats. Do you understand?" When he didn't reply, she cupped his chin gently and raised it. "Repeating myself displeases me."

He nodded emphatically. His body was shaking uncontrollably as it tried to recover from the waves of pain it had just endured. She was also pretty sure he had soiled himself. It was a good thing this wasn't her car.

"Good." She pulled out a hundred thousand yen and offered it to him. "For your troubles. I'm keeping your phone. Keep your mouth shut, and I'll mail a hundred thousand more to your house."

Pek stared at the pile of money. He touched it gingerly with the tips of his fingers, as if fearful that it would light on fire, or she would smack him again. When neither happened, he snatched the wad out of her hand and disappeared it into his jacket.

Shura dumped the boy in a nearby alley and watched as he fled to the end of the block and turned the corner. She didn't actually think he was going to keep quiet, but it was a possibility. The money was a nice motivation, but what she really wanted him to know was that she knew exactly where he lived without spelling it out. Too big a threat could send him scurrying off to the authorities. Too little, and he'd warn Io's vessel of her arrival. Just enough, with just the right amount of greed mixed in, would keep him in line. All he had to do was nothing.

Shura gave the driver the new address, then called Kloos to meet her in Nishi Kasai. No yakuza this time.

It took an hour for Shura's driver to get through the congestion on the highway. The entire time she daydreamed about razing the city so it could be reborn a Genjix metropolis. How could humanity not embrace what the Holy Ones had to offer after seeing the grandeur of the reborn Hong Kong, Shanghai and Moscow? Couldn't they see that only the Holy Ones could elevate them to greater and more wondrous things? Yes, they had to give up their freedom, but that was more than a fair exchange for exorcising the hell of rush hour traffic.

This heaven on Earth would of course come at the price of the Holy Ones eventually consuming the planet, but no one alive now would be around to pay that price. Humans weren't doing a great job on their own anyway. Humanity might as well seize the moment and burn brightly while it was able.

Shura was the first to reach Nishi Kasai. The rest of her team was stuck in the same traffic, but over an hour behind. She decided not to wait, and ordered the driver to pull into a parking lot and wait for her return.

She adjusted her clothing and headed out. It had been years since she last worked a solo assignment, and she relished the freedom. She had chafed at the restrictions of the security detail that had been imposed on her ever since she took control of India. Kloos was sometimes more a mother hen than a second in command, and while she appreciated his loyalty and paranoia, she often felt like it was a gilded cage. Free once more, this bird was ready to make her own kill.

Shura entered the main street of Nishi Kasai and played the tourist. She wasn't dressed for the role, nor did she particularly look like one, so she had to improvise.

When a street vendor offered her a taste of a masala dish, Shura became honestly curious about the flavor and texture of the food, and took her time sampling the pieces. When a particularly gorgeous lavender shawl caught her eye, she gushed and eyed it with enthusiasm, and spent several minutes haggling on the price.

When are you ever going to wear that?

"The point of pretty things is to admire and own them."

That is never the point.

"It is not a coincidence that every Adonis vessel is tall and beautiful."

That is only because humans react more favorably to beautiful people and are more likely to listen and cater to their demands. If your species preferred small and rotund, every one of us would be clamoring for the shortest, fattest human we can find.

Shura wrapped her new purchase over her hair and let it fall over part of her face. There weren't as many large screens blasting her image to the world or cameras running facial identification, but one couldn't be too careful. She stayed near the wall, moving from cover to cover, using the awnings and light crowds to hide her movements.

To your right.

A police car was parked at the far end of the street. The car was facing Ella Patel's building. Two officers were inside. Whether this was a coincidence or not, Shura wasn't taking any chances. She ducked into the nearest shop and looked out the window. The officers had no reaction.

A shopkeeper, a greasy young man with slicked-back hair and an arrogant air, appeared from the back room. "My establishment is closed for the evening." He gave Shura a second look and squinted. Uncertain recognition filled his face.

She acted first. She put on a French accent and gave the man a smoldering gaze with just a hint of a smile. Playful yet curious. "I'm sorry, but I heard from so many that your business has the best–" she looked over his shoulders "–bidet selection and customer service in all of Tokyo."

The man's focus changed from trying to figure out why she looked familiar to preening. "Well of course, Raji – that's me Raji Alloo – values all his customers, and they return the love."

Your acting has improved. Finally. It only took most of your adult life.

"It's always been fine. You were always too harsh a critic, Tabs."

Shura met Raji at the counter and leaned in, just slightly, enough to seem interested but without appearing forward or obvious. She pointed past his shoulder, her hand coming very close to this face. "Tell me about that one. The pretty one with all those buttons."

She had intentionally chosen the most expensive unit on the floor. Raji immediately went into full salesman mode. He told her about the seat-warming features and how the auto-clean was best-in-class.

Shura acted as if she was paying rapt attention, which to be honest wasn't that difficult, since she never realized how complicated and advanced bidets had become since the plain porcelain variety she had grown up with. It had never occurred to her that she would want a vibrating toilet seat, but now she really did.

More importantly, Raji the bidet salesman had completely forgotten that he may have seen her on television, that she may be a wanted terrorist and that there may be a huge bounty on her head. She was just a beautiful woman who wanted to buy a bidet that cost two hundred thousand yen and was flirting with him.

Shura was in a bit of a hurry, so she quickly finalized the transaction, with a promise to come back for two more. The address she left for delivery was the Aizukotetsu-kai headquarters, just in case he did recognize her and tried to turn on her. She really did hope to retrieve it from them when she got the chance.

The purchase was also meant to leave Raji with a fond impression of her. Once their transaction was complete, he didn't think anything of it when she asked for a quick tour of his store and then asked to leave through the back door closer to where she had supposedly parked her car.

Shura continued down the alley behind several buildings until she turned onto the side street to Ella Patel's. She looked back once more at the police car still parked at the entrance to the street. The two policemen had not moved. Satisfied, Shura surveyed the street for the building with the red awning.

She scowled; they were all red. "I'm going to go to Pek's home tonight and strangle him while he sleeps."

Look over there on the left side.

It took Shura a moment to realize what Tabs was talking about. There was a storefront called Beds, Baths and Buddhas roughly halfway down the street on the left side. Right next to it was a five-story apartment. As she neared the store, her nostrils were inundated with a strong overpowering scent of sandalwood and agarwood. Inside, she found a random collection of Buddha statues, home altars and porcelain tubs. There was also a small section for bidets.

"It must be a thing in this country."

I have been in half a dozen Japanese vessels in my years. They are some of my favorites: hygienic, follow orders exactly and are always willing to die for a high power.

Shura passed the store and proceeded to the five-story apartment building. She walked up to the mailbox and scanned the names. There it was: Victoria Khan on the fifth floor. Shura checked the police car and the streets once more, then walked around to the back of the building. Even the back alleys of Tokyo were clean.

She tried the door, scanned to either side, then smashed the handle with a sharp downward thrust of her elbow. Shura listened for a few beats, and then stepped inside. She pulled out a handheld Penetra scanner and began her search. It immediately blinked on Shura, then found another target somewhere above her location. Shura began to follow the signal, watching as the scanner bounced back and forth between Tabs and Io.

She stayed near the far wall, pausing every few minutes, listening for activity. There was a family on the second floor, a television blaring on the third, and what sounded like video game gunshots on the fourth. Somewhere on the other side of the building, a dog was letting out a stream of high-pitched barks and an old woman was shrieking something Shura couldn't quite make out. There also had to be several cats in the area. The place reeked of their piss.

She reached the fifth floor and checked the scanner again. Io was close. When the Penetra scanner was first invented, it was as large as a van and even less accurate. As the technology advanced, they became small enough to fit in a backpack and more accurate, able to pinpoint the exact location of a host to within centimeters. But her own vessel interfered with its accuracy.

Shura stood at the top of the stairwell, pivoting left and right as the Penetra scanner blipped. There was no mistaking it. There were two vessels somewhere on this floor within the range of a grenade's blast radius. That was the best it could do. That would have to be good enough.

She walked up to Ella's apartment and put her ear to the door. Nothing. She felt the gap underneath the door. No breeze. In a small apartment like these likely were, if the girl had caught wind of Shura coming and had escaped through the window there would be a draft pushing through. She felt the doorknob.

One of the doors further down the way opened, and an old woman stuck her face out. Shura's hands clasped together and she shot the woman a bright smile, immediately taking a more deferential stance. Old people loved her.

The old woman scowled. "What are you doing here?"

Maybe you are losing your touch.

"I'm here to see a friend," said Shura sweetly, raising her voice just a pitch. "Do you by chance know if your neighbor is in? We have a dinner date and she didn't make it. I'm worried."

The woman studied her for a brief moment. Finally, she spoke, "What am I, the doorman? Get out of here." She slammed the door shut.

That was a strange exchange. She is hiding something. You may need to investigate.

"Let me check the apartment first." Shura checked the Penetra scanner once more. Still two signatures, including herself. As long as Ella Patel was still near, she could take her time.

She picked the lock and went inside. The lights were already on. The window on the far end was indeed shut. She closed the door behind her and began to search, checking the bathroom and closets, running her fingers along the bed and even opening the garbage can. The drawers were partially open. There were no electronics lying about. More importantly, there were no cables either.

Shura spun around the room slowly. "She was here very recently."

She looks like she is about to run.

"The scanner still sees two signatures."

The girl is either hiding from you or has stepped away. Wait, footsteps approaching.

Shura hurried to the door and listened. Someone was coming up the front stairwell. The walls of the building were paper-thin. Each step shook the walls. The echoes made it sound like a stampede. There had to be several coming. Their footsteps rumbled in the hallway just outside, growing louder. A female voice with an Australian accent. Could this be Ella? She was soon joined by another with an Icelandic accent.

Shura positioned herself beside the door. It could be a coincidence. They could be just passing through. Someone tried the door knob. Maybe not. It began to swing open.

A third voice, a man's, was speaking. "It's unlocked? We're not alo–"

"Oh crap," was all the old man managed to utter before Shura punched him in the face.

CHAPTER TWENTY-SEVEN

Meeting of the Minds

Ella's second year at the Prophus Academy in Sydney was when things really started to fall apart. Nabin began leading his own team and running his own operations. His visits became less frequent.

She found herself with more time on her hands and not sure how to spend it. Part of it was her lack of friends. Another was her lack of disposable funds. She chafed at the many restrictions imposed on her. The girl from the streets began to bubble back up to the surface and her natural instincts began to speak over her good senses. Her mind wandered as she hatched new schemes and her focus at the Academy suffered.

For the third time this month, someone cracked Roen's dentures. This time, they completely shattered and the pieces flew out of his mouth as the punch connected with his jaw.

He had made a bet with Nabin that Ella wouldn't be stupid enough to go home after what happened at the bar. Just in case, he had pulled out a Penetra scanner to check, and was vastly disappointed when the blip of a host popped up on the scanner.

It was a good thing the only things at stake were pizza dinners, which Roen was more than happy to pay for. Jill had banned pizza five years ago, citing his skyrocketing cholesterol and his new allergy to exercising. He would have to get all of the pizza out of his system before the mission was over. Or into his system, as the case may be.

When he opened the door, he fully expected to find Ella either packing or doing something stupid. Something stupid covered just about everything that wasn't packing or literally walking out the door at that very moment. He would also perhaps accept being in the process of climbing out the window as something non-stupid as well.

Roen wasn't the only one lining up to yell at the poor girl. Josie was ready to lecture her on basically failing to follow every protocol in the Prophus agent textbook. Nabin, well, poor Nabin, he was so worried about Ella's safety that he looked like he was finally ready to consider kidnapping her. That or asking her to marry him. All in all, everyone was looking forward to a chat with Ella.

Imagine his surprise when Roen opened the door and instead of finding Ella, he found a rather attractive woman.

They were both holding Penetra scanners in their hands. No one used Penetra scanners unless they were involved in Quasing business.

He took a moment to take in everything. The only very good-looking people involved in Quasing business were Adonis vessels. If this were an Adonis vessel, then not only had the Genjix reached Ella first, Roen and his band of merry people were in deep trouble.

Roen added two and two and two together and came up with, "oh crap."

The result of all of these shenanigans was a legit punch in the jaw from the hand of the attractive woman not holding the Penetra scanner. That got his dentures. It may just be his imagination, but he had been on the losing end of a lot of fights this mission. In fact, he may have lost just about every single fight since he volunteered for this job. Even the fight with those kids.

By the way, that woman hit damn hard.

Roen's feet lifted off the ground and he flew backward. The world became a mush of colors and stars. His vision strobed, and then time sped and slowed up. He remembered this feeling; it was called a concussion. He slammed into the opposite wall and slowly slid to the ground like water rolling down a window.

If Tao were here, he would tell Roen to hang it up. Roen agreed; that was likely the right assessment. He came to a rest on the floor, arms and legs splayed out, and watched the events unfold. His mind was still clearing the cobwebs and his body refused to cooperate.

Fortunately for Roen, his team was nearby. All five surged at the woman as he lay in the middle of the hallway, the wall propping up his head. Unfortunately for Roen, and his team as well, this woman was definitely an Adonis vessel.

Tarfur got to her first, before she could draw her pistol. He managed to wrestle it away, but an uppercut snapped his chin back. She took his legs out from under him. Hekla leaped over the body of her countryman and threw several punch combinations at the Adonis vessel.

Roen didn't have a great view from the floor, but he was pretty sure she hit only air. After Hekla's last attempt, the Adonis vessel struck back, stunning Hekla with a blow to the throat, and then grabbing a fistful of her hair ramming her face into a mirror.

Someone grabbed Roen's collar and pulled him aside. Josie shouted something that he couldn't quite make out. She left him where he lay and charged into the fray. The colonel had barely stepped into the room when a foot connected to her midsection, sending her tumbling to the floor next to Roen. Pedro and Nabin were the last to charge inside together. They must be having a little more success, since neither had been tossed out yet.

Roen groaned to his feet. He gingerly touched his aching jaw and spat out any remaining loose fragments of dentures. Unbelievable. He was going to have to liquid-diet the rest of this mission, and that infuriated him more than anything else at the moment. Wondering if he could blend pizza, he stepped over a writhing Josie and joined the fight.

He entered the apartment and his jaw dropped. Nabin and Pedro had wrapped up the Adonis vessel pretty good. Nabin had her neck and left arm in a tight lock while Pedro had shot low and was pinning her hips to the wall with his arms and shoulder. Yet somehow, they were still losing.

The Adonis vessel snapped her head to the side and smashed Nabin's eye, sending him reeling. She brought an elbow down on the center of Pedro's spine until he loosened his grip on her. She followed up with two jabs of the knee that flattened him on his back.

Roen tried to blind-side her. She turned and caught his punch with her hand, because of course she did. She retaliated with a punch of her own, which to her surprise – and honestly Roen's as well – he blocked. Barely. Her fist hovered inches from his face.

He barked a loud laugh. "Hah, I bet you didn't think–"

The Genjix flicked her middle finger and snapped him in the nose. Roen's eyes watered, and he tripped over Pedro's legs as he stumbled back. Luckily, the bed caught his fall.

The Adonis vessel towered over him. "Are the Prophus in such poor shape they recruit out of retirement homes?"

That voice, that accent. She sounded familiar. He had heard recordings of her in intelligence surveillance reports. This was not only an Adonis vessel, but someone prominent. He squinted. Her face was familiar, too. That was when it hit him.

"Wait a minute, you're Mengsk's little girl! Alexandra! The

one they call the Scalpel. I cooked you pancakes once when you were a kid."

Her face darkened. "Now I recognize you, Roen Tan. What is someone like you doing here?"

"I could ask you the same."

"I meant someone as old and used up."

Roen grimaced. He had kind of walked into that one.

Hekla staggered into the room and blocked the doorway. She was visibly in awe of Shura. "That's Shura the Scalpel? Wow, I never thought we'd run into someone like her here."

"You can ask for her autograph later," growled Roen.

"How is dear Cameron?" asked Shura. "Last time our paths crossed, he wasn't doing so well."

"I'm glad you two didn't work out," he shot back. "You would have made the worst daughter-in-law."

"Wait what?" Nabin sputtered. "She dated Cameron?"

"Please," spat Shura. "You should probably let me walk out of this room. It's the only way some of you may survive."

Roen scrambled to his feet. "We have the numbers, lady."

"How's that working out for you so far?"

Roen checked. His team was ready for round two. Nabin and Pedro were to his right, Hekla and Tarfur to his left. Josie was standing outside, because this apartment couldn't cram any more people in. No matter how good Shura the Scalpel was, there was no way she could overcome these odds. She had to know that.

"We don't have to fight. We outnumber you," said Roen. "If you surrender, we will treat you humanely and with respect."

"If you surrender," she countered, "I won't."

Roen considered pulling out a blade, but decided against it. In a space this small with this many bodies, bare hands was safest, especially against someone of her skill. They were probably more likely to accidentally cut one of their own. Since all of them were wearing body armor, knives would be rendered mostly ineffective anyway. Shura must have come to the same conclusion, as she had not reached for her knives either.

The team synced up by sight and converged. Nabin and Tarfur took the brunt of the damage going in. Roen took a knee to the neck as he wrapped up her legs. She managed to buck him off once, but not the second time. Shura was hard to pin down. There was something about the way she relaxed her body so that it felt like you were trying to wrap your hands around a bag of sand, and then when she did move it was sudden and quick, like a hard jolt or a snake striking.

Just as they thought they had her tied up, she threw a hard elbow to Josie's chin and buckled the older woman to her knees. It gave Shura just enough room to reach down to her thigh. A blade appeared in her right hand, and Shura the Scalpel lived up to her moniker.

She moved like a blur, first slicing Pedro in the arm and then nicking Nabin in the neck. Hekla suffered a gash to the crown of her head while Roen's head got the butt end of the handle. Instead of charging for the door at Josie, the Adonis vessel managed to plunge the blade beneath Tarfur's armor and into his chest. She slammed the blade in deeper and drove him backward.

The two exploded through the window and onto the fire escape. For a second, it looked like the momentum would send them over the side, but Josie managed to dive out and grab her teammate by the pant leg, so only Shura went flying.

As she fell, the Adonis vessel grabbed the shoulder of Tarfur's armored vest, and caught herself dangling five stories above ground. Josie yelled and held onto his legs while Shura threatened to drag him over the side with her. Nabin was there a moment later, adding his weight to hers. Hekla and Pedro joined in, helping haul him back through the window.

They got to work trying to stem the blood immediately. Hekla unfastened his armor and applied pressure to his chest. She looked up at Roen. "The cut is deep. He needs a hospital."

Roen nodded and made the emergency call to 119. He crawled onto the stairwell just in time to see Shura agilely monkey her way down the fire escape and then drop to ground level. She looked up at him and waved. It wasn't smug. She wasn't gloating. It was just a wave, one that said, you had the odds heavily stacked against me, but I escaped, and I will see you soon. Then Shura took off down the end of the alley, around the corner and out of sight.

CHAPTER TWENTY-EIGHT
Captured

The Prophus Academy in Sydney took care of all of their students' needs. By her second year, Ella lived in her own dorm room, had access to as much food as she wanted, and even had clothing and toiletries provided. Ella wanted for nothing.

What the Academy did not provide for her was disposable funds and focus, in reverse order of importance. Nabin had previously occupied most of her time and thoughts, but now that her hands were idle, Ella began to revert to her Crate Town ways. The gears in her head started to turn every time she saw an opportunity to make a profit.

The world was dark and hot. The bag had been tied firmly around Ella's neck, making it hard to breathe. Her lungs labored. She was lightheaded and short of breath. The constant jostling in the back of the moving vehicle disoriented her sense of direction. The only sensations Ella could feel were the numbness in her wrists, the ribbed surface of the van bed, and the damp tingling of perspiration matting the bag to her face.

That, and her breath.

I tell you to brush your teeth all the time.

"You never said it was that bad."

Quasing do not have a sense of smell.

That was new. "You can hear and touch and see, but you can't smell?"

We actually do not do any of those either. We interpret your reactions when you use those senses. It is the same with smells, but we do not know exactly what is considered a good or bad smell.

That took her mind away from reality. Someone had just kidnapped her, and she was probably going to die. She wasn't scared of dying exactly. Death was growing up on the streets. It was just what happened when you lost. Ella didn't like losing though.

"So," she pondered. "When we were in Crate Town, and you said something smelled bad, you didn't really mean it."

Not one bit. It is the same with the other senses as well. When you admire an attractive person, I do not see him as beautiful or ugly, but almost as a formula based upon subjective societal preferences. It honestly is math. You humans interpret your senses in a similar way. It is just more subtle with many variables that influence your decisions.

"You call Nabin ugly all the time."

He is objectively not a good-looking man.

"Don't talk about my guy like that. He's not that ugly."

He is also no longer your guy. And according to math, he is. I also do not like you two together.

"Is it something about him specifically you don't like, or just any man?"

Mostly any man, but a Prophus agent especially. You also tend to get a little crazy with regards to him, but that is usually the case with most humans your age. Puberty is the worst.

These were all points rehashed from countless arguments. Ella couldn't fault Io's logic or reasoning, and she would have actually agreed with her Quasing on almost all of it when they had first met, but things were different now. She was older, had experienced more, desired more. That's what made all of this difficult.

In any case, Ella was relatively certain that she was going to die tonight or tomorrow or at least very, very soon. She decided to take this opportunity to make peace with herself. She forgave the three hundred and thirty million gods for her lot in life, forgave her mother for dying on her when she was a kid, and forgave Nabin for being boneheaded. She even forgave all the jerks in Crate Town who gave her a rough time: the Fabs family, the cops, and the street rat gangs who stabbed her in the back.

The only people she left out of her pardons were her dad and that asshole politician who killed Burglar Alarm. Ella would gladly stab them both if she saw them in her next life.

The gravity of the situation set in. She hadn't lived the best of lives, but she was going to miss it. She honestly never thought she would survive this long, especially after she lost her parents. But now that she had, there were still so many other things she wanted to try. Dying felt premature.

"Cameron once said that a part of every one of his hosts lives within Tao. Is that true? When I die, will you carry a little piece of me in you? Does that mean I'll live forever?"

Honestly? No. It is just something we say, like 'to the Eternal Sea' or 'a part of you will live forever through me'. Platitudes we tell our hosts when they are about to pass.

There was a long awkward pause. Ella's eyes began to water.

Would you like me to say something nice? Ella, a part of you will live forever through–

"It's too late for that, you jerk!"

Uh, to the Eternal–

"Shut up."

The van came to a screeching halt. Ella tensed. The back doors swung open, and an artificial white glare shined through the tiny holes of the cloth bag. Rough hands grabbed her elbows and dragged her out. A cool breeze raised the hair on her arms. More doors slammed. Shadows passed nearby.

We must be underground by the sound of the echoes, maybe a cave? By the number of voices and footsteps, there is anywhere between four and twenty people around us.

"Between four and twenty? You might as well say between two and a thousand, and where the hell are there caves near Tokyo?"

I am simply helping interpret what I sense from our surroundings. No need to get angry.

"You are not helpful. What am I going to do? Make a break for it with a sack over my head and my hands tied behind my back while four or twenty people chase me in what may or may not be a cave?"

I do not see you volunteering anything useful. My life is at stake as much as yours.

"You're the one who is supposed to be ancient and smart."

I AM ancient and smart. I told you to leave Tokyo days ago, but you wanted to stay and hang out with your little friends and try to make one last score.

"They're the only friends I have."

Another lengthy awkward silence passed.

Ella, I am your–

"Shut up, Alien!"

Ella was moved from the "cave" into what sounded like a hallway. The lights changed from white to yellow, and the echoes were replaced by the hum of central air. She was marched into an elevator, and they ascended several floors. She caught alternating glimmers of white and black – fluorescent ceiling lights likely – and heard what sounded like someone talking through a PA system above her. The elevator dinged open and she was dragged once again down another corridor.

"Do you have an idea where we are?"

This feels like an office building. Possibly a military base.

"Please be an office building. Please be an office building.

Do you think the yakuza have us? The Genjix? The Prophus?"

I am not sure. It could be a government agency as well. Japan has been very strict regarding their neutrality on the Quasing conflict.

"Why does everyone want my head? Why can't they just leave me alone?"

You are forgetting about the bounty.

"That's just great."

Ella finally came to a stop when she was tossed roughly into a metal chair. The plastic straps around her wrists were cut off and her hands yanked onto a hard surface in front of her. Chains rattled as something hard and cold clipped around her wrists, cutting into her flesh. A yellow light clicked on, poking a hundred tiny beams through the cloth fabric.

A moment later, the bag was pulled off her head and she was momentarily stunned by the harsh glare of a desk lamp. She averted her eyes and blinked the exploding dots away. Ella raised her arms and heard the rattling of chains. She looked down and saw handcuffs around her wrists. They were attached to a ring bolted onto the table. To her left was a large mirror that covered the top half of the wall. It looked like a scene from a bad Hong Kong cop movie.

It is exactly what you think it is.

"Wait, we've been rescued by the police?" For a second, Ella's hopes skyrocketed. The police were here to serve and protect, and the Japanese police tended to be more civil than in other countries. Maybe the police had somehow caught wind of her situation and were protecting her. By kidnapping her. And throwing a sack over her head. Tossing her in the back of a van. And bringing her into an interrogation room.

OK, maybe not.

It was still better than the alternative. While Ella generally disliked cops, getting kidnapped by the yakuza would be awful. The Genjix, even worse. The Prophus was honestly hardly a better option, because they would kidnap her and throw her in a prison in the Arctic just to keep her away from the Genjix. Why did the Genjix want her anyway?

More immediately pressing, why did the Tokyo police pick you up?

Ella could name half a dozen things right off the bat: theft, gun-running, working with organized crime…

Assault, embezzlement, fraud…

"Racketeering, money laundering, forgery…"

Now that Ella thought about it, she hadn't been giving herself enough credit. She had been awfully busy. For the past few months she had felt guilty about spinning her wheels, but she had gotten quite a bit accomplished.

Pride is not what you should be feeling. The police could throw you in prison for any of these crimes.

"Still better than the alternative." Ella was practically cheerful.

The door opened with a stuttering creak, and a police officer walked in. Ella was almost happy to see him. She tried to wave, but her chained wrist did not make it very far off the table. He did not return the greeting.

"Hello," she said. "May I get something to drink?"

The cop ignored her and placed a watermelon-sized disk on the table. Ella eyed it suspiciously. It didn't look like a torture device.

It is a communication projector.

"What does it do?"

The cop pushed a few buttons, and the air above the projector began to shimmer, then coalesced into a three-dimensional bust of a person. Ella was confused. She had never seen this person before, but he was awfully handsome. Disturbingly so, like he had just stepped out of a beauty magazine. He had a shock of dirty blond hair and a chin that ran for miles, cheekbones that looked as if they were etched from a side of a mountain. That set off several alarms in her head.

Oh no.

That was when it hit Ella as well, and her stomach dropped to the tips of her toes.

The projection of the cover model looked her over and shook his head. "So you're the Receiver's vessel. I expected more."

"You're not much to look at either. Who the hell are you?" Ella shot back. That was a lie; he looked very impressive. She didn't expect the man to answer, but he gladly volunteered.

"I am Rurik Melnichenko," the projection of the cover model said, "and you are now my property."

CHAPTER TWENTY-NINE
Her Way

In Ella's defense, this was who she was. It was how she had survived years on the streets. The Academy had no system in place to help her transition from her old life in Crate Town to that of a student. Because of the Host Protection Program, they were not even aware of her history. As Nabin's presence had saved Ella, his absence doomed her.

In hindsight, that was probably a mistake on the Prophus's part.

Shura was in a mood by the time she returned to Aizukotetsu-kai corporate headquarters. She kicked the glass door open and stormed through, nearly taking it off its hinges. Fortunately, it was late in the evening by the time she arrived, but the yakuza were a twenty-four-hour shop.

The situation had escalated quickly after Shura had her run-in with the Prophus agents. No sooner had she escaped them than the police swarmed the entire neighborhood. She had to flee before anyone managed to identify her as the Blonde Bombshell Bomber. If so, the entire district would have been locked down within minutes.

She ended up having to jump a few walls to circle back to the car. By the time she reached the place she had left it, her ride was gone. Her stupid yakuza driver, the man whose job was to chauffeur her around, had failed in his only duty. Shura had no choice but to walk halfway to the Aizukotetsu-kai office before she risked a taxi.

Hailing one in this city was brutal. By the time she finally made it back to the yakuza office, she could hardly contain her rage. Kloos and the rest of her team was waiting in the lobby. They fell in behind her.

"Where were all of you?" she spat.

"Traffic," admitted her second in command. "And then when we arrived at Nishi Kasai, the police were everywhere. One of the cops recognized Roxani and me. We ended up having to kill him and pull the heat away from the area in order to facilitate your escape."

Shura grunted. That was a reasonable excuse, but it didn't make things any better. Another dead cop wasn't helpful. She could have used the backup; she should have kept them close.

A few of the yakuza lounging in the front lobby almost drew their weapons – she was itching for a fight.

We still need them.

Shura pushed the violence out of her mind and walked to the tea room. Her path was blocked by four guards and the young tattooed woman she remembered as the boss's granddaughter and heir.

Bashira, the granddaughter, bowed. "Oyabun is expecting you."

They stepped aside.

Be wary.

Shura allowed herself a beat at the door before heading in. She left the simmering rage and sharp irritation outside the room, offering the elderly Tanaka Nishiki a gracious bow. "Thank you for seeing me at such a late hour."

"The honor is mine, great Genjix," bowed Tanaka.

"We have run–" she began.

Tanaka gestured toward the small table. "Tea?"

He is trying to make amends for today's mishap.

"Meaning he recognizes his people's incompetence?"

I would not go that far in your assessment. Stay humble.

"A difficult task."

For you, especially.

Shura relaxed her shoulders and offered Tanaka a tilted bow, showing she was ready to talk. She joined him at the table, lowering herself slowly to her knees as if this ceremony was second nature to her. Shura poured them both a cup of tea. The pot was piping hot again. How many guns were pointing at her right now?

Tanaka took his time inhaling the scent of the black tea before sipping gingerly. Shura went along with the charade for several more minutes. Her patience was just starting to wear thin when the leader of the Aizukotetsu-kai spoke.

"I understand you experienced difficulties retrieving the girl."

Shura made sure not to assign blame. "She is lost for now, but I am confident that is only a temporary setback. I need your sources to locate her again."

Tanaka sipped his drink. "The conditions of our agreement were to locate the girl the first time, nothing more. The assistance we offered was simply a courtesy."

"Your people were the ones who lost her."

"An unfortunate occurrence," he countered, "but they were attacked by your enemies. The blame cannot rest upon the Aizukotetsu-kai."

That is a fair point.

"The men you sent with me were not your best. They outnumbered my enemies over three to one." It took effort to maintain a steady voice. "Their boss insisted I not get involved. He ordered me to stay in the car. I could have handled the Prophus if I were there."

"For his failure he will lose a finger, but it was for your own protection. You are a wanted terrorist."

Shura decided to end the charade. She hated tea anyway. She put the cup down on the table. "Let us talk plainly."

Tanaka followed suit. "That is the preferred method in which old men wish to converse."

"I intend to get the girl back. Failure is not an option. You will help me or there will be consequences for both of us."

"The Aizukotetsu-kai do not take kindly to ultimatums."

"The Aizukotetsu-kai should take kindly to facts," she countered.

Here we go. You better make this work.

"I have a plan."

I am reading your mind. You actually do not.

The leader of the Aizukotetsu-kai spoke in a measured tone. "You may be Genjix, but you are only one of several within your organization. We can sell this information to your rival tonight and be billions richer."

"You do not want to go to war with me," she said in a deadpan voice.

Several red dots painted Shura's chest. Tanaka was stone-faced. "You dare make threats in the heart of the Aizukotetsu-kai. You forget your place."

Shura looked down at the small dot dancing above her heart. "I can reach out and kill you before your people can pull the trigger."

"I am an old man and have lived a long life. It would be a good trade."

Shura hated to admit it, but she really liked Tanaka. "What about your granddaughter, Bashira?"

Tanaka scoffed. "I thought you had more honor than this. Bashira is beyond your reach. Once you are gone, we will ally ourselves with your rival, and then we will be untouchable by those who seek to avenge you."

Shura put her hands up to her sides as if surrendering. She leaned in and whispered. "I'm not talking about my people. Who will protect her from yours after you are gone?"

To Tanaka's credit, his hesitation was brief. If she had blinked, she would have missed it. His eyes narrowed, and he put up a hand. The red dots dancing on Shura's body disappeared.

The yakuza boss let loose a long sigh and then stood up. The door behind him opened. His arm waved in invitation. "Would you join an old man in his garden?"

Shura kept her face even, but she wanted really badly to roll her eyes.

Stay in control. You almost have him. Here is all the relevant information regarding the factions within the Aizukotetsu-kai.

Shura followed Tanaka through the back door, accompanied by two guards. The old man offered his arm, which Shura accepted, and they strolled together to a private elevator which began to climb. They were greeted by the cold breeze as they stepped out onto the rooftop of the fifty-story building. One of the guards handed the old man a coat, which Shura helped him don, and then the two strolled down a stone path leading toward a gazebo at the far corner.

"This is my sanctuary," proclaimed Tanaka. "I enjoy the solitude here."

"I would find it difficult to be alone with my thoughts with such wind singing in my ears," Shura admitted.

The old man chuckled and tapped the side of his head. "I am always alone with my thoughts. It is my words that are often shared, even when they are not meant for others. This sanctuary allows my thoughts and my words to remain my own when I desire it."

They reached the gazebo, and Tanaka gestured to a bench at a small stone table. A pot of what Shura could only assume was more tea was waiting for them. This time, Tanaka poured. Shura was surprised to discover it was bourbon.

"I tired of tea decades ago," the yakuza boss admitted. "But tradition and doctors dictate the life of an old man."

"Tradition – and doctors – are harsh mistresses," agreed Shura.

"You haven't met my mistress," chuckled the old man. He sighed. "In any case, my time on this world is short."

"What stage?" asked Shura. She had suspected the man was unwell, but Tabs had confirmed it during her research. It was not a well-kept secret.

Tanaka gave a start, then nodded. "The famed Genjix spy network is as good as its reputation. It has metastasized. I have a year perhaps, no more than two." He downed his drink. "The good news is now I can drink whatever I wish."

According to his medical records, he will not live six months.

"And the bad?"

"The vultures are out. I fear Bashira is too young, strong as she is. She is not ready to lead. She has not consolidated the support of the other bosses. The knives will be out at my funeral."

Shura placed her drink on the table. Bourbon had always been too sweet for her. "Help me recover the girl, and I will throw the whole weight of the Genjix behind your granddaughter."

Tanaka shook his head. "Attacking your enemies – other powerful Genjix – will have serious consequences. I require further assurances."

They began negotiating. Tanaka not only wanted his granddaughter set up as the next leader of the family, and for the Aizukotetsu-kai to be the only crime family in all of Japan, he also wanted them to be made legal. As in given official recognition as a Genjix entity. The man wanted to set up his descendants as rulers of Japan.

"You wish to restore the imperial family," she said, shaking her head in disbelief.

"The surrender of Japan during the Second Great War was a mistake," declared Tanaka. "My country's neutrality during the Alien World War was one as well. It was our opportunity to restore the divine legacy of my country. I will, with my dying breath, set the path for future generations."

It was completely outrageous. All Shura wanted was to capture one pitiful human, who happened to be the vessel of a valuable Holy One, and this old man, a few months from death, wanted to restore the Japanese empire. Either he was senile, or the shadow of death had freed him to pursue his real life goals.

"Go big before you go," she murmured. Shura respected Tanaka's ambitions. She had thought him too conservative and settled when they first met, content to simply rest on his laurels. She realized how in control of the situation Tanaka Nishiki had been the entire time. She could learn a thing or two from this old fox.

"Very well," she replied. "Bashira will have to become a vessel for a Holy One, but we can see to that. Now, for your part of the arrangement."

Tanaka was all smiles. "The police have the girl. Our plants have already gathered the data you are seeking and know where she is being held." He pulled a paper from his inner pocket, placed it on the table, and slid it toward her.

A smirk grew on Shura's face. Of course the old man already had this information in his possession. The rascally old fox had set this up from the beginning. She wouldn't even be surprised if he had orchestrated the earlier failure in order to revisit their negotiations.

That would either make him a mastermind, or an idiot.

"Two sides of the same coin, Tabs."

In any case, the deal was struck, although all she could do was open the door for the Aizukotetsu-kai. It was up to his granddaughter to do the rest. If Tanaka thought yakuza politics were brutal, wait until he saw how the Genjix operated.

Shura memorized the address on the paper and crumpled it, then Tabs flashed a map of the city and the surrounding area in her head. She bowed to Tanaka. "How much support can you provide?"

"I can summon fifty soldiers within the hour."

"That should be sufficient. We attack tonight." She bowed to the father of the Aizukotetsu-kai. "It has been a pleasure, Oyabun. Welcome to the Genjix."

CHAPTER THIRTY
Dwindling Choices

Without any source of income, she began to make money the only way she knew how. At first she started a gambling ring on campus, taking bets and running games. When that got busted, she escalated to embezzling, stealing from the Academy and selling items on the black market.

She did whatever it took to survive. Her education became secondary. Unfortunately, she did not understand what survival here meant.

As soon as the team realized the severity of Tarfur's injury, they moved him into the street where emergency medical units could easily pick him up. Then, following protocol for enemy or neutral territory, they fled the scene. It was the only thing they could do, and it gave Tarfur the best chance of survival.

They moved to a safe distance and waited until an ambulance arrived, then tailed it to the hospital. Hekla stayed to keep tabs on Tarfur while the rest of the team returned to the estate. Roen started working the diplomatic channels to extract Tarfur out of the country.

The team tried to hide their worry. As agents and soldiers, all of them had experienced death, but that made it no less painful every time it happened. The military was close-knit.

Roen excused himself to his room. He stared at the comm device resting on the desk. He dreaded making this call, but it was long overdue. It wasn't unusual for agents to be out of communication for extended periods of time. It was the nature of their business. Months could go by before he could report in. However, this particular situation was unique. Roen activated the line. Even at this age, he hated getting yelled at.

Especially by his wife.

A three-dimensional projection of Jill Tesser Tan, newly retired Keeper of the Prophus, floated in the air in front of him. The smarter and more competent half of their thirty-plus year marriage had her arms crossed: a bad sign. She also wore the same facial expression she used when she was about to order an air strike. "You're not in Australia."

"Hi love," chirped Roen cheerfully. "How's retirement? Are you keeping the garden alive?"

"Most of it was dead by the time I got home. Answer the damn question."

"But you didn't ask..." Roen swallowed the rest of the sentence. When you ran a global military and financial empire like Jill had for the past quarter-century, every word that came out of your mouth tended to sound like an order. "Ella Patel wasn't there. They expelled her six months ago. I tracked her to Tokyo and made contact when the Genjix got involved."

"You weren't supposed to go after her, Roen," seethed Jill. "The moment the Genjix attacked the Academy, you should have pulled out. I would have sent Cameron or another team to track Ella down. Instead, the last I hear, you head straight into Genjix territory and go dark for weeks. I thought you were dead!"

"I couldn't risk it." He withered under her gaze. "The safehouse here was compromised; they went on lockdown.

I was also busy trying to track the girl down. She's a slippery fish."

"Roen, we have Prophus teams who specialize in deep-cover retrieval. Teams like the one your son leads. You should have discussed your next move with me before you ran off into the heart of Genjix space. You're not a young man any more." Jill's eyes narrowed. "Admit it, you didn't call in sooner because you knew I'd pull you off the mission."

She didn't need him to respond. "I only went on this job because Cameron knew I was bored out of my mind at home," he snapped back. "If I had known you were going to retire, I would have bought that sailboat and planned our trip down the west coast."

His wife shot him the same look she gave whenever she caught him breaking his diet. "I know, Roen. You already bought the boat."

He was shocked. "You know?"

"When will you ever learn? I know everything. You have it docked at the harbor under–" she picked up a tablet and held it up "–Ricky Manuto. You christened her *The Basskicker*. Really? That's the name you're going to go with?"

Roen held up both fists. "What? It's a play on words."

Jill held up a hand. "Oh no, I get it. I love you more than life itself, almost as much as I love my son, but you are an idiot. You cannot use that name, Roen."

"Why not? I think it's fine. We can agree to disagree."

"No, Roen. You can't."

"OK."

She took a deep breath. "Give me a sit-rep."

"We found Ella, but she ran. The yakuza attempted to kidnap her. We went to her apartment, got our asses handed to us by Shura the Scalpel. You remember her, right? She's a real piece of work these days, and I mean that kindly. She beat all of us up with her bare hands."

"I hate to remind you of this, darling, but you're an old wrinkly fart now."

Roen reflexively rolled his shoulders, feeling the aches shoot down his back. "Tell me about it. By the way, can you call Dr Stevens and order more dentures? I broke mine."

"Of course you did. Where is the girl now?"

He hesitated. "We lost her again. After our dustup with Shura the cops arrived and we had to bail. One of our guys took a knife to the chest."

Jill dropped her jaw. "Wha–"

"He's in the hospital at the moment. He may need extraction."

Her face turned ashen as he spoke, then red. Roen could see her hands curl into fists. "Let me get this straight." She ticked off her fingers. "I brought you out of retirement so this could be done quietly. But now the yakuza, Genjix, police, probably the Japanese government, and even the Prophus are officially involved? How did you manage to get the entire world in on a clandestine retrieval job?"

"You make it sound a lot worse than it actually is." He paused. "No wait, you're right. It's that bad."

"Do you at least know why they're after her?"

"I'm still working on that. We have a few more leads to follow." That was a lie.

"I'm sending a team to pick you up," said Jill. "The situation has gotten too hot for my senior citizen husband to handle." She paused. "But you're having fun, right?"

"I am," he admitted. "I haven't had this much fun in years. I always did think I took a desk job way too early."

"That's not what you told me when you took the liaison position with the United States's Alien Task Force."

"That's unfair," he protested. "I was literally in body cast at the time they made the offer. In any case, I'd rather be home with you. Thanks for giving me a heads-up about your retirement. How did that go down so quickly?"

"I was in a meeting with the entire Prophus Command talking about maritime lanes in the Gulf of Aden, and I just started daydreaming about you, our house, and that sailing trip you keep going on about. I called Angie to my office that night and told her I was done. The woman probably could use another year of seasoning, but she'll be fine."

Roen was stunned. "So it was your idea to retire? She didn't force it?"

There was a twinkle in Jill's eyes. "She begged me to stay for another year, but my mind was already on *The Basskicker* with the wind blowing through my hair."

Roen's grin spread ear to ear. "Give me a few days. I'll make it happen. Other than that, how's retirement treating you?"

"I hate to say it, but I'm bored," laughed Jill. "It's only been a week since I got home, and I'm already getting cabin fever."

He missed her laugh. It had been a long time since he heard her so unrestrained. "You'll get used to it," he said, softly. Roen really hated this assignment right now. "It'll get better once I come home."

There was a pause. Both of their brains were switching from powerful agents of a covert alien organization to two people who had loved each other for a very long time.

"You look like you've been eating well." She squinted. "Too well."

"I miss you," choked Roen.

They spoke differently. They were no longer two of the most important people in the world. They were used to never having time for small talk, even with each other. For the first time in a long time, their conversation was unhurried, and they could dwell on the details that only a couple with decades together could care about.

Roen asked about her day and told her about how good it felt being back in the field. Jill spoke about how wonderful it was being in the kitchen again, and regaled him with a story of her adventure trying to make poached eggs. He reminded her that she was allowed to sleep in late, now that the weight of the world no longer rested on her shoulders, but that it was of life-and-death importance that she order a new set of dentures for him. She ribbed him gently to watch his diet and to stretch before he got into another fight.

"You have to especially take care of your knees," she said. "I plan to have many long walks with my husband, and those woods in the backyard aren't conducive to wheelchairs."

There was a knock on the door. Pedro stuck his head in. "Sir, I'm sorry to bother you, but there's something out here you need to see."

"What is it?" asked Roen. Then he heard it. A metal clanging echoed in the room outside. At first he thought it was gunfire or someone hammering on water pipes, and then he perked up. It was a gong. Someone was buzzing on the intercom at the estate's front gates. He turned back to Jill. "I have to go."

"Go, go," she waved. "Find Ella Patel and come back to me."

"I'm coming home soon." Roen's voice took a steely note. "I don't care if I have to throw Ella in a potato sack and stow her in–"

Jill held up a hand. "Just be safe. By the way, I'm sending in a retrieval team. They'll arrive within two days."

"That's not necessary," he protested. The look she gave him told him she thought it was.

"I'm also sending in the 3rd Pacific Fleet."

"Funny," grinned Roen. Then he realized she wasn't joking. "Keep the garden alive. Also try to clean the pool. I expect tasty poached eggs by the time I come home."

The projection died. Roen leaped out of his chair and left the room. Pedro handed him a shotgun and fell in beside him. The rest of the team was already armed, each at a window facing the front gate. Even Asha had joined the fun. She may have a hole in her stomach, but there she was, crouched next to the kitchen window with a sniper rifle in hand.

Roen checked the rounds and cocked the shotgun. He turned off the lights and clicked the intercom. "Who is it?"

There was a series of high squeaks and excited chatter. Finally, a girl spoke. "We're Ella's friends. We think she's in trouble."

"Who is with you?"

A boy answered this time. "It's just us. You guys helped us against the yakuza."

Their reasons were as good as any. It still sounded like a trap though. If it were the Genjix, yakuza, or police, the team was as good as dead anyway. That's what Roen generally hated about safehouses above ground: they were vulnerable from every angle. The upside was he didn't have to wade through sewage every day.

He decided to spring it rather than waiting for someone else to make the first move. He had promised Jill he'd hurry up and return home this week. Roen signaled to the team to hold their fire and buzzed the outer gate to open. The team tracked the group of kids walking onto the estate grounds. They cowered as he opened the front door and beckoned them to approach with his shotgun.

The fear on their faces was real. These kids weren't faking. He closed the door behind them and signaled for the team to stand down. They followed orders, but no one looked friendly. The atmosphere in the room was as thick as soup. Nabin, Asha and Pedro were openly scowling, and their gazes followed the kids as if they had stolen something, which of course they actually had a week ago. That was beside the point. Asha still held the rifle in her hand, daring the kids to make a move. Josie had her arms crossed as if she were a Catholic school teacher watching for students to cheat on a test.

None of this was helping matters. Roen decided to defuse the situation. He beckoned for the kids to follow him to the couch. "You're among friends." That was more to his team than Ella's people. "You guys are safe. Anyone need a drink?"

Most of them raised their hands. One of the younger ones piped up, "Do you have any more of that chocolate cake?"

Pedro broke into a chuckle. "So that's where the bite marks came from. I'll get the cups."

The girl bowed and offered to help. That broke a little of the tension. Within a few minutes, the team and Ella's friends were sitting on the couches with a pitcher of water and snacking on shrimp chips. No cake though; Josie had polished off the last of it.

Once everyone settled in, Nabin pressed forward. "What is going on with Ella?"

The kids exchanged glances, and then one of the older ones – a young tattooed man who introduced himself as Hinata – spoke. "She's missing. After you helped us get away at the World-Famous, a woman tried to kidnap Pek. She made him tell her where Ella lived." He nudged the youngest boy. "Tell them, Pek."

"We ran into her at Ella's apartment," grimaced Pedro. "What about her?"

Pek exchanged looks with Hinata and then piped up shyly. "The pretty woman's driver was yakuza. I saw his tattoos."

Roen nodded. "We suspected Shura could be working with them. Now we know, but I don't know how that gets us any closer to locating Ella."

"We think the yakuza may know where she is," said the one named Lee. "Their boss was after Ella because she beat up his son. He was also the one who tried to lure her into a trap at the World-Famous Bar & Udon. We think he has her."

"We don't know where the gang's base is located," said Josie.

Hinata raised his hand. "I can take you there. They're based in a warehouse near the docks. I used to work for them."

Josie looked dubious. "That's a pretty tenuous lead."

"It's the only one we have," said Nabin.

"What do you think, Roen?" asked Josie.

There were no strong options. It was either follow a weak lead or wait. Wait for what though? They were at a dead end. Still, Roen hated going fishing off weak intel, particularly around the yakuza. That was just asking for trouble.

The main gate gonged again. Someone else was coming. The guns rematerialized in his people's hands. Even some of Ella's friends pulled out their sports equipment.

It was Hekla. She walked through the front door of the main house and stared. "What's going on? Am I interrupting something?"

The weapons lowered. The team was far too on edge right now.

"It's nothing," said Roen. "These are Ella's friends. We're wondering if we should follow up on a lead. How's Tarfur?"

Before the words left his mouth, he knew the answer. Hekla's gaze lowered. "He didn't make it."

Roen's stomach clenched. Over thirty years as a Prophus agent, and every death was still a punch to the gut.

"How?" exclaimed Pedro. "It was just a stab wound. I've seen that guy take worse playing rugby."

Hekla's face was grim. "Poison on the blade."

The room became still. It took a few moments for the news to sink in. Then Pedro slammed his fist onto the table and screamed. Asha embraced him and the two huddled silently.

"If you will excuse me," said Hekla, "I need to notify his wife."

Roen stared at the cup of water in his hand. He wished it was something like vodka right now. He had thought his days of losing people were over. A wave of remorse washed over him. He thought he had written his last death notification when he had quit the field. Hekla may disagree, but this one was on him.

He stopped her as she passed. "I'll do it."

Hekla shook him off. "He's my man."

"I'm the one running this crap show."

"With all due respect, over my dead body, sir."

He nodded and let her go.

Josie touched his shoulder lightly. "The kids are still here. What do you want to do about Ella?"

Roen downed the water, crumpled the plastic cup in his hand, and threw it angrily at the garbage can, missing his mark by the length of half the room. He had never played baseball as a kid. "What the hell. We're sitting on our asses anyway. Let's go check it out."

CHAPTER THIRTY-ONE
Prisoner

Ella began bending rules to suit her goals, sometimes outright breaking them. Her demeanor worsened, if that was even possible, as did her restraint. What little patience she had with the other students who looked down on her also thinned. By now, the girl had a chip on her shoulder the size of her home country. She began to retaliate against her bullies, often with a blade.

Ella was woken from an uncomfortable and restless sleep by the annoying door rubbing against its joint. She lifted her head up from the metal table, groggy and disoriented, and stared at the silhouette that walked in. The light was still shining in her face, and her back was stiff as a board from falling asleep at the table. Her wrists were raw from being handcuffed for so long, and her throat cracked when she swallowed.

She didn't know how much time had passed after the brief call with Rurik. The cop had left the room without saying a word, and no amount of yelling, whistling or banging on the table got anyone else's attention. Ella had finally passed out where she sat.

She took back everything nice she had ever said about the Japanese police. It appeared cops were universally assholes, regardless of country.

This is not good.

It took a few more seconds for the gears in Ella's brain to get cranking. She recognized that face; she had seen his projection but now Cover Model Boy was here in the flesh. His last nauseating words rang in her head and sent shivers down her spine. The Genjix Adonis vessel – what was his name – Roger Melno… Melodomo. Melanoma.

Rurik Melnichenko.

"Right."

Rurik sat down opposite her and interlaced his fingers. He rested his chin on his hands and studied her as if she were a pinned butterfly. Or property. Ella glared back.

His voice filled the room as he spoke, as if he were giving a speech. "I am Rurik Melnichenko, soon to be of the Grand Council. You may be the vessel of a Holy One, but you are not worthy."

"You've already told me your name."

"I am the one asking questions, vessel. You may have a Holy One inside you, but you do not deserve such an honor."

"OK, Roger. Whatever you say."

"It's Rurik," he growled. "Rurik Melnichenko, you uneducated scum."

"You really like saying your own name," said Ella. "You speak it like you're talking about a boy you have a crush on."

"You have a smart mouth, vessel." Rurik leaned in and squeezed her cheeks. His grip was like a vice. "Be careful lest I have it sewn shut."

"Like hell you will, you puffed-up buffoon." Ella couldn't help it. There was just no filter between her brain and her mouth. She instinctively reached for her dagger, but the handcuffs tied to the table didn't let her get very far.

Stop antagonizing him if you want to live. This Genjix is on a whole other level. Rurik is an Adonis vessel of very high standing. His Quasing, Sabeen, has been a major player in Russian politics since the House of Romanov.

Ella took Io's advice. She swallowed the spit that she was about to splash on Rurik's twisted and now-ugly face. "What do you want from me?" she seethed.

"From you, nothing. You are worthless. If you want to live, you will do as you are told. You are property now."

"Why should I do anything you say?"

Rurik wrapped his hand around her neck. He squeezed. "I can easily snap your neck and offer one of my men as a vessel for the Receiver."

Listen carefully. If you want to live through this, follow my lead.

"Io and I are very close. If you kill me, she says she will never cooperate. You will get all the blame." Ella barely got the words out as she became short of breath.

I did not say that.

"Well it's true, right? You're not going to help them if they kill me."

Io didn't reply.

Many Quasing were indeed very attached to their hosts. The relationship was often as close as that between a parent and a child. To kill a Quasing's host was often the ultimate crime. That is, if the Quasing liked their host.

The threat, however, appeared to have worked on Rurik. Ella and Io did not have the cosiest relationship, but Rurik didn't know that. His grip loosened around her neck just enough to save Ella from passing out. She collapsed into her chair and rubbed her neck, shooting bad thoughts at the asshole blond cover model.

She tried to speak, but her throat hurt too much. She looked at the pitcher of water off to the side, and then back at Rurik. It took a moment for him to register her request. He complied reluctantly, scowling the entire time. Ella took her time drinking.

You are pushing your luck. Find out what they want. We need to know what they need so we can make the best of the situation.

"Shouldn't our goal be to escape?"

Io was again silent.

Ella smacked her lips and put the cup aside. "Io wants to know what you want with her."

"Is that really what your Holy One wants, or are you playing a game?"

The Russian studied her for a few moments, and then finally decided that her Quasing had to be in control. His tone became more respectful. "The Genjix require services that only Io can offer. It is time she once again fulfills her purpose in service of the Holy Ones."

What does he mean by that? What have they found?

Ella repeated the question aloud.

"It means the Holy Ones have established contact with Quasar."

"I don't get it."

What?!

Io's shock was palpable, and surprising. Quasing were not emotional beings. They understood and displayed emotion, but their bandwidth in showing them was at best restricted when compared to that of their human counterparts. Io's reaction, however, was practically a full-throated scream in Ella's head. A wave of emotion coursed up and down Ella's body. She winced as she sorted through all of Io's thoughts and feelings bouncing in her head.

Do they know we are marooned on this planet? Are they sending the Collective? Is the Eternal Sea within reach? When can we expect a carryall to bring us back into the fold? When can we expect to get off this disgusting planet?

Io peppered her with a dozen more questions. Ella did her best to parse the barrage, but they came out in a jumble. She didn't understand most of what Io was talking about.

"What did the messages say?" asked Ella finally.

"We do not know. We are unable to decipher it," admitted Rurik. "The message from the home world came in the form of a sub-phase signal. Like all things from the Eternal Sea, the signal is biological and requires the expertise of a Holy One specifically bred for that task. Unfortunately, Holy Ones with that ability were rare, even on Quasar. The portion of the original ship that housed the Receivers rests in the ocean basin in the Gulf of Mexico. As far as we know, there is only one Receiver left alive."

"Wait, what? You mean Io?" Ella was stunned. She pointed at her head. "This goof in my head is the linchpin for the Genjix? She's that important?"

Hey!

"You will watch your tone when speaking about a god," snapped Rurik. "You didn't know, did you, you foolish girl? The Holy One residing in your pathetic body is one of the most important Quasing alive."

"Well then," said Ella. "You guys better keep me happy. For starters, I would like some dinner."

Rurik smirked. "You are a container, nothing more. All your Holy One needs is a body. In fact, Sabeen wishes now to bypass you and speak directly with Io."

"Well, that's too bad," she replied. "Sabeen's going to have to go through me to talk to–"

The open-hand slap came so fast Ella didn't have time to steel against it. It smacked her flush on the cheek so hard she fell off the chair and would have crumpled to the ground if it weren't for the fact that she was handcuffed and chained to the table. The right side of her face was on fire, and the room shimmered as her vision blurred. She dangled by her wrists for a few seconds, struggling to get her rubbery legs under her. No sooner had she pulled her head above table level than a strong hand grabbed her shirt and hauled her body completely onto the table. He pinned her in place.

Rurik towered over her. "You mistake your value, vessel." He raised a hand up in the air and smashed it down on Ella's face.

Io opened her eyes just as Rurik was about to hit Ella's face for the fourth time. The first blow had already knocked the girl unconscious. Any more could kill her, and without a host nearby it could kill Io.

"Stop, Sabeen," she said in a calm voice. "I am here."

Rurik stayed the blow, and slowly released his grip around Ella's neck. Io shuffled back into the chair. Her movements were slow and deliberate. The girl had suffered several fresh injuries from Rurik's beating, and the pain coursing through her nerves made control of the body particularly difficult.

Rurik was still standing, almost as if at attention. He watched until Io was situated, then lowered himself into the chair on the other side of the table. He pulled out a thick piece of red rope and, in a practiced motion, looped it around his own neck. The Russian crossed the ends of the rope and began to pull. Rurik's face immediately turned purple. A labored breath hissed from his lips, and then he slumped over.

Io was pretty sure Rurik choking himself out to allow Sabeen to take control was more a display of power than it was the Quasing really wanting to talk to Io in private. He probably realized how difficult Ella was as a host and wanted to show off exactly how much control he had over Rurik. The Genjix had historically not shown their Prophus siblings any mercy in the war, let alone actively recruit them. Something big and important must be happening.

A few seconds later, Rurik's eyes opened and he sat up. "Io. It has been centuries."

"Hello Sabeen. It is good to speak with you."

That was not the truth. Io was dreading this conversation.

Sabeen continued to stare at Io for several moments. Finally, he spoke, "I believe it is time to put our petty war aside and do what is best for all Quasing. Do you agree?"

That statement was a mouthful of nothing. No Quasing argued against that.

Io played along. "I would like nothing more than to see peace between the Prophus and Genjix, and to work together to find a way home."

"Many great things are happening among the Genjix. The Bio Comm Array has been a great success. The project has surpassed expectations and has already established a sub-phase line with Quasar. All we need now is a Receiver to translate and establish the link. Only you can save us. You will be a hero among all Quasing. Can we count on you to deliver us to our salvation from this wretched planet?"

A wave of emotion swept through Io, and she temporarily lost control. Ella's body tilted to one side and nearly fell off the chair. Only by grabbing onto the table did Io save the girl from more injury. Damn these bi-pedal humanoid bodies. Io righted herself and absorbed the ramifications of Sabeen's words.

"All I ever wanted was to serve our people as a Receiver," said Io. "If I could save and return us to the Eternal Sea, then it would be my greatest wish."

"Good," said Sabeen. "I am glad to see that your time with the Prophus has not dulled your dedication to our kind. Therefore, I will allow you the opportunity to rejoin us. Here are my terms."

"Terms?" frowned Io. "What happened to putting aside our petty struggles and working toward the greater good?"

"You are Prophus, a betrayer," said Sabeen. "As far as I am concerned, you are barely a Quasing any longer. For that, you must pay penance and earn your way back to the fold. If you want to see our home world one day, bathe in the warmth of the Eternal Sea and regain your standing, you will swear your allegiance to me. Your work will fall under my ownership.

From this moment on, I absorb all of your standing. Is that clear? Our glories and earned achievements will be shared."

Io was stupefied. She had thought Rurik's claim of Ella being property a poor choice of words, but now she realized how exact and serious the man was in his phrasing. "How can you offer this? This is not our way. This is slavery. No Quasing has claimed the barbaric ownership of another since the early days of the Eternal Sea."

Sabeen shrugged. "It appears humanity's taint has rubbed off on all of us over the eons. And you may not, but I still intimately remember the mighty Receivers ordering the rest of us around as if we were your lowly subjects. Have you forgotten, Io?"

Back on the carryall that had brought them to Earth, Sabeen was part of the cleansing contingent responsible for keeping the membrane of the ship clean from space debris. It was a responsibility for a Quasing of the lowest standing.

Io, on the other hand, as a Receiver, was responsible for maintaining the communication link to the greater Quasing cluster. It was an important and difficult responsibility, reserved for only the most accomplished and perfectly-bred Quasing and one near the highest standing. Their positions could not have been farther apart. That had been the case then, and it seemed the case now, although the tables had turned.

The two had met a century after the crash, when the remnants of the main section of the ship were still trying to get organized. Sabeen was part of the contingent that wanted to explore the planet while Io and many of the other elites wanted to stay on the ship to try to either repair it or reestablish communication. The two had personally butted metaphorical heads, and Io, as she was wont to do back then, had flaunted her standing quite badly in Sabeen's face.

In the millions of years since the crash landing, after all hopes of reestablishing communication with the home world had been shattered, Io had failed to find her place on this world, while Sabeen had found a purpose other than cleaning ship hulls. Now Sabeen's standing put him steps away from being on the Genjix Council, while Io had somehow ended up near the bottom of both organizations.

"That was a long time ago," said Io. "We have all been changed by this planet. What happened to working toward the greater good?"

"If we are to return home," snarled Sabeen, "I intend to do so with my current standing intact. That means I will be the one who receives the standing for getting us home."

"And if I refuse?"

Sabeen shrugged. "You will not. In the end, when we return home, you will lose nothing. You will still be a Receiver. Not all of us will be so lucky. To be a Receiver, even without the glory of being the Quasing's savior, is still better than who you are now."

As much as Io hated to admit it, Sabeen was right. Every fiber in Io's being pleaded with her to just accept Sabeen's terms. The allure of being able to do her job again, of returning home, of being free from the need for hosts, was too great. It was a painful dream she had long thought dead.

To be done with this planet and end the constant cycle of failure. To once again operate as a Receiver. It meant more to Io than she could possibly imagine. The thought that she may actually see the ringed skies of Quasar again hit her so hard, Ella's body wept. It was more than Io dared to hope. All she had to do was say yes. She could begin her work immediately. Everything she had lost could once again be hers.

"I see by the look on your face," said Sabeen, "that you wish for this as much as the rest of the Genjix. This is your chance to save us. Not only the Genjix, but the Prophus as well. Once they learn that we can go home, this silly war with these primitive beings will finally end. You can be the final cure for the violence that has plagued our people."

Still, the terms Sabeen offered were too barbaric to accept. Io had to show her resolve and negotiate better. "You overplay your hand, Sabeen," she said. "I am willing to recognize that you play a small part in returning me to my important purpose, but you need to recognize that I am the last Receiver. You need to agree to my terms."

Sabeen leaned forward in his chair. "Or I can kill your host. Lock you away in a dark, tiny bottle of ProGenesis, and let you think it over. I will open you up once a year to see if you have changed your mind. You may not in the first year or two, but what about after a decade, or a hundred years?"

Sabeen stood up and headed for the door. He opened it and looked back. "I do not know if your relationship with your vessel is as close as she claims. If you do value her, you will accept my terms. Otherwise, I guarantee you she will be dead within days. I give you some time to consider my offer. We leave for China in a few hours."

The door slammed shut with a heavy click, leaving Io alone with her thoughts.

CHAPTER THIRTY-TWO
Finding Ella

Nabin's once guiding and calming presence began to lose its influence. The few times he was able to visit, they bickered constantly. The honeymoon was over. The rose-colored lenses were off, and both began to see the other for who they were. The faults and imperfections showed.

Nabin considered her wild, ungrateful and out of control. Ella accused him of putting his work above her. They were both correct. He demanded she change her ways. She rebelled at his authority. Their fights worsened. Both thought the other in the wrong. Neither was willing to see the other's side.

And where was I during all this?

I encouraged it.

It was raining, because of course it would be the one time Roen and his team had to squat outdoors for a few hours. His knees were acting up in the worst way. If he had any advice to offer the next generation of Prophus agents, it would be to do whatever it took to save their knees and ankles.

He glanced up at the warehouse attached to the rear of the pachinko parlor and averted his eyes from the main street where the constant assault of flashing lights threatened to send him into a seizure. The entire team was here, save for

Asha, who was on the roof of the building across the alley in a sniper nest.

Ella's friends, who for some weird reason called themselves the Burglar Alarms, were here as well. The group had led his team to the yakuza base and was now crouched behind him with their golf clubs and tennis rackets. Excuse him, racquetball rackets.

Roen looked up at the dreary midnight sky; the light drizzle that had been teasing them for the past hour was turning into something more. He pulled his jacket tighter around his body. He could be on *The Basskicker* kicking some bass on the open waters with Jill right now. Soon, very soon.

He caught sight of a silhouette scaling a drainpipe and skulking across the roof of the warehouse. The shadow disappeared from view, and the comm buzzed a few minutes later. "I'm on top of the skylight looking down at the main area of the warehouse. Two floors with catwalks lining the edge. Offices up front on the second floor. Large garage doors in the back. There are rows of equipment lining the center area. Looks like old arcade and gambling machines."

"How much activity?" asked Roen.

"We got a full house, boss. I count fifteen easy at first glance. Who knows how many more are upstairs and in the loading dock."

"Outnumbered three to one isn't my idea of a good time," said Hekla.

"It gets worse," added Nabin. "From what I can see, they're heavily armed."

"Attacking an enemy position while they're on high alert," muttered Pedro. "That's just great. We have wonderful timing."

"Sir," buzzed Asha through the comm, "movement in the back alley. I have eyes on two black sedans and a caravan of transports pulling up to the garage."

The smart money was to wait out the yakuza and even up the odds, but who knew how much longer that would keep him in the rain. Roen had to watch out for his health. Pneumonia was a leading cause of death for people his age. That would be ironic. Survive almost half a century of war, die to a drizzle. In the end, smart money won out, especially when it came to the safety of his team.

"Hold until the herd thins out," he ordered. "Nabin, can you get closer and find out what they're up to?"

"You got it, boss." A few seconds later, Nabin whispered into the comm. "I'm inside. It's one-way though. Had to shimmy through an open window and drop down."

Roen grew more impressed with the lad with each passing day. He was competent, adaptable, and cool-headed. Nabin's skills were being wasted running small-lance operations. He was ready for greater responsibilities, bigger and more important things. Some Quasing should have claimed him long ago.

He signaled to the team to creep closer to the warehouse to provide support in case things got hot. Hekla took lead, and they crept single-file toward the chain-linked fence between the two buildings. Ella's friends began to follow.

Roen put his hand out. "Listen, we appreciate your help, but we'll take it from here."

"Ella's our friend," the one named Daiki said hotly.

"You've done a lot already, but those are armed thugs in there. This isn't a game."

"You can't just leave us out here," said Pek. "It's raining."

Wasn't that the truth.

Roen admired their loyalty and courage, but there was no way in hell he was going to let a bunch of kids wielding gym equipment into a hot zone. He decided to make something up. "If you're keen to help, we need to cover all the escape routes. There's probably a passage to the storefronts, so we need someone stationed there to stand guard. We'll need a few more watching the sides and back as well."

"I'm not old enough to go into the pachinko parlor," whined Daiki, one of the younger ones.

"Another reason why you should be home and studying," muttered Roen under his breath.

Lee raised his arm. "I'll watch the parlor."

"I'll go with you," added Kaoru quickly, clutching his hand.

"I guess I'll watch the side door," said the tattooed guy, Hinata.

"No fair," Pek huffed. "There's cover there from the rain."

"I'll saisho wa guu you for it."

Roen left them to divvy up their assignments and then crept up to the rest of the team, who were squatting in the shadow of a row of dumpsters. All of his people appeared relaxed, almost resting, as they waited for the signal to start. It was the sign of seasoned professionals.

Roen nudged the chain-linked fence with the tip of his boot. "Why isn't this cut?"

Pedro shrugged. "Fence is only six feet tall. We thought we'd just jump it and spare some property damage."

Roen grimaced. "Do you know how old I am?"

"Uh," stammered Pedro. "Actually, I do. You are–"

"–too damn old to climb a fence. Get the wire cutters."

"Sorry, sir. Right away, sir."

Roen looked up at the roof. "How are we looking up top?"

"Vans are parked. One is loading grunts now," said Asha. "Most have handguns. I count three assault rifles and at least five shotguns. I also see a battering ram. They're getting ready for war."

"This is Nabin. I've found Hito Kinata's office. He just threw on his coat and holstered a pistol. He's giving orders to a small group. My Japanese sucks, but here goes: um, um, restoring honor, risk, something, safeguard, police. He definitely said the words Genjix and girl… kill the heir. Oh oh. The group is leaving the office and heading downstairs."

"First van just pulled away," announced Asha. "Second loading now."

"The boss has left the office and gone downstairs to join his entourage. Hang on, footsteps approaching my position. I need to hide."

"Stay safe." Roen checked the row of dimly lit windows just below the roof. They weren't too high up, but there was no way to reach Nabin's position quickly. He stared at the drainage pipe Nabin had used; no way for him to get up, at least. The rest of the team would have to go from ground level.

"Second van pulling out," said Asha.

One of the windows lit up, closely followed by a loud gunshot. Two more pierced the night, and then they were soon joined by the rattling sound of automatic fire adding to the rain's pitter-pattering on the ground.

More rattling followed on their comms. "They found me," said Nabin. "Took two out, but they're swarming."

"Second van just stopped halfway down the street and is reversing course. I'm taking the shot," said Asha urgently. The crack of a sniper rifle joined the night chorus.

"Go, go," yelled Roen. "Asha, don't let the ones in the van back inside. Hekla's team, up through the back. Josie and I will enter through the side door." He turned to the kids. "And none of you even think about stepping foot inside."

Hekla's team crawled through the fence first and disappeared in the shadow of the warehouse. Roen tried to take point and squeeze through next, but was held back by Josie, who looked at him as if he were crazy.

She rolled her eyes and pushed past him. "Beauty before age, old man."

"Beauty before age, sir," he shot back.

"You're retired," she replied, sprinting away.

Roen decided to let her win this round, mostly because he didn't have a clever retort ready. He ran after her.

"We have the ones in the van pinned down," reported Hekla. "There's a whole army back here. We'll keep them busy."

"More like they have *us* pinned down," corrected Pedro.

More sniper shots punctuated the air, and then the all-too-familiar exchange of a gunfight erupted near the loading dock.

"Just keep them busy," said Roen.

He and Josie hugged the walls of the warehouse and they crept up the steps toward the side door situated underneath a green awning. Roen checked the rounds in his shotgun, eyed the Australian to make sure they were on the same page, and breached the door with a short-range blast to the knob.

Sucking in his breath and then slowly letting it seep lightly through clenched teeth, Roen proceeded inside. Frantic yells blasted his eardrums from the side while heavy footsteps rang on the metal catwalk above. He spun to his left and watched for signs of movement. Someone shoved him from behind, knocking him to the ground. An assault rifle rattled over his shoulder.

He looked up just in time to see a yakuza fall. Josie grabbed him by the collar and hauled him back to his feet. "That was too close. I am not taking you back to the Keeper in a body bag."

"She's retired," he replied.

"Once a Keeper, always a Keeper."

Roen pointed at a set of metal stairs to his right. "Let's go save our boy." He touched his comm. "We're in, Nabin. What's your position?"

There were several seconds of silence, long enough to worry Roen. Then Nabin clicked over, breathing heavily. His words came out slurred. "I'm in a tight spot, boss. Holed up in what looks like the break room behind the refrigerator door. Bogeys cornering me in on both sides."

"We're on our way up. Are you all right? Your voice sounds all gummed up." Roen stopped. "Are you eating?"

"They have mochi in the freezer."

Static overcame their comm link. Something hard slammed near the microphone. More gunfire followed.

Roen rushed up the stairs two at a time, took a quick second to catch his breath at the turn, and then went up the rest of the way one step at a time. He reached the second floor completely out of breath. A catwalk lined the perimeter of the warehouse, leading to offices. An open space over the garage kitty-corner to where he stood looked like some sort of break room. It came to life as bursts of gunfire illuminated the darkened area like a firecracker.

Roen weaved his way to Nabin, crouching over as he sped down the catwalk. He could see a dozen people running past through the grating below. One of the side doors opened, and a burly yakuza with a laughably small revolver in his beefy hand jumped out. Roen slammed down on the man's arm with his shotgun and put a slug in his chest.

Another appeared on the catwalk along the opposite wall and opened fire. The glass behind him shattered with a crash, and then three slugs punctured the wall perilously close to his head. Roen flattened himself against the floor, somehow getting his shotgun trapped awkwardly under his body. Cursing, he rolled to his side and opened fire, but his four shots hit nothing. He reached for more shells to reload and then rolled onto his back with his shotgun raised, just in time to see Josie trip a guy and toss him over the railing.

He nodded his thanks and continued to move. He made it halfway across the length of the building when the metal catwalk around him began to spark. Roen dove to the ground again as dozens of tiny yellow sparks exploded around him. He tried to return fire, but the barrage was too thick.

"They've zeroed in on you from below," yelled Josie. "Keep going. I'll cover you."

The colonel dove behind a paneled section of the railing and began to lay down suppression fire, pausing only long enough to swap magazines.

The pressure around Roen abated just enough for him to continue crawling forward on his hands and knees. He made it only a few meters before his knees hurt far too much to go on. He got to his feet and tried to move forward in a crouch. That made his back ache. Finally, deciding to screw it all, he righted himself and ran. He reached the corner and stumbled into two yakuza running in the opposite direction. His shot went wide left, and then they were too close for another. Roen clubbed the first across the side of the head, and then put the second in a choke hold using the barrel of the shotgun.

The second move, in hindsight, was a mistake. Roen had forgotten how much pressure and effort he needed to apply to cut off a man's circulation, and while the shotgun helped, it didn't help enough. The yakuza writhed and wiggled, nearly breaking free of Roen's grip several times. The man threw elbows and punches, and annoyingly kept slapping Roen in the face as his struggles weakened.

Roen's arms began to burn, barely able to maintain the pressure. Choking the man unconscious felt like it would take all night. It became a race to see who passed out first, the yakuza from suffocation or Roen from exhaustion.

Suffocation won out, if barely. The yakuza fell to his knees, and after a few strangled cries, went limp. Roen went limp as well, falling onto all fours and gasping for breath. A nap sounded really good right about now, but the noise of the gun battle below kept him going. He gave himself a second more to recover and then pawed for the shotgun.

Roen got to one knee and looked to the side; Josie was still battling the yakuza below. He touched his comm. "Everyone still here?"

"We're mopping up now," said Asha. "Most of the yakuza are either down or have fled. Two black cars pulled away in the middle of the fight."

"Pedro and I have the rest," said Hekla. "We should have the situation under control in the next few minutes."

"Any injuries?"

"Bullet from a pistol got under my armor," growled Pedro. "I'm not running any marathons any time soon."

"Nabin, you still there? Nabin?"

Roen willed himself to his feet and staggered into the breakroom. He found Nabin on the floor next to an overturned table tussling in close combat with at least half a dozen men. It looked like a tornado had whipped through. All of the chairs were broken, and the refrigerator door was torn off its hinge.

Roen aimed his gun at the tangle of arms and legs. "Everyone freeze."

No one froze. No one was even paying attention.

"Hey," yelled Roen. "I have a shotgun here."

The mob continued to attack Nabin. The Nepalese was a force of nature, however. This wasn't graceful this time; he was fury in a bottle, a torrent of savagery that tore down those who got too close. He was bloodied and cut, but was giving as good as he got, although the yakuza were definitely winning.

Roen aimed his shotgun upward and pulled the trigger. The blast in such a small space sounded like a bomb had gone off. Everyone froze and looked his way.

Roen pointed the shotgun at the mass of bodies again. "Now that I have your attent–"

Debris from the ceiling drizzled down on him. A piece of sheetrock the size of a dinner plate broke over his head. Roen spat out the chalky soot. One of the smartass yakuza tried to take advantage of his distraction by reaching for his gun. Roen shook away the obstruction in his eyes and pulled the trigger again, blasting a hole between the guy's feet. This time the man got the message, throwing his hands in the air.

Roen flipped the shotgun up to his shoulders, grabbed four shots from his hip, and reloaded expertly. Just to show off, he let go of the shotgun and let it roll down to his hip where his finger came back on the trigger.

"What do you know, I've still got it," he grinned. Thank God he had caught it. It would have been awfully embarrassing otherwise. He gestured with the shotgun. "Let him go."

There must have been five sets of hands clawing at Nabin. They let go, and he squirmed his way free, throwing a few extra elbows on his way up.

"Thanks for the assist, boss," he said.

"You mean thanks for the rescue."

"I had it handled."

"Sure you did." Roen touched his comm. "How are we looking downstairs?"

"The warehouse is secure," said Hekla.

"Round them up. Move them to the first floor," replied Roen. "Nabin, clear the upstairs and scour for intel."

As with most things, the action was always the briefest while the cleanup afterward took forever. The team rounded the survivors up into a corner of the warehouse while Nabin searched for information regarding Ella or the Genjix. It didn't surprise him that no one was talking. They had assumed Roen and his team were police, which likely meant they had some sort of catch-and-release agreement set up. Several of them had turned white when they realized otherwise.

Hekla and her team, still hurting from Tarfur's death, wanted to take the screws to some of the yakuza. Nabin, anxious about Ella and feeling they were short on time, agreed. Roen forbade it, instead opting for finesse.

Over the years, he had honed his interrogation skills. Intelligence-gathering was an art, and true interrogation was just a matter of holding negotiations with an individual's psyche. While violence and pain was one method, it was rarely efficient and reliable.

The first step was always jury selection, or in this case, finding the right person to hold negotiations with. Roen walked the lines of prisoners and picked out a particularly well-dressed and haughty-looking young man with a bandage over his nose. As the saying went in their line of work, bravado breaks. Those who show it don't have it.

Roen had Nabin yank the kid into the boss's office for questioning. His choice quickly proved to be the right one; the young man was the boss's son. Roen patted himself on the back for his quality instincts and deduction skills. There was just a stink of nepotism about him.

Nabin sifted through the young man's wallet. "Kid's name is Masato."

"There's also a picture of him and his dad on the wall," pointed Roen.

"You do not realize who you are dealing with," spat the boy. "When my father–"

Roen put a finger to his lips. "Hush. It's not going to be OK."

It took Roen all of five minutes to get the information he needed, all with just a few words. All he had to do was lead Masato to his father's office and read his cues. The boy's eyes gave everything away. It took just a few more softball questions and an angry-looking Nabin playing bad cop for the boy's bravado to crumble like old cheese and to give everything away.

Within minutes, Roen was able to find the hidden safe, was able to determine which drawer held the important papers, and the general logistics of tonight's activities. It looked like a pretty large operation. The one thing he still did not have, however, was an address. Fortunately, young Masato was a sieve, and Roen was able to relatively easily get the kid to give up the password to his father's laptop, which incidentally was *Yakuza123*.

From there it only took a few more minutes to locate the orders from the leader of the Aizukotetsu-kai for Kinata to supply fifty armed men for battle. This mission was to collaborate with the Genjix on an attack on a police facility this very night.

Roen frowned as he read the information. "The Genjix and the yakuza are going to attack other Genjix and the police?"

"Competing factions," Nabin whistled. "They must want her badly. What has Ella gotten herself into?"

"It has to be Io." Roen waved the paper in front of Masato. "There are orders here, but it doesn't have a location. Where did they go?"

Masato shrank back. "I don't know. The orders never mention a place. Just to be ready for battle."

Nabin slammed his fist onto the desk. There was a knock on the door. Ella's friends walked in. Kaoru bowed. "Sorry to disturb you, but we have a problem. Pek's missing. He never returned after the fight."

"What do you mean missing?" asked Nabin.

"After we took the warehouse, the rest of us met up. Pek never showed," said Hinata.

"Why are you telling us this now? We've been here half an hour," said Nabin, waving his hands.

"Pek sometimes gets bored and takes a nap," said Daiki. "We thought perhaps he just got tired."

"But he never showed up?" demanded Roen.

The Burglar Alarms shook their heads.

Roen took a deep breath. The last thing he needed was a dead kid. "We need to look for him right away."

Kaoru held up a phone. "Actually, we know where he is.

He thought it was a good idea to hide in one of the black cars to stay out of the rain. Then the car pulled away."

Roen took the phone. "Pek, is that you?"

"Hellllllllppppp! I'm trapped inside the trunk," replied a high-pitched, panicked scream. "The car is moving. It smells like something died in here."

"Hang on, kid. We're coming." Roen rushed out of the office and leaned over the railing. "Hekla, get me a GPS trace on that phone!"

CHAPTER THIRTY-THREE
The Hunt

I do not deny it. I encouraged and actively worked against Ella and Nabin's relationship. The last thing I wanted for the girl was for her to become a Prophus agent. Being in a relationship with one was just as bad. In either case, Ella would be bound to the Prophus.

It was a connection I could not tolerate. My influence over the girl was limited enough as it was. I did not need to have to compete with someone else. Any chance I got, I tore at the dangling threads of their commitment and watched as it slowly unraveled.

Shura stood on the crest of the hill and scanned the cluster of buildings nestled in the valley at the bottom of Mount Tateshina three hours northwest of Tokyo. It looked like a training facility. To the eastern end near the lone road was the main group of buildings. An impressive obstacle course took over the southwest corner of the camp and a cluster of hollowed-out structures that looked like they were used for urban warfare drills occupied the northwest. The near south end was a sprawling parking lot that housed military and police transports and vans. A tall barbed-wire fence lined the perimeter of the entire base with a good fifty meters between the edge and the nearby forest.

Shura had at first questioned why Rurik would choose such a remote facility to hold Ella Patel instead of, say, a centralized and accessible location like the Tokyo Metropolitan Police Headquarters. That building downtown was a veritable fortress now, nearly impregnable no matter how many yakuza she brought.

Rurik's decision is smart. It is always better to hide than to fortify. You blasted your way through the police headquarters once, so who is to say you could not do so again?

"I *am* rather exceptional," Shura said without any hint of arrogance. "Still, his choice of venue is questionable. The nearest airport is over an hour away."

Look at that open area on the far end, next to the hollowed-out shells. Parallel to those three warehouses.

Shura noticed for the first time the long stretch of runway parallel to the trees on the far perimeter. Now she knew Rurik's plan. By flying out directly from this camp, he mitigated the risk of moving the girl multiple times. Tokyo was a perfect sort of city to ambush a vehicle in transit.

Abbi had informed Shura of a military cargo plane leaving Moscow for Tokyo earlier today. Rurik could have saved time by dispatching one from China, or even chartering one from a commercial liner in Tokyo, but it appeared he was leaving nothing to chance. That meant Shura had to move quickly.

The plane had just entered Japanese airspace. Shura had originally assumed it would be at Narita or a military air base, and had hoped to ambush the transport carrying the Receiver when it left this facility, but now she realized that was not feasible.

She summoned Bashira Nishiki, who was leading the yakuza side of this operation, to her side. "Gather your people for a frontal attack on my command. Draw the police to the front. My people will take care of the rest."

The heir of the Aizukotetsu-kai frowned. "That was not the plan."

"The transport will not depart the base again. This is its final destination."

"There is a tremendous difference between attacking a transport and an actual police base."

"Nobody said becoming the leader of the Aizukotetsu-kai would be easy."

That was not lost on the young woman. She stiffened and bowed. "They will be ready."

After Bashira left, Shura summoned Kloos and the rest of her people. "Change of plans. Kloos, take the team and infiltrate the base to those shelled-out structures. Take over the plane when it lands. Once I have the Receiver, we will commandeer it and depart directly for India."

"I'm not leaving you alone with amateurs," said Kloos.

"Roxani will stay with me then." Before he could protest, Shura added, "You will need everyone else to overtake Rurik's elite guards on that plane."

"His elite guards are already inside that base."

"It's a good thing I have an army of yakuza to play fodder. To your positions."

"Your will, Adonis," they said in unison.

Shura stayed on the hill to oversee the revised operation. The four bodyguards were in position inside the shells of the tactical training buildings within twenty minutes. Bashira had her people organized another half hour later.

They waited and waited. And then waited some more. Shura checked the time. Two hours had passed. Sunrise was an hour away.

Bashira was the first to ask. "What are we waiting for?"

Shura sent her back without an explanation.

Kloos followed up soon after. "Adonis, we are rapidly losing darkness."

Shura was about to reply when she saw the flash of blinking lights in the distance. The sound of engines came soon after. The Antonov military transport maneuvered the turbulent air currents like a pregnant whale, diving from the clouds through the valleys of the mountains. Shura waited until the military transport touched ground and came to a halt.

Wait until the cargo doors open.

The few extra seconds burned in Shura's veins. Her heart beat harder in her chest, her fingers tingled. She yearned for the euphoria of the battle. She didn't revel in death like many of her sisters and brothers at the Hatchery. However, she enjoyed the beauty of the fight.

As soon as the transport turned off the runway and came to a complete stop, Shura spoke into her comm. "Kloos, you're on." She waited several more beats before adding, "Bashira, go."

Five sets of headlights sprung to life in the darkness off the main road. They moved quickly toward the front gates of the base. The gate guard was about to have a very bad night. The poor soul stepped out in front of the vans waving his arms, and then dove to the side when he realized, almost too late, that the lead van was stopping neither for him, nor for the barrier arm. The second van plowed through the chain-linked fence, and all nine vans skidded to a halt perpendicular to the main building. Within moments, dozens of tiny yellow bursts, like fireflies dancing in the sky, lit up the night. Gunfire echoed in the air. Glass shattered, people screamed.

The noise from the battle was soon joined by more further to the west. The rattles of assault rifles and more blinking lights erupted near the airstrip as Kloos and his team moved in toward the cargo plane. An explosion mushroomed into the sky as a nearby fuel truck jumped and crashed onto its side.

Shura took off down the hill, moving at a relaxed jog. The pre-dawn sky was still dark, and the last thing Shura needed was to twist an ankle moments before the most important battle of her life.

Roxani sped away in front of her. The Greek operative was a good half-head taller and several weight classes higher. She carried an assault rifle in hand and had a machete swinging at her hip that was so ridiculously large it could have been mistaken for a cavalry saber. As they neared the chain-linked fence, Roxani drew the machete and, swinging with both hands, hacked at the fence, cutting through it in a matter of seconds.

Shura didn't miss a beat. She charged through, drawing her two pistols and keeping her head low as she fell into a full sprint. They weaved through the rows of trucks and armored vehicles in the parking lot. With most of the attention up front, Shura expected to reach the main building unhindered.

That may have been too optimistic. They encountered a patrolling officer with a guard dog at the row of cars closest to the building. The officer barked a warning and aimed his rifle, simultaneously letting the dog off the leash. The creature growled and charged Shura at full speed.

She dropped to a knee and squeezed both triggers. The first bullet hit the guard in the head, dropping him instantly. The second shattered the nearby truck's driver-side window. The guard dog pounced at her throat. She punched with her left arm, feeding her pistol into the dog's maw. She twisted its mouth aside, wrapped her arms around its body, and shoved the dog through the shattered window in one fluid motion. It yelped as its body cracked against the truck's cabin. The poor creature was cut and injured, but it would live.

You should have just shot them both.

Shura scowled and checked the body of the downed police officer. "I'm civilized, Tabs. I would never shoot a dog." She hated the abuse of innocent animals in service of humanity's disgusting work. She motioned to Roxani to keep moving.

The two reached the loading dock and made their way to the double doors on the far end, staying behind the pallets of supplies and stacks of oil drums.

Halfway down the length of the dock, they found five officers clustered around a set of doors. Shura signaled Roxani to take out those closest to them on her mark. She jumped down to ground level and crept around the concrete peninsula jutting out toward the outer gate.

All five armored. The one crouched against the side wall will be a difficult shot.

"Noted. Not that difficult."

Once she was in place, Shura peeked over the side walls to note their positions relative to each other, and then pulled back. It was barely a momentary glance, but that was all her Holy One needed. Tabs replayed the image in her head several times for her to identify the necessary angles.

When ready, Shura exhaled and turned the corner. Her arms were in place before she could lock in her sights. She pulled the triggers anyway: right, left, left, right. Within a breath, three were down. The first shot missed its mark, it being the difficult one, but the fourth made up for it. The remaining two officers drew their weapons, but were put down by Roxani as she moved in from their blind side. Shura patted the body of one of the officers for keys.

Roxani suddenly moved behind Shura. "Adonis, laser sight on your back. Move to cover."

Without missing a beat, Shura stepped to the near wall and swept her gaze toward the parking lot behind her.

I see movement. Two figures. The laser sight is no longer on.

Shura trusted her Holy One's heightened use of her senses. It was likely another patrol. Why did they not open fire?

Roxani pulled out a Penetra scanner. "I detect six signatures including yours, Adonis. Three near the front of the building. Two on the fifth floor."

Rurik and Sabeen likely have vessels in his personal guard. It speaks to their ego.

"What about behind us in the parking lot?" asked Shura aloud.

"Nothing, Adonis."

"Then whoever is out there is irrelevant to our mission." Tabs checked one more time for any laser sight signals before giving Shura the all-clear. She hurried and unlocked the loading dock doors, and then the two crept inside. "Rurik's personal guards are probably signatures engaging the yakuza. That leaves the Receiver and one other likely on the fifth floor."

Take the turn at the end of the hallway. It should snake to the right to a staging area. Go through it. Afterward, the stairwell will be on your left. Head upstairs to the fifth floor, which should take you to a series of small holding rooms. The odds of the Receiver being kept there are high.

They had managed to find an old blueprint of the facility while planning for the attack. Tabs had taken one look and memorized their route to what was likely the holding cells. The two moved in a crouch with Roxani in the lead and Shura behind with one hand on a pistol and the other on the Greek's back. They hugged the left wall and followed as it curved around the bend. They were about ten meters from the staging area when Roxani stopped and pressed against the wall.

Shura dragged them both down to the ground, her pistol pointed forward. Tabs may have memorized the blueprint of the facility, but that intel was limited. What they didn't realize was that the walls to the staging area were entirely made of glass. Directly on the other side were ten or so people putting on riot gear. Three had their backs leaning on the glass wall.

Too many to take on. Head back the way you came. Go around the right path. You will need to enter a cafeteria section. It should adjoin another stairwell.

She tapped Roxani twice, then palmed her hand down her operative's back: do not engage, pull back. They did not make it more than four steps before one of the officers turned to face them to adjust the straps near her groin. As she looked up, her mouth dropped.

Shura shot to her feet, arms extended. She squeezed three shots: the first shattered the glass and punched the officer in the chest, the second shattered the adjacent window pane and struck the person next to her in the back, and the third struck that same target in the knee. She surged forward, moving with an unnatural grace as her body tilted from side to side, firing continuously.

Three officers went down before they even knew what hit them. Then she jumped through the shattered glass panes and was among them. Shura pulled the trigger point-blank on a man, and dodged a rifle shot that went off so close to her face that the burst burned her cheek. She went low and swept her leg out, tripping two officers. She ended her flurry standing with her pistols trained downward. A pull of each trigger finished off the two laying at her feet.

Shura turned to the man who had nearly put a hole in her face a second earlier and kicked him in the chest, sending him tumbling back into two others. She flowed to the side, dodging a handgun raised to her eye level, and put two rounds into a woman's gut. Her left pistol blocked a kick and sent a slug into an officer's thigh, and then she spun, spraying three shots, of which two hit their marks.

Shura ducked as one fool sprayed the room with his assault rifle, taking him out with a well-placed shot to his ankle. She finished him off with her other gun, tapping him in the head as she moved to her next target. Out of the corner of her eye, she saw someone else dive for her. She jabbed her in the face with the muzzle of her pistol without even looking, and then shot her in the back as she fell. Before Shura had the chance to take ten breaths, all ten of the police in the staging area were dead.

Roxani had just reached the wall and was carefully stepping over the broken glass. She stared at the carnage, her eyes wide. "By the Holy Ones..."

"I told Kloos I didn't need help." Shura slammed the pistols into her gun belt and reloaded. "Let's move."

They continued past the staging room to the stairwell. Shura caught three officers in transit and one more heading downstairs as they exited onto the fifth floor. They alternated their pace and ran a door-to-door sweep, but the area had long been deserted.

They were about halfway across the floor when Roxani called her over. "Adonis, there's something here."

They discovered a pool of blood just inside one of the rooms. The trail dribbled further down the hallway. An overturned chair rested just inside, and four bullet holes showed through the cracks of the mirror on the opposite wall.

Whatever happened here occurred only seconds ago.

Shura stepped inside and examined the table. The chair on the other side of it was still upright, but pushed back. Dried blood rimmed both handcuffs chained to the top of the table, and strands of dark hair were scattered everywhere. Someone had been tortured here, or at least beaten.

Shura glanced at the large mirror across the upper half of the wall. She raised a pistol and unloaded a close grouping in the center. Roxani walked up to it and began to smash the butt of her assault rifle at the cracks, causing the entire wall of glass to collapse.

On the other side of the mirror was a small room with a bank of monitors. A camera on a tripod stared back at them, its lights still blinking. Shura cleared away the jagged fragments of glass and climbed through to the other side.

She rewound it and watched the events that had unfolded.

The timestamp put the scene at less than two minutes ago. Shura broke into a smile. Her appreciation for this Ella Patel grew. Satisfied, she erased all of the footage and hurried out of the room.

Rurik likely has a substantial lead on you.

"From what I saw, I trust in the girl's ability to keep him at bay for a few minutes."

"What are your orders?" asked Roxani, falling in line.

Shura couldn't help but smile. "We have a live one here. We'd best hurry though, before our prey falls victim to the wrong hunter."

CHAPTER THIRTY-FOUR
The Escape

The last straw was when the administrators discovered Ella's theft of Academy supplies, which happened to involve the sale of a utility van as well as several crates of weapons. Not even Cameron Tan, her guardian angel, could save her then. The Academy expelled her. She was actually lucky they did not throw her in prison.

When Nabin heard of this, he broke up with her. He said she was incorrigible and a negative influence on his life.

Their breakup shattered Ella.

The door opened. Rurik walked into the room. Ella tilted her head up from where it rested on her bent arm on the table. Right away, she knew something was different. Io flashed the image in her head: three men stood just outside. Two in police uniforms, one in a fancy suit.

"Our transport has arrived." He walked to the mirror and preened. "Our salvation begins. Tomorrow, Io will be given the opportunity to fulfill her destiny."

"Io needs my permission to fulfill anything," replied Ella. Not even she sounded convinced by that any more.

"You are a vessel," said Rurik. "A body that can be easily replaced. Know this. The only reason you still breathe is because your Holy One has made it known that she fancies remaining in you."

One of the officers grabbed Ella's arm. She yanked it away and bared her teeth. Rurik looked at her in the mirror. He turned and swept the back of his hand across her face, just hard enough to sting. He leaned in. "Listen, you unworthy piece of flesh. Give me any more trouble, and I will execute you where you sit."

It is time you consider what is best for you.

"I'd rather die than do what he says."

That is what is going to happen if you do not keep your mouth shut. We will figure something out when the moment is right. Go along for now until I can come up with an escape plan.

Ella's hackles were raised. "Io, you don't want to go with this jerk, do you?"

I promise you, Ella, that I do not want to cooperate with this human, nor do I wish to align with his Quasing. We have to be smart. Bide our time.

Io's response resonated in Ella's head. "Fine, but it better happen fast. If they get us on the plane, we're finished."

Agreed, so stop antagonizing them. Make yourself appear less of a threat. Cry or something.

"Forget it. I'm not going to cry in front of these assholes."

Think about Burglar Alarm then.

That immediately got Ella weepy. She cursed Io for knowing her weakness. Well, if she was halfway there, she might as well play it up. Ella deflated and moaned, and let one of the officers pin her wrist to the table. The other one kicked the chair from under her and dragged her to her feet.

She kept her body limp, putting up no resistance. The cuffs unshackled and fell away with a clatter. She gingerly rubbed her raw and blistered wrists. It felt like a heavy weight had been lifted. Even this momentary freedom felt good.

Rurik was still preening when the room became bathed in

a deep red light and the unsettling calm was disrupted by the ugly wail of sirens. Sounds of gunfire in the distance soon joined in the cacophony.

The jerk cover model nodded at the reflection of his two men waiting outside. They departed from view. He pulled up his comm and began to dictate orders in Russian.

Get ready. The cop behind you has a holstered gun. The strap is closed, though.

"What about a knife?"

There is a knife on his other side, but go for the gun. Now is not the time for this debate.

"I want the knife too. Just tell me where it is."

Fine. It is in reach just behind your left elbow.

The officer in front of her produced another set of handcuffs while the one behind struggled to hold her up. He slapped the back of her head. "Stand up."

Ella did, but kept her weight back just enough to keep him working on holding her up as opposed to gripping her tightly. As soon as the cuffs were about to go back on her wrists, Ella acted. She leaned on the officer behind her and lifted her legs, kicking out and pushing off the officer in front. The man fell onto his back on the table.

The momentum of the push caused the officer behind her to stagger back. Ella felt herself falling, but she was ready for it. She twisted her body and reached out with her left hand. It missed the hilt of the dagger, and instead she got a handful of the man's belt. It was almost as good. She used the leverage to pull herself to her knees and grabbed the gun from its holster. She turned toward Rurik and fired.

All four shots were errant, the bullets splattering in a horizontal line across the glass. Rurik probably didn't even have to move from where he was standing to dodge. Regardless, he was more confident in her shooting ability than she was. The Genjix ducked and dove to the ground.

A hand grabbed Ella's leg. She turned around and clocked the officer across the side of his head with the pistol.

Go. Get out of here.

Ella decided to grab the officer's knife.

No, leave it.

She struggled with the strap and managed to free the blade. She gripped the knife in her left hand and turned to escape, only to find Rurik blocking the doorway. Ella raised her pistol and unloaded the entire magazine at him. Eight shots, and she missed every one.

The man knew where she was aiming and was somehow quick enough to get out of the way every time she pulled the trigger. It was an impressive display of reflexes. Ella would have complimented him if she didn't hate him so much.

"Why don't you just stay still?" Ella chucked the gun at his face.

He caught it, because of course he did. "I gave you a chance out of respect to your Holy One. Now your life is fore–"

Ella gripped the knife and dove toward his feet. The Russian almost dodged that as well, but almost didn't count when it came to the sharp kiss of a blade. The edge bit into his flesh and gashed his ankle. Rurik stumbled, grabbing a fistful of her leg as she slid by him. Ella abandoned all technique and slashed back and forth at the man's face.

Stay in control. Remember Manish's training.

Io's interruption snapped some calm back into her. Ella buried the frenzied panic growing in her gut before it could take hold. She focused her mind and locked in on the target. She sliced at Rurik again, this time cutting the back of the hand holding her leg. He let go immediately. She kicked out and scrambled to her feet, escaping to the hallway just ahead of the Russian's clutching hands.

Ella picked a direction at random and fled, sensing Rurik a few paces behind her. She turned the corner and slammed the door to the stairwell open, dashing up the stairs immediately.

What are you doing? Go down.

"I'm not heading down into a battle."

If you go upstairs, you will be trapped.

"But..."

The door behind her swung open with a bang and Rurik dove at her. Instinct took over. Ella jumped over the railing to the lower steps. She landed awkwardly and fell, her body feeling every step as she tumbled down. She was on her feet a second later, counting her blessings for not breaking her neck or knocking herself unconscious from that stupid stunt. Her small feet continued paddling down the stairwell as fast as they could move. Rurik came after her, each time just barely missing again as he bounded from landing to landing.

Ella crashed out into the first floor hallway and flattened to the ground. She found herself in the middle of a firefight between the police and an unknown group at the far end. Bullets sprayed the walls, kicking up puffs of drywall and cement. Glass exploded, raining sharp debris around her.

On hands and knees, Ella scrambled behind cover and came face-to-face with a police officer doing the same. They stared at each other, both surprised and unsure of what to do. They looked down at the assault rifle at his feet at the same time. They looked up again and locked eyes.

More gunfire exploded around them. For a moment, Ella thought they had come to a temporary truce. Then the officer shoved her away. He went for the assault rifle. Ella went for *him.*

As soon as he grabbed it and raised the rifle at her, Ella was on him. One cut to the elbow followed by a downward stab to the shoulder put him flat on the ground. Ella kicked the rifle away and, still on all fours, scrambled like a tiny pony through high weeds to the other end of the room.

She wasn't sure who the police were fighting, but these cops had kidnapped her and sold her off to the Genjix.

Anyone was better than them. Ella didn't know why, but she harbored a deep-seated irrational hope that it was Nabin and his Prophus friends swooping in to save the day. If it were him, she would forgive him for everything. Maybe even tell him she loved him.

Can you not do that right now?

"I'm probably going to die any second. My last thought should be whatever I want it to be."

Fair enough.

Ella stopped in her tracks when she saw a greasy tattooed older guy, in sunglasses, leaning out of cover. "Crap." Of course it would be the yakuza. She turned and began to crawl to the wall instead. She reached the safety of a shredded-up cubicle and curled into a ball, her hands over her ears to drown out the loud automatic fire exploding close by.

Police on one side, yakuza on the other. Maybe hiding upstairs was the right decision after all. This place is a death trap.

"You are so not useful."

Ella watched as the police began to rout. It started with an officer getting shot. Another ran out of bullets and abandoned his position. Then the panic spread.

The yakuza, sensing their opportunity, surged forward. Several roared and rushed past her position. More gunfire. Ella had thought they might have overlooked her hiding spot when one of the less eager ones walked past. He looked at her and frowned, pointing his rifle.

Ella prepared to leap at him.

No, he is too far out of range. You will never cover that distance.

Io was right. Ella reluctantly put her hands up.

The yakuza looked to the side and yelled to his associates. "Hey, I've caught her. I got the girl we're looking for. I–" He stiffened and fell. Another yakuza was tossed like a rag doll and bounced off the wall. Two more charged past her position; two more were knocked over like bowling pins.

Rurik stepped into view a moment later. Ella froze, partially hidden under a desk behind an overturned office chair. The Russian sidestepped and tilted his head as a yakuza appeared from his side and fired several times. Rurik contorted his body and dodged the hail of bullets. It was like magic, almost. He proceeded to take the man out with a single shot.

Another yakuza appeared to his right, wielding a shotgun. Rurik grabbed the barrel and pushed the muzzle away from himself. The two struggled over the weapon, then Rurik struck him three times quickly in the throat. The yakuza gagged and staggered, clutching his neck. The jerk cover model snatched the shotgun out of the man's hand and swung it, striking him down. He followed up with a double-tap into the unfortunate soul's chest at close range.

The action fell into a lull. Rurik appeared to be listening to the air. Shouting and gunfire still punctured the night, but it sounded far away. Only the low creaks of the shattered office furniture and broken glass interrupted the temporary lull.

He has not seen you yet. Stay calm.

Easier said than done. Ella froze in place and waited. With just a little luck, he would overlook her and continue to the next room. Then she could go the opposite way and find an exit. The shotgun fell from his hand and Rurik took another step forward. Just as he was about to step out of view, he turned to the side and noticed her.

Ella was ready for it. She was expecting her luck, as it had been the past few weeks, not to hold up. She burst out of her hiding place, her knife slashing. She sliced only air, but it pressed him back far enough to give her room to run.

Ella took off, jumping over bodies and ducking under broken pieces of wire and lights hanging from the ceiling. She could sense Rurik just a few steps behind. There was no way she was going to outrun him. She had just neared the end of the hallway when a police officer stepped out to block her way. Ella didn't miss a step and juked to her left. Her knife shot out and nicked the man's arm.

Grab his gun.

"Oh fine." Ella again didn't care for it, but her hand was right there. Besides, she had to get Rurik off her back. She pulled the gun out of the police officer's holster and spun around to face Rurik, who was only a few steps behind. The Adonis vessel pulled up to a stop, but it was too late. He was in point-blank range, just outside of arm's length but still so close Ella couldn't miss even if she wanted to.

"Die, asshole." She squeezed the trigger.

Nothing happened. The trigger wouldn't budge.

Rurik smirked. "The safety, stupid."

Watch out!

Ella looked up just in time to see Rurik spin gracefully in place. The last thing that occurred to her before his leg whirled around and smashed her in the face was that Rurik would have made a pretty good ballet dancer.

CHAPTER THIRTY-FIVE
Last Hurrah

Unlike some of the other creatures I have inhabited, humans rarely mate for life. Sometimes I think they should, just to avoid having to deal with the repeated emotional trauma.

Ella took the breakup as she took most things: badly and angrily. At that moment, she had declared that she was done with the Prophus, and intended to strike off on her own.

This was a positive development.

Roen was worried they had arrived too late for the party. They had run into traffic on the way out of the city. Some Japanese three-letter boy band had just finished a concert, and the roads were crammed. Fortunately, it cleared at the city limits, and they were soon speeding dangerously down mostly deserted streets.

The wide and well-lit highway ended at the edge of the city. The roads began to snake and weave through the mountains and valleys of the Japanese Alps. To Roen's distress, the van did not slow whatsoever as it cornered perilously close to the edge. He gulped at the sheer drop of the cliff and then looked uneasily over at Nabin, whose face was grim as his eyes focused on the road. The Nepalese's hands were in a perfect ten-two position, his arms were taut, and the veins on his neck were bulging.

"We're not going to do her any good if we drive off the mountain," he said quietly. "My wife will definitely kill you then."

"We've wasted too much time already, sir," said Nabin. His tense arms shuddered and he hammer-fisted the steering wheel. "Ella's probably already gone."

"I wouldn't bet on it. The yakuza will get there ahead of us," said Roen. "They probably already have her. We just need to go in and clean up."

"Not with the way they fight," growled Nabin.

That much was true. If the amateur-hour display at their base was the best the yakuza could do, the Genjix were going to wipe the floor with them. Still, it was their best shot.

"Sir," said Nabin. He stopped. "I need to ask you for a favor."

"What is it, son?"

"I need a transfer. If we do rescue Ella, the Prophus are going to have to hide and protect her. You can't lock her up. Hide her someplace safe where she can be happy. And..." he stopped and swallowed, "...and assign me to protect her."

"Nabin," Roen's voice was soft. "That's going to kill your career. You're one of our finest. You're up for host whenever you want. You're on the shortlist for command operations. Cameron calls you the best agent he's ever worked with."

Nabin shrugged. "I don't care. Can you pull these strings for me? Otherwise, I'll just quit. I'll still end up in the same place."

Jill was going to kill him if Roen agreed. First of all, he'd never had the authority to promise anything, even before he was retired. Second, he wasn't sure if the Prophus would or even could protect Ella. Wasn't that what they were trying to do by enrolling her in the Academy? To allocate a high-value resource like Nabin to a rogue like Ella felt exactly like something Jill and the new Keeper would absolutely forbid.

Still, from what he had seen here, maybe this arrangement was the best course of action. The Genjix had committed tremendous resources to finding Ella, more than at any other time he could remember. As far as Roen could tell, the Genjix had two high-level Adonis vessels hunting her, and were leveraging not only local government, but local organized crime as well.

They hadn't even tried this hard to assassinate Roen, and he had peaked on their top ten most-wanted list. It was almost insulting. Now that he thought about it, the Genjix hadn't tried this hard to assassinate Jill, and she'd been *numero uno* on that list for two decades. Whatever they wanted – or needed – from Ella, they wanted it badly.

The girl had already proven difficult to control. Her stint at the Academy spoke to that. Maybe having Nabin – the kids were obviously still in love – watching over her would be the best thing. At the very least, she might listen to him. God knows she didn't listen to anyone else.

"I'll see what I can do," said Roen. "No promises."

"Thank you, sir."

Nabin turned off the headlights as they climbed the crest of the last hill before reaching the police base. He pulled the car off to the side into a grouping of trees, and the team continued the rest of the way on foot.

Josie tugged on Roen's sleeve as they walked up the hill. "Hey old man," she said with a wry smile on her face. "We're probably either going to die, spend the rest of our life in a Japanese military prison, or get captured by the Genjix. You know that, right?"

"Or, sunshine, we can rescue Ella Patel and spirit her into the loving arms of the Prophus."

She snorted. "Fat chance." She leaned in. Her voice fell to a whisper. "Listen, I think you should stay behind."

"What? Get out of here." He pushed her aside playfully. He

actually tried to shove her for the outrageous suggestion, but he wasn't able to nudge her very far.

She shook her head. "I would love to say I'm watching out for your welfare because you've served the Prophus for a long time and deserve to live out the rest of your life in peace, but that's not it." She grabbed his shoulders. "You once had the highest clearance within the Prophus. If they capture you, they'll break you. You'll leak and break faster than a fishing boat during a monsoon."

"Thanks for the vote of confidence," said Roen dryly. "It's not a suicide mission."

"If you were running ops on this against these odds, would you send your people in?"

"Probably not," admitted Roen. "However, it depends on the stakes, and I would say the stakes are high enough we have to at least try."

"We don't even know the stakes. We have no idea why the Genjix want the girl. For all we know, they just want to capture her because her Quasing was bunk buddies with the Genjix leader back in their alien spaceship."

"I doubt our enemies want Io simply to reminisce about their old gassy alien days," said Roen. "The Genjix have leveraged substantial resources over the past several months trying to find her. Tens of thousands of man-hours, we've traced over hundreds of millions of dollars in bribes, and almost every single surveillance and spy network was tuned to finding her. Whatever she has or knows, they want it badly, and the more they want it, the more we want them to not have it."

She shrugged. "Suit yourself, sir. It's just that you're one of our seniors. People look up to you. You've served the Prophus well for nearly half a century. You deserve peace and rest. I hate to see you throw your life away like this."

"I'm not..." His voice trailed off as she walked on ahead.

What *was* he doing here? Hadn't he told himself that once he retired, he was done? He had served the Prophus and this planet, had given them everything he had. Regardless of what the Genjix wanted with Ella Patel, it should be someone else's problem. Josie was right. What *was* he doing here?

Roen knew the answer. This was his last hurrah. He wanted to see if he still had it. Just because he was retired, didn't mean he had retired his sense of duty to the Prophus and humanity. He was also one to see a mission through. He hated letting the Genjix win. After fighting against them for most of his life, the idea that he would walk away and hand them a victory – after all that they'd put him and his family through – was completely unacceptable.

Not bad for an out-of-shape goof who hadn't been able to throw a punch when the Prophus had found him. Tao would be proud. No, Tao *was* proud. "And Tao would definitely tell you not to attack that base," he chuckled. "It's too late now. We didn't get all dressed up for nothing."

"Sorry sir? Did you say something?" said Hekla, as he approached the crest of the hill and stood next to her. She handed him a pair of night-vision binoculars.

"Never mind." He scanned the grounds. It was quiet, sleepy almost. Other than a few spotlights scattered along the fenced perimeter, there was little light and no movement. He became worried. "Did we get bad intel?"

"We're too late. They already left," choked Nabin. He clutched his head in his hands.

Then he heard it. It was the sound of a plane. He scanned the skies and found the blinking lights of a military transport. He followed its path as it landed on the far end of the base.

No sooner had it taxied than a row of headlights turned on to the right of the base. Several vehicles charged through the fence, and then the sounds of gunfire filled the night. Within seconds, the entire valley exploded into a battlefield.

Roen signaled to Asha. "You have your positions figured out?"

Asha was staring through the night-vision scope of her sniper rifle as she walked alongside him. She nodded and pointed into the distance. "The yakuza have two cars that fit the description Pek gave us. The kid's not answering his phone, but don't worry, I'll find him. After I haul his butt out of the trunk, I'll send him back to our car, and then take position on that mound further up the hill. I should have a clear line of sight on two sides of the building and the airstrip." She paused. "Why did the kid hide in the trunk anyway?"

Roen shrugged. "His friends said he almost got caught in the open while moving across the parking lot, and the opened trunk was the first hiding place he found. He hid behind a piece of tarp and then they closed it on him."

"Just not his night."

He grunted. "It is if he's still breathing."

Hekla, Nabin and Pedro were up next. The three of them were masked and dressed like yakuza. They had decided to insert into the main building through the front entrance and attack the yakuza from behind, figuring they would be the force with the superior strength. Once they were inside, Hekla and Pedro would scour the first floor while Nabin covered the upper levels. There was the possibility that the police could win this exchange and that their disguises would betray them, but it was a chance they had to take.

That relegated Josie and Roen to the perimeter, which everyone assumed would be the safest and easiest part of the mission. Everyone surmised that most of the fighting would occur inside the building. All Roen and Josie had to do was keep the plane grounded. It wasn't something the two of them shouldn't be able to handle. Roen chafed at being relegated to auxiliary duty, but it was the right call. He was a distant shadow of who he used to be, but it still bruised his ego.

The team reached the bottom of the hill and made their way across the field to the fence. To his surprise, they found part of the chain already cut, albeit poorly. The yakuza must have been in a hurry. A little further study revealed that the grass in this area had recently been trampled. There must have been another team of Genjix or yakuza attacking from this side. Someone close by pulled a trigger and then glass shattered. The team fell into a squat. More gunfire, and someone's dying cry echoed in the night. A dog's high-pitched whine followed.

They waited several beats before Roen nodded to Hekla. The team crept through the cut fence and then split apart. Josie and Roen moved through several rows of parked vehicles and made their way west to the back of the base. The sounds of the fighting crescendoed. They reached a transport truck parked in an inner row and paused.

A police officer lay dead next to the driver's side and there were glass shards scattered all over the ground. Roen peeked inside the front cab and found a bloodied and injured German Shepherd, whining as it licked its paw. The dog looked up and began to growl.

He retreated from the poor animal and raged a little. "Those monsters. I'll make those Genjix assholes pay."

He motioned to Josie to continue. They made it a few more meters before a gunfight near the docks erupted, presumably between the yakuza and the police. Josie and Roen dropped to the ground and aimed their rifles at the sounds of battle. He found the action through his scope. A couple of the yakuza had just taken out a squad of police and were about to head into the building.

"I have a bead on the one on the left." Josie clicked off the safety, and her finger drifted onto the trigger.

"Stand down." Roen put a hand over the scope. "That's not our mission. Eyes on the prize. Last thing we need to do is get bogged down in a firefight out here while the plane takes off."

Asha buzzed in over the comm. "I found the boy. He was snoring in the trunk. You believe that? Anyway, I sent him back to the car. I'm heading up the hill. ETA five minutes. It's a big hill."

"What's our situation inside?" asked Roen.

"It's a zoo," replied Nabin. "The yakuza and police are going hard at each other. Best thing to do is stay out of their way and find Ella."

Josie nudged Roen, and they continued to the west end of the parking lot. They reached a cluster of darkened buildings and crept alongside the furthest structure from the base. The two of them flanked a window opening and glanced in. There was no frame and incidentally nothing inside. The building was completely hollow, just four walls and a leaky roof.

Roen touched her shoulder and pointed at a silhouette standing on the far side near the corner. He signaled in both directions and they split apart. Josie circled around to the side door while Roen crawled in from the far window.

She got into position first, creeping through the entrance on the other side and rushing the target. Roen was several seconds late, having a little trouble swinging his leg through the window while holding his rifle.

Josie dragged the target to the floor and jabbed her rifle into their face. She relaxed. "Target dummy."

He helped her up. "Even better. We should be able to get closer to the plane without anyone noticing."

They left the empty building and sneaked from cover to cover. They were now in view of the transport. It had moved over from the end of the runway and made a U-turn. A fuel truck approached it from the side. The plane kept its engines running. The rear cargo door began to lower. The plane was obviously not meant to stay on the ground for long.

"We're moving in," said Roen. "How's it look from up on high?"

"I've got eyes on you, sir," replied Asha. "I do not have a clear view of the back, but I have clear sights of the area between the transport and buildings, so try to keep the action west."

Josie, who was tracking the plane through her scope, held up three fingers. Roen's hopes rose. That wasn't too bad, especially if they had the element of surprise. Three visible, probably one or two more inside, including the pilots. All they had to do was take out two in the initial ambush to even up the odds, and then take over the plane.

"Wait," hissed Asha sharply. "I have movement coming from the building two over from you. I count five more approaching the plane from the port side. Possibly a patrol."

Roen's hopes sank just as quickly as they rose. Nine versus two were worse odds than if he were to go five rounds in the ring with Cameron, and Roen had not been able to beat his son in a fight since the damn kid was fifteen.

Roen suddenly really missed his miserable garden. "If I make it out of this alive, I'm going to pave it over and make a basketball court," he muttered. "Life's too short to grow asparagus."

"Something is not right," continued Asha. "The new group is approaching the transport in an attack pattern."

A crack hammered through the air, and one of the guards at the plane fell. Several more gunshots followed. Within seconds, the airfield had turned into a full-blown battle, all without Roen or Josie firing a shot.

The two fell back to their hiding place. "What the hell are they?" she shouted.

He had hoped it was the yakuza, but he needed only a glance to recognize the movements of a professional outfit.

"It's Genjix on Genjix violence," he replied. "I couldn't be happier. Maybe we should wait them out and let them kill each other."

She peeked over the side. "I don't think we have that luxury. The ones on the plane are already getting overwhelmed. If we want the plane for ourselves, we need to hit them while they're preoccupied."

Roen agreed. "Let's go."

The space between their hiding place and the plane was a good hundred meter stretch of open field. They were sitting ducks, but it would probably be all right as long as no one turned around.

Roen didn't make it ten steps out of cover before one of the attackers, who had taken position at the base of the ramp while the others had gone inside the transport, turned and noticed their approach. So much for stealth. The yellow burst of gunfire exploded as the ground near their feet kicked up. Roen and Josie split and ran in opposite directions. The trail of bullets followed him, because that was just his luck.

He sprinted as fast as his tiring legs could carry him. He considered diving to the ground and returning fire, but he was pretty sure his constant movement right now was the only reason he hadn't eaten half a dozen slugs. Besides, his eyes weren't good enough to shoot someone at fifty meters with an automatic rifle. He weaved side to side and had just made it onto the tarmac when a bullet grazed his foot, sending him tumbling forward. He crashed onto the runway and felt his body crunch along the cement. He finally landed unceremoniously on his side and groaned. He felt as if his skin had just been raked by a cheese grater.

"Get your ass up, old man," shouted Josie, hiding on the other side of the tarmac. She had found cover behind a signpost and was trying to pin his attacker down.

Roen stared in resignation as the burst of the muzzle exploded a chunk of cement inches from his face. The next shot wasn't going to miss. A crack rang through the air, and then their attacker went down.

"I got you covered, sir," Asha's voice blasted in his ear.

"Thanks for the assist," he replied, picking himself up off the ground.

"Good, then I suggest you stop napping, old man."

Roen scowled. Kids had no respect these days. He felt a sharp pain when he put weight on his right leg, but nothing that would prevent him from staying in the fight. It wasn't like he was throwing many kicks these days anyhow. He limped slightly as he met Josie at the ramp.

"Are you injured?" she asked.

Roen kept a brave front. "I've hurt myself worse shaving."

She grinned. "That's why I stopped shaving years ago."

They crouched again and crept up the ramp to see a firefight waging in the belly of the transport. They stayed close to the floor and snuck from cover to cover. The sound of fighting was erratic. The air was thick and hot, filled with smoke.

Somewhere in front, a gruff voice with an Indian accent shouted, "Light them up!"

Another barrage of gunfire followed. Roen and Josie reached several stacks of oil drums tied down on top of a pallet and held their position. He peeked over the side. The original transport crew was desperately holding a center staircase just outside of the cockpit while the attackers were behind cover in the main hold below. As far as he could tell, the defenders were down to the two pilots while the attackers still numbered four.

He signaled to Josie to go on five, and ticked his fingers down: five, four, three…

The fighting stopped. Someone called for a ceasefire. Roen hesitated and froze.

A large man with a gruff voice yelled out in an Indian accent. "That's the last of them. Secure the plane. Shoot any survivors."

Roen cursed under his breath. They had missed their opportunity to take out the Genjix while they were preoccupied with each other. Josie mouthed silently, asking for orders. They had little other choice. Roen held up three fingers, finished the countdown, and then stood up.

He and Josie opened fire, taking down two of the four attackers before they knew what hit them. The remaining two ducked and disappeared from sight. Josie yelled something and moved forward, also disappearing from view.

Roen had no choice but to do the same, lest he risk Josie getting flanked. Clutching the rifle close to his body he crept forward, his back rubbing along the side of a wooden pallet. He reached the corner just in time to see a flurry of action on the other side. Josie was locked in close combat, grappling with one of the Genjix. They were spinning in circles, bumping into the walls and containers as they wrestled for her gun.

Roen was unable to get a clear shot. "Stop dancing, you two," he muttered. It was too risky. He decided to move in closer. No sooner had Roen left his cover than a flash out of the corner of his eye grew larger. His ribs cracked, and then all of a sudden he was flying through the air.

A second later, Roen found himself staring up at the ceiling, gasping like a fish flopping in the sand. He tried to raise his head, but his body vetoed the impulse as he struggled to catch his breath. A shadow towered over him.

A large man with a fierce mustache squinted. Recognition flashed across his face, and he smirked. "I know who you are, Roen Tan. You look a poor shadow to the last time our paths crossed, but I never forget a face. Know that Mayur Kloos is your executioner." He raised his pistol to Roen's face.

A gunshot cracked through the hold, and the man stiffened and stumbled forward. He spun and pointed his pistol to the side and took two more hits to the chest. He managed to return fire and was rewarded with Josie's cry of pain.

Roen kicked out, connecting his heel to the side of this

Kloos fellow's knee. He picked himself up off the ground and punched at the guy. That was a mistake. The Genjix, even injured, easily avoided his attack and, with one beefy hand, swatted him in the face. Ears ringing, Roen lunged and grabbed for the pistol.

He would have loved to say later on that he gave the man a tough fight, but in reality Mayur tossed him around like a rag doll. Three hard shakes later, Roen was flying in the air again, this time landing hard against the metal steps leading to the cockpit, his head bouncing off one as he crashed.

His body had finally had enough and told his brain to shut down. Roen began to lose consciousness. He heard some distant shouting, more gunshots, his ears rang. Then someone had the audacity to slap him. Roen woke with a start to see Josie leaning over him.

"Wake up, wake up," she said, panting heavily.

"What happened?" His head was woozy and the room spun. He looked to the side and saw Mayur Kloos slumped against the far wall. "Oh, we got him. Hooray us."

"You distracted him enough for me to recover and shoot him," she replied.

Roen looked Josie over and realized there was blood caked down the left side of her face. Her clothing was also dark and wet. "You look awful."

The colonel's breathing was labored. "He got me pretty good. Shoulder, thigh, chest. My armor absorbed the brunt of it, so I'll live, I think. I also cut my scalp when he slammed me into the wall. Otherwise," she grinned, "I feel great."

Josie helped him to his feet and then he had to help her stay upright. Together they managed to get up the stairs, past the three bodies of Genjix soldiers, and into the cockpit.

She collapsed into one of the chairs, her body heaving. She coughed, and blood poured out of her mouth. "I can't seem to catch my breath."

Roen helped tear off her armor and checked for wounds. "Your lung's collapsed."

Asha's voice crackled in his ear. "Sir, I've lost sight of you. Are you in the transport?"

Roen touched the comm. "Yeah we have control of the plane. The Genjix aren't going anywhere. Josie's hurt though. We need to..."

"You have company coming," she yelled. "Get out of there now!"

Roen stood up and looked out of the cockpit window. A small army had emerged from the main building and were making their way across the field toward the transport. They were a mix of police and Genjix operatives. Two of the Genjix near the front were dragging a small slumped figure by the arms. Leading the entire entourage was the unmistakably familiar sight of a tall, good-looking pretty boy.

"Oh crap," muttered Roen.

He went over and tried to pick up Josie. A moan escaped her lips. She shook her head and pushed him away. "Get out of here, Roen Tan. I'll hold them off at the cockpit as long as I can."

"I'm not leaving you."

"We'll never make it out together. I'm hurt and you're old." She coughed. More blood poured down her chin. "You've done your time. Go enjoy retirement. You've earned it. It's been an honor, sir. Say hi to the Keeper for me. Tell her I've always admired her."

"Don't you dare die on me, Josie. We're riding off into the sunset together." Roen clenched his fist and shouldered his rifle. He had never abandoned anyone in his entire career, he wasn't going to start now. "Nabin, where are you? What's your ETA?"

"We're trying to fight our way out of the building. There's still a ton of gangsters running around the base," Nabin called back. "We're not going to be able to make it to you in time."

Roen considered his options, and then came to the conclusion that he really had none. At least not one that he was willing to live with, retired or not. He picked up Josie's rifle and put it in her hands. He then checked his own and reloaded. Roen positioned himself behind cover next to the doorway.

"We'll hold them off as long as we can, Nabin. You'd better hurry, son, or you'll have my wife and kid to answer to."

CHAPTER THIRTY-SIX
The Final Standing

Ella and I devised a plan to leave Australia. The Academy had offered to fly her anywhere in the world. I had at first recommended returning to India, which was now a solidly Genjix country.

Ella wanted to strike off on her own, away from both the Prophus and the Genjix. Her original destinations had been Namibia or Tanzania. Fearing to be taken too far from my original goal, I proposed a neutral country, but one still close to the Genjix.

We settled on Japan.

Shura was running out of people to kill. She retracted her blade from the throat of one of the police officers and wiped it on his shirt. He sagged and slid down, a streak of red staining the wall. Roxani was at the other side of the room, checking the bodies and double-tapping anyone still breathing.

The two had descended upon the police from the rear while they were preoccupied with the yakuza up front. Shura and Roxani had swept the entire upper levels of the main facility, and had yet to come across Rurik or Ella Patel. Shura was beginning to wonder if her rival had captured the girl and slipped through her grasp.

"Kloos," she called. "What is your status with the transport?"

His voice crackled. "We're in the main hold. Should have it secured in a few minutes."

"No survivors," she replied.

"Your will, Adonis." Kloos shouted so loudly it hurt her ears. "Light them up!" The sounds of battle renewed over the comm.

As long as the plane stays grounded, our quarry is close by. It is equally in Sabeen's interest to see to the welfare of the Receiver as it is in yours.

Roxani checked the Penetra scanner again. "There are still six signatures in the building, including you. Two on the ground floor moving toward the back of the building. Two more together on this level near the western stairwell. There is also a lone signature four rooms over."

There was little chance Rurik would stray far from the Receiver unless the girl had managed to evade him. It was worth checking out. Shura reloaded her pistols and slowly pushed the heavy metal door open a sliver. The hallway was empty and absent of sound. She closed her eyes.

Rapid breathing just on the other side.

Shura shoved the door open hard and wide, and was rewarded with resistance and a muffled cry. She swept her arms out and encountered two police officers laying in ambush. A rifle swung close to her face. She dodged and swept her right arm out, parrying the barrel of the rifle away with the pistol in her right hand. She punched two slugs into the police officer's chest, and then shoved the falling body aside. She turned to kick the rifle out of the hand of the remaining officer, and then put another bullet from each pistol into his chest.

Roxani came out into the hallway and looked down at the two bodies. One of the officers was still moving, so she finished him off with another shot. She checked the scanner and pointed in the other direction. "This way."

Shura and Roxani found the source of the signature in the corner stall of a men's restroom. A young yakuza, looking more boy than man, huddled in a fetal position next to the toilet with his arms wrapped around his knees. He wore a thousand-mile stare as he rocked back and forth. Incoherent mutters dribbled out of his lips. Shura put a hand on the young man's forehead.

It is Mammay.

That had to mean Sogolov, Rurik's head of security, was dead. The world – and the Genjix – were better for it. Sogolov was a brutal man who had tortured and killed several of Shura's troops over the years. Her fingers twitched. There were no windows and one exit out of the room.

Do not be sacrilegious.

"Of course. My apologies, Tabs." She couldn't help her thoughts, but even then it was inappropriate to wish death on a god. They were all still Genjix after all.

The young man looked up at her. "Voice... take away... no leave."

Shura closed the stall door and signaled to Roxani to go. Trapping Mammay in a broken mind was punishment enough. The boy was obviously in shock from the presence of a Holy One in his head. He may or may not eventually recover, but this was one of the best ways to keep one of Rurik and Sabeen's dedicated sycophants out of action for a few decades.

"Where to next?" she asked.

Roxani checked the Penetra scanner again. "Two clusters of signatures. Both are on the move. Rurik's people appear to be pulling back to the transport."

Shura touched her ear. "Kloos, what is your status?" No answer. Shura called the rest of her team. Again no answer. She next contacted Bashira. "Move all of your yakuza to the air strip."

At least the heir to the Aizukotetsu-kai was still answering. "There are still pockets of police in the building."

"They are irrelevant," snapped Shura. "Only the girl is important."

Roxani motioned to Shura. "Two of the signatures are passing right below us on the ground floor. If we hurry, we can intercept them."

Do it. If something has happened to your team at the transport, and Rurik has the Receiver and escapes to the field outside, your chances of capturing them will be slim.

Shura burst into the stairwell with Roxani close behind. She leaped over the side and dropped down to the railing below. She stepped to the adjacent lower railing as it snaked around the bend and then continued on down. Roxani, who was sprinting down the stairwell, had just reached the second landing by the time Shura was on the ground.

You should wait for her.

There was no time.

Shura left the stairwell and realized her mistake far too late. The two signatures were two of Rurik's lieutenants alongside four of his bodyguards. She recognized Nilaksh and Halston from Hong Kong. The group looked tired, as if they had just been dragged through a war. All sported minor injuries. Halston, who was the one Shura had beaten, was holding his arm.

One of the vessels – Shura forgot his name – began to bark orders. "It's Shura. Take the Adonis. Alive preferably. Dead just as–"

Shura shot him twice between the eyes.

His Holy One's name is Pollack.

"Whatever."

The remaining Genjix attacked. Shura dodged a punch from the nearest bodyguard, blocked Halston's right cross, but took a punch square in the jaw from Nilaksh. The other vessel, Kang, drew his sidearm and clubbed her across the side of the face. The room swayed as he hit her again and then jabbed the muzzle of his gun over her heart as he pinned her against the wall.

As soon as she felt him pull the trigger, Shura jerked her body to the side and shoulder-checked his arm, deflecting the shot. She tied her arm around his wrist and angled it to the side. Kang continued to squeeze shots and only succeeded in hitting one of his own.

Shura elbowed the vessel in the face to create a little distance between them, then smashed the butt of her pistol over Kang's nose, exploding a spray of blood. She tapped him once in the abdomen as he fell to the floor.

To your right.

Someone large slammed into her from the side. The air fled her lungs as she flew out of control and her body spasmed uncontrollably. Even then, as she fell backward, she lashed out, pulling the trigger blindly. One shot hit nothing, but the other struck one of the unknown bodyguards. The last thing she saw before crashing to the floor was blood spewing from his neck as the man spun to the ground.

Then the remaining Genjix were on her.

It was an inevitable result. Even Adonis vessels could be overwhelmed, especially fighting their own people, some of whom were almost as skilled as her. Shura struggled as best she could, but dozens of blows continued to rain down on her. Eventually, human instincts took over, and she stopped fighting back and attempted to just cover up.

That was when Shura knew she had lost.

Just as soon as the fight had started, it ended. One second Halston had his knee on her chest striking her repeatedly in the face, the next, he was thrown off of her and held his stomach from a gunshot wound.

Roxani stood over Shura, her rifle sweeping over the surviving guards. "Are you all right, Adonis?"

Shura sat up and clutched her bruised forehead. "You run too slow."

"Apologies, Adonis."

She spat out a tooth and climbed back to her feet. She walked over to where she had dropped her pistols and checked the bodies. Halston would take days to die with that painful stomach wound. Nilaksh looked roughed up, but no worse for wear.

She determined which vessel Pollack had chosen and left him alive. She did not do any more to Kang, either, though she would not lift a finger to aid either of them. Their Holy Ones guaranteed them their lives, nothing more. With Halston, she gave him a dismissive glance and then shot him once in the chest.

As for Nilaksh, Shura walked over to her while she was crawling toward and pawing for her rifle. Shura kicked it away. The woman, now resigned to her fate, looked up expectantly.

Shura considered her options. "Want a job?"

Nilaksh blinked. "Adonis?"

"You get one chance. Pledge to me until death and you will live a while longer."

"I am honored by your request, Adonis, but my loyalty can't be bought so easily," replied Nilaksh, rising to her knees. "However, if you would consider sparing–"

Shura shrugged. "I can respect that choice." She double-tapped the trigger.

You cannot convert everyone.

"Pity."

She reloaded. "Now where is Rurik?"

"He has the Receiver and is making his way to the transport."

"Let's go." The two exited through the nearest door and found themselves on the northern end of the building. They sprinted westward and turned the corner to find another shootout boiling in the open field. The remaining police had established a perimeter around the plane and were battling the last of the yakuza, who had just exited the building. There weren't many left on both sides, but there didn't need to be for the fight to get bogged down.

That was when Shura spied Rurik and the Receiver's host, Ella Patel. They were near the bottom of the transport's ramp. For some reason, they hadn't gone up yet. Shura thought she knew why. "Kloos, are you there?"

Still no answer.

The uncertainty grated on her. Shura signaled for Roxani to follow. They gave the battle a wide berth, moving to the far side and circling around the port side of the plane. They jumped down to a drainage ditch that ran parallel to the runway and proceeded through ankle-deep muck toward the transport. Shura kept her eyes locked on the plane, watching for any signs of it starting to take off. She didn't know why the plane hadn't done so yet, but she wasn't going to question the gift.

They reached the nearest point between the ditch and the plane. Rurik was still at the bottom of the ramp. Two of his guards ducked behind cover and looked as if they were engaging someone inside. The girl was crumpled on the floor, likely unconscious or drugged.

"Stay quiet. Maintain the element of surprise." Shura took point and began to creep out of the ditch. No sooner had they left the cover, a loud crack punctured the air from somewhere afar. Roxani, who was standing next to Shura, pitched forward.

From your left! Find cover.

Another crack followed, kicking up the dirt half a meter away from Shura. She took off, sprinting the fifty meter distance to the plane. More dirt exploded around their feet.

Sniper weapon. Whoever is shooting at you is getting off shots in rapid succession. Likely someone highly skilled, so probably not police or yakuza.

"It has to be the Prophus."

That would explain the confusion, and possibly why the transport has not taken off yet. Kloos and his team would have responded to you by now if they were still alive.

Shura was almost on top of Rurik by the time the Russian noticed her. He had picked up Ella Patel's unconscious body and was dragging her into the transport. His bodyguard stayed behind at the base of the ramp to engage her.

Another rifle shot from the sniper zinged perilously close to her head. Without missing a step, Shura dodged three shots from Rurik's bodyguard before finishing him off with a single bullet between his eyes. She walked up to the ramp to finally confront her rival. She found him hiding behind a pallet of metal drums as weapons fire pinged around him. He had his arm wrapped around Ella Patel's neck and was holding her close, like a toddler with his favorite stuffed animal.

"Hello, brother," she said. "We are long overdue for a talk."

He used the girl's body as a shield and aimed his gun at Shura. "Stay back."

"You might as well let the girl go, Rurik. There are no other viable vessels around. Sabeen will not allow you to risk the Receiver's life. It's time you and I settle our differences the way it was meant to be."

A flurry of bullets rained down on them from somewhere deeper in the transport. Rurik flinched when a bullet ricocheted close to his head. Shura took advantage of his momentary distraction to charge forward. She covered the distance between them and kicked his gun out of his hand. Then she grabbed the girl and pried her out of his grasp.

Disarming Rurik and getting the vessel to safety had its cost. In the split second it took her to clear away the weapon and hostage, Rurik attacked. Three blinding punches to her body and face sent her reeling backward. Rurik followed up with a kick that lifted Shura off her feet. She landed hard, tumbled over and slid down the ramp on her face. She groaned as her consciousness temporarily flashed.

Get up. Control your breathing.

She had less than a second to recover her wits as Rurik stomped toward her. Her injuries were adding up, and her body wasn't responding as sharply as she expected. She just managed to get back onto all fours when Rurik charged forward and punted a steel-tipped shoe at her head.

Move left.

Shura managed to roll aside just in time as the foot came back down: once, twice, three times. She got to one knee and kicked out, missing badly, and then Rurik got his hands on her. He was strong and relatively fresh. Shura felt the breath squeeze out of her body as his vicelike grip clenched around her throat. He slammed her down on the metal ramp. The air whooshed out of her lungs as he pinned her to the hard surface and applied pressure. Shura clutched and batted at his arms, but it was like beating against heavy iron rods. The stars in the sky disappeared. The darkness at the edge of her vision grew.

His left arm is exposed. Now!

Shura, using what little was left of her fading energy, scissored her legs and wrapped them around his exposed arm. She heaved and straightened her body out, toppling Rurik over and trapping him into an armbar lock. Rurik desperately tried to keep his arm bent, grabbing and punching her repeatedly in the body and head. Shura went for the break relentlessly, clutching his wrist with both hands and applying pressure. His strength slowly deteriorated, and she finally snapped his elbow.

To his credit, Rurik barely grunted in pain. No sooner did his arm crack than he escaped her grasp and attacked her again. A forearm to the face separated the two, a kick to the arm nearly broke her arm as well, and then a final uppercut sent her crashing back onto the ground.

Just as he was about to pounce on her again, a spray of bullets from inside the plane rained near them. Shura just managed to avoid getting strafed in the chest, but Rurik took a bullet to the leg and fell.

A voice called out from somewhere inside. "Are you both dead?"

Shura had found cover, but Rurik was still lying in the center of the ramp, so she decided to reply. "No. You should keep shooting."

There was a lengthy pause. "Is this a trick?"

"No, really," she encouraged. "Keep shooting."

So of course he stopped.

She would have to finish her brother off herself. Shura scanned for her dropped pistols and managed to find them. She checked her rounds and advanced on the other Adonis vessel. Just as she left her cover, a wooden container very close to her head exploded from a gunshot.

"Did I miss?" the voice yelled.

Shura gritted her teeth and crept closer to the other Adonis vessel. Sweat beaded down his brow as he tried to crawl away. The haughty confidence that was usually permanently plastered on his face was nowhere to be found.

He pointed into the transport. "There are Prophus there. We should be working together for the good of the Holy Ones, not against each other. Why don't we settle our differences after the battle is won, and the Receiver is secure in Genjix hands?"

Shura's gaze followed where Rurik was pointing. Weapons fire was still coming erratically from the cockpit entrance. She noticed a balding head and a fluff of white hair sticking out from behind the doorway. She waved. "Roen Tan, is that you?"

The shooting stopped again. A wrinkly head popped out from the cockpit door. He waved back. "Hi."

"What are you doing up there?" she asked.

"Stalling for time. You?"

"I'm about to take care of some family business, kill my brother, you know. Would you be so kind as to stop shooting for a bit so I can sort this first? Then I can kill you."

"Take your time. I have all night. By the way, if you guys were planning on leaving on this thing, you might want to consider Plan B. I smashed all of your consoles and blew the windows out. I'm also using the cockpit chairs as a barricade." There was a pause. "And I dumped all of your fuel."

"I'm going to kill you!" screamed Rurik.

"You're the last thing I'm worried about right now, kid."

Shura turned her attention back to Rurik.

"You can't possibly side with a Prophus over one of your own," he gasped, crawling to his knees. He begged, "We are Genjix. The Receiver is not safely in our hands yet. It is our duty to the Holy Ones to put their will above our petty squabbles... sister."

"*Now* you acknowledge me as your sister," she replied. "It only takes putting a gun to your head while you beg for your life for you to consider me your equal."

You are playing with your prey again. Just remember, no harm can come to Sabeen. Upon your life.

"You don't much care for Sabeen, Tabs. Are you sure you'll mind?"

Your sacrilege pushes even my leniency, daughter. Any Quasing life matters more than any human's.

"I'm sure there's plenty of wildlife for Sabeen out there." Shura raised her gun.

"Wait, wait," pleaded Rurik. "You need me to get the girl to safety. The Receiver's host is not cooperative. She'll turn on you as soon as she wakes. The rest of your people are dead. You need Genjix support."

He has a point. The Receiver is the priority. If Kloos and the rest of your team are dead, you will be hard-pressed to smuggle the girl out by yourself. Especially if she is being uncooperative.

Shura lowered her pistol and gnawed at her lip. This was her chance to end her rival. The very idea of working side by side with Rurik made her skin want to break out in hives. He would betray her at first chance, and if they were successful he would absolutely take the credit. And since he had the backing of the Japanese government, chances were the two of them would have to go to his supporters for aid.

Especially since you are a wanted fugitive and have now attacked a police base with your yakuza allies.

Or Shura could just pull the trigger, end his life, and figure out the details later. She raised her pistol again.

I forbid it. Securing the girl is the top priority. Failure to follow through with that priority and the loss of the Receiver will result in the loss of your status as a vessel. Do I make myself clear?

She was still tempted to go it alone. Risking death was almost more enticing than having to work alongside Rurik and share in the glory.

"Excuse me," said a voice behind them.

Shura whirled to see Ella Patel getting up and standing on wobbly feet. "Welcome back to the land of the living. Now sit down before I knock you out again."

"This is Io. The girl is still unconscious."

"My apologies, Holy One. Please sit down or I will still have to incapacitate you."

"I could not help but overhear the conversation between you and Rurik," said Io. "I have a proposal for you, Tabs."

Hear her out. Io wants something.

"Tabs is receptive to your request, Io," nodded Shura.

"I wish to reclaim my standing among the Quasing. More importantly, I wish to fulfill my destiny. However, Sabeen has only offered me slavery, with all of my work attributed to him. I would become his property, my accomplishments adding only to his standing. If I go with you willingly, what would be your terms?"

I can see why Io rejected Sabeen's proposal. It is an old arrangement rarely used by our kind any longer. Tell her we can offer better. Here is what we propose.

Shura recited Tabs' terms. "As a valued Receiver, your standing will rise alongside mine. We will rise and fall together. You will be treasured and honored as you were on the home world. That is the least we can offer the Holy One who brings us salvation."

"What?" sputtered Rurik. "No, this is an outrage."

Shura, without taking her eyes off Io, pointed her gun at Rurik and shot him in the leg. Or close to the leg. His cry of pain told her she had not missed, nor had she accidentally killed him.

"I offer you standing by my side," said Shura, continuing Tabs' terms. "You will follow your destiny unimpeded and your achievements will be your own."

"What about my host? What about Ella?"

"You may keep your vessel if you wish, as long as you have her under control."

Io considered her words for several moments before finally nodding. "I accept this arrangement. Praise to the Holy Ones."

"Is that acceptable?" Shura thought to Tabs.

It is.

She turned to Rurik.

"Wait, no," the Russian screamed.

Shura emptied her magazine into her Hatchery brother. She reloaded and put twelve more rounds into his body, her hand still squeezing the trigger after she had long run out of bullets. Seeing Sabeen lift from Rurik's body was cathartic. The Quasing's hazy gaseous form, filled with hundreds of glittering lights and tiny explosions dancing inside its membrane, expanded and contracted as it rose into the air.

It fluttered in a circle around the body for a few turns before drifting away into the night, its blinking light joining with the stars in the sky.

A huge weight lifted off Shura's shoulders as she watched the Holy One struggle against the mountain breeze. Sabeen had been with Rurik's family for generations, and it was his family who had named her parents betrayers, who had seized Shura's place within the Genjix hierarchy, who had exiled her from Russia. Now her vengeance was finally complete.

We are one step closer to earning our place on the Grand Council.

A bullet tore through Shura's extended hand. She gasped as the pain crawled up her arm. Roen Tan appeared a moment later. The old man looked pretty worn and beaten up. Sweat poured down his face as he limped between her and Io.

"I think we should see what Ella has to say about all this," he replied. "Thanks for stabbing us in the back, Io."

"Actually," stuttered Io, "I was just trying to–"

"Don't actually me." He pushed the girl to the ground and shook her. "Ella, you awake? Your Quasing is back to her old ways."

The girl began to emerge from her slumber. "Huh, what?"

"Welcome back to the land of the living. As I was saying–" Roen Tan took his eyes off Shura for just an instant, barely longer than a heartbeat. That sliver of an opening was all Shura needed.

She took advantage.

CHAPTER THIRTY-SEVEN
New Terms

As much as I have come to sympathize with Ella Patel, she is still just a human and a vessel. I have a higher purpose calling me, which is to fulfill my destiny. It is always a delicate balance when dealing with this primitive species.

The desires of the vessel, if not in the right mindset, can be unwieldy. I trust that you see the wisdom of what had to be done, and why certain decisions had to be made.

Ella woke to a blinding headache. A voice called her name over and over again, and something was rocking her back and forth. Everything was so dark. That was when she realized her eyes were closed. She stirred and groaned.

"Ella, you awake? Your Quasing is back to her old ways."

That voice sounded familiar. She was about to reply when Io began to catch her up on what had happened since she was out, cluttering her mind with a barrage of words.

Listen Ella. A lot has happened. I am trying to play both sides to ensure our survival. The Genjix were winning, so I worked out an arrangement with Shura. Now it seems the Prophus are winning. The problem is, Roen overheard me talking to Shura. If they win, which it looks like they now might, you need to convince him that I was just playing along to survive.

"Wait, what? You're talking too fast. You're hurting my brain." Io's million words a minute sounded like someone was gurgling water between her ears.

No matter what, we have to be on the side of the winner. I am doing everything I can to keep us alive. You just have to follow my lead. The situation is extremely fluid right now. I am no longer sure who will come out of this victorious.

"Shut up for a second. By Krishna, my head feels like a crushed melon."

Ella squinted. Roen Tan was standing next to her, and had a gun pointed at Shura, who was standing off to the side. It looked to Ella like the Prophus were winning. That was a good thing, right? They were the only people who so far had not tried to kidnap her. Roen was saying something. Ella tuned in on the sounds escaping his mouth.

"Welcome back to the land of the living. As I was saying–"

Shura did this thing Adonis vessels did that made people stop and stare in the middle of a fight. She pounced on Roen like a snake, moving so quickly Ella could have missed it.

Roen managed to squeeze off a shot, but Shura avoided it with ease as she closed in. One karate chop sent the gun spinning out of his hand. It was followed by a breathtaking sidekick that sent the old guy crashing into the inner wall of the transport. Roen slammed into the metal wall with a thunk like a gong, then slid to the ground. He coughed, spewing a small spray of blood.

Shura looked at Ella as she stalked toward Roen's broken body. "Are you the Holy One or the girl?"

Ella, still frazzled and now a little in awe, barely managed to mutter, "the girl."

"Good. As soon as I kill him, we depart."

A blade slid out of its sheath with a hiss and appeared in the Adonis vessel's hand. She knelt in front of Roen and waved it in front of his face, carving the air as if a predator toying with its prey. "Killing you will do little for my standing. However, you were once a worthy opponent, Roen Tan, and as you surely know, the Holy Ones hold long grudges. The Council, Zoras especially, will be pleased to hear that you died by Genjix hands."

OK, so things are fine again. As long as you play along, we should be in the clear. Just follow Shura's lead, and we will both live through this night.

That didn't sound right. Ella's fingers itched to do something. Both Shura and Roen were within arm's reach. She grasped for her big dagger, which of course was not there. She looked around for a weapon – any weapon – to help the old man. Her hand crept toward a knife holstered on the thigh of the corpse of the asshole magazine cover model guy.

Listen closely, Ella, do nothing. You cannot help Roen Tan. You owe him nothing. Let Shura take his life.

Ella didn't like the sound of that one bit, but it wasn't like there was anything she could do to help Roen. She knew enough about Adonis vessels to know that trying to take one on was guaranteed suicide. Still, the idea of doing nothing while Shura killed Cameron's dad didn't sit well with her. She pulled the knife out of Rurik's sheath and stood up.

If you try to help Roen, she will kill you. Let this play out.

"Why should we do anything for the Genjix, anyway? We should be helping the Prophus. It was the Genjix that tried to kidnap us. What arrangement did you make with them? Why do they want me?"

They do not want you. They want me. The Genjix need my skills as a Receiver. We can use that as a bargaining chip. I can keep us both alive this way.

There was a tone in the way she spoke that raised Ella's hackles. The Quasing was hiding something. Io was trying to mask it, but it sounded – Ella couldn't quite put her finger on it – as if she was sincere.

What is wrong with being sincere? I thought we agreed to work together as a team. That we should be forthcoming and honest with each other from this point on.

Shura turned to her and stared, amused, as if daring Ella to make a move. When she didn't, the woman shrugged. "Find a gun. It may be several hours before I can secure extraction."

She put a hand on Roen's throat and touched the point of her blade on his neck. Roen futilely grabbed her wrist and tried to bat her arm away, writhing in her grasp like a fish flopping out of water. The Adonis vessel easily held him in place. Irritated, Shura bopped him on top of the head as if he were a child. "Stop it. Die with some dignity."

A flash streaked by. Shura was suddenly skidding across the ramp, tumbling head over heels. They landed near the bottom of the ramp with Shura pinned to the ground. They struggled, the man on top pried the knife out of her hands, and then she knocked him off her. The two stood and circled each other.

Ella's heart sang: Nabin was here!

Nabin, looking stone-faced and scary (and hot), feinted and attacked the Adonis vessel, charging like a rabid animal. He forced Shura backward even as she snapped his head back with an elbow, then doubled him over with a knee. He continued to smother her with his big hairy hands, lifting her off the ground and crushing her into the wall. It was a brutal, ugly dance, with their bodies pressed close as in a lover's embrace.

The fight continued, but it was painful to watch. Nabin fought valiantly, but as the seconds passed it was obvious he was getting the worse end of the melee. In a few more seconds, he would succumb to her continued beating.

Ella balled her hands into fists. She pulled out her knife and stalked the two, looking for an opening to plunge the thing straight into that bitch's heart. Or back, or thigh, or anywhere really.

Ella, no. The smart thing to do is let things play out.

"Shut up, Alien."

What if–

"I'm through listening to you, Io."

The opening came when Nabin, noticeably slowing and trying to not take any more damage, charged to smother Shura once more. She reversed his desperate attack and ended up pinning him to the wall with her elbow on his neck.

Shura's back was completely exposed. Ella wielded the blade in her hand and readied to charge. Before she could take two steps, another man and woman appeared. They jumped on top of Shura, striking her from behind. They each locked one of the Adonis vessel's arms in place and dragged her off Nabin.

Nabin collapsed to the ground, and then Ella was there, wrapping her arms around him and holding him up. "Are you OK, darling?" she asked, stroking his face.

He blinked and broke into a bloody grin. "So that's what it takes to get a hug. Just another woman beating me senseless."

"You stupid, stupid man," she growled, squeezing him tighter.

"I… I thought you were gone forever," he said, in between heaving breaths.

"You can't dump me that easily."

"I dumped you?" he gasped, indignant.

"Excuse me," said the woman. "A little help?"

She and the man were still holding onto Shura, but barely. The Adonis vessel was obviously drained from her fight with Nabin, but she was still putting a beating on the two. It took all of the Prophus agents there to finally subdue her. Once she realized that she was captured, a calm passed over Shura, and she became quiet, almost docile. Upon closer inspection, Shura's face was its own mass of purple bruises and cuts.

She is conserving energy. Listen, Ella. It appears the Prophus once again have the upper hand. We just need to play it cool and things will be fine. Do you understand?

"I hate you, Io."

"Where's Josie?" asked the man.

"I left her guarding the cockpit. She's in pretty bad shape," said Roen. He still hadn't moved from where Shura had dropped him. Ella had forgotten all about the old guy. He struggled to his feet and called into the transport. "Hey Josie, are you still alive?"

"I will not let you outlive me, asshole," replied a weak voice.

"Good to hear." Roen waved. He turned to the others. "Did we win?"

"The police got reinforcements and have regained control of the facility. The yakuza appear to be retreating," said the man holding Shura by the arm. "What do we do about the Adonis vessel?"

Nabin got to his feet and picked up a rifle. He aimed it between her eyes. The Adonis vessel stared back defiantly.

"Don't shoot her," barked Roen. "Unless any of you are interested in becoming a Genjix host. Does anyone have a flamethrower? If you do, then by all means blow her head off. Anyone?"

Everyone shook their head.

"Drat," snarled Roen. "My kingdom for a flamethrower. I guess we'll have to–"

A gunshot cracked, and then the group found themselves surrounded by half a dozen figures, each with a gun trained on them. It was the surviving yakuza.

A young tattooed woman stepped forward. "Hands up. Drop your weapons."

At the same time, Shura, who had fallen into a relaxed, almost meditative state, came alive. She broke free from both her captors' grasps, tripping the woman, and then got behind the man with her arm squeezed around his neck.

Within an instant, the tables were turned.

Again.

Then Ella noticed Nabin. The pistol had tumbled from his hand. He clutched at his neck as a stream of blood leaked out from between his fingers and down his forearms, then he crumpled to his knees and onto his side. She screamed and fell to the ground alongside him, clutching his head as he stared blankly into the sky.The cries that escaped out of Ella's lips tore through the air. Loud, wracking sobs spasmed her body. It was an ugly cry, her grief pure and agonizing, cutting deep into her being.

She cradled his head in her lap and stroked his hair. The sounds of the violence all around her faded, like the wind whistling overhead or the insects chirping in the distance. None of it mattered. Not any more.

Ella could count on one hand the living beings she had ever loved, truly loved, and now she did not need to count any longer. Everyone she had ever cared for was gone. Her mother, her dog, her home, the love of her life. And it was all because of her. She was the cause.

She caressed his face, feeling the stubble on his chin. She hated its prickliness. It was like kissing sandpaper, she often complained. She wrapped his curly hair around her finger. His knotty wiry hair, oily as always. Ella looked into his blank stare, and had to look away. His eyes used to be so full of life, mischievous and bright, his smile ready to pull into a grin. They were all gone now. Ella brushed her hands over his face and closed his eyes for the last time.

Ella, listen to me. I feel your loss. May Nabin find peace in the Eternal Sea, but you have to snap out of this. We are still in real danger. Shura believes you ally with the Prophus. She will kill you.

"I don't care."

Grieve later. You are needed right now.

"I DO NOT CARE, ALIEN. TO HELL WITH EVERYONE!"

People are going to die, Ella. Is that what you want? What would Nabin want?

That pulled her back from her grief. She looked around and saw Shura next to the young yakuza woman who appeared to be in charge. The yakuza were rounding up Roen and his friends, and lining them up inside the plane. A firing squad. Ella had seen those in her early days in Crate Town.

Listen to me. If you love Nabin, do this for him. If you want to honor his memory, then do something.

Ella raged internally even as she shed her grief outwardly. "Why Io? Why do you care what happens?" Then it hit her. "You want to go! You want to join the Genjix."

No, Ella. That is not true. I admit my greatest desire is to fulfill my destiny and continue my work as a Receiver. To do what I was bred to do. I have always made that intention clear. But not like this. You are also my host, and I do not wish to see you harmed or killed. I also admit I do not relish being transferred to a Genjix fanatic.

"They killed Nabin. I can never be with the Genjix."

Let us reach a compromise then.

Io made her case. Ella shook her head, not liking what she heard, but she realized what few options she had. Ella had had to learn at a young age how to survive. She often had to do whatever it took to make sure she would live to see the next sunrise. Sometimes it meant eating rotten fruit or stealing from good people. Other times it meant hurting innocents. These were all sins she knew were wrong, actions that grated against her character, but survival was a cruel teacher who offered little sympathy or the luxury of deciding what was right or wrong. This was one of those times.

Ella stood up. "Stop," she commanded stridently, in a loud strong voice she did not know she possessed. The yakuza, who were lining up to finish off the Prophus, did as she ordered. All eyes turned to her, even Shura's. Ella crossed her arms.

"Shura, you and I have an agreement. I want to fulfill Io's destiny and aid the Genjix. I will go with you willingly and Io will help you, but we need a token of goodwill." She pointed at the Prophus. "Let them go."

Shura studied her, shrugged and turned away. "No."

"Let them go or you will never get my cooperation."

"I'll just kill you and Io will find another vessel, one less belligerent."

"These are Io's wishes," said Ella.

That gave Shura pause. "I don't believe you. Why would Io care one way or another if the Prophus live or die?"

"Because I care, and Io wishes this. If you do not listen to her, then she knows you cannot be trusted," said Ella, with as much conviction as she could muster. "Io and I are one, and that is the price I demanded to follow her to the Genjix, and she accepted."

Shura walked over to Ella and looked into her eyes. Ella stared back defiantly. Both knew the bond a Quasing and their host could possess. The question was, was Shura willing to gamble on the strength of Ella's bond with Io? Anyone who spent more than a few minutes with either Ella or Io would know that answer.

Fortunately, Shura had never bothered to take the time. "Very well," she said finally. "It isn't like any of these Prophus are of high value. At least, not any longer." She signaled to the yakuza. "Tie them up and let them go. Let the police deal with them. If we're lucky, they will finish this job."

When they were done, Shura led Ella and the remnants of the yakuza into the mountains away from the base. As they reached the crest of the hill outside the base perimeter, Ella paused and looked back as clusters of lights swarmed around the transport. She wondered if her sacrifice was for naught.

"Come, girl," said Shura, beckoning to her. "We have great things ahead of us."

"Goodbye, Nabin." Ella's lips barely moved. The words came out hardly more than a whisper. "I'm going to see you again." Then she nodded to Shura and followed her down the slope of the hill. They were picked up by a group of yakuza a few hours later and spirited straight to a private airport. By the next afternoon, Shura and Ella were on a plane flying over the Sea of Japan. By that evening, Ella was in the heart of Genjix country.

CHAPTER THIRTY-EIGHT
Epilogue

I like to think that Ella and I have succeeded. I have achieved my goals, and have provided Ella with a path to hers. The journey to this outcome may not have been anticipated or even desired, but the reward cannot be disputed.

I have regained my standing with the Quasing and am now responsible for our salvation. Ella is alive and prospering, and has access to a life she could only have dreamed of. One day, I am sure she will see the wisdom in all that I have done.

For now, I am content with where I am and insist on remaining with this vessel.

Io, Vessel debriefing to Genjix Internal Affairs after Ella Patel's defection in Tokyo. Summary judgment leading to allowing Holy One to remain with the vessel. Forced transfer deemed unnecessary as of this time.

Roen Tan had been arrested many times in his life, and getting arrested by the Japanese was by far the politest and most pleasant of those experiences. When police reinforcements found them shortly after the Genjix escaped, they were whisked directly to the hospital, where they were treated and seen to humanely for several days. Roen even got fitted for new dentures. Then they were escorted to the cleanest prison cells he had ever seen.

Roen was put in a cell with the nicest old geezer he could ask for in a cellmate. The guy was ex-yakuza, so the two of them had a lot to talk about. It was a good thing Ohta belonged to another family, or he would have been obligated to try to kill Roen in his sleep, he had said. Roen wasn't sure if Ohta was joking or not. He decided not to pry.

He spent much of his time sleeping, got caught up on his reading, and even took up calligraphy. During the day, he played games and ping pong, and sang karaoke at night. All in all, Roen's stay in prison was all sorts of pleasant.

His vacation ended two weeks later. Roen was taking his post-lunch nap when there was a polite knock on his cell door. The door being made of iron, the knocking reverberated through the cell. It still took half a dozen polite knocks for him to stir.

He sat up, stretched his arms toward the ceiling and turned his torso back and forth. He stood up, patted his cellmate on the shoulder as he wedged past him, and waved at the officer who was looking at him through the open slit.

"Good afternoon, Souta."

The guard bowed, so deep that his head disappeared from view. "You have visitors, Roen-san."

The cell door unlocked with a deep, hollow thunk, and then rattled as it slid open. Roen adjusted his food-stained shirt. Other than the very nice doctor who made sure he didn't keel over, he had very few visitors. Whoever was visiting him now was probably a government official or attorney, or if he was lucky his favorite person in the world.

Today was his lucky day.

The prize behind door #1 opened to reveal Jill Tesser Tan, standing with her hands sternly resting at her hips. If she was happy to see him, it didn't show on her face. Roen grinned from ear to ear and gave her an enthusiastic double five-finger-spread-out wave. "Hi honey, thanks for bailing me out." Then he noticed the large entourage of old men standing behind her. "Who are your friends?"

Jill started from left to right. "This is the United States Deputy Secretary of State, Admiral of the Seventh Fleet, Japanese Minister of Internal Affairs, Minister of Defense, the Deputy IXTF director…" The list went on and on. By the time she was finished, Roen was pretty sure they could hold their own summit right here in his cell.

"All that for me?" he finally said.

"That's what it took to get you out of jail," she snapped. "Come with me."

"Hang on," he said, hurrying back into his cell. "Let me say goodbye and get my calligraphy."

"Your what?"

Roen didn't bother trying to explain. He retrieved his drawings, gave Ohta one last bro-hug, shook Souta's hand, and left the cell for the last time. As he was being escorted out of the wing, several inmates shouted their farewells. Some told him to visit when he got the chance. Others offered to visit him once they got out. That one glance Jill shot him was enough to know to keep from extending that invitation.

They entered a holding room, where Jill thanked and shook hands with all the dignitaries and officials. It took a little longer for all of them to say goodbye than one would think, since every single one of these people wanted a photo op with her. Although she was retired, Jill was still one of the most important and powerful people in the world.

When they were finally alone, she whirled on him. Before he could say a word, Roen's wife threw herself in his arms and gave him a bone-crunching embrace.

He hugged her back, with reservation. "Ribs still cracked," he croaked sharply while his mouth was buried in her hair.

After a solid five minutes of the best hug he ever had, Jill pulled back and gave him the eye. She glanced at his chest and poked. "Is this the cracked rib?"

"No," he replied. That was the wrong answer.

She poked him again. "Right there?"

Roen bit his lip. That one was a little closer. A wince nevertheless escaped. "Maybe."

She poked once more. "Serves you right for starting an international crisis."

"The mission got a little wild," he admitted, taking his wife's hands, mainly because he liked holding them, but also to make sure she didn't poke him again.

"You were supposed to babysit Ella Patel," she continued. "Not go traipsing off to a foreign country. You not only got tangled up with their organized crime, Roen, you also went to war with the police."

"That was unintentional."

"You were supposed to avoid the Genjix at all costs."

"That couldn't be helped."

"You attacked a military base."

He held up a finger. "Technically, civilian defense."

Jill jabbed him in the ribs again. "You could have gotten killed, damn it."

"What about you?" he said defensively. "You didn't tell me you were going to go off and retire the second I took a mission."

Her eyes widened. "Are you comparing my retirement to nearly kicking off World War IV in a neutral country?"

"Hardly World War IV," he muttered. Then for the first time, Roen noticed the tightness around Jill's eyes. A tsunami of guilt washed over him. He was an inconsiderate idiot. She had probably thought him hurt or dead. Thought of him lying in a ditch somewhere bleeding out from a gunshot wound or a heart attack or falling down the stairs. At his age, all of those were equally likely to kill him.

"I'm sorry, hon." His voice broke. "You're right. I got carried away. I should have called for backup or help or anything. I was just a few steps behind Ella the whole way, and thought I could do it." He bowed his head. "I thought I still had it."

"Oh Roen, you big lug," said Jill, embracing him. "I'm just glad you're all right."

"See, I told you I didn't need the retrieval team."

She smacked him lightly on the back of the head. "That's because you were already in jail by the time they arrived, dummy. The retrieval team wasn't dumb enough to try to break you out."

"I would have."

"Cameron was planning on it if I couldn't secure your release," she admitted. "Like father, like son."

"He's a good boy."

They stayed there for a while longer, swaying together as if dancing to a silent song, letting their hearts beat together in rhythm. Roen cupped the back of her head, blew away the stray wisps of hair, now mostly gray with just streaks of brown.

He thought about the decades they had been together, and how the world around them changed, and how they had changed with it. They were unrecognizable now. The world they had lived in when they first met was long gone. Yet through it all, Roen had loved Jill, and she had loved him. No matter how far apart they were, no matter how difficult things got, or how perilous and hopeless the situation became, their love for each other was always there, always strong. It may have been tested, but their love had never broken.

Jill transitioned from their embrace and wrapped her arm around his waist. "Let's go home."

Roen rested his arm on her shoulder, and they walked toward the exit. They leaned on each other as they strolled through the prison hallways. Roen waved at the guards, shook hands with the warden, and gave knowing stares to a few hard-looking men practicing aikido in the play yard.

"I taught them a thing or two," he said smugly.

"I'm sure you did, dear."

A black car was waiting for them outside the prison. Roen looked back one last time before getting inside. As he climbed in the back, he noticed the reinforced windows and armored lining, the overlapping plating on the floor designed to protect against bombings. This wasn't just a normal ride, so he wasn't too surprised to find two familiar and not necessarily welcome faces sitting across from him.

He waved at the one on the left. "Hi, Liesel."

Jill's long-time assistant – now former assistant – offered him a curt nod. Liesel never really cared for him. Tolerated him more like it. "Roen."

He turned to the person sitting next to her. "Hi, Angie. Congrats on your promotion. How's your first few weeks on the job?"

Angie – the new Keeper – did not return the warm greeting. "Off to a rough start, thanks to you. Nothing like a crisis to kick off an administration."

"Thank you for taking time away from your busy schedule to see me get released from prison," he said cheerfully.

"This isn't a social call," she replied curtly. "We need–"

"How are the rest of my people?" he asked.

Irritation flashed on the new Keeper's face. She looked as if she were going to dress him down, but changed her mind. "They're all out. Hekla and her team are rotating off the line for the next three months. Josie is recuperating in a hospital in Sydney. She's already filed her retirement papers. You're the last one, Roen."

"Good. What about Tarfur and Nabin?"

"Tarfur was sent back to Finland. Nabin's been in cold storage ever since your arrest. We've made arrangements to have him flown back to his family in Atlanta."

Roen nodded solemnly. "I'll need to write letters to their families."

Angie shook her head. "That will not be possible or appropriate. You are not even supposed to be here, Roen."

"But I'm–"

This time she did cut him off. "Shut up, Roen. We have more important things to worry about than condolences."

He had known Angie since she was a little girl. She had never been the warm and fuzzy type to begin with. She was probably even colder and even less fuzzy now that the Keeper had regained her position as the leader of the Prophus. There was also the fact that the Keeper hated Roen's guts, and the feeling was mutual.

He crossed his arms and leaned back. "I see you've inherited the Keeper's sunny disposition. Very well, what's on your mind, mighty Keeper?"

"I trust you did not reveal anything to the Japanese authorities," said Liesel.

Roen snorted. "Come on, I'm a professional. Ex-professional."

"If you can call it that," muttered Angie. She gave a start and withered under Jill's gaze. "I'm sorry, Jill."

"I trained you better than that, Keeper," said Jill.

Roen couldn't help admiring how beautiful his wife looked, and sounded. God, he loved that woman.

"We need to know what happened to the girl," said Liesel. "This Ella Patel."

"She went with the Genjix voluntarily." Roen became thoughtful. "I'm not sure, but she may have done so only to save our lives. Shura and the yakuza were about to execute us. She made a deal with them to let us live in exchange for her cooperation."

Angie cursed. "Do you know where the girl is now?"

"Probably in the heart of Genjix territory. Way out of our reach," shrugged Roen. "Why, what's her significance?"

Angie exchanged glances with Jill, who nodded, and then signaled to Liesel. "Show him."

Liesel brought out her tablet and pulled up several files. She handed it to Roen. "It took a while to piece everything together, but we finally found out what the Bio Comm Array does, and how it works. We also uncovered what it has to do with Io."

Roen skimmed the report. His eyes widened as he handed it back to Liesel. He whistled and put his arm around Jill's shoulders. "Well, it looks like you have your work cut out for you over the next few years. I for one am really glad I'm retired. Good luck!"

Shura stepped through the outer gate of the abandoned estate and scanned the premises. It was quiet, peaceful. A little itch in the back of her head told her this would be the perfect place for an ambush. If it were her, she would put a shooter to her right behind the parking structure, one in the second-story window directly above the main entrance – for additional cover – and the last in the thickets to her left where the ground sloped downward. The ground there formed a tiny ravine that became a stream after rain. Shura used to play Genjix agent there as a little girl.

It was a lifetime ago. Back when she went by another name, one that she hadn't dared use since her parents had died. No, they were killed, murdered by their rivals. It had taken most of her life, but the deed was done. She had avenged them after all these years. Setting foot back onto her homeland was a sign of her triumph and revenge. Walking through the front gates of her ancestral home was just a victory lap.

Today, Shura not only claimed Russia as her territory within the Genjix, she had also reclaimed her name. She could finally be Alexandra Mengsk again. "I am home, papa," she said quietly. "Finally free to be my true self. I will reclaim our family's glory, and then I will take it to heights greater than we could ever dare dream."

Are you done?

"I am just getting started."

Finish quickly. Taking an encore after the first act is in poor taste. Act like you have won before.

"Let me have this, Tabs."

Shura entered the main building, past the large double doors with her family's emblem, the paint long since flaked off, and into the foyer. She was greeted by the twins, two massive staircases that curved to the second floor. As a child, she had spent hours gazing from the top banister, waiting for her papa to come home after his many business trips. He would always bring gifts, exotic treasures from other parts of the world. She looked up at the ceiling. The giant chandelier she had nicknamed the Glass Moon as a child was gone, probably fallen or stolen over the decades.

Shura toured the decrepit mansion, stepping into her memories back when times were simpler and her worries less lethal. She walked through the overlarge dining room with the long dining table where her mama would host dinner parties. The back courtyard with the garden and the fountain, where the statue of a Cossack stood ready, his curved sword pointing toward the sky. The shooting gallery where Shura had first learned to shoot at the age of four.

She continued back inside the mansion and up one of the twins. She stepped through her bedroom, which was actually three smaller rooms linked together. Her bed was still there, at least the frame. The canopy had caved in years ago, and rats had eaten most of the rest. Her tea set and small tables mostly now rested in tiny shattered pieces. Some of her dolls remained, although they all looked more like decayed corpses than a little girl's best friends.

Last, Shura went to her father's study, the true heart of the home and the place where he had run his financial empire, hosted cigar sessions with government officials, where he had strategized with other high-ranking Genjix. She stood in the middle of the room and spun in a slow circle.

This was a place filled with fond memories. That torn high-back chair in the corner was where he used to read to her before she went to bed. The small table next to the wall of bookshelves was where he taught her to play chess. She had written her first sonata lying on her belly on the rug next to the fireplace.

Shura walked to the nook and peered out the window overlooking the mansion's inner courtyard. The giant beech tree remained, taking up the entire view of the window with its branches extending outward in every direction.

Her father hated that tree. Her mother loved it deeply and spent hours reading under its shade. Shura's memory of her mama was hazy. She just remembered a beautiful, gentle woman who commanded every room she entered. A woman who moved with the grace of a falling leaf, who was equally skilled dancing the waltz or with the saber. This mansion was her family's ancestral home.

Shura turned and studied the library once more, taking in each detail as her gaze swept the room. Yes, there were many happy memories here, but this was also a room filled with shattered dreams. In this room, her papa had met and declared his allegiance to Vinnick. Vinnick was going up against Enzo, Zoras's previous vessel, for leadership of the Council and of all Genjix. That marked the beginning of the end of her family.

It was in this room that Enzo's men had arrested her father. She walked to the window and looked outside. The weeping willow next to the lake was where they had shot her mother during the family's escape. And it was inside that gazebo where Shura, newly embedded with Tabs, had killed her first human to save her father's life.

This estate was the source of all her happy memories, but where her life had fallen apart as well. Shura took a deep breath and let the cold air burn her nostrils. She exhaled forcefully, pushing out of her body the last childish attachments she had clung to.

"Now I am done, Tabs."

Bury your dead and move on. There is still much to do.

Tabs was right. The past was dead. Dwelling on it served little purpose for the future. Shura hurried down the stairs. She was met at the front door by Bashira Nishiki and a dozen of her newest Genjix Russian direct reports, who were waiting patiently for her orders. They bowed in unison.

"Your will, Adonis?" asked Popov, the lead architect.

"You may begin demolition of the mansion. I want the grounds excavated within the month, and my new headquarters ready for operation by year's end. Spare the large beech tree. Under no circumstance should it be harmed."

She signaled to Bashira to follow. Shura had taken the heir of the Aizukotetsu-kai under her wing as her protégée. The next step for the girl was to earn a Holy One, one who would be loyal to Tabs and Shura. The girl was raw but talented. If she had had a proper upbringing, she may have survived the Hatchery. It was too late for that now, but her connection with the yakuza was an important step in Shura's plans.

Both India and Russia were now hers. Soon Japan would be as well. That would mark her within the top ten – perhaps five – most powerful and influential Adonis vessels in the world, well within a stone's throw of the grand prize. To climb any higher at this stage, however, would be a much more difficult task. Standing at this level was a different sort of game, one that required more than territory and brute force.

One step at a time. You have surpassed my already-lofty expectations, my daughter. Take this time to consolidate your domain. The next phase of our ambition can wait.

A small smile emerged on Shura's face as she walked by the bulldozers rumbling past. A moment later, the loud crashing of falling walls and caving roofs began to sing through the otherwise quiet morning.

"We shouldn't wait too long, Tabs," Shura thought to her Holy One. "Weston knows we're coming for him next. Unlike Rurik, he will not underestimate me. He'll be ready."

Ella hated to admit it, but the life of a Genjix vessel wasn't half bad. In fact, it was positively posh. After the events of Tokyo, she was whisked away to Shanghai. Within a day, she was given a bonkers apartment on the 109th floor of the Shanghai Tower, and a complete staff waiting on her every whim. A security detail was attached, although she suspected that had more to do with keeping her in line than it did with protecting her. This was the heart of Genjix power, where vessels were looked up to as almost divine beings. From that moment on, there was very little Ella wanted for. All she had to do was make Io available for whatever work the Genjix required of her.

As for Io, to Ella's extraordinary surprise, the Quasing had blossomed right before her eyes, figuratively. Ever since they had met, Ella had known Io to be insecure, indecisive, pensive and – to be honest – sort of an asshole. However, as soon as she was placed in her element, working with the massive biocomm receivers, which honestly looked like green and purple organs the size of buildings submerged in gooey red liquid in gigantic glass vats, Io became an entirely different alien.

She became decisive, competent, self-assured. The Genjix had provided her with a veritable army of scientists and engineers, and she organized and commanded them efficiently, like a captain of a battleship. Within the first few weeks, Io had all of the raw organic data of the bio comm facilities sequenced. Ella was shocked to learn the subspace communication signals were living creatures, their raw data imprinting onto the mindless Quasing living within the giant vats in each Bio Comm Array facility. Once imprinted, these Quasing were aggregated and then sent to Io in Shanghai by the tankers to compile into plain messages. The first message, less than two hundred words in Mandarin, required one oil tanker and six thousand Quasing to decipher.

This process went on for months. Io explained that in the past, she would work with thousands of other Receivers to process the data rapidly. Now, working by herself, it would take years. Still, that dribble of information gave Ella the chills, the exact opposite reaction from the rest of the Genjix.

As the weeks turned to months, Ella grudgingly became comfortable with her new life. She got used to the luxury of her position. She came to enjoy being important and special. Most of all, the awful reality of humanity's future became normalized, an aftereffect of her everyday life. Part of it was because of Io. The Quasing was so euphoric and focused on her work that it bled into Ella. There was a joy and satisfaction radiating from her that Ella could feel every single day. Io was now fulfilling her destiny as a Receiver.

Being Genjix almost felt natural and normal.

Almost.

On the eve of their one-year anniversary as Genjix, Ella decided to go on vacation. It was well-earned. Io had forced Ella to work twelve-hour days for months trying to catch up on the mountain of raw organic data that the subspace communications were imprinting onto the live Quasing at each center. By this time, Io had earned enough trust from the Genjix Council for this to be allowed, as long as she stayed within their domain of control.

That trust and freedom apparently only went so far. No sooner had Ella checked into Lebua in downtown Bangkok than she received a call not three steps into her penthouse suite.

"Thailand is beautiful this time of year," said Shura, her huge head floating in the air in the center of the living room. The Adonis vessel had blond hair again. It was now cut into a bob. It looked better this way.

"That's what I hear." Ella did her best to keep the edge out of her voice. She had only seen Shura twice since Tokyo. The Adonis vessel was now a very important person and was spending all of her time in Russia. That was probably best for both of them. "I figure, if I don't get to go now before the rainy season, I won't be able to for another six months. By then, the Western Hemisphere cache will be ready for processing."

"Just two weeks?"

Ella nodded. "That's all the time Io can spare. The Sector Six Bio Comm Arrays will have finished sequencing their Quasing by then. I'll get back just in time to start extrapolating the message."

"Very well. I hope you enjoy yourself." Shura paused. "I trust you, Ella."

She nodded. "Praise to the Holy Ones."

"Praise to the Holy Ones."

The screen went dark.

After settling in, Ella left her room and proceeded to the suite's private elevator. The numbers on the elevator began to descend. It was a long journey down.

Are you sure about this?

"That was the deal."

It was. I will honor it. I am just saying. There is nothing wrong with changing your mind. If you get caught, your life is forfeit.

"I've made up my mind, Io. What about you? What happens if I get caught?"

A gurgling growl grew out of the Quasing. Ella had long recognized that as Io's way of chuckling. *I am untouchable. No matter what you do, the Genjix and Prophus must now embrace me. I am the only Quasing on this planet who can decipher the organic imprints.*

"So if I get caught, you can tell them to pardon me?"

If you get caught, they will execute you. Nothing can be done about that. They will then assign a fanatic to be my new host. Religious fanaticism in a host is obnoxiously tiring. I enjoy our independent streak and still prefer you as my host as long as it does not take me away from my work.

"Aw, that's the nicest thing you ever said to me."

The elevator dinged, and the doors opened to the ground floor. Ella put on her sunglasses and strutted out into the lobby as if she belonged there, because she did. It was amazing how quickly one could adapt to this highfalutin' lifestyle. All a person needed was to be free from hunger, violence and need, and they too could easily change their outlook and demeanor.

Out of the corner of her eye, Ella caught sight of Peng, her handler, falling in line a dozen or so paces behind her. Peng was one of those fanatic Genjix operatives Io was so down on. His job was to protect Ella at all costs. Well, that was part of his job. She was pretty sure the other part of his job was to make sure she didn't escape. The second part was easy. It was incredibly difficult to escape or infiltrate any area that was now considered the Genjix heartland, of which Thailand was definitely a part.

Ella stepped out onto the bustling Bangkok street and casually meandered across the intersection and through the busy shopping district. The crowds parted before her like the sea – the diamond emblem on her coat signifying her position and importance saw to that. Every citizen in Genjix territory recognized that emblem, and no one would dare bother or impede her path. She could shoot someone on the street without any problem.

The thing had been a novelty at first, but now it just made her feel lonely. Ella fought the urge to hide it. Peng would notice that for sure and grow suspicious. Out of habit, she glanced back; he was just outside of arm's reach. Unobtrusive enough to never get in her way, but always close enough to protect her.

Peng was actually the thirteenth bodyguard assigned to her security detail over the past three months. For some reason, Ella had recently become very particular with her personal protection.

Fourteenth actually.

The first four were women. Ella had problems with all of them and requested a new bodyguard after only a few days with each. The next nine were an assortment of both genders whom Ella found varied reasons to replace. Peng, the fourteenth, however, was the right guy. It wasn't that he was nicer to Ella or more lenient or more accommodating; far from it. Peng actually was sort of a droll grump. He was very good at his job. The Genjix spared no expense or resource to protect her. He had one specific trait, however, that Ella was looking for. One that made him acceptable where the other bodyguards were not.

She picked up the pace and turned the corner toward the night market. A cacophony of noise hammered her ears: vendors hawking, shoppers haggling and music blaring. Underneath all of it was the low buzz of a community going about their evening. Something spicy wafted into her nostrils. It was followed by the smell of something rotten, which was soon covered up by the sickly sweet scent of musk. A smile broke on Ella's face and all her senses perked up. It felt like home.

She reached her destination at the dead-end of a busy street at the edge of the market and looked up at the glowing neon sign: Spirit Hands. The door jingled when she walked in. She didn't know how Peng did it, but the guy somehow slipped in with her.

She walked up to the counter where a young-looking old woman or old-looking young woman was watching a Thai drama. She coughed.

"We are booked for the evening," said the strange madam of indeterminable age. She gave Ella a lazy glance. Her eyes widened and she straightened. "My deepest apologies, mistress. I can kick one of my other clients out."

"That won't be necess… good, I mean. Kick them out now. I expect nothing less." Ella still was not comfortable wearing the skin of someone important. She waited patiently as the madam kicked a half-dressed patron out of one of the back rooms and shooed him from the massage parlor.

A different woman, one definitely old, walked out a few moments later, bowing profusely and averting her eyes. "This way please."

Ella eyed the woman up and down. She shook her head dismissively. "Those aren't spirit fingers."

Surprise and fear flashed across the madam's face, if only for an instant. She probably hadn't expected that phrase from someone like Ella. The pause was only a breath long, and then the madam shooed the old woman away. "Yes, yes, you are correct." She held out her own hand. "*These* are spirit fingers. I will see to you myself."

She motioned for Ella to follow. The madam glanced uneasily as Peng silently fell behind them. Ella was escorted to the room in the far back. Before she could enter, Peng pushed past her and did a thorough search of the premises. When he was satisfied, he stepped back into the hallway and motioned to her that it was safe to enter. Then he placed himself directly in front of the door outside.

A small smile crept onto Ella's face. That was why she had chosen Peng as her bodyguard. The man was so modest. All the rest would have waited in here while she got the massage.

Ella entered the room and closed the door. She let loose a long sigh, not realizing that she had been holding her breath the entire time. She shed her clothes and climbed onto the massage table. She waited. The next minute was the longest of her entire life. Finally, after forever, part of the wall swung open and a shadowy figure stepped out.

Ella sucked in her breath. "I didn't realize you would come personally."

He offered his hand. "Hello Ella. It's been a long time."

She threw her arms around his waist. "Hi, Cameron."

"Are the Genjix treating you well?"

"Better than the Prophus ever could," she joked. Ella glanced at the door behind her and then removed a small data chip hidden under her tongue. "We don't have much time. Here is the newest cache of raw data from the Bio Comm Arrays. I included the aggregates this time."

The chip disappeared on Cameron's person so quick she didn't even notice where he hid it. "What we really need is to shut down the Arrays. Can you give us the locations of the facilities? Can you provide those? What about access codes and logistics?"

Remember, Ella.

Ella hesitated, and then shook her head. "I can't give you that."

"Why not?"

"I just can't."

Someone was shuffling just outside the door. She jumped back on the massage table. "Just put that information to good use. No matter what, though, you have to leave the facilities alone."

"But..."

"That's the deal," she hissed. "Use the data any way you like, but the communication link has to stay open."

Cameron looked as if he were about to say something else, and then nodded. Someone knocked on the door. His hands flashed to the gun at his hip.

"Mistress?" said the madam. "Are you ready? May I come in?"

"Just a minute," called Ella. She shooed him away. "Go. Tell your dad hi for me."

Cameron was about to leave when he stopped. He put his hand on her wrist. "Come with me. We'll figure a way to smuggle you out."

That is not part of our agreement.

Ella closed her eyes. To be honest, she wasn't sure if that was even what she wanted. She shook her head. "I made a deal. I have to keep it. I have to stay with the Genjix. At least for now."

"Why are you helping us?"

Ella's face took a hard turn. "This is for Nabin."

He nodded and squeezed her arm. "I miss him too. If you ever change your mind. Whenever you're ready. You give the word. I'll come for you."

A moment later, Cameron Tan was gone and the secret door closed, as if he had never been there. The knob squeaked and turned, and the door swung open. Yellow light from the hallway flooded inside. The madam poked her head in. Relief flooded her face when she saw that Ella was alone. She became all business.

"Please lie on your stomach, mistress."

Ella did so, catching Peng standing outside, averting his eyes from her naked body.

The madam began to knead her shoulders. "You are so tense. You need to relax more."

Ella grunted and sighed. "Tell me about it."

Acknowledgments

I dedicated my debut novel *The Lives of Tao* to my parents, Mike and Yukie Chu. Now publishing my eighth book it feels way past time to do so again. Because let's be honest; it's almost impossible to give the people who gave us life and raised us, and who love us unconditionally despite all our faults, enough credit.

For those who stuck with me through *The Fall of Io* all the way through to the end, you know the day I wrote those acknowledgements was a heck of a day. Well, it's been a wild two and a half years since and everything has changed. We've left the plains of the Midwest for the beaches of the West Coast. I have to mow the lawn every week. I am also now terrified of nature (fire, earthquakes, traffic, and rattlesnakes, oh my!). Most importantly, our family has grown to include Hunter.

Hunter is the joy of my life and for the first time I understand the work, effort and time my parents had to give to raise me and my siblings. I can reflect with a clear lens on my childhood and see how awesome my parents were and how difficult I was. I finally appreciate their sacrifice to nurture a (mostly) functional adult human being.

Paula and I are extremely fortunate that my parents now live close by. They help take care of Hunter every chance they get, and it has been a lifeline. So now not only have they raised me, they're helping raise him. Their support has meant everything.

So, to my Mom and Dad, and to all moms and dads everywhere, thank you for doing your best for us. You all rock!

With love,

Your children who can never repay you enough.